TO CHARM A PRINCE

She is Samantha Douglas, second daughter of a scan-
dalously impoverished earl, a quiet, unassuming miss
who is literally swept off her feet at her first London
ball by a dashing, mysterious stranger who awakens
the passionate woman inside. . . .

He is Prince Rudolf Kazanov, heir to the Russian
throne, who has fled his homeland with his English
mother and young daughter—and most of the
Kazanov fortune. Though hard and cynical when it
comes to matters of loyalty and love, he is enchanted
by Samantha's delicate beauty and sweet innocence.
And as passion draws her into his world, they race to
outwit his enemies, hoping with all their hearts that
their story will end happily ever after. . . .

Books by Patricia Grasso

TO TAME A DUKE

TO TEMPT AN ANGEL

TO CHARM A PRINCE

Published by Zebra Books

TO CHARM A PRINCE

Patricia Grasso

ZEBRA BOOKS
KENSINGTON PUBLISHING CORP.
http://www.kensingtonbooks.com

ZEBRA BOOKS are published by

Kensington Publishing Corp.
850 Third Avenue
New York, NY 10022

All Kensington titles, imprints and distributed lines are available at special quantity discounts for bulk purchases for sales promotion, premiums, fund-raising, educational or institutional use.

Special book excerpts or customized printings can also be created to fit specific needs. For details, write or phone the office of the Kensington Special Sales Manager: Kensington Publishing Corp., 850 Third Avenue, New York, NY 10022. Attn. Special Sales Department. Phone: 1-800-221-2647.

Zebra and the Z logo Reg. U.S. Pat. & TM Off.

First Printing: June 2003
10 9 8 7 6 5 4 3 2 1

Printed in the United States of America

CHAPTER 1

The damned limp ruins my appearance.

Eighteen-year-old Samantha Douglas watched herself in the cheval glass as she limped across the bedchamber. With short Spanish-shoulder sleeves and square-cut neckline, her blue silk gown matched her eyes. Her aunt's maid had dressed her ebony hair in an upswept fashion and then adorned the coiffure with diamond florets that glittered like stars in the midnight sky.

Samantha stared at herself in the cheval glass and decided that she had never looked so pretty. No one would ever guess from her appearance that she hadn't led a pampered life as a member of the Quality. She felt like a princess . . . *until she walked.*

Why was I the one run over by the carriage? Samantha wondered. *Why couldn't it have been—?*

Samantha banished that uncharitable thought. She could never wish what happened to her on anyone else.

Turning away from the mirror, Samantha tried to calm her nerves by focusing on her bedchamber. The four-poster bed was enormous, seeming larger than her old bedchamber at the cottage, a room she'd shared with her two sisters. Everything in the bedchamber—textiles, carpet, wall hangings—had been created in pinks, gold, and cream.

A lady's chamber, Samantha thought. She'd only been in residence at the Duke of Inverary's for two weeks and was still unused to the opulence. She could hardly believe that her aunt and her parents had lived almost their entire lives with this luxury.

"Are you ready to meet society?"

Samantha turned at the sound of her younger sister's voice. "I'm not going to the ball," she told her.

"Are you ill?" Victoria asked, hurrying across the chamber.

"My limp prevents me from walking gracefully, never mind dancing," Samantha said, her expression glum.

Hopping Giles . . . Hopping Giles . . . Hopping Giles.

Samantha recalled the jeering name reserved for cripples and hurled at her since the carriage accident. Like an old friend, heartache for being different swept through her. The little girl who limped was always chosen last for games with other children; there was no reason to think the young woman who limped would be anything other than a wallflower.

"No gentleman will ask a pathetic cripple to dance," Samantha said, unable to control the catch of emotion in her voice.

"A slight limp doesn't make you a cripple," Victoria argued. "Besides, we have more to worry about than your limp. If anyone discovers we're frauds, we'll never find husbands."

"We are *not* frauds," called Angelica, the oldest Douglas sister, walking into the bedchamber. "Father was the Earl of Melrose, and since his passing, I am the Countess of Melrose."

"Father lost the Douglas fortune," Victoria reminded her.

"He didn't lose it," Angelica corrected her. "Charles Emerson swindled him out of it."

"We have nothing to recommend us but our wits and the Duke of Inverary's generosity," Samantha said. "We are pretending to be wealthy."

"Everyone pretends to have more than they do," Angelica said, waving her hand in a gesture of dismissal.

"Aunt Roxie said you're going to marry the marquess and become a duchess when the duke dies," Victoria said, and then sighed. "I wonder whom Samantha and I will marry."

"Are we ready to take our place among the Quality?" Angelica asked, changing the subject.

"I'm not going tonight," Samantha told her.

"Get Aunt Roxie," Angelica ordered Victoria. Then she turned to Samantha, saying, "Why don't you want to go? You look beautiful. Think how much fun our first ball will be."

Samantha leveled a skeptical look on her. "All my life I've listened to children calling me *Hopping Giles*," she said, unable to keep the raw pain out of her voice. "I couldn't bear for society to whisper behind their hands about me. What gentleman will ask a cripple to dance?"

"Sister, do not let a simple limitation ruin your life," Angelica said.

"That's so easy for you to say," Samantha replied. "No one ever had a cruel word for you. You're beautiful, talented, and intelligent. The Marquess of Argyll adores you."

"You have gifts, too," Angelica said, touching her sister's shoulder. "Besides being exceptionally lovely, you are the kindest and most charitable lady I know."

"Gentlemen do not value kindness and charity," Samantha told her. "Gentlemen prefer beauty and talent and intelligence." When her sister arched a brow at her, Samantha gave her a grudging smile and amended herself, saying, "Perhaps gentlemen do not value intelligence in a woman."

The door crashed open, gaining their attention. Auburn-haired and voluptuous, Aunt Roxie marched into the bedchamber. "What is the problem?" she demanded.

"I told you," Victoria blurted out. "Samantha isn't going to the ball. She—"

Aunt Roxie glared at her youngest niece, and Victoria clamped her lips shut. "Don't sit down," she cried, turning her attention on Samantha.

Samantha bolted to attention. "Why can't I sit?"

"Your gown will wrinkle."

Samantha's expression became mulish. "I am not attending the ball."

"What has changed your mind?" Aunt Roxie asked, her tone soothing.

"Charles Emerson ran me over with his carriage," Samantha said. "Should I and my deformed leg now attend a ball at his house?"

"That unfortunate accident happened long ago," Aunt Roxie replied. "He never intended to hurt you."

"Accident or no, Emerson will pay for what he has done to the Douglases," Angelica spoke up.

"Darling, you must put aside this ridiculous notion of being inferior," Aunt Roxie said, ignoring her oldest niece. "You are not merely a limp. Others will accept you when you accept yourself. Don't you want to meet a suitable gentleman and marry?"

"Find me a man who won't mind that his bride is deformed," Samantha said, "and I'll marry him tomorrow."

"You are *not* deformed," Aunt Roxie insisted, her frustration apparent in her voice. "I have spent the inheritances from my three late husbands keeping you girls alive, and now the Duke of Inverary has opened his home to us. Both His Grace and I intend to secure advantageous marriages for each of you. Is this attitude of yours a poultice to my old age?"

"You are not old, and I do appreciate your sacrifice and His Grace's generosity," Samantha told her aunt. "Neither of you understands how daunting a task it is for me to go into society. I have none of Angelica's blond beauty or Victoria's free spirit."

"You possess other gifts like a warm heart and a nurturing nature," Aunt Roxie told her.

"Men don't care about those things," Samantha argued, feeling as though she was losing this battle to remain home for the evening. She should have feigned an illness.

"Darling, I know more about men than the three of you combined," her aunt drawled. "Trust me, men flirt with blond beauty and free spirits but marry nurturing natures."

"Why, thank you, Aunt Roxie," Victoria said.

"You've made us feel so much better about going into society," Angelica added.

Aunt Roxie ignored them. "Did I mention that your future husband will be in attendance tonight?" she asked.

"What do you mean?"

"I had one of my visions," Aunt Roxie told her. "You will marry a man who is not quite what he seems, but a prince among men, nevertheless."

Could Aunt Roxie be correct? Her aunt had been blessed with special, otherworldly talents and knew things before they happened. Was there a gentleman capable of looking beyond her limp?

"If Angelica is marrying the marquess and Samantha is marrying a prince among men," Victoria said, "whom did you see for me?"

"Nobody," her aunt snapped. "You are going to die an old maid on the shelf."

Samantha burst out laughing at the expression of horror on her sister's face. Angelica joined in her merriment.

Taking pity on her youngest niece, Aunt Roxie told her, "I saw an earl and a prince."

"I'll marry twice?"

"I didn't say that."

"You speak in riddles," Victoria complained.

Aunt Roxie gave her youngest niece an ambiguous smile and turned to Samantha. She held out her hand, saying, "Will you trust me about this?"

Samantha hesitated for a fraction of a moment and then placed her hand in her aunt's. "Very well, but I cannot promise to enjoy myself."

"Darling, tonight you will experience the most enchanting evening of your young life," Aunt Roxie promised.

A short time later, Samantha sat beside Victoria in the ducal coach. Magnus Campbell, the Duke of Inverary, and Aunt Roxie sat across from them. The marquess had persuaded Angelica to ride in his coach.

"Remember, my darlings, do not dance more than twice with any gentleman," Aunt Roxie instructed, as their coach halted in front of Charles Emerson's Grosvenor Square mansion.

"We don't need to be so particular about that old rule," the duke said.

"I won't take chances with my nieces' futures," her aunt replied.

What future? Samantha thought, her spirits sinking at the sight of the graceful, fashionably gowned women entering the Emerson mansion. Not one of them limped. *No gentleman will ask me to dance, and once I'm categorized as a wallflower, no man will even look in my direction.*

The Duke of Inverary stepped down from the carriage first and assisted her aunt, her sister, and then her. Angelica and the marquess waited for them at the stairs.

"Sisters, take a good look at this house," Angelica said, staring at the mansion. "We lived here until ten years ago."

"I don't remember," Victoria said.

Instead of looking at the mansion, Samantha turned to stare at the street. "Is this where the carriage ran me over?" she asked.

"Tonight is not the time to dwell on the past," Aunt Roxie said. "Let's go inside."

Samantha felt her sister's touch on her shoulder and heard her say, "This is where it happened."

"That day eludes my memory," Samantha said.

"Emerson will pay for his crimes against you and Father," Angelica promised.

"I hate the dirty weasel," Victoria exclaimed.

"So do I," Angelica said.

"No one hates him more than I," Samantha added.

"I'm so glad that's settled," Aunt Roxie drawled. "Can we go inside now?"

"Would you rather return home?" asked Robert Campbell, the Marquess of Argyll. "My driver can take you back if you want."

"Attending tonight's ball is imperative for Samantha," Aunt Roxie insisted.

"I'll be fine, my lord," Samantha said, managing a smile for the marquess.

Long forgotten memories surfaced when Samantha walked into the foyer. She remembered her parents in evening dress, kissing her good night before they went out. She could almost smell the reassuring scent of her mother's lilac fragrance.

"Do you remember any of this?" Victoria whispered.

"Vaguely, but Angelica would remember best," Samantha answered.

Their party walked upstairs to the second-floor ballroom. Charles Emerson, his son Alexander, and his daughter, Venetia Emerson Campbell, stood at the top of the ballroom and spoke with guests. The orchestra played at the opposite end of the room and consisted of a cornet, a piano, a cello, and two violins.

Samantha saw Angelica and Robert step onto the dance floor. The marquess and her sister seemed made for each other. Perhaps Aunt Roxie was correct that Angelica would marry Robert Campbell and, one day, become the Duchess of Inverary.

Turning to speak to her aunt, Samantha froze as the uncanny feeling of being watched overwhelmed her senses. She looked around but detected no one paying her any particular attention. Still, the uncomfortable feeling persisted.

And then Robert Campbell stood in front of her. "May I have this dance?" he asked.

Damn her sister for putting the marquess up to this, Samantha thought, her face reddening with embarrassment, and panic rising in her breast.

"I—I . . ." Samantha had trouble finding her voice.

"Would you mind terribly if I postponed our dance until later? I'm feeling a bit overwhelmed by this crowd."

The marquess nodded in understanding. "Whenever you feel ready . . ."

"I'll dance with you," Victoria spoke up.

"Tory, ladies do *not* invite gentlemen to dance," Aunt Roxie scolded, sounding scandalized.

"I was just about to ask," Robert said, holding out his hand to Victoria.

Angelica sidled up to Samantha and whispered, "Why don't you dance?"

"I have no wish to become a spectacle."

"I promise, you will not—"

Again, Samantha felt uneasy. Someone was definitely watching her. And then she saw him.

With his arms folded across his chest, the gentleman leaned against the wall and ignored the circle of female admirers surrounding him. Easily the handsomest man she'd ever seen, the gentleman in black evening attire stared at her with an intensity that made her feel weak-legged. After holding her gaze captive for a long moment, he dropped his gaze and perused her body slowly, as if savoring each curve. He lifted his gaze to hers again and inclined his head in her direction by way of a long distance greeting.

What an insolent man, Samantha thought, her face flaming with embarrassed anger. She gave him a cold stare and then turned away. A moment later, unable to control the impulse, Samantha peeked at him.

He was still watching her. His gaze locked on hers, and the corners of his mouth turned up in a smile. When he nodded at her again, Samantha inclined her head in his direction. Her lips turned up in an answering smile.

"Did you hear what I said?" Angelica asked.

"I beg your pardon?" Samantha asked, focusing on her sister.

"Never mind."

The dance ended. Robert and Victoria joined them.

"Here comes trouble," Robert whispered, his lips quirking.

Samantha glanced in the direction he was looking. Venetia, the marquess's widowed sister-in-law, walked in their direction. With her was the gentleman who'd been staring at her. She shifted her gaze away from the man and prayed he wouldn't ask her to dance.

"Lady Angelica, here is Prince Rudolf to renew your acquaintance," Venetia said.

Samantha struggled to keep from laughing. Her sister was caught in an outrageous lie, having bragged to the other woman that the Russian prince had once proposed marriage to her.

"Your Highness, how good to see you again," Angelica said, apparently deciding to bluff her way out of a bad situation. "You remember my sisters, Samantha and Victoria."

Samantha nearly swooned when the prince looked at her and said, "I could never forget such beauty."

"You haven't danced with me, Robert," Venetia said, feigning a pout.

"I was looking forward to our dance," Robert replied, holding out his hand. "Shall we?"

Once they'd gone, Angelica smiled at the prince and blushed, saying, "Thank you, Your Highness, for going along with my fabrication."

"I suppose we were the closest of friends?" Prince Rudolf asked.

"In a manner of speaking," her sister hedged.

The prince smiled. "Did you leave me broken-hearted?"

"Absolutely devastated," Angelica drawled.

Samantha studied the prince while her sister spoke with him. Prince Rudolf was as tall as the marquess, a few inches over six feet. Like the marquess, the prince was broad-shouldered, narrow-waisted, and magnificent in his formal evening attire. Fathomless black eyes shone from his handsome face, accentuated by his black hair.

Prince Rudolf turned to her unexpectedly and asked, "Would you care to dance?"

His invitation surprised Samantha. How could she refuse a prince?

"Your Highness, I-I suffer from an old injury," Samantha said, a high blush staining her cheeks.

Concern etched itself across his features. "Are you in pain?" he asked.

"No, I-I limp when I walk."

Prince Rudolf fixed his dark gaze on hers. Samantha felt her knees go weak and knew why he'd been surrounded by so many admirers.

"Then, you will dance with me," he commanded her, holding his hand out.

Samantha dropped her gaze to his hand. Nervous indecision gripped her. More than anything else, she wanted to dance with him.

Acting on instinct, Samantha placed her hand in his. He gave it an encouraging squeeze, as if he knew her fear, and escorted her onto the dance floor.

Samantha relaxed as soon as she stepped into his arms. The prince danced with the practiced ease of a man who had waltzed a thousand times.

Swirling around the candlelit ballroom in his arms, Samantha felt as if she were floating on air and became intoxicated by the music and the man. The thought that her aunt had been correct about this being an enchanted evening flittered through her mind.

"I feel as if everyone is staring at me," Samantha said.

"They are watching *me*, not you," Prince Rudolf told her. "People are always curious about royals. By the way, you dance divinely."

"You mean, divinely for a woman who limps," Samantha corrected him, dropping her gaze to his chest.

"Speak to me, not my chest," Prince Rudolf commanded. When she looked up, he told her, "I meant, *you* dance divinely."

Samantha felt the heated blush staining her cheeks. "You dance divinely, too."

That made him smile. "I thank you on behalf of the myriad dance masters who tutored me," he said dryly.

Samantha smiled at that.

"You have a beautiful smile and should use it more often," the prince told her.

"People who smile for no apparent reason are considered unbalanced, Your Highness," she said.

"Unfortunately, that is true," Prince Rudolf agreed. "Please, call me Rudolf."

"I can't do that, Your Highness," Samantha said. "Familiarity with someone of your stature would be improper."

"I am a man as well as a prince," he told her. "I want to call you Samantha and cannot do it unless you call me Rudolf."

"Very well, Rudolf, but only when no one is listening," Samantha acquiesced.

"I like the sound of my name on your lips," Prince Rudolf said, making her blush again.

The music ended, and Samantha turned to leave the dance floor with him. The prince held her arm in a firm but gentle grip and silently refused to budge.

"You will dance with me again," he commanded.

Her aunt had said no more than twice with any gentleman but hadn't specified if the dances could be back to back. "Is that proper?" she asked.

"Royalty must be humored."

Samantha inclined her head and stepped into his arms for the next waltz. She glanced in her aunt's direction and saw the older woman smiling and nodding at her.

Circling the ballroom in the prince's arms felt like a dream. Samantha couldn't help thinking that her fear of dancing had been foolish.

The prince and the pickpocket, she thought. Perhaps Jane Austen would write a story about her.

"Speaking while waltzing is customary, Samantha," the prince said.

"I'm sorry, Rudolf."

"What were you thinking?"

"I was thinking you speak perfect English," she lied.

"Your thoughts were not about my lack of an accent," Prince Rudolf said. "However, I will admit my mother is English and tutored me herself."

The music ended before she could reply, but again the prince refused to let her go. "I'm sorry, Your— Rudolf," Samantha said. "My aunt insisted that I should not dance more than twice with any gentleman."

"Your aunt did not intend for you to offend a prince by refusing to dance with him," Rudolf told her. "Dancing two times with the same man applies only to common-ers."

"I am the second daughter of an earl," Samantha said. "That makes me a commoner."

"Then, I will compromise," Rudolf said, his hand on the small of her back as he guided her off the dance floor. "You will accompany me to the refreshment room and share a glass of champagne with me."

Samantha didn't know what to do. Her aunt hadn't

given her instructions about drinking champagne with a prince. She supposed that left her free to do what she wanted.

"I would like that." In truth, she didn't want to see the prince dancing with another woman.

Together, they left the ballroom. Samantha refused to look in her aunt's direction lest she see disapproval stamped across the woman's features.

"Strange, I don't remember the ballroom, only the foyer and my mother's fragrance," Samantha said without thinking.

The prince gave her a curious look. "I don't understand."

"I lived in this house until I was seven years old," she told him.

"Your parents sold the house to Emerson?" Rudolf asked.

"The villain stole it from my father," Samantha said, a bitter edge to her voice. *I am speaking too much*, she realized in the next instant.

The prince had stopped walking and turned to stare at her. Surprise had etched itself across his features.

"I should not have said what I did," Samantha said, touching his arm. "Please, do not repeat it to anyone."

"I would never betray a trust," the prince assured her. "Under the circumstances, I cannot understand your parents accepting Emerson's invitation."

"My parents are deceased," Samantha told him. "The gentleman you saw is the Duke of Inverary, and the lady is my Aunt Roxie."

"The Duke of Inverary?" the prince echoed, his dark eyes gleaming with interest. "I must hear this story."

"Another time, perhaps," she said, glancing around. "I wouldn't wish to be overheard."

Prince Rudolf led her to the stairs instead of the refreshment room. "We will postpone our champagne to walk in the garden while you relate this story to me."

Samantha halted at the top of the stairs. "Is that proper?"

"You are safe with me," the prince assured her. "I would never compromise your reputation."

Samantha relaxed but began to have doubts as they followed several other couples downstairs and headed for a stroll in the garden. She felt certain her aunt would not approve, but when she looked at the prince, she was unable to turn back and let him go. If she was going to live a lonely, miserable existence, she might as well have one evening to remember.

A few minutes later, Rudolf and Samantha stepped into a summer's night created for romance. Fog clung to the ground like a lover, but the sky overhead was clear, a full moon shining down on them. Torches had been lit, providing light for the couples who strolled around the garden. Mingling flower fragrances wafted through the air.

Rudolf took her hand in his and led her across the garden toward a silver birch tree. "Do you recall this garden?" he asked.

"No, perhaps in the daylight—"

"Tell me about the Duke of Inverary," the prince said.

Heedless of her gown, Samantha leaned back against the birch tree. The solidness of its trunk comforted her.

"His Grace, an old friend of my father's, opened his home to us and insisted on sponsoring my sisters and me," Samantha told him.

"How generous of him."

"Your Highness, you have been waltzing with a pauper," Samantha whispered, merriment shining from her blue eyes and a smile on her lips. "I have nothing to recommend me."

The prince stepped closer and, with one finger, lifted her chin. "You have a great deal to recommend you," he said, his voice seductively low.

Samantha stared into his eyes, mesmerized by their dark intensity. His handsome face inched closer.

Great Giles' ghost, he's going to kiss me. And then the scent of sandalwood, so arrogantly masculine, assailed her senses and made thinking impossible.

His face hovered above hers for one brief, tantalizing moment. And then their lips touched.

His lips are warm, Samantha thought, surrendering to this new sensation. Standing within the circle of his arms and pressing her lips to his felt as natural as breathing. And then it was over.

"You are as delicate as a Bulgarian rose and more mysterious than Asian jasmine," Rudolf whispered, his lips hovering above hers. "You intoxicate my senses."

Dazed by his kiss, Samantha stared at him through enormous blue eyes but remained silent. Rudolf traced a finger down her cheek. "Thank you for the gift of your first kiss," he said.

That jerked her into awareness. How did he know she'd never kissed a man? Was her inexperience so obvious?

"How—How did you know?" she managed to ask.

Prince Rudolf placed the palm of his hand against her cheek and told her, "Your skin burns with embarrassment, surely a sign of a first kiss."

Samantha smiled with relief. Apparently, she hadn't done anything incorrectly. "Tell me something more about yourself," she said, looking at him from beneath the thick fringe of her sooty lashes.

"What do you want to know?"

"Tell me about Russia."

"My homeland is cold."

"You told me your mother is English," Samantha said. "What about the others in your family?"

"They are Russians."

Samantha realized he was teasing her. She cast him an unconsciously flirtatious smile and asked, "How do princes really pass their days?"

"We issue commands to inferiors," Rudolf told her, a smile on his lips, "while we are wearing our crowns."

"Wearing the crown is necessary to issue commands?" Samantha asked, tilting her head back to look into his dark eyes.

"A prince should never be far from his crown," he told her, a smile flirting with his sensuously chiseled lips. "Sometimes we princes rescue maidens like you from dragons."

"Is that what you are doing tonight?" Samantha asked, growing serious. "I mean, rescuing me from society's dragons?"

"Do you need rescuing, my lady?" Prince Rudolf asked, staring into her eyes.

Samantha tore her gaze from his, feeling as if he could see into her soul and knew her deepest secrets, fears, and insecurities. Only family knew of her pain. She had too much Douglas pride to let anyone else, especially this man, see her pain.

"How do English ladies pass their days?" the prince asked, changing the subject when she remained silent.

I picked pockets until two weeks ago, Samantha thought. She looked at the prince, forced herself to smile, and said, "I play the violin."

"Will you play for me sometime?" he asked.

"I would be honored," she answered.

"How about that glass of champagne, my Bulgarian rose?" Rudolf asked.

"I would like that very much."

With her hand in his, Samantha limped toward the mansion. At the door, they met Angelica and the marquess on their way into the garden. Her sister appeared none too happy and cast her a look that said Aunt Roxie was displeased with her behavior.

Samantha cared not a whit. Her future loomed long and bleak in front of her. She knew the prince could never be interested in her, but he had given her an evening to remember. Perhaps other, more suitable gentlemen would follow the prince's lead and become acquainted with her instead of dismissing her because of her limp.

"Rudolf, I need to ask you a question," Samantha said, pausing in the foyer. When he inclined his head, she dropped her gaze to his chest and asked, "Why did you single me out tonight?"

"I love the way you look at my chest," he said in a husky voice.

Samantha lifted her gaze to his face. He was laughing at her.

"You are a desirable woman," Rudolf told her. "Why should I not be attracted to you?"

His answer surprised her. "But I limp—"

Interrupting her, a gunshot boomed from outside the mansion. Sounds of alarm reached them.

"Stay here," the prince ordered, heading for the door.

"I'm coming, too," Samantha said, following him outside.

They started down the street where a crowd had gathered. In the distance, Samantha saw her sister and the marquess.

"Oh," she cried in surprise when an enormous man, dressed in black, stepped from the shadows and blocked their path.

"Good evening, Your Highness," the man greeted the prince.

"Good evening, Igor," Rudolf replied in a tight voice, obviously displeased by this man's appearance. "How is Vladimir?"

"Return Venus to her rightful owner or suffer the consequences." With those words, the man disappeared into the night.

"What was that about?" Samantha asked, frightened.

Ignoring her question, Rudolf lifted her hands to his lips, saying, "I must take my leave now. May I call upon you?"

Samantha's smile lit the night, and hope swelled within her breast. "Yes, Rudolf, you may."

The prince gifted her with a devastating smile and then retraced his steps down the street. Samantha watched him disappear inside one of the coaches.

He never called upon her.

CHAPTER 2

December 31, 1812

"Alexander Emerson is excruciatingly boring," Victoria announced. "I don't understand why she wants to marry him."

"What a terrible thing to say," Angelica scolded her youngest sister.

"Well, it's true."

Ignoring her sisters, Samantha stood at the window of her second-floor bedchamber at the Duke of Inverary's country estate. She stared absently at the curving brick drive and the courtyard's three water terraces.

Tonight was a special night. Not only would her family celebrate the new year with a gala ball but would also announce her betrothal to Alexander Emerson. So why didn't she feel especially happy?

You don't love him, an inner voice reminded her.

Through sheer force of will, Samantha silenced that disturbing voice and sent it back to the suburbs of her mind. She turned away from the window and smiled at her younger sister as if the other woman were an imbecile.

"I want to marry Alexander Emerson because he *is* boring," Samantha told her.

She had passed a soul-searching week alone at the old cottage, trying to decide what to do. Her decision had been relatively easy, though, because a woman who limped wasn't exactly the height of fashion.

"You should have gone to Sweetheart Manor instead of the cottage," Angelica said, as if she'd read her thoughts. "Robert spent a fortune restoring and renovating it, complete with staff awaiting a visit from the Countess of Melrose and her husband."

Samantha looked at her older sister knitting a bunting for the babe she expected in four months. "The cottage at Primrose Hill is closer than Scotland."

"A complete change of scenery would have been good for you," Angelica said.

"You may have arrived at a different decision," Victoria said. "You don't love Alexander."

Her sister's remark surprised Samantha. Was it that obvious?

"Father and Mother would never have expected you to marry a man you don't love just so their bodies can rest on Douglas land," Victoria added.

"Out of the mouths of babes comes wisdom," Angelica said with a smile.

"Almost seventeen is *not* a child," Victoria informed her oldest sister. She glanced at Samantha and said, "Too bad Prince Rudolf never called upon you."

Samantha kept her face expressionless, but her stomach knotted at the sound of his name. "Tory, you cannot have believed that a man of his esteem would call upon me."

"You don't need to marry a man you don't love because you fear no other man will ask you," Angelica told her.

"I fear nothing, especially spinsterhood," Samantha said, lifting her chin a notch.

"Hello, my darlings," called a voice from the doorway.

The three sisters turned and watched their aunt cross the bedchamber. Aunt Roxie sat on the settee in front of the hearth and asked, "Is everyone excited about tonight?"

"I can hardly wait for the midnight fireworks," Victoria gushed. "His Grace certainly knows how to celebrate New Year's."

"Yes, he certainly knows how to celebrate," Aunt Roxie drawled in a sugggestive tone.

Samantha and Angelica exchanged smiles. Their wonderful aunt had recently made the duke her fourth husband, and the two seemed to spend a lot of time closeted within their bedchamber.

"Be careful, or you'll find your belly as big as mine," Angelica teased, patting her own pregnancy-swollen middle.

Aunt Roxie laughed. "Swallow your tongue, child."

"You look young enough to become a mother," Samantha said.

"Bless you, darling." Aunt Roxie reached into her pocket and produced a necklace, a ruby pendant hanging on a gold chain. "I've brought you a gift," she said.

Samantha let her aunt place the necklace over her head and then looked down at the ruby. "Thank you, but what did I do to deserve such a reward?"

"Darling, you deserve to be drenched in jewels for being your wonderful self," Aunt Roxie said smoothly. She gazed into her niece's blue eyes and told her, "This necklace possesses powerful magic."

Samantha managed to keep her expression serious and the laughter out of her voice. "What kind of magic?"

"Legend says the star ruby will darken to the color of blood if its owner is threatened," Aunt Roxie said.

"Then, I will keep a guarded eye on it," Samantha promised, unable to control the skeptical smile flirting with the corners of her lips.

"Remember, child, life doesn't always turn out as planned," Aunt Roxie said, putting her arm around her.

"Did you have another vision?" Victoria asked. "Can you tell me which gentleman will invite me to supper?"

"Tory, you are beginning to give me a headache," Samantha complained.

"Well, you are a pain in the—"

"Victoria," her aunt cried.

"I need some fresh air," Samantha said, rising from the settee. She donned her hooded, fur-lined cloak over her blue dress. Then she grabbed her special violin case with the wide leather strap that hung over her shoulder.

"Good-bye, darling, have a wonderful time," Aunt Roxie called. "Remember, your ruby will warn you if danger threatens."

Samantha paused at the door. Her aunt sounded as if she was going on a trip instead of the gazebo to play her violin.

"I won't forget," Samantha assured her aunt, and then left the chamber.

Armed with her violin, Samantha limped down the corridor to the curving staircase. She paused when she reached the first-floor foyer and looked up at the second-floor balcony where the duke's statuary of the Three Fates stood.

What did the Fates have planned? Samantha wondered. Whenever her aunt behaved mysteriously, something unexpected happened, and the unexpected was always a turn for the worse.

"Is something wrong, miss?"

Turning at the sound of the majordomo's voice, Samantha shook her head. Then she started down the corridor leading to the rear of the mansion.

A crisp December afternoon greeted Samantha. The sun warmed her face as she limped across the expanse of snow-dusted lawn nearest the mansion, yet the crispness of the air spoke of winter.

Samantha opened the iron gate that separated the lawn from the marquess's garden. Before passing through the barren garden, she looked over her shoulder at the mansion as an uncanny feeling of being watched made the fine hairs on her nape prickle.

Flicking her cloak open, Samantha glanced at the star ruby. It remained placid. She shook off the uncomfortable feeling and continued on her way past the maze and across another, larger expanse of lawn.

The gazebo stood beyond the lawns at the edge of the woodland. Samantha sighed as she seated herself inside. Scented with woodsmoke from the fireplaces within the mansion, the afternoon was a gem of blue sky and sunshine.

Why didn't she feel happy and lighthearted? Samantha wondered. Alexander Emerson was intelligent and kind and possessed blond good looks. He was excellent husband material, and she intended to be the best wife ever.

The image of the Russian prince stepped from the shadows of her mind. Her heart ached for what could never be. Why had he asked to call upon her? If he'd said nothing, she would never have expected to see him again. Instead, she had waited weeks for a visit that never materialized.

Samantha told herself she should be grateful for that one enchanted evening. Many women never had that much. Opening her instrument case, Samantha lifted her violin and bow. Then she began to play a haunting melody that mirrored her feeling of loneliness.

Two pairs of eyes watched Samantha crossing the grounds. Robert Campbell and Prince Rudolf stood at the window in the duke's study and watched the petite, ebony-haired woman limping toward the gazebo.

"Samantha Douglas is a lovely woman," Prince Rudolf said, breaking the silence.

"Yes, too bad about her limp," Robert replied.

"Limp?" the prince echoed, glancing sidelong at the other man. "I hadn't noticed."

Robert gave the prince an amused smile but made no reply. He walked away for a minute and returned to hand him a dram of whiskey.

"I would prefer vodka if you have any," Rudolf told him.

"I'm sorry," Robert replied with a shrug.

"I'll send you a supply at first opportunity," Prince Rudolf said. He downed the whiskey in one gulp and added, "Vodka is a man's drink. Save the whiskey for the ladies." He returned his attention to the young woman sitting alone in the gazebo. She appeared as lonely as he felt.

"Samantha will be announcing her engagement to Alexander Emerson tonight," Robert told him.

"Wasn't there trouble between the Douglases and the Emersons?" Rudolf asked, without taking his gaze off the woman in the gazebo.

"Alexander is determined to make amends for his father's misdeeds," the marquess replied.

"Samantha deserves a husband who loves her," Rudolf said.

"I spoke those very words to my wife this morning," Robert agreed. "However, unless that man makes an appearance within the next few hours, both Samantha and Alexander will be bound to spouses who don't love them."

Rudolf turned to meet the marquess's dark gaze. "Samantha does not love him?"

"I think not."

Turning his back on the window, Rudolf scanned the duke's study filled with mahogany furniture and bookcases built into the walls. A burgundy, blue, cream, and gold carpet covered the floor.

Though his gaze was on the study, his thoughts were on the woman sitting in the gazebo. Samantha Douglas probably despised him for not calling upon her, but what could he do? Other, more important obligations had demanded his attention. Perhaps if circumstances had been different—

The door swung open at that moment, and the Duke of Inverary walked into the room. Magnus Campbell was an older version of his son—tall and well-built, black eyes, black hair beginning to silver at the temples.

"Shall we get down to business?" the duke said, gesturing toward his desk.

Prince Rudolf inclined his head and sat in one of the chairs in front of the desk. The marquess sat in another chair while the duke took his place behind the desk.

"We haven't seen you about town for several months," Duke Magnus remarked, a polite smile appearing on his face.

"I've been rusticating on my new estate," Rudolf told him.

"Where is that?" the marquess asked.

"Sark Island in the Channel," Rudolf answered. "I settled my mother and daughter there and decided to stay for a prolonged visit."

"You have a daughter?"

Rudolf heard the surprise in the other man's voice and knew he was probably thinking about his young sister-in-law. "I lost my wife," he told the marquess.

"I'm sorry."

Duke Magnus cleared his throat. "Your English is perfect, no trace of an accent."

"My mother is English," Rudolf told the older man, watching his expression. "Elizabeth Montague. Perhaps you remember her?"

Rudolf noted the flicker of recognition in the duke's dark eyes. Within an instant, the older man had shuttered his expression.

"I never had the pleasure of making her acquaintance," Duke Magnus said, shifting his gaze away from him.

The duke was lying. That much was obvious to Rudolf. Had his mother spoken truthfully about the Duke of Inverary? She did have many lucid moments.

"What can we do for you, Your Highness?" Duke Magnus asked.

"I have come to do for you," Rudolf said, looking from the duke to the marquess. Both men wore puzzled expressions.

"I am not in accord with my brother," Rudolf explained. "Last summer, my agents pirated a ship they thought belonged to Vladimir. Unfortunately, *The Tempest* belongs to you."

Rudolf reached into his jacket pocket and produced an envelope. He placed it on the desk, saying, "I am an honorable man with more money than I could hope to spend. Here is a banknote for the money my agents stole. With interest, of course. I hope you won't press charges."

Both the duke and the marquess sat in stunned silence for a long moment. Finally, Duke Magnus said, "We'll call it a misunderstanding."

"I appreciate your generous spirit," Rudolf said.

"Your brother and you play roughly with each other," the marquess remarked.

Rudolf rose from his chair and looked out the window again at the woman sitting in the gazebo. Without thinking, he told them, "Vladimir wants me dead."

Silence greeted his revelation. Apparently, he'd shocked the Campbells again. These descendents of Highlanders thought they were strong, stalwart men but could learn real brutality from his own countrymen.

Duke Magnus cleared his throat. "You'll stay for tonight's celebration, of course."

The last thing Rudolf wanted to witness was Samantha Douglas becoming engaged to Alexander Emerson. "I haven't brought evening attire with me," he said in refusal. "As a matter of fact, I rode alone from London so I could complete the round trip in one day."

"Your horse needs to rest," Robert said, rising from his chair. "We're about the same size. You'll borrow my clothes."

Rudolf flicked a glance out the window again. Like a siren's song, the sweetness of the woman playing the violin called to him. "I accept your invitation," he said. "Would you mind if I walked outside to offer Samantha my best wishes?"

"I'm certain she'll appreciate that," the marquess replied, but his concerned expression said something else.

Rudolf inclined his head and started to leave. The duke's voice stopped him at the door.

"Your Highness, may I ask how old you are?" Duke Magnus asked.

His question surprised Rudolf. He glanced at the marquess, who looked as surprised at the question as he felt.

"I will be twenty-eight on the fifteenth day of May," Rudolf answered, and then left the chamber.

Trying to clear disturbing thoughts from her mind, Samantha had stopped thinking about Alexander and had let her violin take her wherever it would. Caught up in her music, she closed her eyes and poured all of her heartache and longing into her song.

"My Bulgarian rose."

Samantha opened her eyes and stared at the prince. Her heart lurched at the sight of his handsome face, and she couldn't seem to find her voice.

Was he real, or was she imagining him? Why had he decided to come here today when she was about to announce her betrothal? Was this his idea of a joke?

"I promised to call upon you," Rudolf said, his voice intimately husky, "but you do not seem pleased."

"You are slightly tardy, Your Highness," Samantha said, steeling herself against him.

"Rudolf," he corrected her.

Samantha placed her violin and bow into their case. Then she slung the leather strap over her shoulder and stood, saying, "If you will excuse me, *Your Highness.*"

"Sit down," Rudolf ordered.

"I am not one of your—"

"Sit down, I said."

Samantha sat down, her cloak opening with the movement. She never felt the cold, though. Her blue gaze on him glinted with anger.

"I wish to explain why I never called upon you," Rudolf told her.

"An explanation is unnecessary," Samantha said, forcing an insincere smile onto her face.

"Yes, I know," Rudolf agreed, and smiled infuriatingly at her. "I had an emergency."

"A six-month emergency?"

"I needed to settle my mother and my daughter—"

"You have a daughter?" Samantha interrupted, surprised by his words.

"Interrupting is impolite," Rudolf said.

Samantha blushed and dropped her gaze to the gazebo's floor. It was then she noticed the star ruby had deepened into the color of blood. Was she in danger from the prince? She couldn't credit that. Perhaps her heart—

"As I was saying," Rudolf continued, running a hand through his black hair in apparent frustration, "I needed to settle my mother and daughter into the estate I purchased. Several other problems surfaced then."

"I understand," Samantha said, starting to rise.

"I have not dismissed you," Rudolf said, his voice stern with authority.

Great Giles' ghost, Samantha thought, staring in surprise at him. Who did he think he was? The bloody King of England? And then she realized that as a royal, no one had ever refused him anything. Apparently, the prince had led a parochial life. She would love to teach his arrogance a lesson, but she was getting engaged and had no time for games.

"You will postpone announcing your betrothal," the prince told her.

"I will do no such thing," she cried.

"You do not love this Alexander Emerson," Rudolf said.

"You know nothing about me," Samantha shot back.

"I know you are as delicate as a Bulgarian rose and as mysterious as Asian jasmine," Rudolf said, the hint of a smile touching his lips.

"Are you proposing marriage?" she challenged him.

"I cannot offer marriage at this time," he replied. "I want to become better acquainted with you which I cannot do if you are betrothed to another man."

"You want me to cancel my betrothal so that you can become better acquainted with me?" Samantha echoed, arching an ebony brow at him.

Rudolf nodded. "That is correct."

"Your Highness, have you been indulging in spirits?" she asked, and laughed out loud.

"Help . . ."

Samantha whirled around and stared at the woodland behind the gazebo. She glanced at the prince, who was also staring at the woodland.

"Help . . ."

Samantha brushed past the prince and hurried as fast as her limp would allow toward the woodland path. Prince Rudolf was two steps behind her.

"You will wait here," he ordered, grasping her upper arm.

Samantha shrugged his hand off and kept going. Twilight had already descended inside the dense woodland, and she could barely see where she was going.

"Help . . ." The cry seemed to be coming from behind them now.

Samantha whirled around in time to see an enormous man cock a pistol at Prince Rudolf. "No," she cried, starting toward them. Someone grabbed her from behind, but she stomped her assailant's foot with the heel of her boot.

"Owww, she broke my toes," a man cried.

"For Gawd's sake, she don't weigh more than a few ounces," a second man said.

"She weighs enough to make me a Hopping Giles," the first man replied.

"Igor," Samantha whispered, her gaze on the giant with the pistol.

The giant flicked a glance at her and said to the prince, "Your ladybird remembers me."

"You are not easily forgotten," Prince Rudolf said. "Release the woman before you shoot me. She has no part in my disagreement with Vladimir."

Igor remained silent for a moment. "I cannot release her now that she has recognized me, but I will not murder a prince either. If Vladimir wants you dead, he will need to do it himself." He gestured to the path, ordering, "Turn around and start walking."

"I'm not going anywhere," Samantha cried, her panic rising. "I'm announcing my betrothal tonight."

"I'm sorry," Prince Rudolf said, "but you are not a princess. Igor would suffer no qualms about shooting you."

Igor pointed the pistol at her as if to emphasize the prince's words. Samantha curled her lips at him but fell into step beside the prince.

With the two men in the lead and Igor pointing the pistol on their backs, Samantha and Rudolf walked through the woodland. Her limp slowed them down, but fifteen minutes later they emerged from the woods and saw a coach waiting on the road. The sun had set outside the woodland, and dusk was rapidly darkening into night.

One of the men opened the coach door and gestured them inside. Samantha hesitated, saying, "I really must protest—"

Igor leveled the pistol at her, and Samantha climbed into the coach. The prince climbed in and sat beside her.

Igor slammed the door. A moment later, the coach started up.

"I'm sorry for involving you in this," Rudolf said, putting a comforting arm around her. "I promise to rescue you from death."

Samantha looked at him. His handsome face was barely visible within the darkness of the coach. "I'm getting engaged," she told him.

"Not tonight," Prince Rudolf said, and gave her an infuriatingly satisfied smile.

"Buff your crown," Samantha snapped, leveling a disgruntled look on him.

"Your fear is speaking," Prince Rudolf said. "I know you would never wish to be disrespectful."

"The hell I don't," Samantha said, unable to credit what she was hearing.

Whirling away at the moment the coach began to pick up speed, Samantha fell back against him. She felt the prince's arms going around her and jerked herself into an upright position. After giving him a warning look, she turned away. This time she held on to the edge of the seat lest she fall on the floor or the prince's lap.

Great Giles' ghost, Samantha thought in irritated frustration, pulling her fur-lined cloak tightly around herself. How had she managed to get herself involved in this untenable situation? More importantly, how would she extricate herself?

She had passed her entire eighteen years living in the shadows cast by her talented older sister, who wanted revenge, and her vibrant younger sister, who wanted fun.

Nobody ever noticed her, and she had never thought she would be fortunate enough to marry and have her own family.

Then along had come Alexander Emerson, who wanted to make amends for his father's crimes against her family. Alexander didn't love her, but he would have made a good husband.

And now? Even if she survived this, her reputation would be ruined. No man would marry her after she had disappeared with a Russian prince, not even Alexander Emerson. To think her dream had been within her grasp and slipped through her fingers. . . .

Samantha lost control of her emotions. Tears streamed down her cheeks, and then a sob escaped her throat.

"I am sorry," Prince Rudolf whispered against her ear.

Samantha felt his arm around her shoulder, pulling her close. His breath was warm on the side of her cheek, and his sandalwood scent teased her senses. She turned toward him and saw the handkerchief he was holding out to her.

Regaining control of herself, Samantha lifted the handkerchief out of his hand. "I apologize for crying," she said. "Weeping never solved a problem."

"Tears purge the soul of negative humors," the prince said. "I know you are frightened, but we will have an opportunity to escape."

"I fear nothing, Your Highness, not even Igor," Samantha told him, feigning courage. "I have no intention of waiting for an opportunity to escape. Douglases make their own luck." Even in the darkness, she saw the white of his teeth when he smiled at her bravado.

"What shall we do?" the prince asked. "Leap out of a moving coach? We would only kill ourselves."

"We're going to die anyway," she reminded him.

"I think not."

"If I wasn't with you," Samantha asked, "what would you do?"

Rudolf smiled at her. "I would leap out the door."

"Let's do it, then."

"The violin will injure you in the leap," Rudolf told her. "You will need to leave it behind."

Accustomed to the darkness now, Samantha looked him straight in the eye and said, "Your Highness, I and my violin are going out that door. With any luck, I can make it back to the duke's residence in time to save my reputation and my betrothal."

"Very well, but I will carry the violin," Rudolf acquiesced. "Listen carefully to my directions. When I open the door, you must jump at an angle away from the direction the coach is traveling. Tuck in your head, arms, and legs so you will not be run over. Roll away from the road when you hit the ground. Do you understand?"

Samantha made no reply. His words "so you will not be run over" echoed within her mind. The memory of excruciating pain flittered through her mind. Panic and dread paralyzed her resolve to escape the coach.

"Do you understand?" the prince asked again, yanking her free of her memory.

Samantha nodded and repeated his directions. "Jump away from the coach, tucking my extremities, and roll when I hit the ground."

"I will jump immediately after you." Rudolf reached for the handle, but the door wouldn't open. He looked at her and shrugged. "Igor locked it."

"Let me try," Samantha said, reaching across his body.

"Do you think you have more strength than I?" the prince asked.

Samantha dropped her hand to her lap and sat back against the seat. "Do you have any ideas?" she asked.

"None at the moment." Prince Rudolf gave her a devastating smile.

"How can you be so cheerful in the face of death?" Samantha asked, irritated by his smile.

"I am actually relieved," the prince admitted. "The locked door precludes injury."

"I am not as delicate as you think," she said.

"I was considering the chance of injury to myself," he told her.

Samantha felt the heated blush rising on her cheeks and was thankful for the darkness inside the coach. Dropping her gaze to his mouth, she recalled how his lips felt covering hers. What a fool she'd been to believe that a prince would call upon her. She would never give her imagination free rein again. However handsome the prince was, he was not the man for her.

"Our continued good health does not concern me," Rudolf told her. "The star inside your ruby is formed by three benign spirits—faith, hope, and destiny."

"Destiny's spirit doesn't seem benign to me tonight," Samantha said, a rueful tone in her voice.

"Your destiny lies not with Alexander Emerson," the prince said.

"Apparently, my destiny is to die with you," Samantha said dryly. "By the way, why does this Vladimir want you dead?"

"That is none of your business."

Samantha couldn't believe she was going to her grave without knowing the reason why. She had the right to know her murderer's motive.

"Did Alexander—" The prince hesitated for a moment. "Did Alexander give you the ruby?"

"That is none of your business," Samantha said, tossing his words back at him.

"Refrain from disrespect, young lady."

Lifting her nose into the air, Samantha moved to sit on the seat opposite him. The prince moved when she did, joining her there. When she started to switch to her original seat, Rudolf put an arm around her shoulder and pulled her back against his body.

"You cannot escape me, my love," Rudolf whispered against her ear.

Love? Samantha wondered at his choice of words. Was this a cruel joke? Or was he trying to make a doomed woman feel better?

"I apologize for failing to call upon you," Rudolf said. "Family obligations prevented me from doing what my heart desired."

Samantha heard the regret in his voice and relaxed against him. "You owe me no apology or explanation."

"When I met you, I sensed that you understood great pain," Prince Rudolf said, his hand on her shoulder beginning a slow caress. "I have suffered pain in my life, too."

Samantha sighed. "I suppose no one lives without pain, even princes."

"Especially princes," he said.

"We may as well become acquainted while we wait to die," Samantha said. "Tell me about your family."

"I moved my mother and my daughter to England, land of my mother's birth," Rudolf told her. "Upon her brother's passing, I inherited Montague House."

"Losing your wife must have been difficult," Samantha said. "Do you have brothers or sisters?"

"I have four younger brothers," Rudolf told her. "Vladimir and Viktor are twins. Then comes Mikhail and Stepan."

So this Vladimir is his brother. "What about your father?" Samantha asked. "Is he deceased?"

"I prefer not to discuss my father," the prince said,

his voice cold. He softened his tone when he said, "Tell me about yourself, little one."

"I am a pauper," Samantha said. "I haven't a penny to my name."

"I measure people by the size of their hearts, not their purses," Rudolf said, his embrace tightening, brushing his lips against her temple.

"How rare for a prince to possess magnanimous integrity," Samantha said, a smile in her voice.

The scent of woodsmoke wafted through the air into their coach. Both Rudolf and Samantha looked out the window. In spite of the hour and the cold, many people filled the narrow street.

"We are in London," Prince Rudolf said.

He reached out to stroke her cheek and then turned her face toward his. She knew he was going to kiss her and closed her eyes as the exotic scent of sandalwood filled her senses.

His lips touched hers, claiming her mouth in a lingering kiss. It melted into another and then another. Only the coach jerking to an abrupt halt broke them apart.

"Stay alert for any avenue of escape," Rudolf whispered.

"Why am I going to die?" Samantha asked in a quavering voice.

"My brother hates me," Rudolf told her. "Vladimir takes after our father."

His admission surprised Samantha, but she had no time to consider his statement. The coach's door swung open.

"Get out," Igor ordered.

Rudolf climbed down first and turned to assist her. Looping the instrument case's leather strap over her shoulder, Samantha steadied herself by grasping the door handle.

No lock registered in her mind. Samantha snapped her gaze toward the prince.

Rudolf smiled like a boy caught in a prank, earning himself a black scowl. "I saved you from yourself," he whispered.

"Follow my companions into the house," Igor ordered, pointing his pistol at them.

Carrying lanterns, the two accomplices led the way into the alley door of the house. Rudolf walked in front of Samantha, who was followed by Igor.

Once inside, Samantha saw that the hallway led into the kitchen. Instead of entering the kitchen, the men with the lanterns opened a door and turned to start down a flight of stairs.

"Owww," Samantha cried, losing her balance. She pushed the prince out of the way and fell into one of the villains.

"Damned Hopping Giles," the man cursed, shoving her back.

The force of his shove sent her careening into Igor. Rudolf grabbed and steadied her.

"Touch her again, and you will die," Rudolf threatened the man.

"I'm shakin', yer lordship," he shot back.

The prince growled and moved to grab the man.

"Please, Rudolf, I am uninjured. If they kill you, I will be alone," Samantha said, placing a restraining hand on the prince's arm. "Do not do anything rash."

CHAPTER 3

The cellar smelled like a dead skunk. Complete darkness lay beyond the circle of light cast by the lanterns. Samantha didn't even want to think about what hid in the cellar's corners.

"You cannot leave us here," Rudolf said, turning to the giant. "This room is unhealthy."

"You won't live long enough to get sick," one of the men said.

"You'll be dead in the morning," his friend agreed.

Samantha didn't want to die. She especially didn't want to die in this cellar.

Rudolf drew her against his body. He turned to Igor and said, "For the lady's sake, leave us the lantern."

The big Russian gestured one of his thugs to leave the lantern. Then he reached into his pocket and muttered, "Where are those damned keys?" He looked at his minions and ordered, "You get the spare keys. And you bring vodka, cheese, and bread."

"You're gonna feed them?" the second man asked. "What a waste of food and drink."

Igor growled like a bear and stepped toward the man, who dashed up the stairs. "I apologize for the accommodations," he said to the prince. "Vladimir will arrive in a day or two. Ah, here is your supper."

"No caviar?"

"My apologies, Your Highness."

"Igor, I always liked you," Rudolf said. "If you ever leave my brother's employ, you are welcome to join my household."

Before the big Russian could reply, one of the villains said, "Dead men don't keep households." The man reached for the violin case, adding, "We'll get a few coins for this."

"Over my dead body," Samantha cried, holding tight to the violin case, refusing to relinquish it.

Rudolf hit the man's arm, forcing him to release it. At the same moment, Igor grabbed the man's throat, lifted him into the air, and tossed him toward the stairs.

Choking and wheezing, the man scurried up the stairs just as his friend appeared in the doorway, calling, "I found the keys."

"Enjoy the vodka, Your Highness," Igor said. The big Russian climbed the stairs, closed the door, and locked it.

Samantha watched the prince lift the lantern high and turn in a circle as if scanning the cellar for an escape route. Finding none, he set the lantern down on the floor and looked at her.

"In a day or two, you will experience the dubious pleasure of meeting my brother," Rudolf said. "I am sorry you have become involved in our quarrel."

Regardless of the filth, Samantha sat down on the bottom stair. "I cannot believe I am sitting here instead of becoming betrothed," she complained. "Alexander will never marry me now."

"You do not love the man," the prince replied. "From what I have heard, he does not love you."

"Love has nothing to do with marriage," Samantha told him. "That is a luxury reserved for a fortunate few . . . like handsome, wealthy princes."

"Thank you for the compliment," Rudolf said, inclining his head. "However, you deserve a husband who loves you."

"You lied about the coach door," Samantha said, ignoring his remark.

Now the prince ignored her remark, asking, "What is Hopping Giles?"

Samantha sighed. "Saint Giles is the patron saint of cripples, and Hopping Giles is a derogatory name given to cripples."

"You are no cripple."

"Are you blind?" Samantha asked in irritation. "I walk with a limp."

"Assume a respectful tone of voice when you address me," Rudolf ordered her. "I am a prince of Russia."

"You are a royal pain in my arse," Samantha snapped. Then she unleashed the full fury of her anger. "Where do you get the gall to correct my behavior? You disappeared for six months and then barged into my life, upsetting my plans and getting me abducted."

"I have apologized for that," the prince said stiffly.

"I haven't forgiven you."

Sitting on the stair beside her, Rudolf gave her a confused look, asking, "Isn't one required to accept an apology?"

Surprised by his question, Samantha turned her head to stare at him. "Your Highness, have you ever apologized to anyone?"

"Not that I can remember." Rudolf took a swig of the vodka and offered her the bottle.

"I do not indulge in spirits," Samantha said, shaking her head. "Why does your brother want you dead?"

"Vladimir has always harbored an intense jealousy toward me," Rudolf answered. "He wants something I have and, apparently, is willing to kill for it."

Samantha couldn't understand what was so important that one brother would murder another. After all, the English throne was not at stake. "What do you have?" she asked.

"I possess the Kazanov Venus," he answered.

"*. . . return Venus to her rightful owner or suffer the consequences.*" Samantha recalled Igor's words to the prince on the night of Emerson's ball.

"The Kazanov Venus is a medallion of gold engraved with the goddess Venus holding the hand of her son, Cupid," Rudolf told her, his pride apparent in his voice. "The piece has belonged to my family for almost five hundred years and is always passed down from father to eldest son. Whoever possesses the Kazanov Venus enjoys prosperity and fertility."

"Why don't you let Vladimir borrow it?" Samantha asked.

"My brother has already stolen several of my possessions," Rudolf told her. "The medallion cannot be shared."

"If your father bequeathed it to you, then I don't understand how—"

"My father is still alive," Rudolf interrupted. "I took Venus with me when I left Russia."

"You stole from your father?"

"Certainly not." The prince sounded affronted. "I took what was mine."

"Why does Vladimir believe the medallion should be his?" Samantha asked.

"I cannot know what dwells in my brother's mind,

but I do know that malice for me fills his heart." Rudolf
put his arm around her and drew her close against the
side of his body.

The prince was much too close for Samantha's peace
of mind. The warmth of his body and his appealing
sandalwood scent conspired against her, and she felt herself falling under his spell and wishing he would kiss her.

Samantha gave herself a mental shake. Great Giles'
ghost, only a blinking idiot would be thinking of kissing
at a time like this.

"Since we are going to die in a day or two," the
prince said, breaking the silence between them, "would
you care to pass tonight making love?"

Samantha turned her head to stare at him. Only a
dead man would have missed her angry shock.

"That was a bad idea," Rudolf admitted, and smiled
unrepentantly. His next words surprised her when he
mirrored her thoughts. "I wish circumstances had been
different for us."

"So do I, Your Highness."

Rudolf and Samantha sat in silence for a long time.
She rested her head against his shoulder and listened
to the sounds of footsteps on the floor above their heads.
Finally, all was silent.

"I think our abductors have gone to bed," Samantha
whispered, pulling a key out of her pocket and holding
it in front of the prince's face. "Shall we leave now?"

The prince dropped his mouth open in surprise.
"Where did you get that?"

"When I fell against Igor, I lifted it out of his pocket,"
she told him with pride in her voice.

"Your tripping was fortuitous," Rudolf said, standing
to offer her his hand.

"Fortuitous, my arse," Samantha said, accepting his
hand. "I tripped on purpose. That foul-smelling assis-

tant of his had empty pockets. Thankfully, he pushed me in the direction I wanted to go."

Rudolf lifted the key out of her hand, asking, "Shall we leave?"

Samantha nodded but paused a moment to flick the bottom edge of her gown up. She reached into her boot and pulled out a small dagger. "I'm ready now."

"You carry a dagger in your boot?" he asked in obvious surprise.

Samantha thought he was asking why she hadn't drawn it before. "The dagger would have been no match for their pistol."

"You seem different from the proper lady with whom I danced at the Emerson ball," Rudolf remarked.

"I am as I always was," Samantha told him. "Do you want to escape or discuss your misconceptions about me?"

Rudolf smiled, lifted the dagger out of her hand, and ordered, "Take the lantern so I can see what I am doing at the top of the stairs."

"We'll make less noise if we remove our boots," she suggested, reaching for the lantern.

"That is unnecessary." Rudolf moved to start up the stairs, which creaked in protest. He stopped short and whispered as if he'd just had an idea, "Take off your boots."

At the top of the stairs, Samantha held the lantern while he unlocked the door. Rudolf opened it slowly and peered into the empty hallway. He led her down the short hall, away from the kitchen, and outside into the night. She set the lantern down, lest it become a beacon for their captors, and together, they hurried down the alley as quickly as her limp would allow. After putting two blocks between them and their abductors, they paused to put their boots on again.

"The Londoners are celebrating the coming New

Year," Samantha said, hearing loud voices only a short distance away.

"Crowds offer safety," Rudolf said. "Let us join them."

Samantha placed her hand in his, and they walked down the cross street to the main thoroughfare. Here crowds of people milled around as if the hour was high noon.

"Where are we?" Rudolf asked.

Samantha looked up and turned in a circle. The torchlit towers of Whitehall were very close. "We're in East London."

"Which way is Montague House?" he asked.

"We must walk west."

Samantha started to pull her fur-lined cloak around herself but glanced at the cloakless prince. She opened her cloak in a silent invitation.

The prince looked stunned by her offer. Hadn't anyone ever shown him a simple kindness?

"You need it more than I," Rudolf refused.

"Get in here, Your Highness," Samantha ordered. "We have a long walk."

"You will be cold," he argued.

"Your body heat will keep me warm," she told him.

Rudolf grinned, stepped into the cloak, and pulled one side over his right shoulder. Samantha wrapped the other side tightly around herself. She felt his left arm encircle her waist and realized how close they needed to be to share the cloak.

"I will carry your violin," he said.

"That is unnecessary," she told him.

"I insist." Rudolf lifted it out of her hand and looked up at the moonlit sky adorned with thousands of stars. "It is a good night for an adventure," he said.

It was a good night for anything as long as she was with him, Samantha thought, startling herself.

Rudolf and Samantha started walking west on Cheapside and passed St. Paul's Cathedral. From there, they headed north to Great Russell Street. Montague House lay between Bedford House and Bedford Square.

Near ten o'clock, Rudolf and Samantha reached Montague House. "This is it," he said.

"Perhaps your coachman could drive me to His Grace's on Park Lane?" Samantha asked.

"You cannot leave me," Rudolf said. "Igor and his men will be looking for us."

"I will be perfectly safe at His Grace's," she told him.

"Your ability to identify our assailants places your life in grave danger," the prince said, guiding her up the front stairs.

Though that frightened her, Samantha wouldn't let go of her dream so easily. "I might still be able to—"

"Your well-being is more important than your betrothal to Alexander Emerson," Rudolf interrupted.

Surrendering to the inevitable, Samantha sighed heavily and inclined her head. She let him lead her into the foyer and felt relieved when the door closed behind them.

"Karl!" the prince shouted.

A moment later, a dark-haired man appeared. "You have returned, Your Highness," the man said by way of a greeting. "I expected you to—"

"Bring us something to eat in the dining room," the prince ordered. "Send Boris and Elke to me."

"Yes, Your Highness."

Rudolf escorted Samantha down a corridor to the dining room. The room's understated opulence reminded her of His Grace's dining room. A dark mahogany, rectangular table and chairs sat in the middle of the room. A matching sideboard perched on one side of the room, and crystal chandeliers hung over the table. An elaborate, gold-framed mirror hung over the fireplace mantel.

Rudolf seated Samantha beside the chair at the head of the table. No sooner had the prince sat down when his three retainers appeared. Between them, they carried slices of cold roast, cheese, bread, and a bottle of spirits.

Samantha judged Karl to be in the vicinity of the prince's age. Boris and Elke appeared to be approaching midlife.

"We have just escaped Igor," Rudolf announced, drawing surprised looks from all three retainers. "Vladimir arrives in London tomorrow or the next day." He looked at Boris and Elke, instructing them, "Pack my mother and daughter. Karl will drive the four of you to my ship. Inform the captain that I have ordered you to return to Sark. He and the ship must also remain there." He turned to Karl as the couple left the room. "Pack supplies for us, and bring the coach around."

"Yes, Your Highness," Karl said, and left the chamber.

Rudolf turned to Samantha, asking, "Do you know someplace where we can hide?"

"I cannot go into hiding with you," Samantha cried. "My reputation will be ruined."

"My sweet Bulgarian rose, your reputation is worth less than your life," the prince said. "I would prefer somewhere in the opposite direction from where I am sending my mother and daughter."

The prince had a good point. What good was an untarnished reputation if one was dead?

"Won't they be safer with us?" Samantha asked.

"Vladimir will look for me first. In case he finds us, I want my mother and daughter in a different location. I have sent for my three younger brothers, but they won't be here until spring."

Recalling her sister's words about Sweetheart Manor, Samantha suggested, "We can pass the night at my old cottage and leave for Scotland in the morning."

"Scotland?" he echoed.

Samantha nodded. "My family owns Sweetheart Manor near Dumfries. As a wedding gift for my sister, my brother-in-law had it renovated and refurbished."

"Then, we shall go there." Rudolf poured the colorless liquid into two small glasses and passed one to her, saying, "Gulp this down in one swig."

Samantha lifted the glass and sniffed its contents. *No smell.* How strong could it be?

Lifting the glass to her lips, Samantha glanced at the prince before drinking and caught his smile. She gulped the liquid down in one swig. Her blue eyes widened as it burned a path to her stomach.

"Eat this," Rudolf ordered, handing her a piece of Swiss cheese.

Samantha ate the cheese and gasped, "What is that?"

"Vodka." Rudolf gulped the contents of his glass and took a bite of cheese. The spirits seemed to have no effect on him.

His retainers appeared at that moment. Boris carried a sleeping, blond-haired girl. Elke had her arm around a dark-haired woman who seemed confused.

The prince rose from his chair. He spoke to his mother as if she were a child. "Mother, I need to leave London for a few days," he said in a quiet voice. "Boris and Elke will take you home to Sark, and I will join you there later."

"Where are you going?" she asked.

Rudolf raised his mother's hands to his lips. "I have

business in Scotland and will feel better about leaving if you are in residence at Sark."

His mother smiled absently and nodded. Her gaze fell on Samantha. She pointed like a child and asked, "Who is that?"

"My friend, Samantha." Rudolf turned to the sleeping child and smiled with obvious love and tenderness. He traced a finger down one of her cheeks. "Take good care of my family," he said to Boris.

"Your Highness, we will guard them with our lives."

"Once the ship has left," Rudolf said, turning to Karl, "visit three or four dockside taverns and let it be known that you work for me, and I am on my way to Scotland."

"I will return shortly," Karl said. Then he led Boris, Elke, and their charges out of the room.

"Do you want your brother to find us?" Samantha asked.

"I wish to lead him in the opposite direction from my family in the event he intends to give chase," Rudolf told her.

Samantha nodded in understanding.

"Where is this cottage?" Rudolf asked, sitting down again.

"The cottage lies on the far side of Primrose Hill," Samantha told him. "How long will we need to stay in hiding? I must write His Grace and my aunt a note to explain what happened."

"No notes," Rudolf told her. "The more people who know where we are, the better the chance of Vladimir finding us. That is why I have given the order that my ship will remain at Sark. No one knows I have an estate there."

Samantha glanced at her star ruby. Its color had lightened. Apparently, her aunt did possess magical abilities. Could she have forseen—? That notion was too absurd even to consider.

"What is wrong with your mother?" Samantha asked. "She seemed a little—" She searched for the proper word.

"Vacant?" Rudolf supplied, a bitter edge to his voice. "You would be vacant, too, if your husband had locked you in an insane asylum for almost fifteen years."

Samantha was stunned. She had never considered there were worse things in life than having one's father swindled out of his fortune and needing to rely on the generosity of others. Even her limp didn't seem too bad a handicap.

"Why did he—?" When he looked at her, Samantha read the anguish in his black gaze.

"My father locked her away when her childbearing days ended," he told her, his voice filled with raw emotion.

Samantha didn't know what to say. She wanted to offer comfort, but the words eluded her. "I-I'm sorry," she managed.

Rudolf reached for her hand and lifted it to his lips like he had done to his mother. "That was a long time ago," he said with a sad smile. "As you can see, I rescued her and brought her home to England."

When he returned, Karl walked into the dining room and handed the prince a cloak, saying, "I saw them safely boarded. The coach awaits you."

"Lady Samantha, this is Karl," the prince said, rising from his chair. "He will serve you as he serves me."

Karl inclined his head. "That is Karl with a *K*."

"I am pleased to make your acquaintance," Samantha said, rising from her chair. "My cottage lies beyond Primrose Hill."

Leaving the mansion, Rudolf helped her into the coach. He joined her inside after giving his man directions.

Samantha remained silent. She wished she hadn't suggested they stay at the old cottage tonight. Now the prince would see how poor she really was. Saying one was a pauper wasn't the same as seeing the poverty.

"What are you thinking?" Rudolf asked.

"Perhaps, we should go to His Grace's," Samantha said. "I'm certain the duke will help—"

"I do not need the duke's help with Vladimir, only time to consider my strategy," Rudolf said in a voice that told her the point was not debatable.

Samantha said nothing. Less than an hour later, their coach started up Primrose Hill. "Stop at the top of the hill," Samantha called to Karl. When the coach halted, she said, "Let's get out for a minute."

Rudolf climbed out and then helped her down. She turned to look at London and said, "I watch the fireworks every year . . . Look!" In the distance, colorful fireworks lit the night's sky.

"Happy New Year, little one," the prince said in a husky voice.

Samantha smiled softly. "Midnight on New Year's Eve, a time that is not a time."

The prince's face inched closer until his lips claimed hers in a gentle kiss. It lingered into another, more demanding kiss.

Samantha no longer felt the night's cold. She gave herself up to the feeling of his mouth pressed to hers, persuading her lips to part.

"Can we leave now?" Karl called. "My sturgeon is freezing."

Prince Rudolf broke the kiss and said, "I cannot think of any other woman with whom I would wish to hide."

"I'm flattered," Samantha said dryly. She turned toward the coach, saying, "Shall we go, Your Highness? I wouldn't want Karl's sturgeon to suffer frostbite." Leaning close, she added in a whisper, "What's sturgeon?"

"Fish," the prince answered.

"Karl has a pet fish?" she asked in surprise.

At that, Rudolf laughed out loud. "Karl does love his sturgeon."

Great Giles' ghost, Samantha thought, climbing into the coach. What would the prince think when he saw how humbly she'd lived for most of her life? Well, she couldn't change the fact that Charles Emerson had swindled her father and left them paupers. However, accepting another's poverty was easier when one was not faced with the grim details.

The coach halted in front of the pink-and-white stucco cottage, the last one at the end of the hamlet's only lane. Without waiting for his man, Prince Rudolf climbed out of the coach and helped her down.

"There's a place in back to shelter the horses," Samantha said, her gaze on the cottage instead of the prince.

"Take the coach around back," Rudolf instructed his man.

Samantha led the way into the dark cottage. She lit the lantern on the table and announced with a blush, "This is where I grew up."

"You should never be ashamed of your origins, little one," Rudolf said. "There are worse things in life than poverty,"

"Your sentiment is kind," she replied, raising her gaze to his, "but those words are easily spoken when one has never known a day of want."

Samantha glanced around the cottage. All was as she'd left it only a couple of weeks earlier. She tried to imagine seeing it through the prince's eyes.

The cottage consisted of a main room with a hearth at each end, one for cooking and one for heating. There were a table and chairs on one side of the chamber and a settee near the second hearth where she and her sisters had passed many an evening wondering whom they would marry. Three small chambers, no larger than closets, were located off the main chamber.

"I lived here from the age of seven until last June when the Duke of Inverary invited us to live with him," Samantha told him.

"How generous of His Grace," Rudolf replied.

Samantha slid her gaze to the prince. There was something in his voice when he mentioned the duke. Was it a tinge of sarcasm?

"His Grace was my father's best friend and wanted to help us," Samantha said.

"Ten years is a long time to wait to offer help," Rudolf remarked.

"His Grace couldn't find us," Samantha said. "When my father died, Aunt Roxie contacted him, and the very next day, the ducal coach appeared at our door."

"I would have liked to see you as a young girl," the prince said, changing the subject, a soft smile touching his lips. "Which room was yours?"

Samantha pointed to the first door, saying, "I shared it with my sisters."

Rudolf opened the door and peered inside. "This closet is hardly large enough for one person," he said. "I suppose the other two rooms were for your aunt and your father?"

"Yes."

Karl returned then. He immediately set to work lighting a fire in the hearth.

"The hour is late," the prince said, reaching out to caress her cheek. "Sleep in your old chamber and know, as you do, that I am guarding you."

Samantha nodded, limped into her old bedchamber, and closed the door behind her. In spite of the room's chill, she removed her blue gown and neatly placed it on one of the other cots. Wearing only her chemise, she wrapped herself in her cloak and lay down on her cot. She could hear the prince and his man talking in quiet tones but couldn't make out their words.

How long would they need to hide in Scotland? Samantha wondered. What must her aunt and her sisters be thinking? They probably assumed the prince had abducted her.

Samantha knew she should be thinking about Alexander, but the prince's reappearance in her life confused her. Her heart ached for what could never be, and yearning swelled within her breast.

Well, her good reputation was permanently tarnished by now. Maybe she should relax and enjoy herself, steal a few days of happiness in an otherwise bleak future. When this adventure ended, she would pass the remainder of her life as a social outcast. Not that her limp hadn't already set her apart from others.

Though she was bone weary, Samantha was unable to fall asleep but then realized what was wrong. She hadn't completed her usual day's ending, thanking God for some blessing she'd received that day.

"Thank You, Lord, for saving my life tonight," Samantha whispered, kneeling beside the cot. "And, thank You for sending the prince to call upon me, though he was a bit tardy in arriving."

Samantha climbed back on the cot, but sleep eluded her still. Intending to count sheep, she only managed to conjure the prince's image in her mind's eye. She fell asleep counting Russian princes, and each one of them looked exactly like Prince Rudolf.

CHAPTER 4

He dreamed of English ladies, and each one of them looked like Samantha Douglas.

Rudolf perched on the edge of her cot and studied the woman who had haunted his dreams the previous night. Even in the predawn gray, she appeared ethereal and much lovelier than any woman he had known. Or was it her inner beauty that made her so attractive? Her face framed by ebony hair cascading to her waist, Samantha Douglas possessed a hauntingly delicate beauty far different from Olga's head-turning blondness.

Banishing his lost wife from his thoughts, Rudolf concentrated on the sleeping woman. He leaned closer and inhaled deeply of her scent, reminding him once more of roses and jasmine. Rudolf reached out to touch her cheek but stopped a hairsbreadth from her skin.

He wanted her. Badly.

Sublime anticipation made him smile. Oh, yes, he would have her before their journey ended. He would touch every inch of her silken skin and know her body better than she did.

Loving, forgiving, nurturing. Samantha Douglas was

everything he had ever wanted in a woman, everything he had thought he was getting with Olga.

"Awaken, my sleeping beauty," Rudolf said softly. "Open your eyes to greet the day."

His sleeping beauty groaned in a decidedly unfeminine manner. Rolling over, she pulled her cloak over her head.

Rudolf leaned close and whispered, "Samantha, you must awaken now."

"Go away," came a muffled moan from beneath the cloak.

A boyish smile touched his lips. Rudolf whipped the cloak off her, exposing her chemise-clad body to the morning chill.

Samantha bolted up. For a brief moment she seemed confused by her surroundings, but then a high blush stained her cheeks. She yanked the cloak up, shielding her near-nakedness from him.

"Drink this coffee," Rudolf said, lifting a steaming mug off the other cot.

"It's still dark," Samantha complained, taking the mug from him. Their fingers touched in the movement.

Rudolf felt her stiffen at the touch and gazed into her incredibly blue eyes. She was as excited by his touch as he was by hers.

"The eastern sky is brightening with the dawn," he said. "I want to leave as soon as possible."

Samantha sipped the coffee and crinkled her nose. "It's strong."

"I have laced the brew with vodka," Rudolf told her, and smiled when she grimaced. He stood then, looking down at her. "I have placed a pan of warmed water for washing on the other cot. We will breakfast in the coach along the way." Still, he stood in silence and looked down at her for a long moment.

"I cannot wash if you stand there," Samantha said, lifting her blue gaze to his.

"Amazingly, you are even more beautiful in sleep," Rudolf said. When she blushed, he walked out of the room, closing the door behind him.

Samantha emerged from her chamber a few minutes later. She had wrapped herself in her cloak.

On bended knee in front of the hearth, Rudolf finished dousing the fire and looked over his shoulder. He smiled at her and stood, saying, "Happy New Year, my lady."

"Happy New Year, Your Highness."

"Are you ready?"

Samantha slung her violin case over her shoulder. Then she nodded at him and limped toward the door.

Having brought the coach around from the back, Karl already waited outside. Rudolf opened the coach door and started to help her up, but Samantha paused to look at the sky and asked, "What time is it?"

"Early," Rudolf told her.

Bright streaks of orange and mauve lit the eastern sky. A deep blue still colored the western horizon.

Rudolf climbed into the coach after her and pulled the fur throw over them when she started to inch away. "We will be warm beneath this fur and warmer if we share body heat."

Ignoring the panic in her expression, Rudolf put his arm around her and drew her close. "The hour is early," he said. "Rest your head on my shoulder and nap."

Great Giles' ghost, Samantha thought, gazing at him through enormous blue eyes. How the bloody hell could she relax enough to fall asleep when they sat so close they were practically one?

When the prince raised his brows, Samantha did the only thing she could do; she rested her head against his shoulder. She would never admit that his closeness frightened her. Douglases never showed weakness.

Samantha gazed out the window at the morning, its beauty even more apparent with the rising sun. Frost feathered the trees, and a handful of crows searched a field for food. Mother Nature rested beneath a blanket of cold, her spirit awaiting to regain her youth in springtime.

"What kind of fur is this?" Samantha asked, comfortably warm snuggling beneath it.

"This is polar bear, a magnificent white beast found in the far north near the top of the world."

Samantha sat up and looked at him in surprise. "You have traveled to the top of the world?"

"My father took my brothers and me hunting while the bears were migrating," the prince told her. "I regretted killing it almost immediately and have never hunted again."

"Violence for pleasure is a despicable pastime," Samantha agreed, pleased by his admission. She'd been in society for less than a year, but that was time enough to conclude that men usually bragged about killing defenseless creatures. Here was a man confident enough to admit he didn't like killing.

"I never intended to harm the bear," Rudolf added. "I was aiming for my father."

Stunned by his words, Samantha stared at him as if he'd suddenly grown another head. She didn't feel quite as safe as she had. "You-You tried to m-murder your father?" she echoed.

Rudolf shrugged. "He was trying to kill me."

"You must be mistaken," Samantha said. "No man would kill his own child, especially the oldest son."

"My father has always hated me," the prince told her. "He wanted Vladimir to be the oldest. Now, tell me how you were able to pick Igor's pocket."

"I would rather not say," Samantha replied. The coach went over a bump, and she fell against him. Blushing with embarrassment, she murmured, "I'm sorry."

"I am not sorry," Rudolf said, his smile devastatingly charming. "You may fall against me any time. Now, tell me how you managed to pick Igor's pocket."

"What time is it?" she asked.

"Do not think to evade my question," he warned.

"Tell me the time," Samantha said, her smile flirtatious. "Then I'll tell you what you want to know."

Rudolf reached inside his jacket pocket for his watch. Unable to find the timepiece in its usual location, he began to check all his pockets.

"Looking for this, Your Highness?" Samantha asked, holding the watch in front of his face.

Rudolf laughed. "Tell me how you did that."

"My hands move faster than my feet," Samantha said, her pride in her talent apparent. After all, she had no future with the prince. Why not share her dubious ability with him? "After my father lost his fortune," she continued, "we needed money to survive. Tory and I practiced picking pockets until we became experts. Angel was skilled at cheating with dice and cards."

Instead of smiling as she thought he would, Rudolf grew serious. He drew her into the circle of his embrace and brushed his lips against her temple, saying, "You should have had someone caring for you."

Samantha didn't know how to reply to that. Leaning against him, she felt secure and tried not to think about him trying to kill his own father, assuring herself his actions were defensive.

She glanced at her necklace. The star ruby remained placid. She was in no danger from him.

"Look at me, Samantha," Rudolf said, his voice husky. When she did, Samantha saw his handsome face inching toward hers. He was going to kiss her. She closed her eyes, but when his lips would have touched hers, her stomach protested its lack of food by growling.

Samantha felt mortified.

"You need to eat," Rudolf said, planting a chaste kiss on her lips. He reached into the basket on the opposite seat and offered her a chunk of brown bread with cheese. Then he passed her a flask, adding, "We need to take one gulp of this each hour to keep warm."

Raising the flask to her lips, Samantha took a tiny sip and felt the burning sensation from her throat to the pit of her stomach. She didn't waste any time taking a bite of the cheese.

"You are learning," Rudolf said.

They passed through the villages of Harrow and Cookham. Then came Henley and Marlow in the Chilterns, chalk hills rising from the north bank of the River Thames in Oxfordshire and stretching northeast for fifty miles.

Leaving the Chilterns behind, they rode through Oxford. In the distance beyond the old market town rose the forbidding walls of Oxford Castle, but the town itself was invitingly picturesque with its partly stone, partly timber-framed houses.

Northwest of Oxfordshire lay the wooded glens and serene streams of the Cotswald Hills, and Stratford-upon-Avon lay beyond that. The late afternoon sun was sinking in the west as their coach crossed the Clopton Bridge over the Avon River.

Within a few minutes, Rudolf and Samantha sat inside the Black Swan Inn. The common room was crowded, but sitting between the prince and the hearth, she felt warm and cozy and safe.

Samantha ate her beef stew in silence but flicked a sidelong glance at the prince. The light from the hearth played on his features, and she admired his noble profile from his straight nose to his sensuously chiseled lips. That made her recall the feel of his mouth covering hers.

The common room seemed suddenly warmer, and Samantha dropped her gaze to his hands with their long fingers. She wondered how those hands would feel stroking her skin.

"Why are you blushing?" Rudolf asked, turning to her.

Samantha felt the blood rushing to her cheeks as the blush deepened. "I'm not blushing," she told him.

Her response made him smile, but she changed the subject, asking, "How long do you think we'll need to remain in Scotland?"

Surprising her, Rudolf covered her hand with his and said, "I hope for a very long time."

Samantha felt a melting sensation in the pit of her stomach, and her thighs seemed to have developed a slight quiver. "That is unacceptable," she told him. "My family will be worried, and my betrothed"—her gaze skittered away—"I probably have no betrothed now."

"I will make up for the loss of your betrothed," Rudolf said, stroking her hand.

"How will you do that, Your Highness?" Samantha asked, looking him straight in the eye.

"I will think of something," he said, and raised her hand to his lips. "Are you ready to retire?"

Samantha nodded.

"Allow me to escort you to your chamber, Princess," Rudolf said, standing and offering her his hand.

Lifting her violin case off the floor, Samantha rose from her chair. She felt the prince's hand on the small of her back as he guided her across the common room.

Upstairs, Rudolf opened the door of the last room on the left and immediately lit the candle on the table.

Samantha surveyed the chamber. The bed almost filled the tiny chamber, and seeing it made her feel uncomfortable. She'd always been the sensible sister, and now, here she was so far from home with a man who was more stranger than not. How had she come to this?

Tossing her cloak aside, Samantha yawned and stretched, saying, "I can't wait to lie down." She heard the bolt being thrown and turned around. The prince was removing his jacket.

"Great Giles' ghost, what are you doing?" she cried.

Rudolf gave her a puzzled look. "I am going to sleep."

"You can't mean to sleep here."

"I am too tired to argue."

"You must get another room," Samantha told him, "or my reputation will be ruined."

"I thought your reputation was already ruined," he said with an amused smile.

"I'll leave." She turned toward the door.

"Princess, you are straining my patience," Rudolf said, his voice stern, blocking her path. "Remove that gown and get into the bed."

Samantha stood in indecision. How could she sleep in the bed with him and not lose her virtue? Sooner or later—She glanced at the star ruby, which remained placid. Either her aunt had lied about the stone's magical powers, or she was in no danger from the prince.

"Very well," she capitulated.

While the prince sat on the edge of the bed to remove his boots, Samantha disrobed down to her chemise and set her gown aside. She glanced at the prince to see if he was watching, but he'd turned his back on her.

No sooner had Samantha climbed into the bed and pulled the coverlet up when she realized she hadn't completed her evening ritual. Climbing out of the bed, she knelt beside the bed and covered her face with her hands. She prayed silently, *Thank You, Lord, for—*

"What are you doing?" Rudolf asked.

Samantha spread her fingers and peeked at him. Good God, the prince had removed his shirt. What a sinfully perfect back he had, all sinewy muscle.

"What are you doing?" he asked again, this time amusement tingeing his voice.

"I am thanking God."

"For what?"

Samantha couldn't concentrate with the half-naked prince watching her. "For—For none of your business," she told him. "Please, put your shirt on again."

Rudolf's lips quirked. "Do not speak so disrespectfully to me," he said. "I am a prince of Russia."

Ignoring him, Samantha climbed into the bed and turned her back on him. How was she to sleep when the prince lay beside her? And then an alarming thought occurred to her. "Do not even consider removing those breeches," she said.

"Princess," he said, a smile in his voice.

"Why are you calling me that?" she asked, afraid to turn around.

"I told the innkeeper you are my wife."

Surprised, Samantha rolled over and was even more startled to find him leaning over her. A light matting of black hair covered his muscular chest.

"Your—Your chest is bare," she said, and then realized how idiotic she sounded.

Rudolf gave her a wicked smile. "Why do you not follow my example?"

Embarrassment flamed on her cheeks. And that was before the prince leaned closer.

"I am teasing you," he said, almost nose-to-nose with her.

Samantha gave him a wobbly smile. She expected him to move away; but he stared down at her for a long moment, and she became mesmerized by the intensity of his dark gaze.

"Pleasant dreams, Princess," Rudolf said in a husky voice. He brushed a few recalcitrant ebony wisps away from her face, whispering, "A sweet good night kiss."

Rudolf lowered his head until his lips touched hers in a chaste kiss. His gentleness seduced her. Teasingly, his tongue stroked the crease between her lips, and when she opened her mouth in response, he slipped his tongue inside, changing the tempo of their kiss.

Samantha pressed the palms of her hands against his chest. Instead of pushing him away, she slid her hands up his chest, enjoying the rippling of his muscles beneath her touch, and then she entwined her arms around his neck. The sensation of his bared chest against her scantily clad body excited her.

Sanity slammed into her consciousness when the prince broke their kiss. Tracing a finger down her flaming cheek, he whispered, "Good night, Princess."

Shocked by her easy responses to his advances, Samantha rolled over and turned her back on him. Her newly awakened body and her rioting emotions confused her. How could she have behaved so wantonly? Did her actions mean she'd fallen in love with the prince? If he hadn't been such a gentleman. . . . How was he capable of such restraint? More importantly, what did his actions mean? Was he developing a fondness for her, or was she merely a convenience?

Samantha closed her eyes. Part of her felt ashamed of her behavior, but the other part wanted more. And then she remembered God.

You probably aren't too pleased with me, Samantha prayed silently. *I want to thank You for allowing me another kiss. I would be especially grateful if You could somehow contrive to save my*—reputation or virginity?

A drowsy smile touched her lips when she made her decision. *If you could contrive to save my reputation.*

Samantha awakened early the next morning. For a moment she felt disoriented but then realized where she was and with whom. Even worse, during the night, she had somehow gravitated toward the warmth of his body.

Lying on her side with her cheek resting against his chest, Samantha felt his arm around her back, holding her close against his body. In her sleep, she'd thrown her leg across his lower body and woven it between his legs. She could feel his erection against the side of her leg. Opening her eyes, she saw that her chemise straps had slipped, leaving one of her breasts exposed.

The prince still slept. Should she pull the chemise up or wait until he moved? She didn't want to awaken him while she was wrapped around his body.

Samantha lay still, wondering what to do. She shifted her gaze from her naked breast to his well-muscled chest with its matting of hair.

Wanting to see his face, Samantha moved her head slightly as if in sleep. She raised her gaze to his throat, his strong chin, his chiseled lips, his straight nose . . . his black gaze.

Great Giles' ghost, the prince hadn't been sleeping at all. While she'd been persuing his body, he had been perusing hers.

Her gaze captive to his, Samantha sensed his hand moving closer to her bared breast. She sucked in her breath when she felt his hand slide across her breast, cupping it in his hand. He kneaded her soft flesh and then glided his finger across her nipple, which hardened with her arousal.

The intensity in his gaze and his finger caressing her nipple made Samantha feel weak. Her breath came in shallow gasps, butterflies took wing in the pit of her stomach, and a melting sensation ignited a fire between her thighs.

"Your breasts are beautiful, Princess, and your nipples are exquisitely sensitive," Rudolf said, his voice husky, drawing the chemise's bodice up to cover her. Samantha felt her face flaming with embarrassment. His words made her throb with need.

And what should she reply to that? *Thank you* seemed out of place, though she did believe he was complimenting her.

"*Krusseevy,*" Rudolf murmured. "*Krusseevy* means beautiful, *ma lyoobof.*"

"What does *ma lyoobof* mean?" Samantha asked.

"It means your leg is crushing mine," he told her.

Samantha laughed. "What does it really mean?"

Rudolf said nothing, merely smiled. . . .

Life became one long coach ride.

Karl turned their coach northeast, and they rode through Coventry, an ancient cathedral city with defensive walls. Exhaustion blinded Samantha to Leicestershire's stark beauty of ancient gnarled trees and stone villages.

Staring out the window at the passing scenery, Samantha smiled at her own foolishness. Growing up, she'd always wished for a ride with a handsome prince in his grand coach. He would be her knight, her champion, and silence the taunts of the neighboring children. She should have been more careful what she wished for.

"Why are you smiling?" the prince asked.

Samantha turned her head to look at him. His handsomely chiseled face tugged at her heartstrings. If only things could have been different.

"I was thinking that, as a child, I always wanted to ride in a grand coach," Samantha answered.

Rudolf smiled. "And now your wish has been granted."

The coach went over a bump, throwing her against him. "Yes, the Lord usually finds a way to torment us with what we want," she said dryly.

"Would you care to learn a few Russian words?" Rudolf asked, obviously trying to entertain her.

"Not really."

"*Glaza* means eyes," Rudolf said as if she hadn't spoken. "Repeat, please."

Samantha sighed. "*Glaza.*"

Rudolf pointed to her nose and said, "*Nos* means nose."

"*Nos.*"

"*Gooba* means lip," he told her.

"*Gooba,*" she repeated.

"Your pronunciation is excellent," Rudolf praised her. "Now, tell me what I am pointing at."

"*Glaza . . . nos . . . gooba.*"

Beneath the fur coverlet, Rudolf put his arm around her and drew her against the side of his body. Gazing into her eyes, he said, "*Ya khuchoo stubboy spart.*"

"What does that mean?" Samantha asked with a smile. "Was it a compliment?"

With his face merely inches from hers, Rudolf told

her, *"Ya khuchoo stubboy spart* means I want to make love with you."

Samantha lost her smile. The prince was becoming entirely too familiar with his words and her person. She wasn't going to tumble into bed with a man who offered no future.

Rudolf gave her an amused smile as if he knew her thoughts. "You must say *utstan,*" he said.

Samantha arched a perfectly shaped ebony brow at him. She wasn't going to repeat any words she didn't know.

"*Utstan* means take your hands off me," he said.

Samantha laughed.

Wearing an expression of regret, Rudolf touched her cheek and said, *"Ya tibya lyublyoo."*

"What does that mean?" she asked.

"Teach me how to pick a pocket," he said, changing the subject abruptly.

Samantha reached for his hand and lifted it up for her perusal. She studied his long, tapered fingers and pressed the palm of her hand against his as if to measure the difference in size. "Your hands are too big," she announced.

"But how would I do it if I wanted?" he asked.

Samantha gave him a flirtatious smile as an imp entered her soul. She entwined her left arm around his neck and pulled his face closer.

"Successful pickpocketing takes years of practice," she said, her lips a hairsbreadth from his. "A distraction diverts the pigeon's attention while you quickly search his pockets."

With that, Samantha pressed her lips against his. She felt his arms go around her and savored the feeling of his mouth covering hers. His lips were warm, and when he caressed the crease of her mouth with his tongue, she parted her lips for him, allowing him entrance to the sweet softness beyond. His lingering kiss melted into another. And then another.

Summoning all her inner strength, Samantha pushed him away and dangled his gold watch in front of his face, asking, "Do you see what I mean?"

Rudolf shouted with laughter. "Do you usually go around London kissing men?"

"Certainly not," Samantha said primly. "Because of my limp, I usually trip and bump into a gentleman who, naturally, reaches out to keep me from falling."

With one long finger, Rudolf tapped the tip of her nose playfully, asking, "Where did you learn to charm a prince?"

Samantha blushed, saying, "Perhaps some people are easily charmed, Your Highness."

They passed through Derbyshire, a midland county of contrasts from low land to high peaks. Samantha yearned to stop in the market town of Derby, known for its silk and lace. She had only the one gown and couldn't wear it for the rest of her life.

Leaving Derby behind without stopping, they rode into Yorkshire. With an austere beauty, the landscape wore many faces from stone-fenced farms to windswept moors to deep, secluded valleys. Nine miles west of Leeds lay Bradford in a small valley on the eastern slopes of the Pennines.

Passing the Church of St. Peter, Karl halted the coach in front of the Boar's Head Inn. Prince Rudolf climbed out first and then led her into the inn's common room. Within minutes, Samantha and the prince sat close to the hearth's warmth and ate roasted beef, Yorkshire pudding, and horseradish sauce.

Samantha saw Karl enter the common room and scan the tables. Seeing them near the hearth, the prince's man approached their table.

"Your Highness, we will make Carlisle by early afternoon tomorrow," Karl said. "Dumfries is a half day's ride from there."

Prince Rudolf nodded. "Take your supper now."

"Would you care to join us?" Samantha asked.

"No, thank you, my lady," Karl answered, looking scandalized by her suggestion.

"He needs to feed his sturgeon," the prince said.

"Where do you keep this sturgeon?" Samantha asked.

Karl looked at the prince and then, wearing a serious expression, answered, "I keep it in a warm place." At that, the prince's man turned away and crossed the common room to a table near the bar.

Samantha flicked a glance at the prince, who was grinning. "What do you find so amusing?"

Rudolf leaned close. "You are the most charming woman I have ever met, like a breath of fresh air in a smoky room."

"Thank you, I think," she replied, giving him a puzzled smile.

"Tell me more about this feud between the Douglases and the Emersons," he said conversationally.

"The feud has been settled," Samantha told him, "or it would have been settled if I had become betrothed to Alexander."

Rudolf frowned at the mention of Alexander Emerson. "Tell me about it."

"When I was a child," Samantha began with a sigh, "Charles Emerson swindled my father out of most of the Douglas fortune. My father lost the remainder when he tried to recoup his losses by gambling. We were forced to leave the mansion in Grosvenor Square, and our last day there was when I-I suffered the accident that left me with a limp."

"Charles Emerson ran over you with his carriage," Rudolf said.

Samantha nodded. "My father's best friend, the Duke of Inverary, would have helped but was in Scotland at the time."

Rudolf cocked a brow at her. "What about when His Grace returned from Scotland?"

"My father was too proud to ask for help," Samantha answered, "and the duke couldn't find us. For ten years, my sisters and I plotted revenge against Emerson, especially after my father became sick with drink."

"How could three young ladies possibly get revenge?" the prince asked.

"My older sister is an expert cheat at dice and cards, but we couldn't contrive to get into the gambling hells," she told him.

"So, how did you and your sisters get revenge?"

"By chance, Angelica met Robert Campbell at a fair but didn't know he was the duke's son," Samantha answered. "When my father passed away, Aunt Roxie sent His Grace a note, and he invited us to live with him. Robert promised to get revenge for us. Before that could happen, Venetia Emerson Campbell—Robert's widowed sister-in-law and Alexander's sister—tried to kill Angelica. Apparently, Venetia had wanted to be the Duchess of Inverary and had killed her younger sister, Robert's late wife.

"In an attempt to avoid a scandal, His Grace suggested Venetia and her father be transported to Australia. That left Alexander with the Earl of Winchester title and the family fortune."

"Why was Alexander spared?" the prince asked.

"Alexander was completely innocent," she answered. "In fact, Emerson had been trying to have him assassinated—"

"Emerson wanted to kill his own son?" Rudolf interrupted, his expression mirroring his surprise.

"Yes, but I don't know why," Samantha told him. "Anyway, Alexander wanted to make amends by marrying me. The Douglas lands and fortune would have been returned to us, albeit indirectly through our marriage."

"Were you the family sacrifice?" Rudolf asked.

"What a horrible thing to say," Samantha replied, surprised by his words.

"You do not love him."

"I respect him." Samantha blushed, adding, "Ladies who limp aren't exactly the height of fashion."

Rudolf covered her hand with his. "Princess, your limp is of no importance."

"It is important to me," Samantha said. "Tell me why your father prefers Vladimir."

The prince's whole demeanor changed. The smile in his eyes died, replaced by anger and something else. Was it pain she saw? Of course he would be angered by his father imprisoning his mother and hurt by his father's lack of love. Why would any man do that to the woman he loved? And, why would a father reject his oldest son in favor of the second?

Unable to bear the angry pain etched across his face, Samantha wished she hadn't asked about his father. She dropped her gaze to her plate.

"Let us retire for the night," Rudolf said, standing and offering her his hand.

Entering their bedchamber, Samantha removed her cloak and tossed it aside. Then she undressed down to her chemise. Protesting his presence would do no good.

Samantha knelt beside the bed and covered her face

with her hands. Silently, she prayed, *Thank You, Lord, for allowing us to get this far—*

"Samantha?"

Spreading her fingers, she peered at the prince, who sat on the opposite side of the bed to remove his boots. She felt a familiar melting sensation in the pit of her stomach at the sight of his bared chest.

"I-I apologize for my curtness," Rudolf said. "However, I do not wish to speak about my father. Please do not ask about him again."

The prince was a man unused to apologizing, but he was making a good attempt. "I will respect your wishes," she said.

The prince nodded and seemed to relax.

Thank You, Lord, for the prince's apology, Samantha thought. She climbed into bed and pulled the coverlet up.

Rudolf climbed into bed beside her. Without asking permission, he drew her against his body, saying, "Come up here, Princess."

Samantha leaned over him and stared into his black eyes. She studied his face, admiring how the flickering candlelight played across his features.

"Kiss me good night, Princess."

Samantha smiled and lowered her head until her mouth hovered above his. Her lips touched his, tentatively at first, and then grew bolder, deepening the kiss.

She flicked her tongue across the crease between his lips, as he had done to her, and heard with satisfaction his sharp intake of breath. When he opened his mouth, she slipped her tongue inside, their tongues swirling and caressing.

Rudolf entwined his arms around her body and held her firmly, gently. Without warning, he rolled over, and she lay beneath him. He kissed her lingeringly, not giving her a chance to think or protest, planting feathery light kisses on her eyelids, temples, nose, and throat.

"I want to touch you," Rudolf said hoarsely. "Only touch."

He didn't wait for permission.

Rudolf kissed her again, his tongue seeking and gaining entrance to her mouth. His hand lightly caressed her cheek and then drifted down to her throat before crossing to her delicately boned shoulder. He ran his hand down the outside of her arm and then traced two fingers up the sensitive inside.

A languorous feeling slowly seeped through Samantha's veins, and she yearned for him to touch and caress every inch of her virgin flesh. Her young body moved instinctively, pressing into his hand wherever it roamed.

Rudolf moved his hand down her chemise-clad body, and Samantha moaned softly as he teased her by sliding his hand across her breasts without stopping. Lower his hand moved, caressing the softness of her belly and then tracing the curve of her hip before gliding down and then up the inside of her leg.

"*Krusseevy,*" the prince murmured, his lips hovering above hers.

He kissed her deeply, passionately, and then drew the straps of her chemise down. Ever so slowly, he slid her bodice down, freeing her breasts to his dark, intense gaze. She opened her eyes. His gaze locked on hers and held it captive while he cupped her breast and then kneaded it gently.

Samantha pressed herself against his hand—wanting, needing his touch. His fingers stroked the soft flesh, and then he brushed the palms of his hands across her nipples. Closing his thumb and forefinger around one nipple, he squeezed it into arousal.

Samantha thought she would die from the pleasure, and then she felt his mouth on her breasts. She moaned as he locked on a nipple, suckling upon her, and she arched herself toward him, wanting . . . wanting. . . . She didn't know what.

With a groan, the prince moved to one side. She opened her eyes. He was staring down at her, a look of yearning on his face.

"Sleep now," Rudolf said, pulling the bodice of her chemise up. He lay back on the bed and gathered her into his arms, saying, "We have another long ride to-morrow."

Samantha moaned, more from embarrassment than the thought of another day in the coach, and buried her face against his chest. And then another, more alarming, thought occurred to her. How would she face him in the morning after her wanton behavior tonight? She would pretend it never happened and demand separate chambers tomorrow night.

CHAPTER 5

"Rudolf?"

"Yes, Princess?"

Cuddled beneath the fur in the coach the next morning, Samantha felt battle ready but refused to look at the prince lest she lose her courage. She kept her gaze riveted on the passing scenery—barren trees and snow-covered fields.

"I-I want my own bedchamber tonight," she said. Silence greeted her announcement.

"Did you hear me?" she asked, turning to look at him, unable to bear the suspense. "I want my—"

"Nyet." Rudolf gave her a stern look, adding, *"Nyet* means no."

"I insist," Samantha said, her voice rising.

"Duty demands that I protect you, which I cannot do if you are sleeping in another chamber," Rudolf told her.

"I can take care of myself," Samantha protested. "I do wear a dagger strapped to my leg."

Without a word, Rudolf leaned forward and lifted the bottom edge of the fur coverlet. Then he flipped her skirt up and removed the dagger from the sheath strapped to her leg.

"Give me that," Samantha demanded, surprised.

Rudolf tossed the dagger out the window. He gave her an infuriating smile and said, "Now you do not wear a dagger strapped to your leg."

"That was my lucky dagger," she cried.

Rudolf burst out laughing. "Your lucky dagger?" he echoed.

His laughter didn't sit well with Samantha. "How dare you steal my property," she said, narrowing her blue gaze on him. "You may be a prince of Russia, but this is England where you are nobody."

"Guard your words," he warned.

"Or what?" Samantha challenged him. "Will you abduct me and take me to Scotland?"

"I did not abduct you," Rudolf informed her. "I merely assumed responsibility for your protection."

"Who is protecting me from you?" she asked.

"I will debate the point no more," he said in stern voice, fixing his black gaze on hers.

"You are an autocratic toad," Samantha replied, turning her head to stare out the coach's window. "You need not have taken me with you. His Grace could have protected me."

"It seemed like a good idea at the time," the prince drawled.

Samantha snapped her head around to look at him. "And now?"

"And now I am not so sure," he said.

"You ruined my life for a royal whim," Samantha accused him.

"I rescued you from an unhappy marriage," Rudolf told her.

"Did I ask you to rescue me?" Samantha shot back.

"You have condemned me to an unhappy, childless spinsterhood."

"Being alone is a much better choice than being married to a man who doesn't love you," Rudolf said.

"I didn't have a choice," Samantha reminded him. "You chose for me. No man will love or marry me now."

"Do not be dramatic," he said.

"I am realistic," she corrected him. "Unless . . . Are you offering marriage?"

In the blink of an eye, Prince Rudolf shuttered his expression, a gesture reminding her of the Duke of Inverary and her brother-in-law, the Marquess of Argyll. "I cannot offer you marriage," he said.

"Cannot or will not?"

"What difference does that make?"

Samantha held his gaze for a long moment and then gave him a look filled with contempt. "I wouldn't marry you if you were the last bachelor in England," she said in a scathing voice. "By the way, refrain from referring to me as your wife. Doing so in Scotland would, in fact, make me your common-law wife."

"Thank you for the warning," Rudolf said, returning the contempt.

The tone of his voice hurt Samantha as much as his words. Tears welled up in her eyes, but she turned her head to look out the window and fought them back. She wondered at his ability to hurt her so easily and reduce her to tears. After all, as a child, she'd had much practice in guarding herself against people knowing her pain. If she hadn't, the other children would have done worse to her, much worse.

Good Christ, Rudolf thought. *Now I've made her cry.* He need not have been so cruel and hadn't meant to imply that he found her unattractive. On the contrary, he found her too desirable and needed to save himself from any complicating entanglements. The last thing he needed was to love a woman. And yet, why had he forced her into hiding with him? She was correct; His Grace could have protected her. Still, he could not give her hope for a marriage where there was no hope. After losing Olga, he had vowed never to marry again and intended to keep that vow.

Rudolf reached for her hand beneath the fur coverlet. Without bothering to look at him, Samantha tried to free her hand, but he refused to let go.

"I promise not to make any more advances," Rudolf said, close to her ear. "Please, understand. Losing Olga was too painful; I cannot allow myself to love any woman."

"Then, give Vladimir the Kazanov Venus," Samantha said dryly. "You have no need for a fertility charm."

Rudolf chuckled. Though Samantha still looked out the window, he sensed her relax. Apparently, the storm had passed.

"We will reach Carlisle early enough to go shopping," Rudolf said conversationally, hoping to regain her favor by offering her a gift.

"Shopping for what?" she asked.

"Karl packed my belongings," Rudolf told her, "but you cannot wear the same gown indefinitely."

"Don't bother yourself about me," Samantha said. "I don't have any money."

"I have more than enough money and would be honored to purchase you a few gowns," Rudolf told her.

"Honored?" Samantha echoed, arching an ebony brow at him. "I accept your offer but will repay you when we return to London."

"That will be unnecessary."

"Ah, but I insist," she said, giving him a sweet smile. "You may also purchase me another dagger."

"I will consider it," he replied.

Situated on the River Eden, Carlisle lay a mere nine miles south of the Scottish border. They reached the market town shortly after noon and stopped on High Street where the shops were located.

After sending Karl ahead to procure accommodations at the Royal Rooster Inn, Rudolf slipped Samantha's arm through his and led her down the street in the direction of Madame Andrews' Dress Shop, the most exclusive shop in Carlisle. Or so they'd been told.

"May I be of service, sir?" a middle-aged woman asked when they entered, looking down the long length of her nose at their rumpled appearances.

"I think we should leave," Samantha whispered.

Rudolf ignored her. Instead, he gave the woman his most charming smile and said, "Your Highness."

The woman looked confused. "I beg your pardon?"

"I am Prince Rudolf Kazanov, and this is my bride"— he paused to lift Samantha's hand to his lips—"Her Highness, Princess Samantha."

The woman looked from one to the other. She wore the most skeptical expression Rudolf had ever seen.

"Excuse our appearance," he said, reaching into his pocket for a wad of bills to hand the woman. "We have traveled north with few belongings, which is why we are visiting your shop."

"I am honored, Your Highness," the woman said, her gaze on the money. "I am Madame Andrews."

"My bride and I leave for Scotland in the morning," Rudolf told the woman, returning her smile. "Ready-made gowns will suffice if you can complete the alterations by tomorrow morning."

"It can be done," Madame Andrews told him. She turned to Samantha, saying, "Please follow me, Your Highness. I will need to take your measurements."

Samantha nodded and then cast Rudolf a warning

look. He grinned at her discomfort and followed them into the backroom. After all, what could his Bulgarian rose do? Complain that her husband was watching her disrobe?

The fitting room was small, containing only a couple of chairs, a table, and a platform for the person being measured and fitted. Sitting in an upholstered chair, Rudolf stretched out his legs and ordered, "Bring us several gowns."

Madame Andrews left the room.

"Are you going to sit there and watch?" Samantha whispered.

Rudolf grinned. "That is what a loving husband would do. Is it not?"

"You are *not* my husband," she reminded him.

Madame Andrews returned before he could reply. She carried an armful of gowns, set them down on the table, and held each one up for their inspection. Most had fitted bodices and long, loose sleeves, and had been created from the best quality materials—silk, velvet, sarcenet.

"I chose colors I thought would suit Her Highness," the woman told them.

"We'll take the white muslin morning dress," Rudolf said. "I like the shell pink and the sky blue silks, the garnet and the midnight blue velvets, the amethyst sarcenet, and that forest green riding habit."

"These gowns are too costly," Samantha interjected. "Only give me the—"

"My bride is unused to spending my money," Rudolf told the dressmaker.

Madame Andrews smiled. "Enjoy the moment, Your Highness. Becoming accustomed to spending money is very easy."

"I am certain you are correct," Rudolf agreed. "My

bride will need cashmere shawls and slippers to match each gown, silk and lace chemises, silk stockings with lace garters, and nightgowns and bedrobes."

"I only make gowns, Your Highness," Madame Andrews answered.

Rudolf stared at her intently. "I wish you to procure them for us and will pay you triple for your trouble."

Madame Andrews inclined her head. "I will gladly do that for you."

"Include the ostrich feather I saw in your window," Rudolf added.

"An ostrich feather?" Samantha echoed. "No jewels?"

"The jewels will come in time, *ma lyoobof,*" Rudolf said.

Turning to Samantha, Madame Andrews said, "If Your Highness will remove your gown please."

Rudolf smiled when Samantha opened her mouth to protest his presence and then thought better of it. She showed the woman her back and let her unbutton her gown.

Catching Samantha's eye when she stood in her chemise, Rudolf slid his gaze down the length of her body. He admired the swell of her breasts above the neckline of her chemise, and remembered their softness and taste. He dropped his gaze to her tiny waist, the inviting curve of her hips, shapely legs, and dainty feet.

Rudolf felt his manhood stirring and wondered at his own sanity. Why was he doing this to himself? The more he looked, the more he wanted.

Madame Andrews finished taking her measurements and left the room for a moment. Samantha stepped into her gown again. Rudolf bolted out of the chair, saying, "I'll button it for you, *ma lyoobof.*"

Wearing a decidedly unhappy expression, Samantha showed him her back. Rudolf began buttoning her gown tantalizingly slowly, admiring the slender column of her back. He nuzzled her neck when he reached the top.

"You promised," Samantha whispered.

"I am playing a role for the dressmaker," Rudolf lied. "She left the room."

"Ah, my mistake," he whispered, planting a kiss on the side of her throat.

Madame Andrews returned and asked, "Your Highness, where shall I deliver everything in the morning?"

"We will be staying at the Royal Rooster Inn." Rudolf helped Samantha with her cloak and folded her hand inside the crook of his arm. They left the shop and walked down High Street in the direction of the inn.

A short time later, Rudolf and Samantha sat near the hearth in the common room of the Royal Rooster Inn. On the table before them lay beef steak and kidney pie, roasted potatoes, and baked tomatoes stuffed with grated onion and chopped ham. There were meringues fastened with whipped cream for dessert.

Rudolf watched Samantha closely. Her mood had lightened considerably. Most women adored shopping, especially with other people's money. Olga had always—

"I love meringues," Samantha said, turning to him abruptly, interrupting his thoughts. Holding the meringue in her hand, she flicked the tip of her tongue out and licked the whipped cream from the sides in an unconsciously sexual gesture.

"Good Christ," Rudolf murmured, suppressing a groan.

"Are you ill?" Samantha asked, covering his hand with her own. "You look pale."

"My leg is cramped," he lied. "I am glad you enjoy the meringue."

Her expression cleared. When she flicked her tongue

out again to lick the whipped cream, Rudolf imagined her performing that particular gesture on his—

"Your Highness?"

Rudolf focused on his retainer. "Yes, Karl?"

"The arrangements have been completed, Your Highness."

Rudolf inclined his head. "Thank you."

"To what arrangements is Karl referring?" Samantha asked when the man had gone.

"I have a surprise for you," Rudolf told her.

"I love surprises," Samantha exclaimed, reminding him of a young girl.

"As much as meringues?"

She smiled at his question. "More than meringues."

"I thought you would," Rudolf said. "Let us retire."

Upstairs, Rudolf unlocked the door and walked inside. He lit the candles on the table and turned to look at Samantha, an expression of joy appearing on her face.

Samantha couldn't believe her eyes. On one side of the chamber stood a wooden tub with steam rising from it—a bath.

"What a wonderful surprise," she exclaimed, turning to him.

"When we arrive at Sweetheart Manor tomorrow," Rudolf told her, "we need to give the staff a good first impression. We do not want to appear bedraggled."

"It's hot," she said, dipping her hand into the tub.

Rudolf placed a bar of soap into her hand, saying, "Save some hot water for me." Then he walked away.

After discarding her gown, Samantha looked expectantly at him and waited for him to leave. Instead, he removed his jacket and then washed his face in the water bowl on the table. She watched him take a razor and a small mirror from his gear, lather his face, and begin shaving.

"I suggest you undress and get into the tub," he said without looking at her. "Unless, you prefer that I bathe first?"

"I cannot strip naked with you in the room," she protested.

"I promise not to peek," Rudolf said, glancing over his shoulder and giving her a wink.

Samantha felt her irritation rising. The prince was tormenting her with this bath and his refusal to leave. She stood perfectly still and glared at him in an unspoken refusal to bathe while he remained in the chamber.

"Very well, I will wait outside the door," Rudolf said, wiping the soap from his partially shaved face. "Remember, I do not wish to bathe in cold water."

Muttering in Russian, Rudolf tossed the cloth on the table and left the chamber. Samantha expected him to slam the door shut, but he closed the door with a quiet click, making her feel a twinge of guilt for insisting he leave.

Samantha dropped her chemise, climbed into the tub, and groaned in pleasure at the heat. She longed to savor the sensation and soak until the water cooled but knew she had no time to waste. The prince could change his mind at any moment and burst into the room. Lifting the soap to her nose, she inhaled deeply of the scent of roses.

After washing, Samantha rose from the tub and toweled herself dry. She donned her chemise and knocked on the door, calling, "I'm finished, Your Highness."

Samantha grabbed her discarded gown. She moved to draw it over her head but paused when the prince spoke.

"Why are you dressing again?" he asked.

Samantha turned toward him. The prince had already removed his shirt and sat on the edge of the bed to remove his boots.

"I am dressing so I can wait in the corridor," she told him.

"Forget about that," Rudolf said, his dark gaze narrowing on her. "Get into the bed."

"Being in the room while you bathe isn't pro—" Samantha recognized the irritated expression on his face. "Oh, very well."

Samantha set her gown aside and limped to the other side of the bed. Intent on completing her nightly ritual, she covered her face with her hands. She heard the prince drop each of his boots and then the creak of the bed when he stood to drop his breeches.

"No peeking, Princess," she heard him teasing, and then came the sound of him climbing into the tub.

An overwhelming urge to part her fingers and peek at him surged through her. She separated her fingers and then smiled. With his wonderfully muscular back turned to her, the prince looked like a giant sitting in the wooden tub.

"Are you watching me?" he called.

Samantha closed her fingers and refused to answer. She struggled to focus on God and prayed silently, *Thank You, Lord, for the new gowns and the bath.*

With the prince sloshing water in the background, Samantha tried to keep her mind on God, but the temptation was too great. She opened her fingers again and gazed at the prince's naked back. In the candlelight he appeared like Adonis.

"What are you thanking Him for?" Rudolf asked.

"I am thanking Him for the gowns and the bath," Samantha answered, snapping her fingers shut.

"*I* gave you those things, not God," Rudolf reminded her.

"God gave you the idea to give them to me," she explained.

Rudolf laughed out loud at that. "You had better climb into the bed and turn your back lest I startle you when I rise from the tub," he warned.

Samantha didn't need a second warning. She leaped into the bed, pulled the coverlet up, and flopped onto her side away from the tub. Hearing the sounds of the prince toweling himself dry, she suffered the urge to roll over and watch, admire his masculine beauty in the candlelight. Fear of the unknown kept her back toward him.

She heard the sounds of him at the table as he finished shaving. Then all was silent for several moments.

Unable to bear the suspense, Samantha rolled over and saw the prince kneeling in prayer beside the bed. "What are you doing, thanking God?"

"No, Princess," he answered with a wicked smile, "I am asking Him for a favor."

"What?"

"None of your business."

Samantha turned away. She felt the bed creak as the prince climbed in beside her.

Long moments passed.

"Samantha?"

"Yes?"

"Look at me."

Samantha rolled onto her back. The prince leaned over her, and she stared into his darkly intense eyes.

"Yes, Rudolf?"

"I am sorry, Princess." His face inched closer. "I cannot keep my promise."

Rudolf claimed her lips in a long, slow, soul-stealing kiss. Swept away on the wave of his passion, Samantha entwined her arms around his neck and returned his kiss in kind, savoring the sensation of his warm flesh touching hers.

Rudolf thrust his tongue in her mouth, their tongues

swirling around each other in a primal mating dance. Tentatively at first and then with maddened passion, Samantha surrendered to her desires and thrust her tongue into his mouth. The prince groaned with the pleasure of her response and clutched her tightly as if he would never let her go.

Rudolf worshipped her with his lips, planting dozens of feathery light kisses on her eyelids, temples, and the corners of her mouth. *"Ma lyoobof,"* he whispered in a voice husky with passion. Then he flicked his tongue across her silken cheek to kiss her earlobe, his tongue swirling wetly around her ear.

Samantha felt hot and chilled all at the same time. Instinctively yearning for something more, she moaned and arched her body against his.

Rudolf kissed the base of her throat while his hands began a slow caress of her body. He glided a hand down her arm and up its sensitive inside. Drawing her chemise straps down, he exposed her breasts to his gaze.

"So beautiful, so perfect," he murmured, planting a kiss on the swell of each breast.

Samantha sighed in answer.

Lowering his head, he teased her by flicking his tongue across the tip of a nipple. Instantly, it beaded into arousal.

"Yes, Rudolf, kiss me there," Samantha panted.

She heard him groan at her invitation. And then he took her breasts in his hands and kneaded them softly. Dropping his mouth to a nipple, he suckled upon it gently.

Samantha felt a melting sensation in the pit of her stomach. His lips on her nipple and suckling noises made the hidden spot between her thighs throb.

Rudolf licked and suckled each of her nipples in turn. At the same time, he ran a hand down her body—caressing the outside of her thighs and then running a finger up the sensitive flesh on the inside. Cupping the mound of flesh covering her pubic bone, he kneaded her gently and inserted one long finger inside her.

His finger made her burn and jerked her into awareness. "What are you—?"

Rudolf silenced her by covering her mouth and kissing her again. Thoroughly. His hand never paused its seductive movement. Her protest died, and she willingly spread her legs for him, her hips beginning to move in tempo with his finger.

"Princess, let me love you," Rudolf whispered, his lips hovering above hers. "Let me show you paradise."

"Yes, take me there . . ."

Rudolf kissed her again and drew her chemise down her body until she was completely naked. Then he knelt between her legs and said, "Open your eyes." When she obeyed, he told her, "You are beautiful, *ma lyoobof.*"

Grasping her legs, Rudolf lifted them high and rested them on top of his shoulders, exposing her moist privates to his gaze. "So beautiful," he murmured.

His words brought a moan to Samantha's lips. She was vulnerable to his gaze and touch yet felt no fear, only the desire to get even closer, so close they would become one.

Rudolf lowered his head and pressed his mouth against the valley between her thighs. His lips kissed her nether lips, her distinct female perfume intoxicating his senses, bringing a primal urgency to mate with her, bury himself in her body, spill his seed deep inside her.

"Do you like my mouth on you like this?" he asked in a hoarse voice.

"Yes, oh, yes," she moaned, her hips moving in tempo to what his mouth did to her.

"Open your eyes," Rudolf ordered. When she did, he

told her, "From this night, you belong to me and no other."

He dipped his head and kissed her throbbing flesh. At the same time, he leaned forward and grabbed each of her nipples with a thumb and forefinger, gently squeezing and releasing.

Samantha moaned low in her throat. Her young body was on fire.

"Shall I give you release, *ma lyoobof*?" Rudolf asked.

"Yes."

Rudolf held her hips firmly and rubbed the tip of his manhood against her wet, swollen nub. He thrust forward suddenly and buried himself inside her.

Samantha cried out at his invasion of her body but slowly relaxed when he remained still. She liked his hands and his lips on her body, and she liked the feel of him inside her.

Opening her eyes when he began to move, Samantha gazed into his fathomless black eyes. She moved with him, slowly at first and then faster, faster until they became one maddened, bucking creature. He stopped suddenly, and she moaned in protest.

"I want to show you paradise," he said in a hoarse voice, as if speaking took extreme effort.

"Yes, take me there," she breathed.

Rudolf withdrew slowly, and then grinded himself deeply into her. He leaned down against her and suckled a nipple while he thrust himself inside her.

Samantha cried out in surprised pleasure as throbbing waves of pleasure surged through her body. She heard him groan and felt him thrust hard and deep, spilling his seed into her.

Within minutes, Samantha realized what she had done. She had fallen in love with the prince, given him the gift of her virginity, and ruined whatever chance she'd had of marrying and having her own children.

She had lost her dream, thrown it away for a moment's pleasure.

Tears of regret welled up in her eyes and rolled slowly down her cheeks. She bit her bottom lip, stifling a sob, but couldn't stop her tears from dripping off her face onto her breast.

"What is this?" the prince asked, moving to one side and gathering her into his arms. "Did I hurt you, Princess?"

Samantha shook her head.

"Why are you weeping?"

Samantha swallowed painfully, a lump of raw emotion sticking in her throat. In a barely audible voice, she told him, "I have killed my own dream. No man will marry me now, not even Alexander Emerson."

"You do not need to marry Alexander Emerson," Rudolf said, holding her tighter. "I will take care of you."

"Are you offering marriage?" Samantha asked, looking into his eyes for the first time.

His expression shuttered like a curtain falling and became impossible to read. The gesture reminded her again of the Duke of Inverary and her brother-in-law, the Marquess of Argyll. Apparently, all men shared some things in common, especially when the subject was marriage.

"I cannot offer you marriage," Rudolf told her, his hand beginning a slow caress.

With a sob escaping her throat, Samantha pulled out of his embrace. She rolled over and turned her back on him.

"Princess, do not turn away from me," the prince said, his hand on her back.

"Leave me alone, Your Highness." She stiffened when she felt him trace a finger down the column of her spine.

"Think of the lovely gowns and geegaws that will be yours tomorrow," Rudolf coaxed.

It was the wrong thing to say.

Samantha moved quickly, catching him off guard. In one swift motion, she bolted up in the bed and slapped his face with all the strength she could muster.

"My virginity was worth more to me than a few gowns," Samantha told him. "If you hadn't coerced me to leave London, I wouldn't have needed them." Her voice rose in anger. "And I would never have had to leave London if you hadn't got me abducted and nearly killed. I saved your royal arse by stealing the key from Igor's pocket. You have repaid me by stealing my dream."

At that, Samantha turned away in a huff and flopped down on her side of the bed. She waited for his angry response, but none came.

"You are correct," Rudolf said in a voice filled with regret. "Unfortunately, no apology will restore your dream to you. It seems I cannot make anyone happy, not even myself."

Samantha wondered at his last pain-filled statement but said nothing. With tears streaming down her cheeks, she determined to face her bleak future bravely. She hurt too much to care about his pain.

CHAPTER 6

"You look lovely in your purple gown."

Samantha glanced sidelong at the prince and said, "The gown is amethyst, not purple."

"There is no difference," Rudolf told her. "Amethyst and purple are the same color."

"Amethyst is a bluish violet," Samantha corrected him. "Purple is true purple."

"Is amethyst a false purple?"

Her irritation rising, Samantha lifted her nose into the air and turned her head to look at the passing scenery. The prince was deliberately being obtuse, baiting her because she hadn't spoken to him since climbing into the coach that morning. Apparently, His Highness couldn't bear to be ignored.

"Are you angry with me?" Rudolf asked.

Samantha sighed. "I am angry with myself," she said, without taking her gaze off the view outside.

"Do not be angry," Rudolf said, inching closer. "Your reputation was already ruined."

Samantha snapped her head around to stare at him. Only a dead man would have missed her displeasure.

"Are you going to strike me again?" Rudolf asked, obviously feigning fear.

Samantha's lips twitched with the urge to laugh. She gave herself a mental shake. Losing one's virtue was no laughing matter.

"Admit it, Princess," Rudolf said. "You enjoyed the intimacy we shared."

"If you wanted to have fun," Samantha told him, lifting her nose into the air, "you should have abducted my sister. Tory adores fun."

"I did not abduct you," the prince corrected her. "Tell me what you adore, *ma lyoobof.*"

Samantha gave him her sweetest smile. "I adore boring gentlemen. I adore people who keep promises. I adore being left alone when I'm not in the mood for company."

"I apologize for bothering you." Rudolf folded his arms across his chest, turned his head, and looked out the window.

Samantha watched him, a wave of guilt surging through her. The prince hadn't forced her to do anything. She was the one with the weak moral character, not he.

"Rudolf?" Samantha touched his arm. When he looked at her, she said, "I apologize for my rudeness."

"Thank you for that," Rudolf said, covering her hand with his own, "but I should be apologizing to you. I will marry you before we return to London and save your reputation."

"No, thank you," she refused.

"No?" he echoed, his expression mirroring his surprise.

"I cannot marry a man who only wants to save my reputation," she told him.

"You were ready to marry Alexander Emerson," Rudolf reminded her, sounding insulted.

"That was different."

"Like purple and amethyst?" Rudolf asked, his tone sarcastic. "Why can you not marry me to save your reputation?"

I love you, Samantha thought, *and I can't marry you unless you love me.*

"Well?" he asked.

Samantha said nothing, merely turned away. She would never share her heart's secrets with him. She had already shared her body, and that was sharing enough.

"Why would you marry him but refuse me?" Rudolf persisted.

"I have a headache," Samantha interrupted him, holding her hand up in a gesture to stop. "Please, let's discuss this another time."

"As you wish," he said curtly.

Samantha closed her eyes and leaned her head back against the coach. Both Alexander and she had ulterior motives for wanting to marry each other. He wanted to make amends for his father; she wanted a family of her own. Neither was in love.

Prince Rudolf was another matter. He thought she was pathetic and offered to marry her out of pity. She loved him and could only marry him if he loved her. Anything less would be too painful to bear.

Two hours of strained silence later, their destination came into view. Located on the shores of Loch Kindar, Sweetheart Manor lay on the outskirts of New Abbey Village. A double octagon formed an imposing approach to the manor. In the center of the first octagon stood the statue of a boar, guarding the house. The second octagon contained a lion statue with its front paw on top of the world.

The manor consisted of three attached buildings. The main house was built in early Georgian times, and the middle structure dated from the reign of William and Mary. The last and original building was erected during Tudor times.

Three footmen materialized as soon as Karl halted the coach in front of the main house. A tall, dignified-looking man who appeared to be in charge stood outside the front door.

Accepting the prince's offered hand, Samantha stepped out of the coach and stared at the manor. She could hardly believe that she was standing outside the house where her father had been born.

Rudolf leaned close, saying, "Let me do the talking."

Samantha inclined her head and slipped her hand through the crook of his arm. Assuming a royal attitude, she lifted her nose into the air and looked expectantly at the majordomo.

"You could have a future at Drury Lane," Rudolf said with laughter lurking in his voice, making her smile.

"Welcome to Sweetheart Manor," the majordomo greeted them. "I am Durwin. I assume you are the Marquess of Argyll"—he looked at Samantha—"and you are the Marchioness of Argyll, the late earl's daughter."

"I am Prince Rudolf Kazanov of Russia," Rudolf said, giving the man an easy smile. "My wife, Princess Samantha, is sister to the Marchioness of Argyll."

Though her expression remained placid, Samantha felt surprised by the prince's declaration. She had warned him to make no public announcement that she was his wife. Doing so made her his common-law wife, in fact.

"Welcome to Sweetheart Manor, Your Highness," Durwin said, leading the way into the foyer where maids and footmen and cooks were lined up for inspection. "My father was the majordomo for the late earl's father. Several other servants have such a history with the Douglases."

"Tradition gives a man strong roots," the prince replied.

The moderately large foyer, modest by London's standards, was almost entirely Italian marble. On the immediate right rose a winding staircase to the upper levels. Several pieces of classical statuary poised here and there, but Samantha saw her brother-in-law's fine touch in the silk greenery and flowers that warmed what would have been an austere foyer.

"This is Prince Rudolf Kazanov of Russia," Durwin announced. "Princess Samantha, his wife, is one of the late earl's daughters."

When the Douglas servants clapped their approval, Rudolf inclined his head and said, "The marquess shows wisdom by keeping the late earl's faithful retainers."

"Annie and Sally, unpack Her Highness's baggage," Durwin instructed. "Kevin, help the prince's man carry the baggage upstairs. The rest of you return to your duties."

As the servants departed the foyer, the majordomo turned to the prince, saying, "I will escort you to your chamber. You will, of course, stay in the master suite."

"Durwin, Russian royalty always keeps their own chambers," Samantha lied, drawing a surprised look from the prince.

"As you wish, Your Highness."

Samantha slipped her hand through the prince's arm and smiled sweetly. He didn't look especially happy. Apparently, she had foiled his plans to seduce her again.

Rudolf and Samantha followed the majordomo upstairs. He led them down a corridor toward the rear of the mansion.

"Here we are," Durwin said, opening a door. "The

marquess desired the quietest chambers overlooking the gardens."

The master suite was grand. Opposite the hearth, an enormous bed sported a rich red velvet bedspread with gold braiding. The room was furnished with a highboy, a French chest of drawers, a leather slipper chair, a round mahogany table, and a mahogany settee with fabric upholstery. A red-and-blue Persian carpet covered the hardwood floor, and the walls had been painted a deep bottle green. Arched windows overlooked the rear gardens and pond; beyond the grounds, Loch Kindar provided a serene background.

"Is this satisfactory, Your Highness?"

Rudolf nodded. "This will do."

Durwin walked across the bedchamber as Karl and footmen carried the baggage into the chamber. The majordomo opened the door to the connecting chamber, saying, "And this is your chamber, Your Highness."

The prince certainly doesn't have far to go, Samantha thought, limping toward the other room. She glanced at Rudolf as she passed him. He smiled at her, obviously satisfied by the proximity of her bed to his.

Her bedchamber was almost as large as the prince's, its color scheme done in jeweled tones. The walls had been painted red, and opposite the hearth, the canopied bed had been decorated with brilliant blue-and-gold textiles. An upholstered settee sat near the hearth, accompanied by a writing table with chair, various occasional tables, and a highboy. A red, gold, blue, and cream Persian carpet covered the oak floor.

A footman was already busy lighting a fire in the hearth. The two maids unpacked the gowns and hung them in the chamber's adjoining dressing room.

"A lovely room," Rudolf remarked. "Don't you think?"

"The chamber is quite lovely," Samantha agreed.

Durwin flicked his wrist at the maids and the footman, who instantly left the chamber. "Will there be anything else, Your Highness?"

"No, thank you," the prince answered.

"What time do you wish to dine?"

"The journey has been long and tiring," Rudolf answered, glancing at Samantha. "We will skip tea and dine early, say five o'clock."

The majordomo started to turn away but then paused. "Your Highness, we didn't expect your visit and had planned a Twelfth Night party for tomorrow night in the Tudor great hall," Durwin said. "Would it be acceptable if—?"

"Do not cancel your celebration because of us," Rudolf interrupted.

Durwin smiled. "Thank you, Your Highness."

"Do you have a key for that door?" Samantha asked.

"A key?" the majordomo echoed in confusion.

"Samantha, my love . . ." The prince's voice held a warning note.

"Never mind," Samantha said, waving the majordomo away. "You may leave."

Samantha turned to the prince as soon as the door shut behind the majordomo. From the expression on his face, she knew he was displeased with her.

"Do nothing to embarrass me or yourself in front of the servants," Rudolf ordered in a stern voice.

Samantha inclined her head. "I would like to rest now."

Instead of leaving, Rudolf stepped closer. With a smile on his lips, he reached out and cupped her cheek.

"Do not deprive me of hope, *ma lyoobof,*" he said. "Hope may be all I have."

"Who knows, Your Highness?" Samantha returned

his smile, thinking how charming he could be. "Miracles happen every day."

"I certainly hope so," Rudolf replied. "Do you want to rest or tour the estate?"

"Both."

"Rest now," he said. "There will be time to explore tomorrow. Turn around, and I will unbutton your gown."

Samantha showed him her back. Within seconds, the prince unfastened her buttons, and she felt him running a finger up the bare skin of her back. He pushed aside the heavy mass of her ebony hair and planted a kiss on the back of her neck, sending a chill down her spine.

Samantha refused to succumb to her desires. She whirled around, ready for battle, but the prince merely smiled and stepped back a pace.

"Pleasant dreams, *ma lyoobof,*" he said, turning to leave.

"What is *ma lyoobof*?" she asked.

"Wicked witch." The door clicked shut behind him.

Samantha disrobed and hanged her amethyst gown in the dressing room. Wearing only her chemise, she limped across the chamber to the bed and climbed between the coverlet and the sheets.

My father's ancestral home, Samantha thought in wonder, leaning back against the pillow. Her father had been born and passed his childhood here. Which chamber had been his? What had his life been like? Too bad they hadn't had the money to move here; on the other hand, she shouldn't forget that her brother-in-law had renovated and refurbished the manor. Who knew what it had looked like after all those years of neglect?

Samantha glanced toward the door connecting her chamber to the prince's. She wished circumstances had been different, but there was no use in thinking about what could never be.

Willing herself to relax, Samantha closed her eyes. Within minutes, she drifted into a dreamless sleep.

Three hours later, Samantha stood in the dressing room and pondered what to wear. Finally, she decided on the sky blue silk with the long, loose sleeves. The color matched her eyes, or so the prince had said.

Why was she tormenting herself? she wondered. No matter what she wore, her clothing could never change the circumstances that kept the prince and her apart. He was a royal and could never marry her, even if he wanted it, which he certainly did not.

Dressed except for her buttons, Samantha grabbed the gown's matching cashmere shawl. She knocked on the connecting door and waited.

Instead of calling out to enter, Rudolf opened the door and flashed her a smile. He looked heartbreakingly handsome in his black waistcoat and breeches.

"Welcome to my chamber," Rudolf said, stepping aside so she could enter.

Samantha pointed to the back of her gown, asking, "Would you please button me?"

Rudolf arched a dark brow at her. "What do you think ladies' maids are for?"

Samantha felt her face flaming with her embarrassment. She started to turn away, but he stopped her.

"I would love to button your gown," Rudolf said in a voice suggesting intimacy.

"You like to tease me, don't you?" she asked.

"In more ways than you can imagine," Rudolf answered, fastening her buttons. He lifted the shawl out of her hand and wrapped it around her shoulders.

Located on the ground floor, the dining room was small by London standards. Its doors and floor were oak, the walls painted red and decorated with portraits. A red-and-blue carpet covered the floor beneath the mahogany dining table, which had seating for only twenty. A crystal-and-gold chandelier provided light along with the fire in the hearth and the candles on the table and sideboard.

Durwin greeted them at the door and escorted them to the table. "Your Highness," he said deferentially, pulling out the chair at the head of the table.

Turning to Samantha, Durwin said, "Please follow me, Your Highness." Then he proceeded to walk the length of the table, obviously intending to deposit her at the other end.

"Durwin, are you stealing my wife?" Rudolf called.

"I beg your pardon?" the majordomo said.

Samantha flicked a glance at the two footmen who stood at attention near the sideboard. From their expressions, she expected the two men to explode with laughter.

"If you put my wife at the other end of the table, I will not be able to admire her beauty while I dine," Rudolf said, laughter tingeing his voice. "I would prefer she sit here beside me."

"I apologize, Your Highness," the majordomo said, escorting her back to the prince.

Beneath the majordomo's supervision, the two footmen served them potato soup with celery for their first course. The main dish consisted of roasted goose, sage and onion stuffing, watercress garnish, and a thickened gravy.

"So, Princess, is your gown true blue or false blue?" Rudolf asked, as the footmen placed the carved goose on the table.

"This color is sky blue," Samantha said, refusing to rise to his bait.

"I can never keep my colors straight," Rudolf replied. "Are you feeling rested?"

"Quite."

They finished their dinner engaged in easy conversation.

"Will you play your violin for me tonight?" he asked. She smiled at that. "Yes."

"And would you care to ride with me one morning?"

"I don't know how," she admitted.

"Then, I will teach you," he said. "Now, shall we walk outside before retiring to the drawing room?"

"I'd like that," she answered.

"Durwin, send one of the footmen for our cloaks," Rudolf ordered, sounding every inch the prince.

"Colin, fetch their cloaks," Durwin instructed one of the men.

Samantha leaned close to the prince. "Why didn't you speak directly to the footman?" she whispered as the man left the room.

"A prince is required to observe the servants' hierarchy," Rudolf told her, lowering his voice. "The major-domo enjoys more status than the footman and would be insulted if I spoke directly to the man instead of him."

"If Durwin is absent," Samantha asked, her blue eyes sparkling with merriment, "do you send the footman for him and then tell him to send the footman on your errand?"

Rudolf burst out laughing. "Speaking directly to the footman is acceptable in that case."

"The whole idea of a servants' pecking order seems absurd to me," Samantha said.

"Why do you not know this already?" Rudolf asked.

"I lived in the cottage until last June," Samantha whispered. "We didn't keep servants."

"And since then?"

"I never noticed," she answered. "I was too busy with other important things."

Rudolf smiled at her. "What important things held your attention?"

"I was required to learn how to make small talk," Samantha told him, a smile tugging at the corners of her lips. "I also needed to learn the latest dances, to hold a fan properly, and to serve tea. God forbid, I should be remiss in learning who to seat with whom at dinner parties."

Rudolf chuckled. "Ah, yes, the empire would be endangered if you failed to learn those things."

Samantha struggled against her laughter when the footman returned to the dining room. Instead of giving them their cloaks, he passed them to Durwin.

"Your Highness, would you like a footman to carry a lantern outside?" the majordomo asked, assisting them with their cloaks.

"No, thank you."

"Is there anything else I can get you?"

"I merely desire a few moments of privacy with my wife," Rudolf said, turning away. "Actually, Durwin, I want someone to get my wife's violin from her chamber and leave it in the small drawing room."

Durwin snapped to attention. "I will take care of that myself."

"I appreciate your effort," Rudolf replied.

Leaving the dining room, Rudolf and Samantha passed through the foyer and then stepped outside. A full moon lit the night.

Samantha breathed deeply of the crisp air, scented by woodsmoke from the manor's fireplaces. "I never thought we would arrive," she said.

"You weathered the journey," Rudolf said. "What is the significance of the boar and the lion guarding the house?"

Samantha shrugged. "My father never spoke of his boyhood here. I suppose he was bitter about losing the Douglas fortune. He found peace when the drinking finally killed him."

"I am sorry for your loss," Rudolf said, putting an arm around her shoulder.

"I am sorry for the loss of your wife," Samantha said.

"Ah, yes, Olga."

"Does your daughter resemble her?" she asked.

"Karl tells me that Dumfries is only eight miles from here," Rudolf said, ignoring her question. "We will take the coach and buy you another dagger."

His wife's death still pains him, Samantha thought. How could she ever compete with the cherished memory of a beloved wife?

"Did you hear me?" he asked.

"Do you think I'll be needing a dagger?" she asked.

Rudolf flashed her a smile. "Fortune favors those who are prepared."

"I warned you not to announce that we were married," Samantha said, changing the subject.

"There are worse things in life than being your husband," Rudolf said, tilting her chin up to gaze into her eyes.

"Thank you, I think," Samantha said dryly.

"Let us return inside," Rudolf said. "I want to listen to your violin."

Arm in arm, Rudolf and Samantha returned inside the manor. As soon as they entered the foyer, Durwin rushed forward and helped them with their cloaks.

"I also left you a bottle of brandy in the small drawing room," the majordomo told the prince.

"Thank you, Durwin," Rudolf said. "If you should ever consider leaving the marquess's employ, you will find a place in my household."

They left the majordomo preening with the prince's compliment and walked upstairs to the drawing room. As promised, her violin awaited her there.

The small drawing room was warm and inviting. The walls had been painted a yellow ochre, their shade matching the gold, red, and blue carpet. There was a mix of textiles, the upholstered chairs and settees offered in jewellike colors.

Samantha reached for her violin case as Rudolf poured himself a brandy. He looked over his shoulder at her and asked, "Would you care for one?"

Samantha smiled. "I never indulge in spirits."

"No one is watching," he coaxed.

Samantha shook her head. "I have learned difficult lessons from my father's troubles."

"I understand," Rudolf replied, sitting in a high-backed chair.

Samantha rested the violin between her head and shoulder, keeping it in place against her neck. She held the bow in her right hand.

Closing her eyes, she began her song, conjuring the lonely moorlands and mysterious mist, light and darkness, and all the shades of shadows in between. The haunting melody gradually increased in tempo like a swirling spiral until it became almost jaunty before fading away to conjure winter's slumber, spring's growth, summer's song, and autumn's rustling.

Samantha opened her eyes and stared at the prince. He sat with his eyes closed as if letting her song lead him wherever it wanted.

When she ended her song, Rudolf opened his eyes and then stood. "Thank you for the concert, Princess," he said. "You play exceedingly well."

His compliment pleased her immensely. Samantha returned the violin and the bow to the case and then set it aside. She rose from the settee and accepted his offered hand.

Together, they walked down the corridor to their chambers. Without an invitation, the prince followed her into her bedchamber.

"What are you doing?" she asked.

"I will unfasten your buttons," he told her.

With the task completed in mere seconds, Rudolf kissed the side of her neck. Samantha turned around to face him but stepped back a pace.

"Good night, Princess," he said, lifting her hand to his lips. "May your dreams be pleasant."

Samantha watched him walk through the connecting door into his chamber. She stood there for a long moment and stared at the door, wishing circumstances had been different, wishing they were two average people, wishing he wasn't a prince and she wasn't a pickpocket.

Giving herself a mental shake, Samantha limped into her dressing room to change into a nightshift and bedrobe. Returning to the bedchamber proper, she gave the door a troubled look and knelt beside the bed.

"Thank You, Lord, for getting us here safely," Samantha murmured, covering her face with her hands. "Thank You for having the marquess renovate Sweetheart Manor"—she spread her fingers and stared at the dresser—"and thank You for giving me the idea to block the door."

Rising from the floor, Samantha limped across the room on bare feet and slowly pushed the dresser toward the connecting door. The prince was an honorable man, but he was a man, nevertheless, and might decide to visit her during the night, catching her in a weakened state.

With her door safely blocked, Samantha climbed into the bed and pulled the coverlet up. She looked at the door and wondered what he was doing.

Bang! Bang! Bang!

"Samantha?"

She stared at the door in silence. Pretending sleep seemed the best course of action.

"Samantha, are you awake?" he called. "What was that noise?"

She heard him trying to open the door. Several muttered words in Russian followed that.

A moment later, the corridor door burst open, and Samantha bolted up in the bed. Looking none too happy, the prince marched across the chamber and then pushed the dresser to its original place.

"What do you think you're doing?" Samantha demanded.

"If a maid walked into this room and saw that door blocked," Rudolf said, his voice stern with anger, "both of us would be disgraced. Perhaps they would doubt who we are and send a message to the marquess. That could bring Vladimir to us."

"I don't believe that would happen," she argued.

"Would I lie?"

"Yes."

"Commoners always watch royals and then gossip about them," he said, running a hand through his black hair in obvious frustration. "Do you want that?"

Samantha felt a flush of embarrassment coloring her cheeks.

"There is no need to block the door," Rudolf assured her. "You are safe with me."

"I wasn't safe last night," she reminded him. "I lost my virtue."

"Virginity has nothing to do with virtue," Rudolf told her, turning to leave.

Samantha had no idea what he meant. She dropped her gaze to his flaming red silk bedrobe. Of all the colors in the universe, she would never have expected the prince to wear a red bedrobe.

"Your Highness?" Her lips twitched with the urge to laugh.

"What is it now?"

"Is that true red or false red?" she asked.

"Red is red," he growled. "Purple is purple." At that, the prince disappeared through the connecting door into his chamber.

Samantha lay back on the bed and stared at the door. She felt relieved that the matter of his sneaking in here was settled. And yet, the bed seemed lonely without him. She'd grown accustomed to his body beside hers.

She missed him.

CHAPTER 7

"I missed you beside me last night."

Seated at the dining table the next morning, Samantha glanced at the prince but said nothing. What could she say? She wasn't about to tell him how much she missed him. That would lead to his crawling into bed with her.

Samantha resumed eating her oatmeal porridge. "I adore melted butter," she said, reaching for a hot scone. "How is your trout?"

"The trout is baked to perfection," Rudolf said, his smile telling her he knew she was changing the subject. "You look very pretty in your white gown. I like the contrasting black shawl."

"Why are we sitting at the far end of the table?" Samantha asked, changing the subject to the mundane.

"Since we will be in residence for several weeks, I thought we could amuse ourselves by sitting in a different seat each meal," Rudolf said, giving her a charming smile. "Changing position does wonders for a person's point of view. One begins to understand how someone else thinks."

She bit into a scone and asked almost disinterestedly, "What does that mean?"

"If you change your point of view," he told her, "the world becomes a different place."

Samantha arched an ebony brow at him. "Are you trying to tell me something?"

"You might think differently about us if you saw the situation through my eyes," Rudolf told her.

"There is no us," Samantha insisted, leaning close to whisper. "What's wrong with my point of view? Why don't you try to see the situation through my eyes?"

The prince caught the majordomo's eye and, with a flick of his wrist, sent Durwin and a footman out of the room. The majordomo closed the door, leaving them alone.

"How did you do that?" Samantha asked, watching the men leave.

"Practice." Rudolf smiled and then said, "The damage to your reputation has been done. Why not relax and enjoy yourself?"

"I told you last night—"

"Lie about your virginity," Rudolf interrupted. A bitter edge crept into his voice when he added, "Others do."

"That would be too dishonest," she said primly.

Rudolf burst out laughing. "Princess, until recently, you picked money out of gentlemen's pockets."

"Circumstances forced me to do that," Samantha defended herself. "My family needed to eat."

"I am not criticizing your behavior," Rudolf told her. "I am merely—never mind." He stopped talking, apparently deciding to drop the subject.

"Finish your porridge. Then we will tour the manor."

When they emerged from the dining room a short time later, Durwin was waiting just outside the door.

Rudolf turned to the majordomo and said, "Give my compliments to the cook."

"Thank you, Your Highness."

"I would like you to seat us in a different place at the table for each meal," Rudolf instructed the man.

Durwin looked puzzled by the request. "As you wish, Your Highness."

"We are starting our grand tour of Sweetheart Manor," Rudolf told him. "The large drawing room is that way?"

"Yes, Your Highness. Shall I escort you around the manor?" the majordomo asked.

"My bride and I wish to explore the house alone," the prince said in refusal and then turned to Samantha. "Are you ready, my dear?"

Samantha smiled at the prince for the majordomo's benefit and slipped her arm through his. She would have preferred that Durwin accompany them, but the man would become suspicious if she didn't want to be alone with her husband.

The large drawing room was formal yet comfortable. The walls sported burnished golden oak from dado to floor as did the mantel above the white marble hearth. The walls above the dado had been papered a deep gold. A red, white, and blue Persian carpet covered the oak floor. Couches, love seats, and settees had been upholstered in various fabrics, the predominate color being a taffeta cream. Here and there tables were positioned, several accompanied by wooden chairs with upholstered cushions.

Samantha was immediately attracted to the portraits of Douglases covering the walls, apparently requisitioned by her brother-in-law. It was the first time she was seeing the illustrious ancestors she'd heard about from her aunt.

"This is Good Sir James Douglas," Samantha said, staring at a portrait. "He fought and died with William

Wallace, Scotland's greatest hero in the wars of independence."

"Independence?" Rudolf echoed.

"Scotland has not always been united with England." Samantha stopped at the next portrait and read the name at the bottom. "This is Archibald the Grim, the bastard son of Good Sir James. When the legitimate Douglas line died, Archibald became the third Earl Douglas."

"A bastard inherited?"

Samantha nodded. "His son, the fourth Earl Douglas, fought with Joan of Arc against the English."

"Your father was not Earl Douglas," Rudolf said.

"My father was the Earl of Melrose, a title granted at a later date to a branch of the Douglas clan," Samantha told him. "There's an interesting tale about the first Earl Douglas," she said, slipping her arm through his. "During the wars of independence, women in the English garrison sang a lullaby to their children which ended with the words 'The Black Douglas shall not get ye.'

"During the recapture of Roxburgh Castle, Black Douglas led his men silently through the dusk to the castle and found an unguarded entrance. The first person he encountered was a woman singing her child to sleep. As she sang 'The Black Douglas shall not get ye,' the Black Douglas laid a hand on her arm and said, 'I am not so sure of that.' "

Prince Rudolf smiled. "So did this Black Douglas get them?"

"I don't know," Samantha said with a shrug. "The story always ended there."

"You must tell me a new story every day," Rudolf said, guiding her toward the door.

"Only if you tell me one," she said, her blue eyes gleaming as she warmed to the man.

Rudolf nodded his head in agreement. "Let us surprise the staff in the kitchen," he said.

Rudolf and Samantha could hear the buzz of laughter and conversations as they neared the kitchen. All of this stopped the instant they walked into the room. With surprised expressions frozen on their faces, the servants snapped to attention.

Warm and inviting, the kitchen was enormous. On one side was a gigantic red brick hearth, and opposite that were dozens of pots and pans hanging from hooks on the wall. Laden with bowls and utensils, a long table with wooden chairs stood in the middle of the room.

"My compliments to you," Rudolf spoke to the cook. "I have not eaten so well since leaving my homeland."

"Thank you, Your Highness." The cook preened beneath the prince's praise.

Samantha glanced at the maids. Sally was staring at the prince with an expression of mingling adoration and hunger, unacceptably bold.

Feeling a twinge of jealousy, Samantha touched the prince's arm and smiled warmly when he turned to her. "Darling," she drawled in a good imitation of her aunt. "The staff is busy with their party preparations. We should continue our walk."

"You are correct, *ma lyoobof,*" Rudolf said, covering her hand with his. He turned to the cook again, saying, "I can hardly wait for your next meal."

"Thank you, Your Highness."

"Do you like gingerbread?" Samantha asked, as they left the kitchen.

"I have never eaten it," the prince answered.

"Gingerbread topped with clotted cream is a taste of heaven," Samantha told him. "I'll make you a batch tomorrow."

The prince looked surprised. "You cook?"

"We didn't keep servants at the cottage," Samantha reminded him.

Rudolf smiled. "I will help you make this gingerbread."

Three more chambers on the first floor awaited their inspection—the marquess's office, the chapel, and the library. The office was located in the rear of the house and overlooked the gardens. A warm, cozy atmosphere pervaded the room—roaring fire in the hearth, sturdy oak desk, oversized chairs.

"What is that?" Samantha asked, spying the heap of papers tossed on top of the desk.

"Karl packed my business ledgers," Rudolf answered with a wry smile.

"What kind of businesses?"

"Shipping, mostly."

"My brother-in-law has shipping lines," Samantha said.

"Yes, the marquess is part of my competition," Rudolf told her. "I was hoping that you would read a book in here later while I worked."

"I would like that," Samantha said, blushing.

Their next stop was the chapel. Samantha merely peered inside the door and then turned away.

"Would you like to go inside and thank God for something?" Rudolf teased her.

"I don't need chapels or clergy to speak to God," she told him. "He hears me no matter where I am."

The two-storied, loft-style library was their final destination in the Georgian section of the manor, the third level being servants' quarters. The library was as big as any ballroom Samantha had ever seen.

A large fireplace heated the first section of the room, and the walls sported built-in bookcases from floor to ceiling. In the middle of the room perched a gigantic globe of the world in a wooden stand.

A double archway served as the entrance to an attached reading room with its own marble hearth. Comfortable-looking upholstered and leather seating arrangements filled the room.

"I never saw so many books," Samantha said, turning in a circle. "My sister would hate this chamber."

"Which sister is that?" Rudolf asked.

"Victoria."

"She does not like books?"

His tone of voice told her he couldn't imagine anyone not liking books. She felt the same way but understood her sister's taste in activities.

"Tory has difficulty reading and ciphering numbers," Samantha told him. "I think something is wrong with her eyesight. She sees *p*'s instead of *q*'s and *nines* instead of *sixes*."

"How frustrating that must be." Rudolf turned to the stairway leading to the second level. "Let us go upstairs."

The loft-style second level had upholstered and leather benches and chaises against the walls. Sconces and portraits hung above them.

When they turned to retrace their steps downstairs, Rudolf flashed her a charmingly boyish smile and said, "Watch this."

Rudolf perched on the well-polished railing and slid to the first level, leaping off at the bottom. Samantha burst out laughing.

"You try now," Rudolf called.

"I'm afraid," Samantha refused, shaking her head.

"I will catch you."

Samantha perched sideways on the railing as the prince had done. Laughing all the way, she slid down the banister.

True to his word, Rudolf grabbed her by the waist before she could fall. He lost his balance in the movement and fell, shielding her from hitting the oak floor as they went down.

Samantha lay on top of the prince and laughed. Keeping her within his embrace, Rudolf joined in her merriment.

Without warning, Rudolf placed a hand behind her head to keep her steady and kissed her. Caught up in the moment, Samantha surrendered to her tender feelings for him and returned his kiss in kind. It was the prince who broke their kiss.

"*Ma lyoobof,* you take my breath away," he said. "Literally."

Samantha laughed again and rose slowly from the floor. She held out a hand to him to help him up. When he seemed to be pulling her down again, she cried, "Don't you dare."

Samantha broke free from his grasp and, laughing all the way, ran out of the library as fast as her limp would allow. Rudolf leaped off the floor and bolted after her. Catching her in the corridor, he threw an arm around her shoulder and pulled her against the side of his body.

"Savoring small moments like this has been missing from my life for a long time," Rudolf said, planting a kiss on her temple. "Thank you, Princess."

Samantha responded to the warmth in his voice. She looked at him through her enormous blue eyes and gave him a jaunty smile, saying, "You are welcome, Your Highness."

The second section of Sweetheart Manor had been built during the reign of William and Mary. The upper level served as servants' quarters, and the first floor had been renovated into a spectacular ballroom. The hardwood floors had been left bare for dancing, and a gigantic crystal chandelier hung over the center of the ballroom. On the far side of the room stood a grand piano.

Rudolf and Samantha crossed the ballroom on their way to the Tudor section of the manor. When they reached the middle of the ballroom, and stood beneath the chandelier, Rudolf paused and turned to her.

"May I have this dance, my lady?" Rudolf asked, holding out his hand, mirroring the night they met.

Falling in with his playful mood, Samantha flashed him a smile. "Are your intentions honorable, Your Highness?" she asked.

"No."

"In that case . . ."

Smiling into the prince's dark eyes, Samantha placed her hand in his and stepped into his arms. With the prince humming a waltz, they swirled around and around the ballroom.

Great Giles' ghost, Samantha thought, how she wished returning to London was not in their immediate future.

"A passing cloud is casting a shadow over your smile," Rudolf said. "What are you thinking, *ma lyoobof?*"

Samantha blushed furiously but said nothing.

"You have a thought you do not wish to share?" he asked.

Samantha inclined her head.

"Then, I will demonstrate how I dance with Zara," Rudolf said. "That will bring the sunshine back to your smile."

"Zara?" she echoed.

"My daughter is Zara," Rudolf told her. "Remove your shoes."

Samantha gave him a puzzled smile but removed her slippers.

"Stand on my boots," he instructed her.

Samantha giggled. "You want me to—?"

"Step on top of my boots and hold on to me."

When she did as instructed, the prince pulled her close. Slowly, much too slowly for a real waltz, he began to dance around the ballroom.

Samantha burst out laughing. Unable to control her mirth, she fell off the top of his boots.

"How odd," Rudolf remarked, the corners of his lips turning up in a smile. "Zara has the same reaction when I dance with her."

Samantha stared at him through blue eyes that shone with love. The prince enjoyed his daughter and was a good father. He was the type of man with whom she had hoped to share a family.

Samantha retrieved her slippers, and they continued their tour. Stepping into the Tudor great hall was like traveling back in time. The floors were wood with no carpeting, and several pieces of furniture had been pushed against the walls in preparation for the servants' Twelfth Night celebration. A huge fireplace ran along one wall, and unlit torches adorned the walls.

Rudolf removed his waistcoat and settled it over her shoulders. "Let us step into the garden for a few minutes," he said, taking her hand in his.

Though the garden was winter barren, Samantha could see that it would be lovely the other three seasons. There was a carved semicircular stone seat with winged lion end supports. On the other side of the pond, five Doric columns supported a stone gazebo with wrought-iron cupola. Stone lions stood guard with a sundial on the near side of the pond.

Samantha inhaled deeply of the crisp air. "This must be paradise in summer," she said.

"My estate on Sark Island is heaven on earth," Rudolf said. "You must visit me there."

Samantha forced herself to smile. She didn't want to think of their lives outside the manor. When the danger had passed, they would return to London and go their separate ways. She would never see Sark Island.

"Look over there," Samantha said, pointing across the pond.

A few yards back from the opposite shore of the pond stood an enormous playhouse. Near that, an ancient oak held a treehouse in its branches.

"The marquess must be planning a large family," Samantha said.

"I always wanted a dozen sons and daughters," Rudolf said, a note of regret in his voice.

"Your wish may still be granted," she teased him. "You do possess the Kazanov Venus."

"I will never marry again," the prince said, his expression grim. "The pain was too great."

Returning the way they had come, Rudolf paused near the piano. "You must bring your violin down here and play a duet with me," he said.

"Do you play the piano?" Samantha asked in surprise.

Rudolf shrugged. "I can carry a tune."

"Play something for me."

Rudolf inclined his head and sat on the bench. He flexed his long fingers a few times, which reminded Samantha of how those fingers had played upon her naked flesh.

The prince's playing combined great strength with gentleness and delicacy. His tune held an irresistibly jaunty air . . . reminiscent of springtime songbirds and dancing wildflowers.

Samantha leaned against the piano and closed her eyes. She let his melody transport her to another, happier place. His energetic playing lightened her spirit and brought a soft smile to her lips. Lord, but she wished for her violin.

Opening her eyes when the music stopped, Samantha saw him smiling at her. "You play divinely, Your Highness."

Rudolf gave her a devastating smile. "I am certain we will make beautiful music together, *ma lyoobof.*"

Samantha was certain of one thing only. She had fallen hopelessly in love with a prince who wore a red silk bedrobe, played the piano divinely, and waltzed with his five-year-old daughter.

An hour later, Samantha sat inside the first-floor office and watched the prince. Rudolf sat at the desk and muttered unhappily in Russian as he tried to bring order to the mountain of papers and ledgers that Karl had dumped there.

"Excuse my impatience," Rudolf said with a sheepish smile, turning to look at her. "At the moment, I could choke the life from Karl and never feel a twinge of guilt."

"You don't mean that," she said.

"Then I would need to train a new driver," he replied. "As they say—"

"—the devil you know is better than the devil you don't know," she finished for him.

"Precisely, but your soothing presence makes my task easier," Rudolf told her.

Samantha blushed, saying, "Now I know why all those ladies were hovering around you at the Emerson ball."

"Why is that?"

"You are an incorrigible flatterer."

Rudolf gave her a boyishly charming smile and said, "I am guilty as charged."

Samantha returned her attention to the books on her lap: *The History of the Douglas Family* and *Pride and*

Prejudice. Which book should she read first? *Pride and Prejudice* would be like visiting an old friend since she'd already read it at the duke's residence. She opened the book about the Douglas family and began to read.

"What is so interesting, Princess?"

Samantha looked up. The prince had put the mountain of papers into order and sat with one of the ledger books in front of him.

"I am reading about Sweetheart Abbey, from which my family named the manor," she told him.

"What is so interesting about the abbey?" he asked.

"Monks named the abbey Dulce Cor in honor of the lady who founded it," Samantha answered. She gave him an impish smile, adding, "Here is the interesting part. The lady loved her husband so much that she embalmed his heart and carried it with her wherever she went for twenty-two years. When she died, the lady had the embalmed heart buried with her at the abbey's altar."

"What a heartwarming story," Rudolf said dryly. Then he asked, "Would you carry my embalmed heart with you, Princess."

"Certainly not." Samantha shook her head. "I have a weak stomach."

"What is the other book?"

"*Pride and Prejudice* by Jane Austen," Samantha answered. "I read it once before."

"With all of those books in the library, why would you read the same book twice?" Rudolf asked.

Remembering how much she loved the story made Samantha smile. "I love happy endings," she answered.

Rudolf smiled at that. "Princess, I adore your gentle heart."

"Will you have it embalmed and carry it with you wherever you go?" she asked.

Rudolf burst out laughing.

"Perhaps, I'll write a romance like Jane Austen," Samantha told him. "I'll call it *The Embalmed Heart.*"

Rudolf laughed even harder at that. They were still chuckling about the embalmed heart when they left the office to dress for dinner.

Wearing her garnet velvet gown, Samantha knocked on the prince's bedchamber door just before dinner. Instead of calling out for her to enter, the prince opened the door and stepped aside to allow her entrance.

"Could you—?" Samantha gestured over her shoulder to her buttons.

"The pleasure is mine, *ma lyoobof.*" After fastening her buttons and nuzzling her neck, Rudolf turned her around to face him. "The ruby looks good with your gown," he said. "What color is that?"

"The gown is garnet," she told him.

"It looks red to me," he teased her, planting a chaste kiss on her lips.

When he reached for a painted wooden box, Samantha asked him, "What is that?"

"A surprise."

Leaving his chamber, they walked downstairs to the dining room where Durwin supervised two footmen as he'd done the previous evening. Samantha smiled when she noted the majordomo had put their place settings side by side in the middle of the table.

"I see you have remembered my request," Rudolf said to the majordomo.

"Remembering your request is my job, Your Highness," Durwin replied.

"Quite so."

The two footmen served them tomato soup, followed by ribbons of cucumbers sprinkled with cayenne pepper in a sharp dressing and accompanied by Geneva rolls with butter. The main course was deviled rump steaks with a tangy marinade of oil, vinegar, cayenne, and mustard.

"I have noticed that most rooms in the manor have a red color scheme," Rudolf remarked. "The marquess must be partial to red."

"So are you, judging by your bedrobe," Samantha teased him.

The prince stared at her gown's neckline until she began to squirm uncomfortably. "The ruby looks good, but you need jewels to accessorize your other gowns," Rudolf told her. "Diamonds and pearls would suit you, I think. When we ride to Dumfries for your new dagger, I will purchase you a gift."

"That is generous but unnecessary," Samantha told him.

"Would you deprive me of that pleasure, too?" Rudolf asked, lowering his voice.

Samantha pinkened. She knew exactly to what other pleasure he was referring.

At dinner's end, Rudolf rose from his chair, grabbed the painted wooden box in one hand, and offered her the other. "Princess, let us retire to the large drawing room and allow these men to attend their party."

In the drawing room, Samantha sat on an upholstered love seat in front of the white hearth. She watched the prince set a small table down in front of her and then drag an ottoman across to the table to sit opposite her. He placed the painted wooden box down on the table and opened it to reveal a chess board and pieces.

"Princess, you must learn to play chess," Rudolf told her. He started placing the pieces on the board, adding, "These pieces represent the heroic warriors from the Great Battle on Ice."

"An ice battle?" Samantha echoed.

"Hundreds of years ago Alexander Nevsky led an army against invading knights on the frozen Lake Chudskaye," he explained.

Samantha lifted her head as the first strains of music drifted into the room. "It sounds like fun," she said.

"I will teach you to play chess another time," Rudolf said, rising from the ottoman and offering her his hand. "We will attend this party. I must speak with Karl anyway."

Samantha stood and placed her hand in his. "We will leave if our presence makes them uncomfortable?"

"You always think of others before yourself," Rudolf said. "We will leave whenever you want." He raised her hand to his lips, adding, "Princess, your wish is my command."

Samantha gave him a jaunty smile. "That is only because you want me to carry your embalmed heart around."

CHAPTER 8

All activity stopped when Rudolf and Samantha walked into the Tudor great hall. The music and conversations died as the servants turned to stare at them.

"We shouldn't have come," Samantha whispered.

"Leave it to me," Rudolf said, and gave their audience an easy smile. "Your music attracted us, especially since I need to speak with my man, who, I hope, has contributed vodka to the festivities."

The prince scanned the crowd until he found Karl. The man inclined his head in the affirmative.

"Resume your activities," Rudolf said. "The princess and I would like to watch this traditional Scots party."

When no one moved, Rudolf looked at the men holding fiddles. They began playing at once, and the partygoers resumed their dancing, conversations, and eating.

"They seem subdued," Samantha whispered.

Rudolf put his arm around her shoulder and drew her close. After kissing her temple, he told her, "Drinking more vodka will cure them of that."

Durwin approached them. "Your Highness, let me escort you to our refreshment table," the majordomo said. "We have some traditional Scots dishes."

"Thank you, Durwin," the prince said. "I would like to taste these foods."

The oak trestle table had been laden with various dishes of hot and cold food. Samantha did not recognize many of the delicacies, and one, the dressed sheep's head, repelled her at once. There were hot and cold puddings, roasted chestnuts, fried herrings, Finnian haddock savoury, sardine savoury, potato and nut savoury, and various sweets. Along with the food were heather ale, whiskey, and vodka.

"We will serve ourselves," Rudolf told the majordomo. Handing Samantha a plate, he began to fill it with several of the selections. "Sheep's head, *ma lyoobof?*"

Samantha gulped back her revulsion and shook her head. She pointed to a hot pudding, saying, "I'll have some of that." After tasting it, she smiled and announced, "This is delicious. What is it?"

"That is haggis, Scotland's national dish," Durwin told her, looking surprised by her ignorance.

Samantha blushed. "My parents never told my sisters and me very much about Scotland."

"Haggis is the heart, liver, and lungs of a sheep minced with suet, onions, oatmeal, and seasonings," Durwin told her. "The mixture is boiled in the sheep's stomach."

Samantha managed a smile for the majordomo and glanced at the prince, who was grinning at her. With great difficulty, she kept from disgracing herself by swallowing what she had in her mouth.

"I'm not hungry," Samantha said, placing the plate on the table.

With the prince and the majordomo watching, Samantha poured vodka into a small glass. She downed it in one gulp and popped a piece of cheese into her mouth.

Rudolf chuckled. *"Ma lyoobof,* you must have some Russian blood," he said, making her smile. "Durwin, you will excuse us? I must speak with Karl."

"Of course, Your Highness."

Rudolf and Samantha walked around the dancers to Karl, who stood near a table of refreshment on the far side of the Tudor great hall. As they maneuvered their way across the hall, Samantha noted that several of the maids were staring with unmistakable adoration at the prince. A twinge of jealousy shot through her.

"I want the coach ready to travel after lunch tomorrow," Rudolf instructed his man.

Karl nodded. "Where are we going, Your Highness?"

"You are going nowhere," Rudolf told him. "I am taking Samantha to visit Sweetheart Abbey."

When the man glanced at her, Samantha asked, "How is your sturgeon enjoying Scotland?"

"He is enjoying himself very much," Karl answered, smiling in the direction of the pretty maids.

"Your sturgeon is a male?" she asked, seeing where his gaze was, wondering why the prince was smiling.

"Yes, Your Highness."

"Why are you calling me that?"

Karl shrugged. "What else would I call the prince's wife?"

"But I am—"

"Let it be," Rudolf warned. He looked at his man again, saying, "I hope you have not supplied them with all our vodka."

"I would never do that, Your Highness," Karl said. "Besides, these Scots seem to prefer whiskey."

Sally, one of the maids, chose that moment to appear in front of them. When she curtseyed to the prince, Samantha noted the young woman's large breasts and deep cleavage.

"Your Highness, would you dance with me?" Sally asked. "I would love to tell my grandchildren about the night I danced with a prince."

"Sally," Durwin called, a warning note in his voice. He started across the hall toward them but stopped when the prince gestured him away.

"You do not look old enough to have grandchildren," Rudolf teased the maid, giving her an easy smile.

Sally blushed and giggled nervously.

"*Ma lyoobof,* you do not mind if I leave you for a moment?" Rudolf asked.

Samantha forced herself to smile and inclined her head. Watching the prince escort the maid onto the dance floor, she felt another twinge of jealousy.

Without thinking, Samantha poured vodka into a glass and drank it in one gulp. Then she ate a piece of cheese.

"You drink vodka like a Russian," Karl remarked.

Samantha looked in the prince's direction, a soft smile on her lips, and said, "I have a good teacher."

Karl nodded.

"What does *ma lyoobof* mean?" Samantha asked him.

"*Ma lyoobof* means *my love,*" Karl told her.

Samantha smiled at the prince's man. Warm feelings for the prince surfaced, wiping away the distaste of jealousy.

"All women want to dance with a prince," Rudolf complained when he returned to her side at the dance's end. "Let us escape into the night, *ma lyoobof,* before another maid traps me into dancing."

Samantha arched an ebony brow at him. "You could refuse."

Rudolf put his arm around her shoulder, pulled her close, and led her toward the door. "I could not refuse to dance with any woman, even a maid," he told her. "That would be hurting her feelings needlessly."

Samantha let herself be escorted outside into the night. She felt relaxed, the two shots of vodka having made her tipsy.

Rudolf and Samantha stepped into a crisp winter's night. Immediately, he removed his jacket and placed it around her shoulders.

"Thank you, but you will be cold," she said.

"Your mere presence warms me, *ma lyoobof,*" he said.

Samantha cast him a sidelong smile. "Are you flattering me so I'll carry your embalmed heart around?"

"How did you guess?" Rudolf replied with an answering smile.

Samantha looked up at the night sky. Accompanied by hundreds of glittering stars, a full moon hung overhead.

"The beauty of the night makes the sun seem garish," Samantha said.

"Seductive night is infinitely more beautiful than the sun," Rudolf agreed. "In Russia, we call this the Wolf Moon. At this time of year, our ancestors would gather around their hearth fires and listen to the howling wolves, which came closer to villages to search for food during the winter."

"That sounds frightening," Samantha remarked.

"Look at the stars, *ma lyoobof,*" Rudolf said. "On New Year's Eve, the midnight stars return to their original positions like horses returning to their stables."

Samantha smiled. "What a pretty thought."

Rudolf pulled her against the side of his body and, with his left hand, pointed toward the biggest star in the sky. "That one is called Betelgeuse, part of the constellation Orion. Do you know the story?"

Samantha shook her head.

"If you drew lines from one star to another in that section of the sky, the finished picture would be a man," the prince told her. "One of the greatest hunters of all time, Orion was the son of the earth and the sea."

When she shivered, the prince asked, "Are you cold? Shall we return inside?"

Though chilled, Samantha was reluctant to end the evening. The prince was at his most charming, and she wanted to savor the moment.

"Tell me about Orion," she said.

"Zeus, Poseidon, and Hermes—"

"Who are they?"

"Greek gods," Rudolf answered. "These three Greek gods were visiting a man called Hyrieus, who showed them great hospitality. They wanted to give him a gift in return, but what Hyrieus wanted was a son. Zeus, Poseidon, and Hermes urinated into the skin of the ox they had eaten and told Hyrieus to bury it. Orion was born from that skin."

"That is an inauspicious beginning," Samantha said.

"Look to the south, *ma lyoobof,*" Rudolf said, turning her in that direction and warming her chilled body by pulling her in front of him and encircling her with his arms. "Sirius is the brightest star in the heavens. It is also called the Dog Star because of its proximity to Canis Major, the Big Dog constellation. Do you see it?"

"Yes, I see it," Samantha lied. She couldn't see a dog, only a bright star. But, she was enjoying her nearness to the prince.

Why am I tormenting myself like this? Samantha wondered. If she encouraged the prince, he would want entrance to her bed. He offered nothing but heartache in return.

"What are you doing?" Samantha asked, feeling the prince turning her in the opposite direction.

"There is Polaris," Rudolf said, pointing to the sky. "The North Star never changes position like the other stars. Sailors use Polaris to guide them across the seas . . . You are cold, *ma lyoobof.* Let us return inside."

Samantha remembered the maids' hungry gazes on him. "Let's walk around to the front," she said. "I don't want to return to the party."

A few minutes later, Rudolf and Samantha walked into the deserted foyer and went directly upstairs. Again, the prince followed her into her bedchamber and gestured for her to turn around. When she showed him her back, the prince unfastened her buttons and nuzzled the side of her neck.

"Pleasant dreams, *ma lyoobof,* " he whispered against her ear.

Samantha turned to face him as soon as he released her, but Rudolf was already walking toward the connecting door. "You should not be so familiar with servants," she said, before she could bite back the words. "You will only encourage their boldness."

"I beg your pardon?" Rudolf said, turning around, a puzzled smile on his face.

"I said, you should not—"

"Are you jealous?"

"Certainly not." Samantha felt the blush rising on her cheeks.

"Princess, do not prevaricate," Rudolf said, walking back to her. "Now you know how I feel when you mention Alexander Emerson."

His admission of jealousy lightened Samantha's mood. Then she realized how little she had thought of her intended betrothed and felt a stab of guilt.

"You are jealous of Alexander?"

"We were speaking of your feelings, not mine," Rudolf reminded her. He lifted her hand to his lips and added, "You should have more faith in me, Princess. I would never share my body with just anyone and certainly never with a servant."

"What is wrong with the poor?" Samantha asked. "I have no money."

"I never mentioned money," Rudolf replied, reaching out to caress her cheek. "As a prince and an employer, I have an obligation to respect my servants as they respect me. Seducing a servant is disrespect."

After the prince had disappeared into his chamber, Samantha readied herself for bed. Guilty remorse gnawed at her. How could she accept a gentleman's proposal of marriage and then never give him a thought? What must Alexander and her family be thinking?

Samantha knelt beside the bed and covered her face with her hands. *Thank You for sending me such an enjoyable day with the prince,* she prayed. *And thank You for making the prince such an honorable gentleman.*

Too honorable, an inner voice whispered.

Samantha peered through her fingers at the connecting door and recalled the prince's words to her. *"Admit it, Princess. You enjoyed the intimacy we shared . . . Your reputation is already ruined."*

Seeing the grain of truth in the prince's words, Samantha steeled herself against her desires. She leaped into the bed and pulled the coverlet over her head to keep herself from walking through the door into his chamber.

Samantha rose late the next morning and limped across the chamber to the window. Though frost feathered the trees and winter-barren lawns, sunbeams danced across the top of the pond, and no clouds marred the vast blueness of the sky.

After lunch, Samantha stood in the foyer and accepted the majordomo's assistance with her fur-lined cloak. She wore her forest green riding habit, and on her feet were the black boots she'd worn on their journey from England.

"What color is that?" Rudolf asked, ushering her out the door.

Samantha smiled at the question. "Green."

"What kind of green?"

"Green is green, Your Highness," Samantha said, tossing his own words back at him.

Rudolf helped her up on the coach's driver's seat and then climbed up beside her. Taking the reins in his hands, Rudolf started the coach down the road leading away from the manor.

"If you are really a prince," Samantha teased, "why haven't I ever seen you wearing your crown?"

"I am a modest man who does not like to boast," Rudolf answered.

Samantha laughed at that, earning a smile from the prince. "When I was a girl," she told him, "I wished that I could wear a tiara. In my innocence, I thought if I was a princess, the other children wouldn't make fun of my limp, and I wouldn't be chosen last for games."

When the prince remained silent, Samantha had the humiliating feeling that she had revealed too much of herself. She glanced at the prince. His expression was grim.

Rudolf halted the coach along the side of the road. Samantha turned to him, puzzled by their stopping.

"*Ma lyoobof,* I apologize for not rescuing you until the Emerson ball," Rudolf said, raising her hand to his lips.

"If I had lived in your village, I would always have chosen you first."

"Thank you, Your Highness," Samantha said, managing a smile for him as he started the coach down the road again.

Samantha regretted her disclosure. The prince pitied her. She would rather be chosen last than pitied. Her leg might be deformed, but her Douglas pride was strong and intact.

"Stop!" Samantha screamed, as a large dog bounded into the road in front of the coach. A loud wail of pain rent the air.

Rudolf halted the coach and leaped down, ordering, "Stay there."

Ignoring his order, Samantha climbed down from the coach and limped after him. She knelt beside the prince, who tried to inspect the dog without touching it.

The dog, an enormous deerhound, lay on the side of the road and whimpered. It stared helplessly at them through huge dark eyes.

"There's no blood," the prince said.

"It could be bleeding inside," she told him.

Recovering itself, the deerhound tried to sit up. The dog made no snapping protest when Samantha lent a hand to help it. The hound sat up but held its injured paw off the ground.

"Never touch a strange dog, especially one that is injured," Rudolf warned her.

"Nonsense," Samantha said, as the dog licked her hand. "Let's lift it into the coach and take it back to the manor."

"This dog must have an owner," Rudolf argued.

"We own the dog," a voice behind them said.

Samantha started to turn toward the voice but felt the cold steel of a pistol touching the back of her head. Glancing sidelong at the prince, she saw the business end of a pistol touching the back of his head, too.

"As you value your life," the voice warned, "make no sudden movements."

"We don't want to kill you," a second voice added.

Samantha realized in surprise that the voices belonged to boys, not men. Where did these children get pistols? Where were their parents?

"You won't get hurt if you do what you're told," the first voice said.

"Raise your hands in the air," the second voice said.

"I'll give the orders here," the first boy told the second.

"I'm helping," the second boy said.

"Just concentrate on holding that pistol steady," the first boy ordered.

Samantha struggled against a smile. If she didn't have a pistol pointed at the back of her head, she would have laughed out loud.

"Stand up slowly and turn around."

With their hands in the air, Rudolf and Samantha rose from the ground. The sight of the boys startled Samantha, and she glanced at the prince, who looked as surprised as she felt.

The boys appeared no older than ten years of age. Obviously brothers, both boys had dark eyes and black hair. Their clothing was ragged, and they were in desperate need of a bath.

"We did not intend to hurt your dog," Rudolf said, lowering his arms to his sides.

The older boy snapped his fingers at the dog, saying, "Come."

The deerhound limped toward its master.

"The show is over," the younger boy said, and the deerhound stopped limping.

"That damned dog is an actor," Samantha exclaimed.

Rudolf opened his mouth to speak, but Samantha touched his arm and said in an angry voice, "I'll handle this." With her hands on her hips, she turned to the boys and asked, "How old are you?"

"I'm eight," the younger boy said. "My brother is ten."

"Don't tell her anything," the older boy ordered.

"Where do you live?" she asked him.

"That's none of your business," he answered.

Samantha arched an ebony brow at him, indicating her displeasure with his attitude. "Your father will be angry when he learns you're trying to rob travelers."

"We don't have a father," the younger boy spoke up.

"Is he dead?" Samantha asked, feeling sorry for them.

"We don't know," the younger boy answered with a shrug. "We never met him."

"What about your mother, then?" Samantha argued, turning to the older boy. "She'll be very displeased with you."

"She's not here," the eight-year-old said.

"Where is she?"

"Ma went to Edinburgh last fall and never came back."

"Don't tell her anything," the ten-year-old ordered.

Samantha felt her heart breaking for these children. She knew what it was to lose a mother and a father, but she'd never been abandoned like these boys. How could any woman do that to her own babies?

"What are your names?" she asked, softening her tone.

"I'm Drake Morton. Drake means dragon," the younger boy told her with pride in his voice. "This is my brother Grant. His name means great."

"Jesus Christ, brother," Grant swore. "Now they know who to send to the gallows."

"No one is going to the gallows," Rudolf told them.

"I am Samantha Douglas. The Mortons are distant relatives of the Douglases," she said. "This gentleman is Prince Rudolf Kazanov from Russia."

"Is that in the Highlands?" Drake asked.

Rudolf smiled. "No, Russia is across the sea in Europe."

"Are you a real prince?" Grant asked, looking skeptical.

"I assure you that I am Prince Rudolf," the prince answered.

"Give us your money," Grant ordered, waving the pistol at him.

"My servants carry my money for me," Rudolf told him. "As you can see, I have brought no servants on this excursion."

"Why not?" the boy asked.

"I wanted to be alone with my wife."

Grant nodded. "We'll take your wife hostage until you return with the money."

Rudolf laughed out loud. "No gentleman would leave his lady with robbers," he told the boy.

The deerhound chose that moment to trot toward Samantha. The dog sat up in front of her and raised its front paws in the air.

"Don't beg, Giles," Drake said. "She doesn't have any food."

Samantha was surprised. "Did you call the dog Giles?"

"That's his name."

"This is a sign," she said, turning to the prince.

"What are you talking about?" Rudolf asked, looking at her in confusion.

"Giles is the patron saint of cripples," Samantha told him. "The dog named Giles is a sign from God. I'm taking them home and keeping them."

Samantha warmed to the idea. With her reputation ruined, she would never marry, but that didn't mean she couldn't have her own family—two sons and a dog.

"You cannot steal another woman's sons," Rudolf argued.

"I'm rescuing them, not stealing," Samantha replied.

"Who will care for them?" Rudolf asked her. "Will you give them a job and put them to sleep in the servants' quarters? What if the other servants do not want to care for them?"

"My adopted sons will not be servants," Samantha told him. "I will care for them, and they will sleep in my chamber."

"Where will you sleep?"

"I'll sleep in your chamber."

"And where will I sleep?"

Samantha smiled sweetly. "You will sleep beside me."

It was a bribe, pure and simple. She knew it, but the boys needed her. And . . . she had an excuse to join the prince in his bed and grab a few weeks of happiness with him. She could pretend the prince was her husband and the boys were their children.

"Give the prince those pistols and climb into the coach," Samantha ordered in a voice of authority.

Without waiting for a reply, Samantha limped toward the coach and opened the door. She looked at the boys and the prince, who hadn't moved.

"Who are you?" Grant asked, apparently suspicious of her kindness.

"I'm your fairy godmother, and this is your lucky day," Samantha answered. "Get into the coach and be quick about it."

"What about Giles?" Drake whined.

"Giles is coming, too."

She looked at the prince for help. He was grinning like an idiot.

"Don't argue with her," Rudolf warned the boys, holding his hands out for the pistols. "You won't win."

CHAPTER 9

"Holy water," eight-year-old Drake exclaimed, entering the manor's foyer.

"Holy hell," ten-year-old Grant said, equally impressed as he turned in a circle to scan the manor's foyer.

Walking behind them, Samantha smiled and glanced at Rudolf, who was also smiling at their reactions. Apparently, the boys had never seen any place quite as impressive as this. Samantha recalled the first time she'd entered the Duke of Inverary's home after living almost her entire life in the little cottage on the far side of Primrose Hill. Her reaction then was similar to the boys' reaction now.

"Your Highnesses," Durwin called, entering the foyer, "why have you returned so—" His gaze fell on the boys. "Ragamuffins! Get out of this house, you dirty brats!" With horrified contempt stamped across his features, the majordomo marched across the foyer toward the boys.

Recovering from her momentary surprise, Samantha stepped in front of the boys. She looked at the prince for help, but he only smiled at her and folded his arms across his chest to watch.

Samantha turned to confront the majordomo. After all, he was the servant, not she.

"What do you think you are doing?" Samantha demanded.

Durwin stopped short. He appeared as surprised by her protecting the boys as he was by their presence. "Your Highness, these boys are—"

"—my guests," she finished for him. Her blue gaze sparkled with righteous anger, daring him to challenge her words.

Durwin looked horrified. "You cannot mean to harbor these miscreant ragamuffins."

"Do *not* speak disparagingly of my soon-to-be adopted sons," Samantha ordered, shocking the man even more. Her gaze drifted to Giles, and she added for good measure, "Or their dog."

The horrified majordomo turned to the prince in a silent plea for help. Samantha looked at Rudolf, whose smile had grown into a broad grin.

"What are you smiling at?" she asked, irritated by his lack of help.

"Be careful, Princess," Rudolf warned, his placid expression at odds with the tone of his voice. "Remember to whom you are speaking."

"You need to show respect for your husband," ten-year-old Grant said, nodding in agreement. "Your husband is your master."

"I think we are going to get along famously," Rudolf told the boy.

Surprised by the public rebuke and the boy's defense of it, Samantha stared from the boy to the prince. Apparently, all men stood together against all women.

Eight-year-old Drake slipped his hand into hers. When she looked down at him, he smiled at her in an effort to offer his own brand of comfort.

"Tell Cook to prepare a mountain of food for the boys and the dog," Samantha instructed the major-domo. "I want the footmen to light a fire in the Tudor hall's hearth and set up three tubs of hot water there. Borrow clean clothing from the stableboys. My husband will replace them. Then send Sally to move my clothing into my husband's chamber. The boys will sleep in mine."

Durwin began to protest, "But, Your Highness—"

"Go now," Samantha ordered.

"Your Highness?" Durwin said in an irritated voice, turning to the prince.

"Do as she says," Rudolf said, looking as irritated as the majordomo. "In the future, do not argue when my wife gives you instructions."

"Yes, Your Highness." Durwin left the foyer in a hurry.

With a smile on her lips, Samantha turned to the prince, saying, "I was beginning to wonder if you would support me."

"How could you possibly doubt my loyalty?" Rudolf gave her a devastating smile. "You give orders as if you were born to it." He gestured in the direction of the dining room, adding, "Let them eat first. They will be more amenable to a thorough cleaning with a full stomach."

"But their hands are filthy," Samantha said.

"They have eaten with dirty hands for months," Rudolf told her. "One more meal will make no difference."

"Your Highness, you are the wisest of men," Samantha said.

Rudolf cocked a dark brow at her. "I will remind you of those words one day."

Grant and Drake were more impressed with the dining room than the foyer. Both boys stood two feet inside the door and surveyed the room from the dining table with seating for twenty to the enormous crystal-and-gold chandelier to the red-and-blue Persian carpet.

"I never saw such a big table," Grant said.

"I never did either," Drake said, still holding Samantha's hand.

"If I never did," Grant replied, rolling his eyes, "then you never did."

"Let's sit down while we wait for the food," Samantha said.

"You mean, we can really sit there?" Grant asked.

Rudolf chuckled and put his hand on the boy's shoulder, saying, "Did you think we would make you eat from a plate on the floor?"

"You really are my fairy godmother," Drake said, looking at Samantha with adoration.

Samantha felt an insistent tugging on her heartstrings. She'd always felt insecure because of her leg, but she'd had parents who loved her and couldn't imagine the loss these boys felt.

Rudolf and Grant sat on one side of the table. Samantha and Drake sat opposite them. Giles chose to sit beside Samantha and rested his head on the table.

"My wife and I play a game by sitting in a different chair each day," Rudolf told them. "Perhaps you would like to play with us?"

Samantha smiled when both boys nodded their heads vigorously. "Ah, here is the food," she said.

Beneath the majordomo's supervision, three footmen walked into the dining room. The first carried a serving bowl filled with mutton hash, the second carried a platter of fried potatoes and onions, and the third carried bread, butter, and gingerbread accompanied by a small bowl filled with clotted cream.

"I'll have some of that, please," Drake said, pointing to the gingerbread.

"The gingerbread is for dessert," Samantha told him, setting a plate of hash and potatoes in front of him.

"Do you know how to read?" Rudolf asked them.

Both boys shook their heads and kept eating as if they hadn't had a meal in days.

"I know the alphabet," Grant said, scooping another spoonful of hash.

"Me, too," Drake said.

"Do you know how to cipher numbers?" Samantha asked.

Again, the boys shook their heads and shoveled food into their mouths.

"We know about money," Grant said in a voice muffled with the amount of food inside his mouth.

"We like money," Drake agreed, his own mouth full.

"You don't need to put all the food into your mouth at one time," Samantha said. She glanced at the prince, saying, "We had better add table manners to our list of what they need to learn."

"What's that?" Drake asked.

Samantha placed a second helping on a plate for the dog and set it on the floor. "Table manners means how to eat properly—"

"We know how to eat," Grant told her. "Put food into your mouth, chew it, and swallow."

Rudolf laughed. "At the moment, you are deleting the chewing."

"As I was explaining, you need to eat without making everyone nauseous," Samantha told them.

"What's nauseous?" Drake asked.

"Nauseous means sick to your stomach."

"Oh. Like puking?"

"Yes."

"What should we call you?" Grant asked her.

Mother, she thought, but said, "You may call me Lady Samantha. The prince is Your Highness."

"In private, you may call me sir," Rudolf told them.

"Lady Samantha?"

She looked down at Drake. His enormous dark eyes were deep, fathomless pools. "Yes, dear?"

"Does your leg hurt?" he asked.

"Are you referring to my limp?"

Drake nodded.

"When I was a little girl, a coach ran me over," she told him. "One leg grew slightly shorter than the other, which makes me limp."

"I bet that hurt," Grant said.

"Yes, but that was a long time ago," Samantha replied. "I am fine now."

Drake stopped eating and slipped his hand into hers. "Your leg must hurt sometimes."

Samantha gave his hand a little squeeze, answering, "When I tire from standing unbalanced for a long time, then my hip aches."

"You never told me that," Rudolf said.

"You never asked," Samantha replied. "Besides, it really is of no significance." She didn't like the pity crouched in the prince's gaze.

Samantha cut two pieces of gingerbread onto plates and then dropped a dollop of clotted cream on each. She passed one to Grant and placed the other in front of Drake.

"What are you doing?" she asked when the eight-year-old lifted the whole piece of gingerbread into his hand.

"I'm putting the gingerbread in my pocket to eat later," Drake answered.

"That's a good idea, brother," Grant said.

Rudolf laughed and caught the boy's wrist before he lifted the gingerbread off the plate. "If you are too full to eat it now, leave it on your plate."

"But we'll lose it," Grant complained.

"If you want the gingerbread later," Samantha told him, "you may ask for it."

"What if that angry man won't give it back?" Drake asked in a loud whisper.

Samantha burst out laughing and glanced at the majordomo. "You mean Durwin?"

"Shhh." Grant put a finger across his lips and then whispered, "If he hears us talking about him, he'll throw us out of the palace."

"Durwin takes orders from me," Rudolf told them.

"He does?" the boys exclaimed simultaneously.

Rudolf inclined his head.

"Tell him to stop looking at me," Grant whined.

"He gives me the creeps," Drake said.

Samantha covered her mouth to keep from laughing out loud and looked at the prince. He seemed to be struggling against laughter, too.

Drake looked from one to the other and then scolded, "Catching the creeps is no laughing matter."

At that, Samantha did burst into laughter as did the prince. After the past seven months in society, the boys' innocence was refreshing, and their banter reminded her of growing up with her sisters.

Samantha flicked a glance at the prince and wondered if he had any pleasant memories from childhood. His father's and brother's hatred made that unlikely.

* * *

Three tubs filled with steaming water stood in front of the hearth in the Tudor great hall. Several torches on the walls had been lit to chase away late afternoon's dimness, the sun having already sunk below the horizon in the west.

"Take off your clothes and climb into those tubs," Samantha ordered, sounding like a general before her troops. "There are soap and a washing cloth in each tub. Do not forget to clean behind your ears."

The boys stripped down to nothing and climbed into the tubs. Rudolf lifted their soiled garments off the floor and passed them to the majordomo, ordering, "Tell a footman to burn these."

With a wholly disgusted look on his face, Durwin lifted the garments out of the prince's hand. He hurried to the hall's entrance where he passed them off to a footman.

"Giles, get into that tub," Rudolf ordered, rolling the sleeves of his shirt up.

The dog sat at attention and wagged its tail.

"Giles doesn't understand," Samantha said.

"Princess, the dog understands." Rudolf looked at the dog again, ordering, "Get into the tub."

The dog lay down on the floor, rested his head on his forelegs, and whined. Samantha and the boys giggled, and the deerhound wagged its tail as if he enjoyed being their entertainment.

Rudolf pointed at the tub. "Giles, get into that tub," he ordered in a stern voice. "Now."

Giles stood and leaped into the tub. Then he plopped down, splashing the prince in the movement.

"Good boy," Rudolf praised the dog. He called over his shoulder, "Durwin, do you want to wash the dog?"

The majordomo shook his head vigorously. Behind him, the footmen smiled at their superior's back.

Rudolf picked up the soap and started lathering the dog. Samantha giggled at the sight of a prince washing a dog.

"Do you find this amusing?" Rudolf asked.

"I never would have thought a royal would stoop to a menial task," she said.

"I am also a man," Rudolf told her. A smile played on his lips, and he dropped his gaze to her body.

Samantha blushed. If his words and his gaze on her could make her blush so easily, how would she survive sharing a chamber with him?

"Princess, hand me that bucket," Rudolf said. "I want to rinse him."

The prince dumped the water over the dog's head. Giles lifted his head and howled his displeasure.

"Out," Rudolf ordered.

Giles needed no second invitation. He leaped out of the tub and shook the excess water off, spraying Samantha.

"I'm wrinkling," Drake called.

Samantha passed the prince a towel and then limped toward the boys, who still sat in their tubs. After checking behind their ears, she handed Grant a towel, saying, "Dry yourself." Then she gave her attention to the eight-year-old, ordering, "Stand up, Drake." When he did, she began to dry him.

"Shall I help the other boy?" Durwin asked, standing beside her.

Samantha glanced at the ten-year-old and noted his grimace. "Fetch those clean clothes," she said.

Finished with the dog, Rudolf took the towel from Grant and helped him. Then he wrapped the towel around the boy until Durwin handed him the clean clothing.

With her hands on her hips, Samantha walked around the two boys and the dog and inspected them. "Now I can see your handsome faces," she said, making them smile. "Giles, I never would have believed you had white markings on your gray coat."

"Come with us," Rudolf said.

Grant took hold of the prince's hand, and Drake clutched Samantha's. Leaving the Tudor great hall, they returned to the main house and walked up the stairs to the second floor.

"Holy water!"

"Holy hell!"

Drake and Grant stood in the middle of the enormous bedchamber and turned in a circle. They stared with open mouths at the chamber's opulence: red walls, canopied bed, upholstered settee near the hearth.

"Kneel beside the bed," Samantha said.

"Why?" Grant asked, giving her a suspicious look.

"You need to thank God each night for a blessing He's given you that day," she told him.

"That's easy," Drake said, casting her a flirtatious smile, which elicited a chuckle from the prince. The eight-year-old knelt beside the bed and folded his hands in front of him, saying, "Thank You for sending us a fairy godmother."

Samantha felt tears welling up in her eyes. The boys were the only people she'd ever met who'd been grateful for her presence. Yes, her sisters loved her, but being family required them to love her. Or did it?

"Thank You for sending us the prince," Grant said, kneeling beside his brother.

"Climb into the bed," Samantha said. When they did, she told them, "I will be in the next chamber if you need me."

"Lady Samantha?"

"Yes, Drake."

"Do fairy godmothers kiss little boys good night?"

Samantha smiled and kissed each boy's forehead, thinking that this was how family life should be. Perhaps she wasn't destined to enjoy life as she'd wished, but sometimes a person needed to make do.

Turning away from the bed, Samantha limped toward the connecting door where the prince waited. She paused when Drake called out to her.

"Lady Samantha?"

"Yes?"

"Why are you weeping?"

"My tears are happy, not sad," she told him, heading for the connecting door.

"I told you girls were stupid," Grant whispered to his brother.

"She's a lady, not a girl," Drake whispered back.

"Ladies are big girls," Grant told him, "and being stupid has no cure."

Rudolf turned to Samantha as soon as the connecting door closed behind them. "You probably want to rest." He gestured to the enormous bed, saying, "Make yourself comfortable. I will awaken you to dress for dinner."

Feeling shy, Samantha dropped her gaze to the red-and-blue carpet, saying, "Thank you, Rudolf."

Samantha removed her riding habit and hanged it neatly in the dressing room. With a soft smile on her lips, she stared at the prince's clothing hanging beside hers. There were few things more intimate than sharing a closet, and a tidal wave of love surged through her.

If only he wasn't a prince. . . . If only Aunt Roxie was here to guide her, she would know how to win the prince's love. . . . If only the impossible was possible.

Though she knew God would disapprove, Samantha decided to grab a few weeks of happiness for herself. She would pretend that the prince was her husband.

Samantha limped into the bedchamber proper and knelt beside the bed. Though it wasn't bedtime, some thank-yous couldn't wait.

Covering her face with her hands, Samantha whispered a prayer to the empty room, "Thank You, Lord, for sending Grant and Drake to me. I promise I will love and care for them to the best of my ability. Giles was an unexpectedly nice touch, too . . ."

While Samantha knelt beside the bed in prayer, Rudolf sat alone in the library and sipped brandy. He tried to concentrate on how to get Vladimir out of his life without having to kill his own brother, but the image of Samantha lying in his bed kept intruding on his thoughts.

Thirty minutes is time enough to take care of her private needs, Rudolf decided. He rose from the chair but then sat down again. Now that he had her where he wanted, Rudolf was reluctant to take her.

Samantha Douglas was everything he wanted in a woman—loyal, sensitive, nurturing. Though blessed with an inner strength, she had an aura of vulnerability that made him want to protect her. She was everything he had foolishly believed Olga was. Loving her had brought him only pain.

And Zara, he corrected himself. His daughter was worth all the pain he had suffered.

Rudolf sipped his brandy and stretched his long legs out. Though he had offered to marry Samantha to save her reputation, he'd been relieved when she refused him. He couldn't chance making another mistake. He wanted never to marry again, especially to a woman he loved.

He loved her.

Rudolf bolted up in his chair. Yes, he loved her but intended to keep his own counsel. Love led to misery and pain. Always.

Again, the image of Samantha lying in his bed paraded across his mind's eye, beckoning him to return upstairs. He set the snifter of brandy down on the table and rose from the chair.

Who knew what misfortune tomorrow could bring? He would grab a few weeks of happiness and pretend she was his wife.

With his mind made up, Rudolf left the library in a hurry. He took the stairs two at a time, pausing to collect himself when he stood before his bedchamber door.

Rudolf hesitated. What if she rejected his advances? She had offered to share his bed because she wanted the boys to sleep in her chamber.

Stepping inside the bedchamber, Rudolf looked toward the bed. Wearing only a silk and lace chemise, she had fallen asleep on top of the coverlet.

Rudolf sat on the settee in front of the hearth and removed his boots. Next came his shirt. Then he unfastened his breeches, letting them drop to the floor.

After donning his red silk bedrobe, Rudolf advanced on the bed. He stood there for a long moment and perused her beauty from the ebony mane of hair to alluring curves and delicately boned feet.

Rudolf knelt beside the bed and covered his face with his hands. She must be a good influence, he thought. Because of her, he'd begun speaking to God again.

"Are you asking or thanking?"

Rudolf dropped his hands. She was smiling at him. "I was thanking Him for sending you back to my bed," Rudolf said, returning her smile. "I was wishing . . ."

And then Samantha did the unexpected. She opened her arms in invitation, welcoming him into the bed.

With a groan of mingling relief and desire, Rudolf climbed onto the bed and pulled her into his arms. One hand cupped the back of her head to hold her steady; the other imprisoned her against the hard, muscular planes of his body. His lips captured hers in a slow, smoldering, soul-stealing kiss . . . a kiss filled with the budding love he refused to express in words. She returned his kiss in kind, pouring all of her love and need into it, pressing the softness of her body against him, instinctively trying to become one with him.

"Let me love you," Rudolf whispered in a husky voice.

"Yes," Samantha breathed against his lips, swept away on the waves of his passion.

Rudolf rolled her onto her back and leaned over her. Dipping his head, he captured her mouth again and flicked his tongue across the crease in her lips, seeking and gaining entrance to the sweetness beyond, possessing her mouth even as his body would soon fill hers, feeling her tremble with desire.

Without relinquishing her lips, Rudolf caressed her soft cheek, her slender throat, her delicate shoulders. Breaking their kiss, he gazed into her incredibly blue eyes and whispered, "So soft, so sweet."

Rudolf felt her arms slide up his chest and hook around his neck. She pulled his face closer until his mouth covered hers again. When she flicked her tongue across the crease of his lips, Rudolf groaned and gave her entrance to his mouth, reveling in the sensation of her wanting to explore him.

Hearing her sigh of satisfaction, Rudolf took control again. His mouth left hers; he sprinkled dozens of feathery light kisses on her eyelids, temples, throat.

Rudolf rose from the bed, smiling when she moaned in protest, and ordered, "Open your eyes, *ma lyoobof.*"

When Samantha obeyed, Rudolf shrugged out of his bedrobe. He recognized the gleam of desire in her eyes as she slid her gaze down the length of his body. Then he leaned close and drew her chemise down her body and tossed it aside, exposing her naked beauty. He worshipped her with his eyes before reaching with one hand to caress her from throat to feet.

Samantha held out her arms again in invitation. Rudolf knelt on the foot of the bed. Lifting her legs, he kissed the bottoms of her feet and flicked his tongue teasingly across her insteps.

Keeping her gaze captive, Rudolf kissed each of her toes. From there, his lips slid to her ankles, her legs, her thighs, her belly, her throat, and her lips. He turned her over and kissed her from the nape of her neck to her ankles.

"Roll over, *ma lyoobof,*" Rudolf ordered thickly.

When she did, Rudolf lay on top of her, his muscular hardness covering her softness completely. His kiss was demanding, his hands reaching down to capture her wrists and gently drawing her arms over her head.

Holding her immobile with one hand, Rudolf slipped his free hand to her breasts and caressed each in turn, flicking a finger across her passion-darkened nipples, already hardened with her arousal.

"Let me touch you," Samantha whispered.

Rudolf wasn't ready to relinquish control yet. "You will touch me, *ma lyoobof,*" he said, staring down at her with arrogant satisfaction. "You will touch me when I allow it."

Samantha moaned in protest. He lowered his head to her breasts and tormented her nipples with his tongue.

When she moaned and squirmed, Rudolf captured a nipple with his mouth and suckled leisurely upon it. Then he lavished the same attention on her other breast, driving her wild with need.

"Your breasts are beautiful," Rudolf whispered. "Watching you suckle a babe would give me pleasure."

Samantha moaned in answer.

Rudolf slipped a hand to the crevice between her legs to caress her there. "You are wet for me, *ma lyoobof.*" He knelt, one leg on each side of her body, and gazed down at her, saying, "Look at me."

When Samantha opened her eyes, he told her, "Touch me now."

Samantha reached out to caress his chest. He closed his eyes and let her hands wander wherever they would. Rudolf groaned when she slid her fingers, like threads of silk, across his nipples as he'd done to her.

Feeling himself losing control, Rudolf grabbed her hands and spread her legs. He caressed her female button with the tip of his manhood and then thrust forward inside her. Instinctively, she wrapped her legs around his waist and met each of his thrusts with her own.

Suddenly, unexpectedly, Samantha gasped and melted against him, flooding him with her juices. Rudolf lost control, plunging deep inside her. He groaned and shuddered and spilled his seed.

Recovering himself a few minutes later, Rudolf opened his eyes and gazed at Samantha. She had surrendered her body to him completely. He wanted her heart and her soul, too.

Falling on the bed to one side, Rudolf refused to let

her go but kept her imprisoned against the side of his body. *"Ma lyoobof,* I think you have killed me," he said.

Samantha raised herself on one elbow and, with love shining from her eyes, gazed at him. A smile flirted with her lips when she said, "Next time, Your Highness, be more careful what you wish for."

CHAPTER 10

Morning had aged into a feeble old man by the time Samantha awakened the next day. She yawned and stretched and then looked down at her nudity. The memories of the previous evening came rushing back to her, making her feel warm all over.

Samantha closed her eyes and tried to recapture her night of love with the prince. Again she felt his lips on hers, his hands caressing her in the most intimate places, his hardness filling her, carrying her with him to paradise.

You are not his wife, an inner voice reminded her, making her feel a twinge of guilt.

Samantha banished that troubling thought. Her reputation was ruined whether she bedded him or not. She would have the next fifty years alone to ponder her sins once she returned to London.

Rising from the bed, Samantha washed the sleep from her face and donned her white muslin morning dress. She could hardly wait to see her pretend husband and sons.

Leaving the bedchamber, Samantha limped down

the corridor to the stairs. She found Giles tied to the banister in the foyer. The deerhound wagged his tail when he spied her.

"What are you doing here alone?" Samantha said, untying him. "Come with me."

After freeing the dog, she limped into the dining room. The room was empty except for the majordomo and a footman.

"I wondered when you would be down," Durwin said, setting a cup of hot coffee in front of her. "His Highness told me not to disturb you. Will you be eating lunch or would you prefer Cook prepare a breakfast food?"

"If luncheon is already made, I'll have that," Samantha answered him. She gestured to the dog, saying, "Sit here beside me, Giles." The deerhound sat at attention beside her and then rested his head on her lap.

Luncheon consisted of a thick and hearty yellow split pea soup. Accompanying the soup was toast as well as a medley of potted mushrooms, chicken, and ham.

"Where are His Highness and the boys?" Samantha asked the majordomo.

"His Highness has taken the boys to Dumfries to purchase them clothing," Durwin answered.

Samantha wondered why the prince hadn't awakened her to accompany them. She was pleased that he'd taken a liking to her soon-to-be adopted sons.

"When His Highness returns, tell him I am in the small drawing room," Samantha said, rising from her chair. "Come along, Giles."

Samantha climbed the stairs to the second-floor drawing room. She sat on the blue-and-gold upholstered settee that perched in front of the hearth.

"Giles, I am going to entertain you," she said, lifting her violin out of its case.

Holding the violin steady on her shoulder, Samantha

lifted the bow and began to play. Her song held a jaunty air with an irresistible rhythm that flowed into a feeling of elemental forces. Her talented bow conjured celestial winds, sunbeams dancing across water, a chuckling brook.

Suddenly, unexpectedly, Giles lifted his head and howled like a wolf. Laughing, Samantha stopped playing and put her violin back in its case.

"Up, Giles," she said, patting the settee beside her.

The deerhound leaped onto the settee and flopped onto his side. Then he rested his head on her lap.

Samantha stroked his head, the motion as soothing to her as the dog. Without ceasing her patting, she relaxed back against the settee and closed her eyes. The handsome image of the prince appeared in her mind's eye, and she enjoyed a pleasant hour reliving their intimate activities and whispered words of love. Like an old friend, insidious insecurity surfaced and wove itself around her heart and mind.

Samantha knew she loved the prince and could never marry Alexander Emerson, even if he still wanted her. She knew the prince felt a fondness for her that could never be validated with marriage. She also knew she would be a social pariah once she returned to London.

"Lady Samantha?" a voice called from the doorway.

"I am here," she answered, recognizing Drake's voice.

Drake and Grant raced across the drawing room toward her. Carrying several packages, Prince Rudolf followed behind them.

"The prince bought us new clothing," Drake told her, his excitement obvious.

Grant laughed out loud. "He ordered that angry man to put the clothes in our bedchamber."

"We ate lunch in a real inn," Drake exclaimed.

"I'm so glad you had an enjoyable day," Samantha

said. She looked at the prince, asking, "Why didn't you awaken me?"

Rudolf didn't answer her. Instead, his dark gaze had fixed on the deerhound. "Do not allow the dog to lie on the furniture," he said. Then, he ordered, "Down, Giles."

In an instant, Giles leaped off the settee. He sat at attention in front of the prince and wagged his tail.

"To answer your question," Rudolf said to Samantha, "you appeared too comfortable to awaken this morning."

Drake leaned close and told her, "We bought you presents."

"You did?" Samantha smiled at him. "I love surprises."

"All girls love surprises," Grant said.

"So do boys," Rudolf said.

"Do you love surprises?" Samantha asked the eight-year-old.

Drake nodded. "I love fairy godmothers more."

Samantha felt her heart melt at the boy's words. Tears welled up in her eyes, but she fought them back.

"Holy hell, she's weeping again," Grant said. "I'm never having a wife."

Samantha laughed through her tears. She glanced at the prince, who winked at her.

"Give this to Lady Samantha," Rudolf told the ten-year-old.

Grant lifted the package out of the prince's hand. Blushing with nervous embarrassment, the boy told her, "I chose this for you."

The box contained a lady's cane. Created from bamboo, the cane sported a top made from hardened rosin and decorated with brass. Making it more appealing, the artisan had painted flowers down the length of the cane.

"What a beautiful cane," Samantha exclaimed, keeping her expression placid.

The last thing she wanted was a cane. Limping was bad enough; she had no desire to announce her handicap by leaning on a cane.

"You can use it when your hip hurts," Drake told her.

"I certainly will," she replied. "Thank you for thinking of me."

"That isn't the best part," Grant told her. "Look here."

The ten-year-old lifted the cane out of her hand and twisted its top. Then he pulled the handle off the cane to reveal an Italian stiletto.

"I will carry this cane whenever I go walking and will feel secure, even if I am alone," Samantha said, flicking a glance at the prince. If she'd had this with her a couple of weeks earlier, she would not be in this untenable position.

"Who wants to give her this one?" Rudolf asked, holding another long, beribboned gift.

"I do," Grant said. Seeing his brother's disappointed expression, he told him, "You'll give her the next one."

Samantha accepted the gift from the ten-year-old. She unfastened the ribbon and then opened the box, exclaiming, "What a beautiful parasol."

She lifted it out of the box. Adorned with ribbons and lace, the parasol had an ivory handle inlaid with semiprecious stones.

"Parasols can communicate a lady's thoughts," Samantha told them. "If His Highness harbors affection for me, he would ask to carry my parasol. If I snap my parasol open decisively"—she demonstrated—"I am telling His Highness I do not like the topic of conversation, and he is being too bold with his attentions."

"Drake, here is your gift to the lady," the prince said.

The boy lifted the slim, rectangular box out of the prince's hand and looked at Samantha. "I chose this for you," he said, giving her a flirtatious smile.

The gift was a fan created from blue silk and feathers. When opened, the fan resembled a spread peacock's tail, complete with ocellar spots and shimmering iridescent color.

"I love it," Samantha cried. "Do you know I can communicate with this fan, too?"

Both Grant and Drake shook their heads.

"Would you like me to demonstrate with the prince?" The boys nodded.

"Are you ready, Your Highness?" she asked.

"I am always ready for you, *ma lyoobof,*" he told her.

Samantha closed the fan and then opened it partially, showing only three sections. "What am I communicating?"

"You want to meet me at three o'clock," the prince answered.

Samantha smiled. "That is correct."

The boys appeared suitably impressed.

Samantha snapped her fan shut and pointed it toward the door.

"You are chastising me for my impudence," Rudolf told her.

"What's impudence?" Drake asked.

"Boldness." Samantha covered her left ear with the fan.

"She wants me to keep her secret," the prince told the boys.

Samantha held the half-opened fan to her lips. In an instant, Rudolf was beside her. He gathered her into his arms and planted a chaste kiss on her lips.

"What did she tell you?" Drake asked.

"The lady gave me permission to kiss her." Rudolf

handed her two small packages and said, "From me, *ma lyoobof.*"

Samantha opened the first and smiled. In the box lay a small, six-inch blade to replace the dagger he had tossed out the coach's window. The second box contained a gold tiara adorned with crystals and semiprecious gems.

When Samantha only stared at it, Rudolf lifted the tiara out of the box and placed it on her head. "No one will ever make fun of your limp," he told her, "and you will always be chosen first for games."

"Here we go again," Grant said.

Samantha felt the hot tears welling up in her eyes, and her bottom lip quivered with her struggle to hold them back. Her tears brimmed over; a teardrop rolled down each of her cheeks. Embarrassed, she dropped her gaze to her lap.

Rudolf wiped each teardrop away. Then he kissed her and and said, "Thank you, *ma lyoobof,* for the magical moments you have given me."

"Thank you for the magical moments you have given me," Samantha said, lifting her gaze to his. She looked at the boys, adding, "This is the best day of my whole life, and I'm very happy."

"Lady Samantha, why do you weep when you're happy?" Drake asked. "I only weep when I'm sad."

"Lady Samantha weeps because she is sensitive," Rudolf told them. "Women's emotions are different from men's."

"I see," Grant said, wearing a skeptical expression.

"I don't see," Drake said.

"You do not need to concern yourself with women's emotions until you are older," Samantha told them. "Why don't we go to the ballroom and play?"

"What will we play?" Drake asked.

"We'll play Society," she answered.

"I never heard of that game," Grant told her.

"In order to play, simply pretend to be in high society," Rudolf explained.

"What do we do?" Grant asked.

Rudolf offered Samantha his hand and said, "Come along with us, and we'll show you."

Rudolf and Samantha, wearing her tiara, led the way downstairs. The boys and the deerhound followed behind them.

The ballroom was empty except for the gigantic chandelier and the grand piano. No carpeting covered the hardwood floor.

"Stand over there," the prince told the boys. "Watch what we do."

Then Rudolf turned to Samantha, saying, "My lady, may I have this dance?"

"Yes, Your Highness." Samantha curtseyed.

Rudolf took her into his arms. While he hummed a waltz, they swirled around the ballroom as if an orchestra played.

Stopping near the boys, Rudolf said, "I will play the piano, and Lady Samantha will take turns dancing with you."

"Who will be first?" she asked.

"I will," Grant spoke up.

"The basic waltz pattern is step, slide, step," Samantha instructed him. She nodded to the prince, who began to play. Hearing the music, Giles lifted his head and howled, making everyone laugh.

"I do believe Lord Giles will accompany His Highness," Samantha said. With the dog's howling in the background, she began moving with the ten-year-old, saying all the while, "Step, slide, step . . . step, slide, step."

Samantha and Grant circled the ballroom once. When they neared the piano, she stopped and said, "Thank you, sir, for an enjoyable dance."

"My turn," Drake said, stepping forward. He winked at her and bowed from the waist.

Samantha curtseyed. Taking his small hands in hers, she nodded at the prince, who began playing a waltz. Beside him, Giles howled.

After circling the ballroom, Samantha stopped when they reached the piano. The prince stopped playing, and the deerhound stopped howling.

Turning to the dog, Samantha said, "Lord Giles, may I have this dance?"

Giles barked. Then he lay down and rested his head on his forelegs.

Everyone laughed.

Samantha limped across the ballroom and gazed out the window. She pointed to the distance, asking, "Do you see that oak?" When the boys nodded, she said, "Tomorrow, we'll walk down there and see the treehouse."

"A real treehouse?" Grant exclaimed.

Samantha inclined her head. "I love oak trees. Do you?"

Drake nodded.

"Oaks are the mightiest of trees," Samantha told the boys. "They spend three hundred years growing, three hundred years resting, and three hundred years expiring."

"I did not know that," Rudolf said, standing close to her.

"What is expiring?" Drake asked.

"Expiring means dying," she answered. "The wider the girth, the older the oak tree."

Grant snorted. "That sounds like people . . ."

Three hours later, Samantha dressed for dinner in her shell pink silk gown with matching cashmere shawl. She settled her tiara on her head and peeked at herself in the cheval mirror. Then she left the chamber, the prince having already escorted the boys downstairs.

Limping into the dining room, Samantha smiled at their new appearance. Both boys wore dark blue breeches and waistcoats, white shirts, and blue cravats. They stood behind their seats for this evening's dinner, as did the prince, and awaited her.

"Great Giles' ghost, you look beautiful," Samantha gushed.

"Boys are handsome, not beautiful," Grant corrected her.

"I'm choking," Drake said, tugging at his cravat.

"Gentlemen always wear neckties to dinner," Samantha told him. "His Highness has been wearing neckties for years and hasn't choked to death."

Rudolf sat at the head of the table. On his right sat Samantha, and the boys sat opposite her.

"Tonight we are going to learn about table manners," Samantha told the boys. "Your Highness, what is the first thing we do?"

"Lift your napkin off the table," Rudolf said, demonstrating. "Give it one shake, and place it on your lap."

"We do this so we will not soil our clothing if we spill something," Samantha explained. "If there is a lot of silverware, you must work from the outside inward during the course of the meal."

"Why can't we use just one of each?" Drake asked.

"The richer the gentleman, the more silverware he uses," Samantha said. "Isn't that correct, Your Highness?"

"Most definitely," the prince agreed.

Beneath the majordomo's supervision, the footmen began serving them dinner. There were crusty rolls with butter, oyster soup garnished with parsley, roasted beef, and potatoes dressed with spiced cream and lemon juice.

"Do not slurp your soup," Samantha reminded them.

"Why are there so many damned rules?" Drake asked, obviously tired from the day's excitement.

"Cursing is not allowed at the table," Rudolf said.

"I'll never remember everything," Grant complained.

"Practice makes perfect," Samantha told them. "Soon enough, you will be following the rules without even thinking about them." She glanced at Drake and asked, "Why aren't you eating your soup?"

"There's stuff floating in it," he told her.

"Those are oysters," she said.

"I don't like oysters," Drake said, a wholly disgusted expression on his face.

"I don't like them either," Grant agreed.

"Did you ever eat oysters?" Rudolf asked.

Both boys shook their heads.

"If you never ate oysters," Samantha told them, "you cannot know if you dislike them." Lord, but she sounded exactly like her aunt.

"Oysters look like something that came out of my nose," Drake said.

Rudolf shouted with laughter, and the boys joined in the prince's merriment. Samantha covered her mouth with her hands to hold back the giggle and glanced at the majordomo. Even Durwin had turned away, but his shoulders shook with silent laughter.

"Don't eat the soup, then," Samantha told them. "We'll need to work on what to do when you dislike something the cook serves."

Hours later, Samantha ushered the boys to bed. She glanced at the prince, who stood leaning against the connecting door. The hint of a smile flirted with his lips as he watched her performing motherly duties, and she wondered what he was thinking.

"Don't climb into bed yet," Samantha ordered. "You need to thank God for a blessing."

The boys knelt beside the bed and folded their hands in front of them. Grant spoke first, saying, "Thank You,

Lord, for the new clothing and thank You for the prince."
Then he elbowed his brother.

Drake paused before speaking and cast Samantha
a flirtatious smile. "Thank You, Lord, for Lady Samantha . . ." He paused for a minute and then added, "I
could do without the oysters, though."

"Me, too," Grant said.

Samantha struggled against her laughter. She didn't
want to discourage their speaking to God, even if what
they said was inappropriate.

After giving each boy a kiss on the forehead, Samantha
turned to leave. With a smile on his lips, Rudolf still
lounged against the connecting door with his arms
folded against his chest.

Samantha took one step toward him but stopped
when Drake spoke. "Lady Samantha, will you tell us a
story?"

Samantha limped back to the bed and sat on the
edge. "What kind of story do you want?" she asked.

"Tell us about when you were a little girl," Drake
said.

She glanced at Grant, who nodded in agreement
with his brother.

"Very well." Samantha paused before speaking and
placed a finger across her lips as she thought of something the boys would like. Then she asked, "Did you
ever go potato knocking?"

Both boys shook their heads.

Samantha looked at the prince. "What about you,
Your Highness?"

Rudolf smiled. "No, *ma lyoobof.*"

Samantha turned back to the boys and began, "My
sisters and I—"

"What are their names?" Drake interrupted.

"Angelica and Victoria."

"How old are they?" Grant asked.

"Angelica is nineteen, and Victoria is seventeen."

"Do they—?"

"Do you wish to hear this story or not?" Samantha asked.

Drake pretended to button his lips together. She glanced at Grant, who also buttoned his lips. When she looked toward the prince, he buttoned his lips, too.

Samantha giggled like a young girl. Then she began again, "When my sisters and I were younger, we went potato knocking. Take a large potato and wrap twine around it tightly. Sneak to a neighbor's closed door and tie the potato around the doorknob. Then, let the twine loose, walking as far from the door as you can, and hide. When you yank the end of the twine repeatedly, the potato knocks on your victim's door. When he opens the door, no one is there."

Rudolf shouted with laughter, drawing her attention. The boys laughed, too.

"I can't wait to try it," Grant said.

"What happens when the victim knows you played a trick?" Drake asked.

"Then you run away as fast as you can," Samantha answered.

"I bet the victim never caught you, though," Grant said.

"Well, none of our victims caught my sisters," Samantha hedged. "I was caught a few times because my injured leg prevented my quick escape."

"What happened?" Grant asked.

"The victim grabbed me and marched me home," Samantha answered with a smile. "Then I became the victim of a spanking."

Samantha rose from the bed and turned to leave. The prince wasn't smiling now. She hoped that wasn't pity crouched in his eyes. Being pitied made her feel pathetic.

Rudolf opened the connecting door, saying, "After you, *ma lyoobof.*"

"Your Highness?"

"Yes, Drake?"

"Do princes give good night kisses?"

Rudolf smiled. "Yes, they do."

With tears welling up in her eyes, Samantha watched Rudolf walk to the bed. He leaned down and gave each boy a good night kiss.

When the prince returned to her side, Drake called, "Good night again, Lady Samantha."

"Good night," she answered, her voice choked with emotion.

"Oh, Lord, she's weeping again," Grant said.

Once inside their bedchamber, Rudolf turned to her and brushed a tear off her cheek. "Why are girls so stupid?" he teased, echoing Grant's words. "Turn around and I will unfasten your buttons."

Samantha showed him her back and felt his fingers on the back of her gown. With his task completed, Rudolf kissed the nape of her neck, sending delicious shivers down her spine. She felt him pushing the gown off her shoulders, letting it slip to the floor at her feet. Stepping out of it, she stood in front of him wearing only her chemise, silk hose, lace garters, and slippers.

When he tossed the gown across the settee, Samantha protested, "The gown will wrinkle."

"Then, I will purchase you a dozen more," he told her.

Rudolf reached behind her and pulled the pins from her hair, letting her ebony mane cascade to her waist. Then he slipped the chemise's straps off her shoulders, and that pooled at her feet, too.

"You are beautiful, *ma lyoobof,*" Rudolf said, stepping back a pace to admire her.

Samantha blushed and dropped her gaze to the carpet. Rudolf lifted her chin and waited until she looked into his eyes.

Holding her gaze captive, Rudolf shrugged out of his waistcoat and tossed it onto the settee. It fell across her gown even as his body would soon cover hers. Next came his boots, his breeches, his shirt.

"*Ma lyoobof,* I have a good night kiss for you," the prince said in a husky voice when he stood naked to her gaze.

Rudolf yanked her against his muscular nakedness, his mouth descending to hers. Samantha sighed, savoring the exquisite sensation of his hardness touching her softness.

Their kiss was long and languorous and melted into another. And then another.

Leaving her lips behind, Rudolf burned a scorching path to her throat and then her breasts. The prince dropped to his knees in front of her, his arms encircling her body. He pressed his face against her belly; his tongue traced a path to the crevice between her thighs.

Rudolf slashed his tongue down and up the secret place between her legs. He kissed her female's nub and then tormented it with his tongue.

With a cry of mingling surprise and pleasure, Samantha melted against his tongue. Spasms of exquisite pleasure shook her body, and she clutched him tightly against her.

Rudolf stood then and kissed her again. He lifted her into his arms and carried her to bed.

Refusing to release her, Rudolf cradled her against his body. Stroking her back, he whispered, "You are all that a man could want in a woman. Sleep now."

"I want to touch you the way you have touched me," Samantha said, looking into his dark eyes.

"I will grant you your wish in the morning," Rudolf told her, his smile filled with love. "For now, I want to hold you close while we sleep."

Samantha dropped her hand to his groin.

In an instant, Rudolf rolled her onto her back, his well-muscled legs spreading hers. "Very well, *ma lyoobof,*" he said. "I think I can stay awake a few minutes longer . . ."

CHAPTER 11

Three months passed, and Samantha's life fell into a routine. Grant and Drake filled her days. In the morning, she tutored the boys in reading while the prince assumed responsibility for their ciphering numbers. After lunching like a real family, they passed most afternoons in play, and Samantha was always chosen first for games.

The nights belonged to Rudolf. Pretending he was her husband proved easier than she had imagined. Each evening when they retired to their bedchamber, Samantha went without guilt or remorse into his arms and gave herself completely to the prince.

January's days lenghtened. Melancholy sunsets, woodsmoke-scented air, and the rhythmic sounds of a piano and a violin playing a duet marked the passing of January.

February's gray skies delivered rain and then waxing sunshine. As the days grew longer, catkins hanged on birch trees while buds adorned the maples.

Courageous crocus opened their petals when the blue skies of March arrived, and pussy willow buds swelled with the changing season. Migrating robins began to appear; the starlings' speckled plumage was replaced by spring's glossy black.

On that fifteenth day of March, Samantha sat in the carved stone gazebo on the far side of the pond and watched the boys playing in the treehouse nearby. Beside her sat Giles, the deerhound. She would have been up in the trees herself if she hadn't been feeling a tad queasy from the enormous luncheon she'd eaten. As spring drew ever closer, she'd begun to dread the idea of returning to London and wished they could remain in Scotland forever. The only thing awaiting her in London was bleak reality.

Samantha smiled when she heard Grant telling his brother, "I will be the prince, and you will be the servant."

"I don't want to be the servant," Drake protested. "I want to be the prince."

"I'm older so I'm the prince," Grant announced.

"That isn't fair," Drake whined.

"Boys, come down here," Samantha called.

Reluctantly, the boys moved toward the ladder. Grant said, "I'll go first."

"I want to go first," Drake argued.

Grant ignored him and hurried down the ladder. He laughed at his victory, which only angered the eight-year-old even more.

"No good, sneaky bastard," Drake shouted.

"Come here," Samantha called sharply. When they stood before her, she said, "Brothers should never argue. Apologize at once."

"Sorry," Grant said sourly.

"Sorry, too," Drake replied.

"I want you to say something nice about each other," Samantha said. "Drake, you go first."

"I like the way you always protect me," the eight-year-old told his brother.

Samantha nodded with approval. "Your turn, Grant."

"I like the way you don't know as much as I do," the ten-year-old told his brother.

"I do so."

"Grant, you are an instigator," Samantha said.

"What's that?"

"A troublemaker," Samantha answered. "Sit here beside me, and I'll tell you a story." When they settled, she began, "Today is the fifteenth day of March, also known as the ides of the month. A long time ago there lived a famous Roman named Julius Caesar who wanted to be the emperor of Rome. A soothsayer told him—"

"What's a soothsayer?" Drake interrupted.

"A fortune-teller," Samantha answered. "Anyway, the soothsayer told Caesar to 'beware the ides of March.' When the ides of March arrived, jealous senators stabbed him to death. Forever after, the ides of March has been considered an unlucky day."

Drake shuddered and looked around, saying, "Holy water, I got the chills."

"Your Highness," a voice called.

The three of them turned around and spied Durwin walking around the pond toward them. "It *is* our unlucky day," Grant said.

"That isn't very nice," Samantha scolded, struggling against the urge to smile. "Perhaps Durwin would consider playing in the treehouse and serving *two* princes."

"His Highness requests your presence in his office," Durwin said when he reached them.

"Would you stay with the boys until I return?" Samantha asked, rising from her seat.

"Of course, Your Highness."

Walking away, Samantha did smile when she heard Grant saying, "Come into our treehouse, Mr. Durwin." "We'll be the princes," Drake added. "You will be the servant."

Samantha knew something was wrong as soon as she walked into the office and saw the prince's grim expression. Then she saw the man sitting in one of the high-backed chairs. Her heart pounded wildly in her chest, and a wave of nausea rolled over her at the thought of losing Grant and Drake.

Rudolf stood as she limped across the office. So did the stranger. She knew she looked frightened when the prince smiled at her, his look telling her not to worry. But, she couldn't erase the **grim** expression he'd worn before masking his emotion.

"Please be seated," Rudolf gestured to the chair.

Samantha sat down and threw a guarded look at the man. Both men sat when she sat.

"This is Mr. Stockwell, an agent of the Duke of Inverary," Rudolf told her.

Samantha felt her heart breaking. She didn't want to return to England. She wanted to remain in Scotland with her pretend family.

"Mr. Stockwell informs me that His Grace requests our immediate return to London," Rudolf told her.

Samantha nodded and studied her hands folded in her lap. "I'll make the necessary preparations," she said in a small voice. "The boys will be joining us, too?"

Rudolf inclined his head.

Later that evening, Rudolf and Samantha walked upstairs behind the boys. She couldn't help thinking that this was the last night they would climb these stairs together, the last night they would listen to the boys' prayers, the last night they would sleep in their bed.

Rudolf had been grimly quiet since Mr. Stockwell's arrival, and Samantha missed him already. She felt like throwing herself down and weeping forever. Tomorrow was the first miserable day of bleak reality. Weeping would not change that fact, would only upset the prince and the boys.

"Thank You, Lord, for His Highness and Lady Samantha," Drake prayed, kneeling beside the bed.

"Thank You for sending us Mr. Stockwell," Grant said, kneeling beside his brother. "Now we'll have a trip to London."

"What if we don't like London?" Drake whispered.

"Don't worry about that now," Grant said.

"I'll be happy wherever Lady Samantha is," Drake said, smiling at the object of his affection.

"Jesus Christ, brother, do you want to make her weep?" Grant asked.

After kissing both boys good night, Rudolf and Samantha went into their own chamber. In silence, Samantha undressed and donned her nightgown. Then she knelt beside the bed and covered her face with her hands.

The bed creaked when the prince sat on its edge beside her. "Are you thanking God for Mr. Stockwell, too?" he asked.

Samantha shook her head but kept her face covered. In a voice aching with emotion, she told the prince, "I am asking Him for—"

Samantha burst into tears, her body wracked with heart-wrenching sobs. She wept for a lifetime of pain and insecurity, for the bleakness of her future, for her soon-to-be-lost love.

"What is this?" Rudolf said, reaching for her. He

lifted her onto his lap, asking, "Why are you weeping?"

Samantha rested her head against the solidness of his chest. She was ashamed to meet his gaze. "I don't want to return to London."

Rudolf tightened his hold on her and planted a kiss on the crown of her head. "You knew we would need to return one day," he said, his tone soothing.

"Pretending that day would never arrive proved exceedingly easy, Your Highness," Samantha told him. "I-I have been happy in Scotland."

"Look at me, Princess," Rudolf said, lifting her chin, waiting until she looked into his eyes. "Happiness is a journey, not a location. If you are happy here, then you will be happy there."

"I don't think so," she said.

Rudolf lowered his head and claimed her lips. Hooking her left arm around his neck and her right arm around his body, Samantha surrendered herself, letting the prince take her wherever he would.

Their kiss was long, slow, soul-stealing. Samantha poured all of her love and her need into that single, stirring kiss. And the prince responded in kind, meeting her unspoken emotion with his own.

They made love with a gentle desperation. Rudolf sprinkled dozens of kisses across her eyelids, temples, and throat, but his lips always returned to hers as if he yearned to steal her heart and soul to keep for himself and to cherish forever.

Rudolf worshipped her body with his hands and lips. His touch on her was soothing yet exciting. He made her forget that, like Adam and Eve, they would soon lose their paradise.

And then they slept, cradled in each other's arms. . . .

* * *

The coach entered London on the first day of spring. Their journey home seemed to have passed more quickly than their flight to Scotland, even though the coach was cramped with the boys and the deerhound.

"Holy hell, look at all the people," Grant exclaimed, staring out the window.

"I never knew there were so many people in the world," Drake said.

Rudolf and Samantha looked at each other and smiled. He lifted her hand to his lips and asked, "Are you afraid, *ma lyoobof?*"

"I am deeply concerned," Samantha said with a rueful smile.

"I will stand by your side," Rudolf promised, and lifted her hand to his lips.

Samantha looked out the window when the coach came to an abrupt halt in front of the Duke of Inverary's town house. "We have arrived," she told the boys.

Without waiting for Karl, Rudolf opened the door and climbed out. He turned to assist Samantha and the boys. Giles leaped down, barked, and followed them up the front stairs.

The foyer seemed crowded. Not only was Tinker, the duke's majordomo, there to open the door, but the entire family was waiting for them.

Magnus Campbell, the Duke of Inverary, and Aunt Roxie stood together. Her sisters, Angelica and Victoria, perched on a bench while Robert Campbell, her brother-in-law, lounged against a wall as if waiting for the entertainment to begin.

"Oh, my darling," Aunt Roxie cried, hugging her to her voluptuous bosom. "I feared for your safety."

"I'm sorry I caused you worry," Samantha said.

Aunt Roxie's gaze shifted to the two boys and the deerhound. "Who are these boys?"

"These are my sons, Grant and Drake," Samantha answered, faltering when she heard a chuckle from the marquess and the prince. "This is our dog, Giles."

Her aunt looked surprised. "I beg your pardon?"

"I said, this dog is—"

"I heard that," her aunt interrupted. "What did you say before?"

Samantha drew the boys close, took a deep breath, and said in a voice that brooked no argument, "Grant and Drake are my soon-to-be-adopted sons." She looked at the duke, adding, "I hope you will agree to help me with the legal aspect of their adoption."

Before he could respond, Aunt Roxie seemed to recover herself. She laughed and gushed, "Welcome to London, my darlings. I am your Aunt Roxie." She gestured to the other young women, saying, "Those are your aunts, Angelica and Victoria, who are going to escort you and your dog upstairs to help you settle in."

Taking their cue, Angelica and Victoria rose from their perch and smiled at the boys. Angelica, eight months pregnant, held out her hand to Grant, saying, "I know the perfect chamber for you and your dog."

Grant stared in fascination at her swollen belly.

Seeing where his gaze was, Angelica said, "I'm soon going to have my baby."

"I thought babies came from Edinburgh," Grant said in obvious confusion.

Angelica laughed. "I'll tell you where they really come from in a few years."

Grant went willingly, but Drake clung to Samantha. Seeing her chance to escape, she stepped toward the stairs, saying, "He's frightened. I'll settle them into their chamber."

"Do not even consider walking up those stairs," Aunt Roxie warned her. "His Grace has business to discuss with His Highness and you."

Without acknowledging that her aunt had spoken, Samantha knelt in front of Drake. "You can go with Tory, can't you? I promise you will be perfectly safe. Tory loves to have fun, just like you."

Drake cast Victoria a shy smile. When she offered her hand, the boy accepted it and went with her.

"We had better get this over with," Rudolf said, once the boys had disappeared up the stairs.

"You're damned right about that," Duke Magnus said.

Dreading what was to come, Samantha felt wrenchingly queasy. She knew she had no one to blame but herself. If she hadn't given the prince her virginity, she would be able to assume an affronted attitude and swear that nothing had happened. Unfortunately, she had never been a good liar.

"You look pale, *ma lyoobof,*" Rudolf said, grasping her arm. "Would you care to lie down instead of accompanying us?"

The prince was giving her an escape route. In that moment, she loved him more than ever.

And then her old friend insecurity stepped from the shadows of her mind. Why did he want her upstairs? What did he think would happen in this interview?

"I will be fine," Samantha told him, managing a faint smile.

"Have you been ill?" Aunt Roxie asked, concerned.

"Samantha has been feeling under the eaves lately," Rudolf answered.

"How do you know?" Samantha asked, snapping her gaze to his.

"I notice everything about you, *ma lyoobof,*" Rudolf said. Duke Magnus cleared his throat and gestured to the stairs, saying, "Let us retire to my study for this discussion."

Samantha sat in one of the chairs placed in front of the duke's mahogany desk. She folded her hands on her lap and then stared at them as if they were the most interesting feature inside the room.

Aunt Roxie sat in the chair beside hers. She reached over and patted her hand, saying, "All will be well, my darling."

With his arms folded across his chest, Robert stood near the window. Duke Magnus sat behind his desk while Rudolf sat in the chair beside her aunt's. Samantha had the sudden feeling the prince was trying to distance himself from her.

"Your Highness, would you care to give us an explanation for the past three months?" Duke Magnus asked.

"Certainly, Your Grace," Rudolf said with a polite smile. "Samantha and I were abducted by Vladimir's agents and taken to London. We escaped and journeyed to Sweetheart Manor to disappear until my three younger brothers arrive in England this spring."

"What a frightening experience," Aunt Roxie exclaimed.

"Roxie, I'll handle this," Duke Magnus said. He looked at the prince, saying, "We managed to keep your disappearances quiet. We gave out that Samantha was visiting friends in Scotland, and you had traveled to the Continent on business."

"I appreciate that, Your Grace," Rudolf said.

Samantha peeked at the prince. He seemed to have relaxed a bit since entering the study. The situation wasn't as bad as she had assumed.

From this moment, she and the prince would go their separate ways. That thought wrenched her heart, and her stomach rolled, leaving her queasy. She closed her eyes and fought the nausea.

"So no harm has been done," Rudolf was saying.

Duke Magnus cleared his throat. "I took the liberty of announcing your betrothal to Samantha in the *Times*."

"What?" Samantha was stunned.

"Oh, my darling, yours will be the wedding of the year, if not the decade," Aunt Roxie gushed.

Samantha stared at her aunt as if the woman had suddenly turned purple. The prince spoke then, drawing her attention, leaving her nearly breathless with pain.

"I cannot marry Samantha," he announced.

"Cannot or will not?" Duke Magnus cocked a dark brow at him.

"What is the difference?" Rudolf replied. "There will be no marriage."

"Are you rejecting her because of her limp?" Robert spoke up.

"How dare you even give voice to such a suggestion," Rudolf replied.

A tidal wave of humiliation washed over Samantha. Because of the prince, she had been abducted and nearly killed. He had seduced the virginity out of her and ruined whatever chance she'd had to make her dream come true. Now he was tossing her aside like used goods.

You must bear part of the blame, an inner voice reminded her. She had allowed the prince to seduce her and, in the doing, had killed her own dream.

The room spun dizzyingly, making her even more queasy, and she heard the pounding rush of blood in her ears. After a lifetime of rejection, she couldn't bear any more and needed to get out of that room.

"I am going upstairs now," Samantha said, rising unsteadily from the chair.

With all the dignity she could muster, Samantha limped across the study to the door. A hand touched her arm to prevent her leaving, and then she heard the prince's voice.

"*Ma lyoobof—*"

"Don't call me that," she snapped.

"You do not understand," he said. "My refusal of marriage has nothing to do with you."

Samantha lifted her gaze from his hand on her arm to his face and gave him a cold stare. "I understand very well. Release my arm."

When he silently refused, she added in a broken voice, "Please, let me go."

The prince dropped his hand. Samantha quit the chamber.

I cannot make anyone happy, Rudolf thought, staring at the closed door. He had never made Olga happy, and now he had brought Samantha pain.

Go after her, an inner voice told him.

Rudolf reached for the doorknob, but the duchess blocked his way. "Where do you think you're going?" she demanded.

"Samantha misunderstood," Rudolf answered. "I need to explain myself."

"I will see to my niece's needs," Roxie told him. "You may explain yourself to His Grace. Do not leave this room until I return." She looked beyond the prince to the marquess.

"If need be, I'll tie him to the chair," Robert promised.

Satisfied, Roxie left her husband's office.

"Your Highness, be seated and explain yourself," the duke said.

The Duke of Inverary sounded infinitely more relaxed than he had a few minutes earlier. Rudolf's stress rose in direct proportion to the duke's relaxation. The

English aristocrats would never listen to reason. He was trapped and would again wear the marriage yoke. How could he have done this to himself?

Trying to appear relaxed, Rudolf sat down in the chair in front of the duke's desk and stretched his long legs out. He fixed his black gaze on the older man's.

"Marrying Samantha will endanger her life," Rudolf told him. "Vladimir wants me dead and will use her against me."

"So you are not actually opposed to marriage?" Duke Magnus asked.

"Generally speaking, I oppose the state of matrimony. No good ever came from marriage," Rudolf said. "In particular, I am not opposed to Samantha."

"I am glad to hear that, Your Highness," the duke said. "My wife has planned the wedding for the twenty-third day of April. Invitations have been sent to six hundred of our closest friends."

The situation was worse than Rudolf had thought. His refusal to marry Samantha would not only hurt her feelings but humiliate her in front of six hundred aristocrats. Of course, those six hundred would repeat the tale to another six hundred who, in turn, would do the same.

"And if I refuse?" Rudolf asked, cocking a dark brow in a gesture that resembled the duke's.

"Did I mention that your mother and daughter are rusticating at my country estate?" Duke Magnus asked with a smile.

"You bloody bastard," Rudolf swore. How dare this man endanger his family.

The marquess bristled at the insult to his father. "Now see here—"

The duke gestured his son to silence. "I assure you, Your Highness, my parents were married."

Rudolf balked at being forced to do anything, especially by this man. "You may be legitimate issue, but you suffered no qualms about scattering your seed far and wide."

The marquess lunged for the prince.

"Sit down, Robert," the duke ordered.

"But he—"

"I said, sit down."

"Are you blackmailing me?" Rudolf asked.

"Call it an incentive," Duke Magnus answered. "I don't care if you marry my wife's niece and divorce her next month, but I will not allow you to tarnish her reputation by refusing to do the honorable thing."

"I find talk of honor amazing coming from your lips," the prince said.

Robert growled. The duke gestured him to remain calm.

"I want my mother, along with Boris and Elke, returned to Sark Island," Rudolf insisted. "Crowds of strangers disturb her. I want my daughter brought to this house and guarded until the trouble with Vladimir is finished."

"I can do that," Duke Magnus agreed. "Do you see an end to it soon?"

"My three younger brothers will arrive in England shortly and will negotiate with Vladimir," Rudolf told him.

"Vladimir is ensconced at Montague House," Duke Magnus told him. "I advise you to leave him there until this trouble is settled. I will have him watched. Why don't you stay here? You will be close to your daughter and Samantha. You do agree to the marriage?"

Rudolf inclined his head. He looked the duke straight in the eye and said, "You will live to regret this, though. You do not know who I really am."

"What do you mean?" the marquess asked.

"I am no prince."

"You're an imposter?"

"I am Prince Rudolf Kazanov," he said. "However, I am not my father's son, but another man's bastard. Fedor Kazanov is too proud a man to refute his first-born and acknowledge that his English bride was less than pure. My mother suffered because she bore me."

"How did she suffer?" the duke asked.

"If you have seen her, then you must have noticed she is vacant at times," Rudolf replied.

The duke nodded. "Yes, I did. She didn't recognize me."

"You knew his mother?" the marquess asked.

Both the prince and the duke ignored the marquess. Their black eyes were fixed on each other.

When Rudolf spoke, there was no masking the hostility in his voice. "My mother was carrying me when she married Fedor Kazanov. When her childbearing days ended, he locked her in an insane asylum. She passed fifteen years there before I was able to free her and bring her home to England."

The Duke of Inverary winced visibly.

"My God, what a monster," the marquess exclaimed.

Rudolf wasn't listening. All of his focus centered on the duke. His voice filled with cold contempt when he said, "She suffered greatly because of you."

"You know?" Duke Magnus asked.

Rudolf inclined his head. "Sometimes my mother has lucid moments."

"What does the prince know?" Robert asked his father.

Duke Magnus was silent for long, uncomfortable moments. He took a deep breath and answered, "His Highness knows that *I* am his natural father."

Robert appeared stunned.

"Your father is admitting I am your half brother, albeit from the wrong side of the blanket," Rudolf said, without taking his black gaze off the duke.

"I am an old man who cares nothing for his reputation and will acknowledge you if you wish," Duke Magnus offered.

"I do not need your validation," Rudolf told him, his voice laced with bitterness.

The duke looked hurt by his words, and a bolt of guilt shot through Rudolf. Why should he care about the duke's feelings? The duke had never cared about his mother or him.

"Fedor Kazanov acknowledges you as his firstborn son," Duke Magnus said. "To the world, you will remain that."

"I do not want Samantha or anyone else to know the relationship between us or my origins," Rudolf said.

"Robert and I will guard your secret," the duke assured him. "May I call you Rudolf?"

"No, Your Grace, you may call me *Your Highness.*"

The duke inclined his head, saying, "I hope you will forgive me someday for the pain I caused your mother and you."

Rudolf stared hard at the man. He seemed sincerely sorry, but Rudolf could not put away the pain of the past twenty-eight years.

"Who knows what the future will bring?" Rudolf said finally. "I passed my whole life waiting for this moment, planning your downfall in myriad, horrific ways. And now that the long-awaited moment has arrived, I am beset by other, more important problems." Rudolf smiled, but it did not quite reach his eyes, eyes that resembled the older man's. "I suppose I should be grateful to you. The thought of bringing you down kept me strong when Fedor beat me."

"I am so sorry," the duke said, his voice hoarse with emotion.

Between Samantha and the duke, Rudolf felt an insistent tugging on his heartstrings but steeled himself against it. He had learned to be suspicious of people.

"I understand your bitterness," the marquess spoke up.

"Do not patronize me," Rudolf said, rising from his chair. "You will never understand what being a bastard and the cause of your mother's suffering means to a man."

Robert inclined his head. Then he asked, "Why does Vladimir want you dead?"

"Vladimir knows he is the true heir," Rudolf said.

"If you left Russia permanently and renounced your claim, Vladimir would inherit," Robert said.

"Vladimir stole some of my valuables," Rudolf told them. "In return, I left Russia with several priceless valuables meant for the heir. I consider these as reparation for the harm done to my mother."

Duke Magnus smiled at that. "I do believe you have inherited some of my finer points of character."

Rudolf would not—could not—warm to the duke. He glanced toward the door, saying, "What is delaying Her Grace?"

CHAPTER 12

"My worst fear is confirmed."

Samantha knelt in front of the commode and gagged dryly. Sweat mingled with the tears streaming down her cheeks. She turned her head at the sound of her aunt and, in a voice that mirrored her misery, said, "I've made myself sick."

Sobbing with humiliation, Samantha turned away from her aunt and again gagged dryly. Her only thought was the prince's words: *I cannot marry Samantha . . . There will be no marriage.*

Feeling her aunt's comforting arms holding her steady, Samantha surrendered to her misery. She sobbed as if she would never stop, which made her gag dryly again.

When her tears were spent, Samantha leaned against her aunt's legs and tried to regain enough strength to stand. Her aunt helped her up and across the chamber to the bed.

"Eat this," Aunt Roxie said, holding a piece of bread in front of her face.

Leaning against the headboard, Samantha began to

shake her head but stopped lest the queasiness return. "I cannot eat a bite."

"I said to eat this," her aunt ordered. "Do as I say."

Samantha would need to have been dead to miss the annoyance in her aunt's voice. She lifted the bread from her aunt's hand and took a bite. Closing her eyes, she breathed deeply.

"I'm so tired," Samantha said, taking another bite.

"Do not get comfortable, my dear," Aunt Roxie told her. "You need to return to the study before you can sleep."

Samantha looked at her through blue eyes mirroring her misery. "I am *not* going downstairs."

Aunt Roxie sat on the edge of the bed. "Darling, arrangements need to be made for your wedding."

There will be no marriage pounded in her head. She couldn't marry the prince unless he loved her. Samantha stared into her aunt's eyes and told her, "There is no need for a wedding."

Aunt Roxie burst out laughing at that as if she were privy to a joke that eluded Samantha. "Are you telling me that the prince and you were not physically intimate?"

"That is precisely what I mean," Samantha said, lifting her chin a notch, a high blush staining her cheeks.

"Do not lie to me," Aunt Roxie said, her gaze narrowing on her.

Samantha looked away in embarrassment. "Yes, the prince and I—" She broke off, unable to finish.

"Have you been feeling poorly?" her aunt asked. "Dizzy? Nauseous perhaps?"

Samantha inclined her head and looked with suspicion at her aunt. What point was she trying to make? What did her health have to do with marrying the prince? People took ill. That was the way of the world.

And then an outrageous thought popped into her mind. Samantha looked with dawning horror at her aunt.

"When did you last have your menses?" Aunt Roxie asked.

Samantha closed her eyes against the reality of her situation. She couldn't recall the last time, certainly before the prince and she fled to Scotland.

"I thought so," her aunt said with a feline smile. "Queasiness without menstruation means you are carrying the prince's child."

"Rudolf doesn't love me," Samantha wailed. "I cannot marry him if he doesn't love me."

"You were ready to marry Alexander Emerson," Aunt Roxie reminded her.

Samantha was unable to suppress a sob. "I love Rudolf and couldn't bear his hatred."

"Why would the prince hate you?" her aunt asked. "His actions speak otherwise."

"Don't you see?" Samantha said. "Rudolf will grow to hate me because you—my pregnancy—forced him into an unwanted marriage."

"All men consider all marriages unwanted," her aunt told her, giving her a dimpled smile. "Darling, the prince's lips say no, but his gaze on you positively screams his love."

"What do you mean?" Samantha asked.

"If you want to know a man's mind, watch what he does, not what he says," Aunt Roxie said. When Samantha dropped her gaze to her hands folded in her lap, her aunt said, "That would require you to lift your head proudly. You would need to look people in the eye instead of keeping your gaze glued to the carpet because you mistakenly believe you are inferior."

Samantha snapped her gaze to her aunt's. She *was*

inferior to other ladies. Had her aunt forgotten her deformed leg?

"That's much better," Aunt Roxie said, cupping her niece's chin. She held out her hand, adding, "Let's return to the study. The prince needs to be informed of his impending fatherhood."

"I can't," Samantha said, shaking her head, fresh tears springing to her eyes. "This whole situation is too humiliating."

Aunt Roxie narrowed her gaze on her niece and shocked her when she said, "Darling, your wedding is scheduled for one month from now. The invitations have already been sent. We need this matter settled before society learns of your return to London. Come to the study willingly, or I will drag you down."

"Please, give me a few minutes to freshen myself," Samantha acquiesced. She worried her bottom lip with her small white teeth. "Could you—I mean, would you—?"

"I will inform the prince of your condition," Aunt Roxie said, patting her hand. "You will not be subjected to anyone's initial reaction."

"I love you, Aunt Roxie."

"And I love you, my darling."

Samantha managed a wan smile. "I do feel better since eating the bread. Why were you carrying a piece of bread in your pocket?"

Her aunt's smile was feline. She breezed out of the chamber, saying, "I had a feeling this would happen."

Her dream was coming true, Samantha thought, but not precisely as she had envisioned. Would the prince despise her for trapping him into marriage? Was there even a slight chance that he could grow to love her?

Stop your damned pretending, Samantha told herself. *For once in your misbegotten life, accept reality.*

The prince would never love her. What man could

love a woman who limped? She was unwanted defective merchandise. But she would love Grant and Drake and the new babe, and they would love her.

Samantha washed her face and brushed her hair away from her face. She limped across the chamber toward the door but paused before leaving.

Her heart sank to her stomach. How would she bear it when Rudolf began to have affairs?

Downstairs, Rudolf fixed his gaze on the study door and wondered out loud again, "What is delaying Her Grace?"

The door crashed open suddenly, as if in answer to the prince's thoughts. The Duchess of Inverary walked into the room, being certain to close the door lest the prince try to flee.

Out of habit, the three men stood at her entrance, but the duchess gestured them to sit. Wearing a feline smile, she paused there for a long moment.

"Magnus, I hope His Highness has come to his senses and is prepared to do the honorable thing," she drawled.

The Duke of Inverary nodded at his wife. Roxie turned her attention on the prince, saying, "Congratulations, Your Highness."

Rudolf gave her a sour look. Congratulations were only in order when the groom desired the union. He watched, puzzled, as the duchess touched almost all of her fingers as if counting.

Roxie gave him a bright smile. "Come November, my niece will be making you a father again."

"That is impossible," Rudolf said, bolting out of his chair.

"Did you have intimate relations with my niece?" the duchess asked.

Rudolf had the good grace to flush. "Yes, I did."

"Was my niece a virgin the first time she participated with you in these activities?" Roxie asked.

Rudolf could feel the muscle in his right cheek begin to twitch. "Yes, she was."

"Did my niece engage in intimate activities with any other man during that time?"

"Of course not," Rudolf barked, his left cheek muscle twitching.

"That makes you the father of the child she is carrying in her body," the duchess informed him.

"Samantha would have told me," he said.

The duchess laughed and shook her head, saying, "She didn't know."

Duke Magnus chuckled, and his son joined him. Rudolf gave them an unamused look.

"How could she not know?" he argued. This whole conversation was ridiculous.

"I blush to speak so intimately with you," Roxie said, with no blush staining her cheeks. "Despite her deflowering, Samantha is an innocent. She admitted missing her menses, and I found her draped over the chamber pot."

"Samantha is ill?" Rudolf said, not bothering to hide his concern. "I must go to her."

This response illicited outright laughter from the duke and the marquess. The duchess blocked his way, ordering, "Sit down, Your Highness. Your panic is tedious."

"But Samantha—"

"My niece will be joining us shortly," Roxie told him. "I do not wish to explain why her husband-to-be has swooned."

While this conversation was taking place inside the study, Samantha stood outside the duke's study. She had never felt more miserable in her life. The prince had told her many times that he could not offer her marriage, and now her family was forcing him to marry her. He would never forgive her for that.

Enticing the prince to love her would be impossible. Even her aunt's expertise with men would do her no good. No woman, especially an unwanted cripple, could compete with the cherished memory of a beloved first wife, the mother of his firstborn. Great Giles' ghost, the woman was almost a saint to the prince. What other reason could there be for his refusing to marry again?

If the prince wanted to dedicate his life to his lost wife, Samantha decided, then she would not force him to marry him. Many women bore children out of wedlock. She was a cripple with a tarnished reputation, a social pariah. So why not add bearing a child out of wedlock to her flaws? There was no reason both of them should be unhappy.

Determined to set matters straight, Samantha squared her shoulders and lifted her chin a notch. She raised her hand to knock on the door but lost her nerve.

Unexpectedly, the door opened a crack, and she heard Rudolf say, "I'm going to see what is keeping—Oh, there you are. Why are you standing there? Come inside."

Rudolf opened the door wider and stepped aside to let her pass. Blushing with embarrassment, she dropped her gaze and limped into the study with the speed of a woman on her way to the gallows.

Escorting her to the chair in front of the duke's desk, Rudolf asked, "How do you feel?"

"Fine," Samantha said in a voice no louder than a whisper.

She refused to meet his gaze. He was being magnanimously kind to her in the face of extreme provocation.

Duke Magnus spoke, "Samantha, dear, these are the plans we—"

"I need to speak before you continue," she said.

Samantha heard the tremor in her voice and could have kicked herself. She had wanted to be more forceful.

"We are waiting," Rudolf said.

Samantha flicked a quick glance at the prince, who stood beside her chair. His towering over her was intimidating. Then she turned to the duke, her legal guardian.

Her words came out in a rush, "I refuse to marry His Highness."

Everyone seemed stunned into silence. Except the prince.

"Like me, you have no choice," Rudolf said, his voice cold with contempt. "You should have thought of the consequences before you spread your legs for me."

Samantha heard her aunt gasping at the prince's crassness, the marquess coughing, and the duke beginning to growl. Her eyes burned with the humiliation she felt. How could the prince insult her? She was sacrificing herself for his happiness.

Usually dormant due to her limp, Douglas pride swelled in her breast, and Samantha felt a rush of anger surge through her. She stood then and faced the prince.

"If you recall, Your Highness," Samantha said, her blue gaze glittering with anger, "I wanted separate chambers."

"You should have insisted," Rudolf replied, his expression grim. "You knew I did not want to marry again."

"I did insist." Her voice rose with self-righteous anger. "You refused to listen."

"Samantha, darling—" her aunt began.

"Be quiet," Samantha snapped, shocking everyone in the room, even herself. She had never spoken rudely to anyone.

Duke Magnus tried to reason with her. "Samantha, dear—"

"You be quiet, too," she told him, less forcefully due to his rank.

She whirled around and narrowed her gaze on her brother-in-law. The marquess held his hands up in a gesture that he would not enter the fray.

When she turned to the prince, he was smiling at her. Great Giles' ghost, what was there to smile about?

"Your Highness, you do not need to marry me," she said, composing herself.

"Do not be ridiculous," Rudolf replied, losing his smile. "You are fit for nothing and cannot live on the generosity of others indefinitely."

"I am *not* ridiculous," Samantha said, tears welling up in her eyes. She took a deep breath. Lord, but the prince was making her queasy. In a calmer voice, she announced, "I will live at the cottage with Grant and Drake."

"Sit down," Rudolf ordered.

Accustomed to obeying orders, Samantha plopped down in the chair.

"I have always been careful about scattering my seed," Rudolf said, his voice tight as he fought for control, his words making Samantha blush. "No child of mine will be raised a bastard. Do you understand?"

Samantha had never seen the prince so angry. Refusing to surrender to her fright, she argued, "What difference does it make if the babe is born a bastard? I will love it anyway."

None too gently, Rudolf grabbed her chin and forced her to look at him. "You have no idea what being a bastard means," he told her. "You would be condemning the child to a life of unimaginable anguish."

Samantha began to sob. "I-I d-don't want to force you to marry me."

"I am not a man who can be forced into anything," Rudolf said. "I want to give my child my name."

"But you don't love me," she whispered brokenly. She just could not survive a marriage to a man she loved if he didn't love her.

"Love has nothing to do with marriage," Rudolf told her, his cheek muscles twitching at the mere mention of the word *love*. "You will understand when you are older."

Unexpectedly, Rudolf knelt beside her chair. Taking her hand in his, he said, "I cannot live in good conscience if my child is born a bastard. Please, Princess, marry me."

Samantha couldn't bear his distress at the thought of fathering a bastard. She acquiesced with a nod of her head.

"Well done, Your Highness," Aunt Roxie said. "My niece gave me a fright."

Samantha wasn't ready to submit just yet. She raised her blue gaze to his, saying, "I can live without love if you can live without affairs."

She heard her aunt moaning, "Oh, dear God, she'll be the death of me yet. Magnus, do something."

"I do not understand," Rudolf was saying to her.

"I want you to promise never to indulge in an affair," Samantha told him.

Rudolf snapped his brows together. "My wife will not dictate to me."

"I have no wish to dictate to you," Samantha said. "I merely want your word of honor never to engage in affairs."

"Your Highness, young women like my niece are incredibly idealistic about matters of the heart," Aunt

Roxie said, trying to explain. "She doesn't know what she is asking."

Samantha looked at her aunt. "I understand perfectly."

"I said I never scatter my seed," Rudolf said. "Why do you believe I would engage in affairs? Your suspicion insults me."

"You scattered your seed on our journey to Scotland," Samantha reminded him.

The marquess burst out laughing. Samantha snapped her head around to glare at him. His laughter ceased abruptly.

Rudolf stared at her for a long moment. Finally, he gave her a curt nod.

"You need to say the words," Samantha told him, little realizing how much she was embarrassing him until she noticed his cheek muscles twitching.

"I promise not to engage in affairs," Rudolf said in a choked voice.

Watching her relax back in the chair, Rudolf bristled at the fact that she had embarrassed him in front of the others. The little witch thought she had the upper hand. He needed to exert his authority now so there would be no misunderstanding later about who ruled in his household.

"Now we can get down to specifics," Aunt Roxie said with a relieved laugh.

"I have several demands of my own," Rudolf said.

"Oh, crap," Roxie muttered.

Samantha looked at him expectantly. A faint smile touched her lips.

"As my wife, you will obey me in all matters and never question my judgment or authority," Rudolf told her, pleased to see a slight furrowing in her brow. "That includes being at my beck and call sexually, socially, or any other way I might require your services."

Apparently, the insult was lost on her. "Can I breathe?" she asked.

"I do not find your sarcasm amusing." Rudolf let her digest that and then added for good measure, "You will not leave the house without escort unless I have given my permission."

Samantha looked surprised. "You don't trust me?"

"And you will not engage in sexual affairs," Rudolf said, ignoring her question. "In other words, you will never spread your legs for another man."

Samantha gasped, and her complexion paled. He knew he had shocked her. Slowly, she rose from the chair and faced him. "Your Highness, do you actually believe I have so little virtue that I would—I would—do what you said?"

His little bride-to-be wasn't as smart as she thought, Rudolf decided. She was no match for his experience, and he went in for the kill.

In a voice oozing with sarcasm, he reminded her, "You spread your legs on our journey to Scotland and welcomed me into your body."

Rudolf knew he'd stunned her into silence. "Be a good girl and sit down in silence while His Grace and I arrange the specifics."

Samantha didn't move. With mutiny in her eyes, she stood there and stared at him.

"I said, sit down," Rudolf ordered.

Samantha dropped into her chair and clamped her lips together. Obviously fuming, she folded her hands on her lap and stared at them.

If she was any angrier, Rudolf decided, steam would be coming out of her ears. "You show remarkable promise, *ma lyoobof*. Perhaps I will not regret marrying you."

Rudolf sat down in the chair beside hers and looked at the duke, who was grinning at him. "Your Grace, shall we get down to specifics?"

Duke Magnus turned to Samantha, saying, "The prince will be in residence with us because his brother has moved into Montague House."

"Zara will be brought here and guarded," Rudolf told her. "I hope you will become acquainted with her."

Samantha recalled the pretty, blond five-year-old and smiled at the prince. Grant and Drake would love his daughter. "I will look after her," she said, relishing the job. "I know you must miss her, but do you think remaining at Sark Island would be safer?"

The duke began to explain, "His daughter isn't actually—"

Rudolf gestured the duke for silence and then turned to Samantha, admonishing her, "Less than five minutes ago, you agreed never to question my judgment. Since I have decided Zara will reside here, I obviously judge her safer here."

"I only asked," Samantha said.

"To ask is to question," Rudolf informed her. "You gave me your word never to question."

Samantha couldn't remember why she had fallen in love with him. The charming prince of her dreams had vanished. In his place was an autocratic ogre.

"Do what you want," she said sullenly.

"I intend to do that," Rudolf replied. "Preferably, without being questioned."

Samantha said nothing. Her face flamed with embarrassment at the public rebuke. She doubted she could survive the next fifty years with this stranger. Remaining a spinster and becoming a social pariah seemed more appealing with each passing moment.

Duke Magnus cleared his throat. "The wedding is

planned for April the twenty-third." He chuckled. "Since it's Saint George's Day, I can guarantee your husband will never forget your anniversary."

"I'm beginning to wonder if I would like to forget it," Samantha grumbled.

"Guard your tongue, Princess," Rudolf warned.

"You'll wear your mother's wedding gown," Aunt Roxie said with forced gaiety. "Isn't that exciting?"

Samantha turned her head to look at the prince and asked, "Am I excited or not?"

She heard the marquess chuckle. Her gaze was fixed on the prince's cheek muscle, which had begun to twitch again.

"I think one thousand pounds a month for pin money is adequate," the duke was saying to the prince.

"I don't need money," Samantha told them.

"You need it if I say you do," Rudolf told her.

"I can have the betrothal contract ready for signing tonight," Duke Magnus said.

Rudolf nodded. "Once Karl finishes unloading the coach, I will purchase a betrothal ring."

Suddenly, a ring seemed so final to Samantha. "I don't need a ring," she said.

"You need one if I say you do," Rudolf told her.

Duke Magnus stood then, signaling the interview ended. He offered his hand to the prince, who hesitated for a fraction of a second and then accepted it.

Watching them, Samantha suffered the feeling that something more than her betrothal had passed between the two men. That was impossible, though. They barely knew each other.

The five of them left the duke's study and walked downstairs. Samantha intended to get herself a cup of tea, check on the boys, and then hide in her chamber for the remainder of the day.

Tall and well built and blond, Alexander Emerson was entering the mansion as they reached the bottom of the stairs. Spying them, he crossed the foyer and, without a word, punched the prince.

Caught off guard, Rudolf staggered back into the marquess. Samantha screamed in horrified surprise.

"You no-good, foreign bastard," Alexander said.

Rudolf shrugged the marquess' hands off, lunged for the other man, and raised his fist to strike. At the same moment, Samantha leaped into action and jumped between the two men. Unable to stop his fist's forward momentum, Rudolf struck Samantha instead of Alexander.

"Oh, my God," Roxie screamed.

Samantha crumpled to the floor. She remained conscious but held her hand over her cheekbone.

"I am sorry," Rudolf said, dropping to the floor beside her and holding her in his arms. "I never intended— I would never purposely strike you." He looked at the stunned majordomo, ordering, "Fetch a cold, wet cloth."

"I will be fine," Samantha assured him. "It wasn't your fault. I placed myself in front of you."

Rudolf dropped his hand to her midsection and asked in a worried voice, "Are you certain?"

"Yes."

Tinker, the majordomo, returned then and handed the prince the cloth. Rudolf folded it and pressed it on Samantha's face.

"Can you stand?" he asked. When she nodded, he helped her up but kept his arm around her.

"Perhaps Alexander should return later," the duke said.

"This matter needs to be settled now," Aunt Roxie disagreed. "Samantha is uninjured." She looked at the prince and said, "Your Highness, see to your man unloading the coach." To Samantha, "Take Alex into the dining room and explain the situation."

The last thing Samantha wanted to do was tell Alexander Emerson that she would not be marrying him. She dreaded admitting that she was already pregnant with the prince's child. Alexander didn't love her, but he would be hurt. She had depleted her courage and inner strength on the prince.

"My face throbs, and I'm very tired," Samantha hedged.

Her aunt narrowed her gaze on her. "You will feel worse if you do not do as I say."

Rudolf tightened his grip on her. "My intended wife will not speak to her former betrothed unless I am present."

Aunt Roxie inclined her head, saying, "As you wish, Your Highness."

Samantha slipped out of the prince's grasp and limped toward the dining room. Behind her walked Alexander, Rudolf, and the marquess.

"Are you coming, too?" she asked her brother-in-law.

"You don't want to be alone with these two," Robert told her.

The marquess closed the dining room doors, and the four of them sat at the forty-foot table.

Rudolf and Samantha sat on one side. Alexander and Robert sat opposite them.

Samantha wondered how to start. She had never thought she would have any husband, and now she had two men fighting over her. She didn't like the feeling at all. How did the acclaimed beauties handle all the male attention?

"Alexander is waiting," Robert said gently.

Samantha nodded. She raised her gaze to her former betrothed.

"I am sorry for this strange turn of events," Samantha said. "His Highness did not abduct me. We were speaking in the gazebo and heard a cry for help coming from the woodland. When we investigated, some men—agents of His Highness' brother—abducted us and took us to London. We managed to escape.

"Rudolf felt we should go into hiding. His brothers are coming to England to help straighten out this trouble.

"I-I cannot marry you now. I hope you will forgive me someday."

Alexander flicked a glance at the prince and said, "I will marry you anyway."

Samantha felt her heart sinking to her stomach. This was going to be more difficult than she had ever imagined.

"You don't love me, Alexander."

"I like you and respect you and know you will make an excellent wife and mother," he told her.

Close to tears, Samantha couldn't control her quivering bottom lip. In a soft voice, she said, "I am going to marry the prince."

"You don't have to marry him," Alexander said.

"Yes, she does," Rudolf said in a harsh voice. Then, "Tell him."

Samantha raised a badly shaking hand to her mouth. She took a deep breath and said, "I am carrying the prince's child."

"You bastard," Alexander said to the prince. "You coerced her to Scotland and then took advantage of her innocence. I ought to call you out."

Before the prince could accept the challenge, Samantha sobbed, "No, please—" She burst into tears, and the prince leaned close to put his arm around her.

"If you ever need me, don't hesitate to seek me out,"

Alexander told her, standing. To the prince, he said, "If you ever hurt her, I will kill you."

When the four of them returned to the foyer, Aunt Roxie was waiting and looped her arm through Alexander's. "Stay a moment," she said. "I want to speak to you."

Without a word to anyone, Samantha turned toward the stairs. Rudolf caught her hand, asking, "Where are you going now?"

Samantha removed her hand from his. "I am going to my chamber to rest and promise not to leave the house," she told him. "If you don't trust me, my aunt will vouch for my whereabouts while you are gone."

Rudolf snapped his brows together. Of course he trusted her. How dare she imply that he didn't.

The marquess laughed out loud. "She sounds like my wife," he told the prince. "I never would have believed that sweet Samantha could be as snippy as her sister. Motherhood will cure her of that, though."

Samantha watched them leave the house and then turned to climb the stairs to her third-floor chamber. She had never felt so tired, and her damned cheekbone hurt.

From below, her aunt's voice drifted up to her. "Dear Alexander, I was so looking forward to welcoming you into the family. I have another niece that will suit you better than Samantha. Victoria is a tad impetuous and not as sweetly biddable. You men like a bit of spice, though. Victoria needs a strong, solid man like yourself who can control her wilder impulses. I know you are up to the task . . ."

CHAPTER 13

She had a black eye.

Samantha grimaced at her image in the cheval mirror. Limping wasn't enough? Now God had sent her a bruised cheek and a swollen black eye.

And an autocratic ogre for a betrothed, Samantha reminded herself. She was certain the prince hadn't meant to strike her; she should never have placed herself between two fighting men.

In spite of her disappointment in the prince's attitude toward her, Samantha had tried to make herself especially attractive and dressed in the shell pink silk gown he'd bought her. Their marriage would be a sham, but even an unwanted bride deserved pleasant memories. She would have only one betrothal and one wedding in her life. She didn't want to look back with bitterness.

If Rudolf had transformed himself from a charming prince into an autocratic ogre, was it possible for him to transform again? How would she go about changing him? Certainly not with arguments.

Whatever she gave to him, he would return to her, Samantha decided. She needed to woo her betrothed with gentle words. She practiced her smile in the mirror, but moving her face hurt because of her swollen cheek.

Disgusted with her own appearance, Samantha turned away from the mirror and limped toward the door. She paused as she recalled her aunt's words of wisdom: *If you want to know a man's mind, watch what he does, not what he says.* She wouldn't listen to what the prince said, only watch what he did.

Samantha left her chamber and limped down the corridor to the boys' chamber. She found it empty, so she went downstairs to the drawing room where everyone met before going to dinner. She hoped the boys would be on their best behavior.

Walking into the small drawing room, Samantha saw that she was the last to arrive. She peeked at the prince and tried to gauge his mood, but he was in a conversation with the duke.

"Lady Samantha!" Grant and Drake noticed her at the same time. Both boys raced across the drawing room and gave her a hug.

"The duchess is making Giles eat in the kitchen," Grant told her.

Drake nodded. "She's very bossy."

Samantha smiled at that and felt her cheek throb. "When the duchess goes out, we'll allow Giles into the dining room with us."

"What happened to you?" Drake asked.

"Your eye is black and you look sick," Grant said, sounding worried.

Samantha refused to tell the boys that the prince had struck her, albeit accidentally. "I bumped into something," she lied.

"What?" Grant sounded skeptical.

"I bumped into an open door," she told them.

"Did you cry?" Drake asked.

"No."

"Do you hurt?" Drake asked.

"Yes."

Drake crooked his finger at her in a gesture for her to lean closer. When she did, he put his arms around her neck and said, "I'll kiss it and make it better."

Then the eight-year-old touched his lips to her bruised cheek. Stepping back, he asked, "How does it feel now?"

"I do feel better," Samantha said. "Thank you for helping me."

"I want to kiss it, too," Grant said.

Samantha leaned close and let the ten-year-old press his lips on her cheek. When he stepped away, she said, "I feel almost like new. Whenever I feel poorly, I want both of you to make me feel better."

Grant and Drake beamed with pride. Drake grabbed her hand and led her across the drawing room. "His Highness is feeling poorly, but I don't think he wants me to kiss him," he said in a loud whisper.

"Did he tell you he was feeling poorly?" Samantha asked.

Drake shook his head. "He's very grumpy tonight."

"Drake, darling, you are going to be a heartbreaker," Aunt Roxie drawled.

"What's that?" Drake whispered to Samantha.

"She means all the ladies will fall in love with you," she told him.

"Yuch," Drake exclaimed, looking disgusted.

Samantha heard a masculine laugh and peeked at the prince. Catching her eye, Rudolf crossed the drawing room. He lifted his hand to touch her cheek.

"I am sorry, *ma lyoobof*," he said. "Can you forgive me?"

Samantha stared into his dark eyes. What had happened to make him start calling her his love again? His moods confused her.

"I don't blame you," Samantha told him. "I learned never to step between fighting men."

"If you kiss it," Drake called, "she'll feel better."

Embarrassed, Samantha blushed and dropped her gaze to the carpet. Rudolf lifted her chin and planted a chaste kiss on her lips.

"Her cheek, Your Highness, not her lips," Drake called, making everyone laugh.

Rudolf leaned close again; his lips brushed her cheek. When she winced, he said, "You are in pain. I will never forgive myself."

Samantha didn't know what to say. She looked at the others. Her aunt was beaming, the duke was smiling, and her sister was giggling.

Dropping her gaze, Samantha realized the three of them wore formal evening attire. "Are you going somewhere?"

"We're going to the opera," her aunt answered.

"After that, we're going to Lady Mayhew's ball," Victoria added.

Samantha glanced at the prince. "I would like to go to the opera, too."

"I thought opera bored you," her sister said.

"Tory, you are the one who dislikes the opera," Samantha said.

"I despise the opera," Victoria said with enthusiasm, making the prince smile. "I do love the intermission, though."

"Darling, your eye is blackened and your cheek bruised," Aunt Roxie reminded her. "We don't want to invite speculation."

"What does that mean?"

"Your aunt means you will not be leaving this house until the bruise disappears," Rudolf said.

Samantha felt irritated. Was she a prisoner in the duke's house?

"What if the bruise is still there on April twenty-third?" Samantha asked.

"A veil will cover it nicely," the prince told her.

Samantha was relieved that oyster soup was not on the menu that evening. Tomato soup enriched with a swirl of cream and chopped green herbs was followed by dandelions dressed with morsels of bacon and a sharp vinaigrette, stewed mushrooms, and baked Dover sole.

Duke Magnus sat at the head of the table. On his left were Aunt Roxie, Grant, and Victoria. Samantha, Drake, and Rudolf sat on the opposite side.

"Angelica sent Mrs. Sweeting to help with the children," Aunt Roxie told her. "She's unpacking her bags now."

"Have you met Mrs. Sweeting?" Samantha asked the boys. When they nodded, she told them, "Sweeting was my nanny when I was a very little girl."

"Well, that explains why she's so old," Grant said, making everyone smile. He glanced at the duchess and added, "You won't believe this, but we didn't have table manners before."

"Is that so?" her aunt remarked.

"Lady Samantha gave them to us," Drake announced. "She taught us reading, too."

"His Highness taught us numbers," Grant told them.

"How did you meet the prince and my niece?" Aunt Roxie asked the ten-year-old.

"The boys went bent on highway robbery," Rudolf

answered, his voice filled with laughter. "Thinking we had struck the dog, we stopped the coach. The next thing we knew, the boys had materialized from nowhere and pointed pistols at us."

Samantha watched the prince as he spoke. He was so heartbreakingly handsome. She yearned for his love, and then she dropped her gaze to his hand on the stem of the goblet. Remembering his hands touching her body, she yearned for something else.

"Isn't that right, Princess?" Rudolf was saying.

Samantha snapped her gaze to his face. She felt the heated blush staining her cheeks and wondered if his smile meant he knew her thoughts. "I beg your pardon?" she said.

"Giles pretended to be injured," Rudolf went on.

Samantha dropped her gaze to his mouth as he spoke. She recalled where his lips had touched, and her breath came in shallow gasps.

"Darling, are you ill?" her aunt asked.

Samantha shifted her gaze from the prince to her aunt. "I beg your pardon?"

"You are behaving strangely tonight," Aunt Roxie remarked. "Are you ill?"

"People in love always act like that," Grant told the duchess.

"Lady Samantha loves His Highness," Drake added. "That's why she stares at him."

Samantha suffered the almost overpowering urge to crawl beneath the table. She heard her sister giggling, the duke coughing, and her aunt's murmured "Is that so?" The prince's reaction escaped her. She absolutely refused to look at him.

What could she do but sit there and blush in silence? She couldn't protest and announce that she didn't love her betrothed, the father of her unborn child. That would be too insulting to him. On the other hand, Rudolf didn't love her and hadn't wanted to marry. Her pregnancy had trapped them into a union.

Samantha did the only thing she could do. She changed the topic of conversation. "Prince Rudolf's daughter will be arriving in a few days," she told the boys. "I do hope you will be kind to Princess Zara and include her in your games."

"I'll play with her," Drake said. "I like girls."

"I like them, too, but they're stupid," Grant added.

"Why do you believe girls are stupid?" Aunt Roxie asked.

"Girls weep all the time," Grant answered. "Lady Samantha weeps whether she's happy or sad."

Again, Samantha felt a blush rising on her cheeks. She peeked at the prince. He was smiling at her.

"Do you mean that Lady Samantha is stupid?" the duchess asked.

"Yes," Grant said, and nodded.

"We love her anyway," Drake said, and smiled at Samantha.

"I'm glad I'm not His Highness," Grant said in a loud whisper, leaning close to the duchess. "It's his job to make her smile whenever she weeps."

"How does he do that?" Aunt Roxie asked.

"We don't know," Drake told her. "He takes her into the bedroom."

Everyone, including Prince Rudolf, laughed at that. Only Samantha remained silent. The joke was on her. She was about to become betrothed to a man who didn't love or want to marry her.

When dinner ended, they walked upstairs to the duke's office. On her way down, Mrs. Sweeting met them in the corridor and took the boys to their chamber. Intending to get her cloak, Victoria went with the boys.

Inside the duke's study, Samantha sat down in the chair in front of the desk. Her aunt sat down beside her.

"Your Highness, would you like to read this first?" Duke Magnus asked, handing him the contract.

Samantha watched the prince give the document a quick perusal and then sign. As her guardian, the duke signed and then handed her the document.

Wetting her lips gone dry from nervousness, Samantha began reading the document in order to delay signing. Once she'd affixed her name to the contract, she doubted she would ever be able to break it.

"Sign it, Princess," Rudolf said, standing beside her. "No matter what it says, you are pregnant and have no choice."

Without acknowledging his words, Samantha lifted the quill from his hands and signed the contract. Now she was well and truly trapped. She watched the duke and the prince shake hands. No one bothered to shake her hand.

"Your Highness, would you care to say good night to Grant and Drake?" Samantha asked, rising from her chair.

Instead of answering, Rudolf reach into his pocket and produced a tiny velvet-covered box. He opened it, removed a diamond ring, and placed it on the third finger of her left hand, saying, "Diamonds are priceless gems, and so are you, *ma lyoobof.*"

Samantha heard her aunt sighing. She looked up at the prince and, blushing, said in a soft voice, "Thank you for the ring and the thought."

In silence, Rudolf and Samantha climbed the stairs to the third floor. She was pregnant with the prince's child but didn't know how to make conversation with him. Strange, she hadn't had this problem in Scotland. Apparently, he had no wish to converse with her.

If only he loved me . . . If only he had wanted to marry me . . . If only I didn't limp.

Why was her life filled with if-onlys? No contentment was possible with if only.

"Thank God for a blessing," Samantha said, entering the boys' chamber. Grant spoke first. "Thank You for Lady Samantha and His Highness. Oh, and thank You for Mrs. Sweeting." Then he elbowed his brother.

"Thank You, Lord, for not serving me oyster soup," Drake said.

Samantha bit her lips to keep from laughing. She glanced at the prince, who was smiling. Both kissed the boys good night and left the chamber.

"Which chamber is yours?" Rudolf asked in the corridor.

Samantha pointed to the chamber at the end of the corridor. Surprising her, Rudolf reached for her hand and escorted her to her chamber.

"Which chamber is yours?" Samantha asked.

Rudolf grinned like a boy caught in a prank. "I have the next chamber," he answered. "I insisted on it." He lifted her hand to his lips and then apologized, "I am sorry for striking you this morning."

Samantha inclined her head. "It was an accident." As he started to turn away, she said, "May I ask you a question?"

Rudolf inclined his head.

"Will you become angry?"

"That depends on the question."

"Why have you changed?" she asked, hating the pleading note she heard in her own voice. When the prince gave her a puzzled smile, she realized he had no idea what she meant.

"You are not the man I knew in Scotland," Samantha told him, trying to explain without insulting him.

Rudolf cocked a dark brow at her. "Who am I?"

"I wouldn't wish to say," Samantha answered, dropping her gaze to the carpet.

Rudolf lifted her chin, and when she raised her gaze to his, he told her, "I am as I always was."

"You are behaving differently," Samantha said, shaking her head. "Your mood—"

"Any man forced into an unwanted marriage would be in a bad mood," Rudolf interrupted her.

His words broke her heart, but Samantha masked her pain with a placid expression. "Why are you trying to keep me a prisoner in this house?" she asked.

"I have learned to guard what is mine when Vladimir is close," Rudolf told her. "As my intended wife and the mother of my child, you belong to me."

Samantha balked at his words. "I belong to myself. I am not property."

"According to the law, a wife and children are the man's property," Rudolf informed her. "He can do whatever he wants with them. Within reason, of course."

"Your Highness, we are not standing in Russia," Samantha informed him in a lofty tone. "This is England—"

"The laws to which I refer are English," he said.

Samantha was startled. She'd had no idea that her homeland considered her some man's prospective property. Of course, since her deceased father had lost the Douglas fortune, she had lived a life of unusual freedom.

Samantha lifted her nose into the air and announced, "The law is an arse."

"The law is the law," Rudolf said. "And violet is purple." At that, the prince left her standing there and disappeared into his chamber.

Feeling dejected, Samantha walked into her bedchamber and closed the door. Tears sprang into her eyes and rolled down her cheeks. She wiped them away with the back of her hand.

Today had been the worst day of her life, excepting the day she'd been run over by the carriage. She hoped it wouldn't get worse.

Her turbulent emotions and pregnancy had taken a toll. As soon as she climbed into bed, she slipped into a deep, dreamless sleep.

When she awakened the following morning, Samantha felt better but a tad queasy. She yawned and stretched and rolled over.

On the bedside table lay a piece of bread on a plate. Sitting up, Samantha read the note beside the plate: *Eat this.* The note wasn't signed.

Samantha ate the bread and leaned back against the headboard. Who had sneaked into her chamber while she slept and left her the bread? Probably her aunt.

A short time later, the queasiness passed without the usual dry heaving. Eating bread must be beneficial.

Samantha rose from the bed and, finished with her morning ablutions, dressed in her white muslin gown. Then she left the chamber and limped down the corridor to the stairs. She hadn't felt this good in the morning for several weeks. Great Giles' ghost, she was even hungry.

Limping into the dining room, Samantha stopped short. Except for the majordomo, the chamber was empty. Her relations were probably sleeping in because of their late night, but she had expected to see the boys and the prince.

"Where is everyone?" Samantha asked, reaching the sideboard.

"The boys have already eaten," Tinker told her. "His Highness hasn't come down yet."

Samantha helped herself to a scoop of scrambled eggs with mushrooms, one slice of ham, and a roll. Then she spied the fried kippers and potatoes and reached for the serving spoon.

"I'm sorry, my lady," the majordomo said, "but you are not allowed to eat the kippers and potatoes."

Samantha laughed, unable to credit what he'd said. "Why?"

"His Highness gave me specific instructions about which foods are forbidden to you," Tinker answered.

Stunned speechless, Samantha could only stare at Tinker. The ogre was now dictating her menus? Not wishing to cause trouble for the majordomo, she inclined her head and sat down at the table.

Reaching for the *Times*, Samantha read while she ate. The gossip column on page three mentioned Lady Mayhew's ball and caught her attention. The more she read, the darker her morning grew.

Recently returned from the Continent, Prince Rudolf Kazanov appeared more handsome than ever to England's acclaimed beauties. Both matron and debutante simply swarmed around the prince all evening. But where is the prince's ebony-haired betrothed? Could the prince be reconsidering his offer? This reporter has it on good authority that Prince Rudolf has always favored blondes.

The son of a bitch, Samantha thought, tears welling up in her eyes. The prince had escorted her to her room and then changed into evening attire and attended Lady Mayhew's ball.

Pushing her plate away, Samantha covered her face with her hands. Her shoulders shook as she fought the silent sobs.

"Lady Samantha, are you ill?" Tinker asked, materializing beside her.

Unable to speak, Samantha shook her head and pointed at the newspaper. The majordomo leaned over the table and read the article.

"I would not believe this," Tinker told her. "If the reporter didn't write scintillating gossip, he would lose his job."

With tears streaming down her cheeks, Samantha looked at the majordomo. She knew he was lying but loved him for it.

Breaking every rule of etiquette, Tinker sat down at the table. "I meant to tell you an interesting story that happened while you were away," he said. "On their way to the opening of Parliament, the Regent and the prime minister rode together in the state coach drawn by eight white horses. Unfortunately, one of the horses closest to the coach was having a problem with digestive flatulence.

"At one point, the whole coach shook with the force of the flatulence. Both men were forced to cover their noses with their handkerchiefs.

"The Regent leaned close to the prime minister and said, 'You see, even a monarch cannot control some things.'

" 'Quite so,' replied the prime minister. 'If you hadn't said anything, I would have assumed it was one of the horses.' "

Samantha burst out laughing. Using her napkin, she wiped the tears off her face.

"I'll bring you a cup of tea," Tinker said.

"I prefer coffee."

"You aren't allowed coffee," he said. "Your condition, you know."

"Does the whole household know about my condition?" she asked.

"I'm afraid so," Tinker said, delivering the tea. "Please, my lady, eat a little bit more." Then he returned to stand near the sideboard.

Drawing her plate close, Samantha picked at the eggs and ate the roll without butter. A sound near the doorway drew her attention.

Prince Rudolf walked into the dining room. "Good morning, Princess," he said, passing her on the way to the highboard.

Samantha remained silent. She watched him scooping food onto a plate and pouring coffee into a cup. When he turned to face her, she dropped her gaze to the *Times*.

The prince sat down beside her, repeating, "I wished you a good morning."

"I'm sorry, Your Highness," Samantha said, looking at him. "Your good wishes come too late."

"What do you mean?" Rudolf asked.

"Simply this." Samantha set the newspaper between them and pointed at the article.

Rudolf read the article and then raised his black gaze to hers. His face was an expressionless mask. "This article ruined your morning?"

Irritated even more by his lack of emotion, Samantha said, "It has ruined my whole damned day."

The prince's placid expression faltered. She saw the angry glint in his eyes. He was angry with her?

"Do not speak disrespectfully to me," Rudolf said in a low voice.

"Or what?" Samantha asked, her voice rising with her anger. "Will you coerce me to flee to Scotland? Will you seduce the virginity out of me? Will you cry foul when your seed hits its mark, trapping you into an unwanted marriage?"

Samantha paused in her tirade to catch her breath. Only then did she notice his cheek muscles twitching and began to doubt her sanity in baiting him.

"I do not answer to you," Rudolf told her.

Samantha rose from her chair. With her head held high, she limped across the chamber to the door.

"Where are you going?" Rudolf demanded.

"Away from you."

"Do not leave this chamber," Rudolf ordered. "I have not dismissed you."

Samantha couldn't believe what she was hearing. She whirled around and told him, "You aren't my prince."

"I am your betrothed and will be your husband in a few days," Rudolf told her. "That means I am your master."

Samantha dropped her mouth open in surprise. Of all the unmitigated—

"I dislike eating alone," Rudolf said. "Sit down while I finish my breakfast."

Samantha lifted her chin. "Keeping you company is not part of the betrothal contract."

Rudolf smiled. "Obedience *is* part of the contract. Now, sit down."

With mutiny in her eyes, Samantha limped toward the dining room table. She didn't stop at the table, though, but went directly to the sideboard.

Grabbing a plate, Samantha filled it with a small mound of fried kippers and potatoes. Then she poured herself a cup of coffee.

Only then did Samantha sit down. She chose a seat across the table from the prince.

"You did not eat this breakfast," Rudolf said, looking at the plate of food in her hands. "Why are you eating a second one?"

Samantha answered by stuffing a large piece of fried

kipper into her mouth. She followed that with a potato and washed it down with coffee.

"You should not be eating that fried food," Rudolf told her.

"Menus weren't stipulated in the contract," Samantha replied. "I'll eat whatever I please."

The prince inclined his head and resumed eating his own meal. He read the newspaper as he ate but glanced in her direction every few minutes. Each time he looked at her, the prince gave her a smug smile.

Rebellion grew within Samantha. Though the newspaper article had stolen her appetite, she was determined to eat the small mountain of forbidden food on her plate.

Samantha kept her gaze fixed on the prince. Each time he glanced at her, she stuffed kippers and potatoes into her mouth.

Almost as soon as she'd forced the last piece of kipper down, an uncomfortable feeling, like the pitch and toss of a boat on waves, began in the pit of her stomach. It grew more pronounced with each passing moment.

Trying to calm herself, Samantha placed one hand on her belly and one hand on her throat. Why was the prince eating so slowly? she thought in distress. She needed to lie down and digest what she'd eaten. She needed to get out of there.

Prince Rudolf looked at her and tossed his napkin on the table. He stood then, saying, "You are dismissed."

Samantha leaped out of the chair and bolted, as fast as her limp would allow, out of the dining room. She prayed to make it to her third-floor bedchamber.

Prince Rudolf caught her outside the dining room doors. With one arm, he grabbed her around the waist while he reached for the enormous flower pot filled with silk flowers.

Rudolf tossed the flowers on the floor and pushed Samantha to her knees, holding her head over the empty pot. This time her gagging wasn't dry.

When her spasms ended, Samantha leaned against his legs and closed her eyes. Never had she been more mortified in her entire eighteen years.

Rudolf crouched down and wiped her mouth with his handkerchief. Then she felt him lifting her into his arms.

Hiding her face against his chest, Samantha began to weep. How could she hope to win his love if she vomited her breakfast in a flower pot. He'd been surrounded by society's acclaimed beauties, and she wasn't a blonde.

Rudolf easily carried her up the stairs to the third floor. He opened her chamber door with his foot and gently placed her on the bed.

Samantha looked at him through blue eyes that mirrored her misery. A sob escaped her.

Sitting on the edge of the bed, Rudolf reached out and brushed her hair off her face. "Are you feeling better now?" he asked.

"Yes, thank you."

"I gave Tinker instructions because I know which foods will sicken you," Rudolf explained.

"How do you know this?" she asked.

"I have been through this before," he answered. "Do you feel weak?"

Samantha nodded.

Rudolf leaned close, dropped a chaste kiss on her forehead, and then stood. "I promise if you sleep now, you will feel much better when you awaken."

Samantha watched him leave. That kiss on her forehead had seemed almost paternal, and his demands on her contained a pinch of parental discipline. Why was he treating her like a child? Was he trying to distance himself from her?

Later that afternoon, Samantha sat with Mrs. Sweeting and the boys in the drawing room. The prince had spoken truthfully. After napping for two hours, she had felt much better. He had known what would happen and let her eat that food anyway. She sighed. Perhaps he had known that she needed to learn the lesson the hard way.

Two difficult lessons in two days. She doubted she would survive the summer.

"Angelica is having the baby," Victoria cried, rushing into the drawing room. "Aunt Roxie went to help the midwife. Imagine, we'll be aunts."

"Did Aunt Roxie say how long it would take?" Samantha asked.

Victoria shook her head. "I suppose this means I'm trapped in the house tonight," she said.

Samantha smiled at her. "Why don't you read a good book?"

"Very funny, you know I hate to read." Her sister turned to the boys, asking, "How about a game of hide and seek?"

"Sweeting, I'm going to my sister's house," Samantha said, rising from the chair. "Perhaps I can be of some small service there."

Samantha left the drawing room and, after fetching her cloak, went downstairs to the foyer. She wanted to leave a message for the prince, but Tinker was nowhere in sight.

Leaving the house, Samantha limped down the street in the direction of the marquess's house, two doors down. Suddenly, a hand grabbed her arm and whirled her around.

"I told you not to leave the house," Rudolf said, his anger apparent. "Where were you going?"

"My sister is having her baby," Samantha explained, and pointed to the mansion two doors down. "She lives right there."

Rudolf relaxed. He looked over his shoulder at Karl, gesturing his man away. "I will accompany you."

Webster, the marquess's majordomo, opened the door for them. He smiled, recognizing Samantha.

"Is the marquess home?" Rudolf asked the man. "I would visit him while my fiancée is helping her sister."

"I'll show you to his office . . ."

". . . His Highness," Samantha supplied.

"Your Highness, the marquess will be glad for your company," Webster said. He looked at Samantha, adding, "I believe you know the way."

Samantha nodded, climbed the stairs, and then limped down the corridor toward her sister's chamber. She heard moaning, which grew louder with each step forward.

Reaching the closed bedchamber door, Samantha stood in the corridor in indecision. She didn't think she could bear to see her sister in pain.

Samantha summoned her courage and opened the door just as her sister screamed. The midwife was feeling her sister's belly.

"It will be hours before the babe arrives," the midwife told her aunt. "She's so big. I'm wondering if there are two inside her."

"Should I send for the doctor?" Aunt Roxie asked.

"There's no need for that yet," the woman said. Then she asked, "Who is that?"

"What are you doing here?" Aunt Roxie asked.

Samantha fixed her gaze on her sister caught in the midst of a contraction. "I thought I could help."

Aunt Roxie grabbed her arm and guided her toward

the door. She pushed her outside, saying, "You'll help us by staying out of our way." The door clicked shut.

Samantha sat on the Grecian chaise in the corridor and stared at the closed door. The sound of her sister's screams pierced the house's silence and echoed in Samantha's mind.

A maid appeared with steaming water and towels. She knocked on the door and handed the bucket to Aunt Roxie, who leaned close to the girl to whisper in her ear. Then the maid disappeared again.

Rudolf appeared several minutes later, sat beside her on the chaise, and put his arm around her. "Your aunt told the maid you needed me," he said. "What is wrong?"

Samantha looked from the closed bedchamber door to the prince and said, "I am afraid."

CHAPTER 14

She is young, Rudolf realized. His betrothed had the stunned look of a fledgling warrior after his first battle. At the age of twenty-eight, he had forgotten how inexperienced an eighteen-year-old woman could be.

Rudolf put his arm around her and gently drew her close. "Are you afraid of me?" he asked.

Samantha shook her head.

That was good, Rudolf thought, relieved. Then he asked, "What do you fear, *ma lyoobof?*"

Before she could answer, her sister let out a piercing shriek. Samantha dropped her hand to her belly and glanced at the closed bedchamber door.

Rudolf knew then what she feared but asked, "Tell me what you fear, *ma lyoobof.*"

Samantha gazed at him through enormous blue eyes that mirrored her near panic. "I have experience with pain," she answered. "I am afraid to give birth."

"There is nothing to fear," Rudolf said, brushing his lips across her temple.

"That doesn't sound like nothing to me," she said, making him smile.

"When your time comes, I will hire the best midwife and physician in England," Rudolf assured her.

"Will you stay with me?" she asked.

"If that is what you wish, Princess." She trusted him, Rudolf thought. In spite of his harsh words, she trusted him to keep her safe. Taking away the pain of childbirth was impossible. If he could purchase her an easy labor, he would spend a fortune for it. Her fear could only make the ordeal worse.

"You should not be listening to your sister's labor," Rudolf said, helping her off the chaise. "Let us go home."

Samantha nodded. Arm in arm, they walked downstairs and returned to the duke's mansion.

Entering the foyer, Rudolf guided her toward the stairs, saying, "I think you should rest."

Upstairs, Rudolf opened her bedchamber door and followed her inside. If he could distract her, her sister's cries would be only a vague, unpleasant memory in the morning.

"Sit here," Rudolf said, gesturing to the bed. He walked into her dressing chamber and returned with one of her nightshifts. "Let me unbutton your gown."

"Is this proper?" she asked.

Rudolf grinned. "I promise you won't get pregnant."

Samantha smiled and turned around. She felt his hands on her gown, and then he ran a finger the length of her back, sending delicious shivers down her spine.

"Turn around," he whispered.

When she obeyed, the prince drew her gown down, and she stepped out of it. He leaned close and kissed her lips and the delicate column of her throat. At the same time, he pushed her chemise down until she stood in her stockings and lace garters.

Entwining her arms around his neck, Samantha pressed herself against him. She wanted him, needed him.

Rudolf kissed her again, lifted her into his arms, and placed her on the bed. He lay down beside her and ran his hand down her body from her throat to the juncture of her thighs.

"Your breasts are beautiful, *ma lyoobof*," Rudolf whispered. "Pregnancy has darkened your nipples."

He dipped his head, his mouth slashing across hers. And she responded, returning his kiss in kind.

"Take off your clothes," Samantha whispered.

Rudolf smiled and slid his hand to the secret place between her thighs. He dropped his head and flicked his tongue across the tip of her nipple. His fingers found her wet, swollen nub and stroked it until she cried out in ecstasy and clung to him.

When her spasms ended, Rudolf kissed her again. Then he sat up and reached for her nightshift. "I do not feel comfortable taking you beneath your guardian's roof without benefit of marriage."

He pulled the bed's coverlet back and gestured for her to slide beneath it. "Once we are married, *ma lyoobof*, I will take you to Sark Island. We will make love for hours, all day and all night if you want."

Samantha smiled drowsily at the thought. Perhaps the prince did care for her. She grabbed his hand and asked, "Will you take me to Sweetheart Manor, too? I was happy there."

"I will take you wherever you want," Rudolf told her. "Sleep now. I will instruct Cook to send up a light supper. I will eat with the boys and listen to their prayers."

"Don't leave me yet," Samantha said.

With a smile on his lips, Rudolf sat down on the bed and leaned against the headboard. He drew her into his arms, saying, "I will hold you until you sleep."

Samantha rested her head against his shoulder and

laid her arm across his body. She closed her eyes and sighed with contentment.

Rudolf planted a chaste kiss on the crown of her head. He stroked her back soothingly until she became a dead weight against him and her hand on his body dropped away.

Gingerly, Rudolf slid from beside her and gently lay her back on the bed. He pulled the coverlet up, leaned close, and kissed her forehead without awakening her. Instead of leaving the bedchamber, Rudolf stood for several minutes and stared down at her.

He loved her, which did not make him particularly happy. After four years of steering clear of marriage and emotional entanglements, he'd done the unthinkable without realizing it. Now it was too late; he'd fallen in love and trapped himself into a marriage.

Samantha loved him now, but how long would her love survive when she learned the truth about him? He was a prince but not what he appeared to the world. His whole life had been a lie. If only he could share the truth with her. If he did that, she would look with revulsion on him. How long would it be before Vladimir appeared and tossed the truth into her face? His brother was perfectly capable of ruining other people's lives in order to get what he wanted.

He should reveal himself to her before that happened, Rudolf thought. On the other hand, what use would that be? She was already pregnant and had no choice but to marry him.

When she awakened the next morning, Samantha was in a better frame of mind. Her sister's cries of pain seemed like a bad dream. Besides, the prince did care about her. She dropped her hand to her belly and decided she could bear the pain. What mattered was giving the prince a child and making him happy.

"Watch what a man does, not what he says."

Samantha recalled her aunt's words. If he didn't care just a little, the prince would have disregarded her fears. Instead, he'd held her until she slept. Perhaps the prince had not wanted to marry her, but he would be a good husband. She would be the best wife ever.

Rolling over, Samantha spied the bread her aunt had left on the table. She sat up, leaned against the headboard, and ate the bread. After resting there for fifteen minutes to allow the bread to do its magic, she rose and dressed.

Samantha limped into the dining room a short time later. Victoria was just finishing her breakfast.

Her sister looked up when she entered and smiled. "Good morning, *Aunt* Samantha," she said, and then held up two fingers. "We are the proud aunts of a boy and a girl."

"Angel had twins?" Samantha said, limping to the sideboard.

"Douglas and Amber Campbell," Victoria said, rising to leave. "I suppose this will be the year for babies."

After her sister had gone, Samantha lifted a plate off the sideboard and dropped onto it a spoonful of scrambled eggs, a lean piece of ham, and a roll with no butter. Then she grabbed the *Times* and sat at the table.

"Excuse my boldness, my lady," Tinker said, standing beside her. "Your breakfast isn't enough to sustain a flea. Please, take a little more."

"I am fine as I am," she told him.

"As you wish," Tinker said, and set a cup of tea beside her plate.

Eating a leisurely breakfast alone was pleasant, but

she'd much prefer eating with the prince. As if her thoughts had conjured the man, Prince Rudolf walked into the dining room. She smiled and set the newspaper aside when he wished her a good morning. Speaking was definitely a more appealing pastime than reading the newspaper.

Without bothering to go to the sideboard, Rudolf set a portfolio down on the table and then sat beside her. He leaned close and planted a kiss on her cheek, making her blush.

"How do you feel this morning?" Rudolf asked.

"Much better, thank you," Samantha answered. "Angelica has delivered twins, a boy and a girl."

Rudolf smiled. "That is excellent news. If I have time later, we will go to Bond Street and purchase gifts for them. When you visit her, I am certain she will be so happy with her babies that the pain of bringing them into the world will be forgotten."

"Excuse me, Your Highness," Tinker said. "May I serve you something from the sideboard?"

Rudolf nodded. "I will have whatever Lady Samantha is having."

Tinker returned within mere seconds and set a plate down in front of the prince. On the plate sat a teaspoon of scrambled egg, a contemptibly small slice of ham, and a roll with no butter.

Rudolf looked at the plate and raised his gaze to the majordomo. Tinker responded by raising his brows and then looking at Samantha.

"Samantha, you need more food than this," Rudolf said. He turned to the majordomo, instructing the man, "Bring us two plates of eggs, ham slices, rolls, and butter."

"No kippers, Your Highness?"

The prince shook his head, his lips quirking into a smile. He burst out laughing when the man turned to Samantha, asking, "Fried kippers, my lady?"

Blushing with embarrassment, Samantha shook her head and said, "I'll have the kippers another time, probably in a decade or two."

Within moments, Tinker returned and set the new plates down in front of them. Turning to walk away, the majordomo smiled in triumph at her.

"Thank you, Tinker," Samantha said, acknowledging his victory to get her to eat more.

Without a word to her, Rudolf opened the portfolio and began to read the first page. Samantha watched him while he ate and read. The prince was easily the handsomest man she'd ever seen, and he cared for her enough to want to ease her fears.

Caring wasn't love, but perhaps a good beginning. At least, he wasn't growling at her.

Now that the prince sat beside her, Samantha decided that her appetite had returned. She didn't want to disturb the prince at his work, so she turned to the *Times* and began to read. The society column caught her attention again.

> *Prince Rudolf Kazanov, recently returned from the Continent, was seen at several balls. Among them were Lady Wesley's and the Countess of Bedford's. Needless to say, the ladies—all blondes—swarmed the dashingly handsome prince. Where, oh where, could his little betrothed be hiding?*

Full-bodied jealousy swelled in Samantha's breast, and outraged anger swept through her. Slowly, she rose from her chair and said, "Tinker, could you please leave us. Close the door on your way out."

With a quizzical expression, Rudolf looked up from his papers. "Is something wrong?" he asked.

"How could you?" Samantha burst out.

Rudolf glanced at the newspaper and said, "Explain yourself."

"You rotten bastard," Samantha said, anger blinding her to his slight flinch. "You made love to me and then left to continue your social life."

"You misunderstand," Rudolf said mildly. "Sit down and finish your breakfast."

He wasn't even taking her seriously, Samantha realized, which only made her angrier. She stared at him unwaveringly, though her bottom lip quivered with her supreme effort to hold her tears back.

"I may be a pathetic cripple to you and that reporter, but I am not stupid," Samantha told him.

When she turned to leave, Rudolf grabbed her left wrist, saying, "I do not think you are—"

Wham! Samantha closed her right fist and punched him, hitting him in the same spot he'd hit her.

Obviously stunned, Rudolf could only stare at her in silence. Though injured, he never raised his hand to his face.

Samantha stared at him in horrified silence and then began to shake. She'd struck him. Even now she could see the bruise forming on his cheekbone and beneath his eye.

Samantha limped out of the dining room and went to her chamber. Losing her battle with tears, she lay on the bed and wept.

How could she have been fooled by the prince again? Hadn't he said he didn't want to marry her? She was exactly what the reporter implied—pathetic. God, how everyone must be laughing at her.

"Watch what a man does, not what he says."

Her aunt's advice came back to haunt her. Except for the day in the duke's study, the prince had spoken kindly to her. His actions were not so kind. He had continued his life as if she didn't exist. Which of those ladies who had swarmed him at Emerson's ball last June had clung to him at Lady Mayhew's or Lady Wesley's?

Samantha knew one thing for sure. She could not live the remainder of her life like this. She would be insane before the end of the year.

Bang! Bang! Bang!

Samantha ignored the knocking on her door. She knew who it was. Great Giles' ghost, how could she have struck him? The prince would exact his revenge somehow. Her only intelligent move had been to order the servants from the room before she slugged him.

"Samantha!"

She might as well get this over with, Samantha decided, sliding off the bed. She crossed the chamber and called, "Yes?"

"May I come inside?" Rudolf asked. The door opened before she could answer, and he walked into the room.

Samantha stared at the bruise rising on his handsome face. Hoping to escape whatever punishment he was about to deal her, she said, "I apologize for striking you. You probably won't believe this, but before I met you, I had never struck anyone in my entire life."

"I believe you," Rudolf said, reaching out a hand to her.

"I'm very tired," Samantha said, stepping back a pace. "Could you possibly punish me later?"

The prince stared at her, his lips quirking at her outrageous request. Samantha did not see that because she kept her gaze fixed on the carpet.

"I never meant to hurt your feelings," Rudolf told her.

"You didn't," she said, too proud to admit he'd hurt her. "Even if you did, I know you never meant it."

The prince relaxed, saying, "Princess—"

"I am not your princess," Samantha told him. "You never wanted to marry again, and my pregnancy forced you into this. Perhaps there is another solution to our dilemma."

Rudolf folded his arms across his chest. His gaze on her made her nervous.

"The problem is you don't want to marry, but you want this child born on the correct side of the blanket, so to speak," Samantha said. "I'll send Alexander Emerson a note. He was still willing to marry—"

His hands shot out, and Rudolf yanked her against his hard, unyielding body. "Do *not* even consider that, or I will be forced to kill him."

Samantha stared at him through her enormous blue eyes, wide with fear. She had no doubt he would do it, too.

Rudolf released her and shoved his hands in his pockets as if he didn't trust himself not to harm her. "Zara will be arriving this afternoon. Will you take your anger out on her?"

"Do you actually believe I would be unkind to her?" Samantha asked, offended.

Rudolf gave her a grudging smile. "No, I trust you with my daughter."

"I'm very tired," she said, glancing toward the door.

"I'll leave you then." He moved to kiss her, but she stepped back.

Samantha stared at the door after he'd gone. He left her depleted of energy, and her damned hip hurt.

That late March afternoon felt more like the beginning of May. The warmth of those early spring days fooled the forsythia bushes, which had begun to open their yellow flowers.

Holding her cane in front of her, Samantha sat with Mrs. Sweeting on the stone bench in the garden. The boys were tossing a ball around the garden in a rousing game of keep the ball away from Giles.

"Lady Samantha, won't you play with us?" Drake called.

"I'll watch today."

"We'll let you be on Giles' side," Grant said, trying to entice her.

Samantha laughed. "I don't think so."

Drake walked over to her, looked at the cane, and then into her eyes. "Do you hurt today?"

"My hip is a bit tired," Samantha admitted.

Offering his own brand of comfort, the eight-year-old put his arms around her neck and kissed her cheek. Then he turned to the elderly nanny.

"Sweeting, if you play with us, I'll let you be on my side," Drake said.

The woman laughed. "That is very appealing, but don't you think I'm too old to run around the garden?"

Drake shook his head. "You're still young."

"Thank you, child," Sweeting said. "If I ran around the garden, I would need to borrow Samantha's cane. What would she use?"

"I'll ask the prince to buy another cane," he answered.

Samantha glanced toward the door. Rudolf stood there, holding his daughter's hand.

With a smile on her lips, Samantha rose from the bench and limped toward them. "Hello, Zara. You are very welcome here."

The little princess smiled but clung to her father's

hand. With pale blond hair and blue eyes, she looked nothing like her father.

Samantha raised her gaze to the prince, but he was staring at the cane. She gave her attention to the girl again, saying, "I have some friends I would like you to meet."

"Are you in pain?" Rudolf asked.

"My hip feels tired today."

"Carrying the child will not be good for your hip," he told her.

"I will be fine," she assured him.

"I'm Drake," said a voice beside her. "My name means dragon."

"My name is Grant," another voice said. "It means great."

The boys stood on either side of Samantha and stared at the princess. "That lady over there is Sweeting," Grant said. "She'll make you wash behind your ears."

"The beastie is Giles," Drake told the princess. "He likes to lick faces. What's your name?"

When the girl remained silent, Rudolf said, "Tell them your name."

"Zara."

"What does it mean?" Drake asked.

"Zara means princess," Rudolf told them.

"Drake and Grant are playing ball," Samantha said. "Would you like to play with them?"

Zara shook her head and tightened her grip on her father's hand. "My daughter is unused to playmates."

"How sad," Samantha said. To the boys, she said, "Continue your game, and Zara will join you later." She held out her hand to the girl, asking, "Would you like to sit on that bench with me?"

Zara looked at her father and then at Samantha. For

one awful moment, Samantha thought she would refuse, but then she released her father's hand.

Together, Samantha and Zara crossed the garden toward the bench. "Sit here between Sweeting and me," she said to the girl. "Tell me, what games do you like to play?"

When Zara remained silent, Samantha rambled on, "When the weather is warm, I like to lie on my back and watch the clouds make pictures in the sky. Does that appeal to you?"

Zara smiled and nodded her head.

Samantha glanced toward the door. With a worried expression, the prince still stood there and watched. She couldn't fault him for that, though. The girl was all he had left of his beloved wife.

"I love to smell the flowers in the spring and plant a butterfly garden," Samantha told the girl. "When summer arrives, I listen for the flower fairies and roll down the grassy sides of hills. Once the leaves of autumn fall from the trees, I love to play in them. Sometimes, I even toss a handful into the air. Whenever it rains, I sit in front of the hearth and play my violin."

"What about winter?" Zara asked.

"When winter comes," Samantha said with a smile, "I make angels in the snow. Did you ever do any of those things?"

"No, but I would," Zara said.

The deerhound chose that moment to appear in front of the girl. He sat at attention and lifted a paw into the air.

"Giles is pleased to meet you and would like to shake your hand," Samantha told her.

Zara gave her a nervous smile and then touched the dog's paw. "I am pleased to meet you, Giles."

Samantha glanced toward the door again. Rudolf

had disappeared inside the mansion. Apparently, she had passed the test of caring for his daughter.

Before an hour passed, Grant and Drake had charmed the princess into playing with them. Samantha smiled as she watched them let the girl win every game. Soon the three of them lost interest in the ball and just gamboled around the garden.

"Take them inside for a snack now," Samantha instructed the nanny.

Sweeting stood and called to the children, saying, "Come along now. We are going inside for cider and cookies."

Standing on either side of the girl, Grant and Drake took her hands in theirs. "Cook makes the best gingerbread cookies," Grant told her.

"You need to hold the cookie high," Drake advised her. "If you don't, Giles will steal it right out of your hand."

Followed by Sweeting, the children went inside. Only the deerhound remained in the garden. Giles sat beside her and rested his head on her lap.

"You want your share of love, too," Samantha said, stroking the dog's head. When she looked down at the dog, she noted that her star ruby had darkened. Or was it a trick of the afternoon light?

Enjoying the feeling of the sun's warmth, Samantha closed her eyes as she stroked the dog's head. Suddenly, the deerhound growled.

"Good afternoon, my lady," a heavily accented voice said.

Samantha opened her eyes. Tall and well built, a gentleman stood there. His black hair reminded her of someone she couldn't quite place, but his blue eyes were cold and his mouth cruelly shaped.

"Giles, relax," Samantha ordered. The deerhound stopped growling but kept its gaze riveted on the stranger.

"Sir, this is private property," Samantha told him. "For whom were you looking?"

"This is the Duke of Inverary's home, is it not?" the man asked, ignoring her question.

Samantha nodded. "Who are you?"

"Prince Vladimir Kazanov," he introduced himself, and bowed to her.

Samantha tightened her grip on the cane, and her eyes widened with her surprise. She opened her mouth to order him away, but he spoke first.

"I see that you recognize my name," the prince said. "And you are?"

"Samantha Douglas."

"Ah, my brother's next victim," Vladimir said. "I would like to speak to you."

Samantha stared him straight in the eye. "Speak and then leave."

Vladimir inclined his head. "I am willing to pay you a great amount of money if you will help me with a minor family matter."

"And that would be?"

"I want you to steal the Kazanov Venus for me," he told her. "It is—"

"I know what it is," Samantha interrupted. "I cannot be bought, Your Highness."

"That medallion is my birthright," he said, stepping closer.

Giles growled and stood, ready to lunge at the prince.

"Sit, Giles." Samantha rose from the bench and, at the same time, twisted the top of her cane off. She pointed the stiletto at the prince. "Your retainers tried to kill me." She stepped closer to him, and he took a step back.

"I do apologize for that misunderstanding," he said.

"You don't sound sorry," she told him.

"Vladimir." Rudolf marched across the garden to

confront his brother. "Stay away from my family, or I will kill you."

"I heard you were looking for me," Vladimir said, his smile not quite reaching his eyes.

"My business with you has nothing to do with my family," Rudolf told him.

"Beware of my brother," Vladimir said, looking at Samantha. "I cannot understand why you would be loyal to a—"

"Leave this garden now," Rudolf interrupted, "and stay away from my family."

Vladimir looked from Rudolf to Samantha and then laughed. "She doesn't know? My dear, your betrothed has secrets."

"I am not your dear," Samantha told him.

"If you change your mind, I am staying at Montague House," he said, and then left the garden.

"What did he want?" Rudolf asked.

"He wanted me to steal the Kazanov Venus," Samantha answered, returning the stiletto to the cane. "What is it that I don't know?"

"Nothing, Vladimir is intent on causing trouble," Rudolf said.

Samantha knew he was lying. "Why don't you trust me?"

"I trust no one," he answered.

"Why do you want to marry a woman you don't trust?" Samantha asked.

"I don't want to marry you," Rudolf told her, his voice cold with contempt. "I want to save my child from the stigma of bastardy."

Samantha felt as if she'd been kicked in the stomach. She stepped back a pace and took a deep breath. Without a word, she limped toward the door, calling over her shoulder, "Come, Giles."

* * *

Too hurt to face the prince across a table, Samantha ate a lonely meal in her own chamber. She did, however, emerge briefly to say good night to the boys and the prince's daughter.

When she walked into the little girl's chamber, Samantha stopped short. Rudolf was there, sitting on the edge of the bed. She would have backed out of the room, but the girl spied her.

"Lady Samantha," Zara called.

Pasting a smile onto her face, Samantha limped across the room to the bed. "I wanted to wish you a good night."

"Daddy is telling me a story," Zara told her. "Do you want to hear it, too?"

"No, thank you, but I would like a good night kiss," Samantha said. "May I have one?"

When the girl nodded, Samantha leaned close and kissed her cheek. "Will you play with me tomorrow?"

Zara nodded. "Will we watch the cloud pictures?"

"We will do whatever you want. Good night." She turned to leave and limped toward the door, calling, "Sweeting, sleep in here tonight."

"Samantha," the prince called.

Pretending deafness, Samantha left the chamber. She did not want to listen to anything the prince had to say.

When she awakened the next morning, Samantha rolled over and reached for the slice of bread her aunt had left there. A short time later, she limped into the dining room, expecting to see the children. Instead, she saw the prince sitting alone and reading the papers in his portfolio while he ate.

"Good morning," Rudolf said as she passed him on the way to the sideboard.

"Good morning," Samantha said without looking at him.

At the sideboard, Samantha selected two hard-boiled eggs, a scone, and vanilla jelly. Then she grabbed the *Times* and turned around. Indecision gripped her. Where should she sit? Next to the prince or not?

Deciding that sitting away from the prince would be churlish, Samantha set her plate on the table beside the prince's. Then she sat down and began reading the newspaper.

"I wish you would not read that anymore," Rudolf said.

Samantha looked at him, which was a mistake. The sight of his handsome face tugged at her heart. Without replying to him, she began eating her breakfast and reading the newspaper. Again, the society column on page three caught her attention.

> *Prince Rudolf was seen with several acclaimed beauties at the opera last night. Where is his betrothed? When will she return to London?*

"Why didn't you escort me to the opera?" Samantha asked.

"You have a black eye," Rudolf said.

"So do you." Samantha turned in her chair to look at him. "Does your betrothal to me embarrass you?"

"If you have finished your breakfast," he said, glancing at her empty plate, "you are dismissed."

That didn't sit well with Samantha. "I will not be dismissed," she told him. "I refuse to leave because you order it."

"Then, I will," Rudolf said, gathering his papers together.

Samantha sat in stunned silence and watched him leave. Her pain was tangible, making breathing difficult.

Too humiliated to look at Tinker, Samantha limped out of the dining room and went directly to her chamber. She lay on her bed and wept until her body had drained of tears.

CHAPTER 15

She missed him.

Rudolf avoided her almost completely after that morning. No matter what time she went to breakfast, he wasn't there. During the day, the prince used the duke's study to conduct his business affairs. Sometimes when she sat with the children in the garden, Samantha felt him watching her. Whenever she looked toward the window, he stepped away.

Dinner was the only time Samantha actually saw him. Immediately after dinner, Rudolf excused himself and left the mansion.

Samantha did know what the prince was doing, though. Each morning she read about his social life in the *Times*. One evening Rudolf attended several balls. Another evening saw him at the opera. A third evening caught him having an intimate supper with a certain flame-haired actress who was London's latest rage.

By the end of the second week, Samantha couldn't bear the pain another moment. She missed the man she had known in Scotland and wanted him back.

Unlike her sisters, she had never in her entire life taken the initiative, but she needed to do something soon.

Arguing and nagging would do her no good. She needed to assume a casual attitude and pretend she didn't care.

Exactly two weeks before her wedding, Samantha stood in front of the closed study door. The prince was working inside.

Samantha felt queasy at the thought of walking into the study and talking to him. Her heart pounded frantically, and her hands shook as though she had the palsy.

Closing her eyes, Samantha took a deep breath. Then she raised her hand and knocked before she could lose her courage.

"Enter," she heard the prince call.

Samantha pasted a smile on her face and opened the door. He watched her limp across the study. Reaching the desk, she was relieved to see two of his ships' captains sitting in the high-backed chairs. The prince couldn't very well refuse her in front of his employees. No, he would be especially polite with strangers listening.

"The children and I are picnicking in the garden for lunch and—" He was staring at her so coldly, she stopped speaking. She suffered the almost overpowering urge to bolt from the room.

"And?" the prince said.

"I thought you might want to join us," Samantha said, her fright making her breathless.

"You can see that I am busy," Rudolf replied, gesturing to his desk.

"You need to eat lunch," she pressed him.

"No."

"You aren't eating lunch?"

Rudolf fixed his black gaze on hers. "Please, leave me to my work," he said in an irritated voice.

Fright and humiliation paralyzed her. Samantha wanted to leave, but her feet wouldn't move.

"Damn it, get the hell out of this room and stay out," Rudolf ordered.

Samantha flushed, her humiliation complete. "I'm sorry I interrupted," she apologized.

Without looking at the captains, Samantha limped out of the study and closed the door behind her. Trying to calm herself, she leaned against the wall.

"My lady, are you ill?" Tinker asked, materializing from nowhere.

"Yes," Samantha said in a small voice. She had never felt worse in her life. "I just need a moment."

Closing her eyes, Samantha took deep breaths in an effort to calm herself. In the next instant, her eyes flew open when she realized the majordomo had opened the study door and was calling, "Your Highness, Lady Samantha—"

"No!" she cried.

"What in hell is going on out there?" Rudolf asked.

"Lady Samantha is ill," Tinker told him.

Samantha turned her back on the door. Holding onto the wall, she took three steps down the corridor.

"What is the problem?" Rudolf asked, his hand on her arm, holding her steady.

His question surprised her. The prince had just humiliated her beyond endurance, and the problem eluded him?

"I'll help you to your chamber," the prince said.

Samantha lifted her gaze from his hand on her arm to his dark gaze and ordered, "Remove your hand from my person."

Rudolf snapped his brows together. "What did you say?"

"Don't touch me." She looked at the majordomo, asking, "Where is my aunt?"

"Her Grace is in the drawing room," Tinker answered.

"Is His Grace with her?" she asked.

"Yes."

"If you will excuse me," she said, looking at the prince.

"I will not excuse you," Rudolf said, tightening his grip on her arm.

Samantha raised her voice. "You are dismissed, Your Highness."

Something flickered in his dark eyes. Almost immediately, he masked his feelings.

"If that is pity I see in your eyes," Samantha told him, "I will shoot you with one of the duke's pistols. By the way, the wedding is off."

"The wedding is *not* off."

"I won't marry you," Samantha cried brokenly, losing control. "They can't force me to the altar. If you want a wife, marry that actress."

"For God's sake," Rudolf swore, lifting her into his arms. "Don't fight me." Turning to carry her upstairs, he ordered the majordomo, "Tell Her Grace that her niece is hysterical and needs her in her bedchamber."

"Put me down," Samantha said when they reached the second floor. "I want to go to the drawing room."

Rudolf paused and then set her on her feet. When he put his arm around her, she turned on him, insisting, "I am not hysterical."

"What are you, then?"

"I am furious and embarrassed," Samantha said. "Don't ever treat me so disrespectfully again. If you do, I swear I'll kill you."

Samantha shrugged his hand off. Turning away, she walked down the corridor to the drawing room.

"Darling, whatever is the matter?" Aunt Roxie asked.

"I need to speak privately with both of you," she said.

"Sit here beside me," her aunt invited her, patting the settee.

Samantha sat down and folded her hands in her lap. She didn't know how to start this discussion without upsetting them.

"Tell us what is bothering you," Duke Magnus said, his voice kind. "If it is within my power, I will fix it."

Samantha looked at him and then her aunt. "I want—no, need—to cancel the wedding."

"I can't do that," the duke said. "You are already with child."

"You care for the prince, darling," her aunt said. "I know you care for him a great deal."

"The prince does not care for me," Samantha said.

"He does care for you," her aunt disagreed. "Your relationship is progressing nicely."

"We don't have a relationship," Samantha told her. "He hasn't spoken to me in two weeks."

"I told you to watch—"

"Damn it, I did watch," Samantha interrupted her. "The prince took himself to several balls, an opera, and supper with an actress."

Aunt Roxie laughed. "Darling, that's a good sign."

Samantha stared in horror at her aunt. She couldn't believe what her aunt was saying. The woman was as crazy as the prince.

"Prince Rudolf is fighting his feelings for you," Aunt Roxie told her.

"His feelings are losing," Samantha said. "He just humiliated me in front of two of his captains." She turned to the duke and pleaded, "Please, Your Grace, cancel the wedding."

"I'll speak to him about his behavior," Duke Magnus said.

"I don't want you to do that," Samantha cried. "I want you to cancel the wedding."

"Think of your baby," the duke tried to reason with her.

"I am thinking of my baby," she said. "The man hasn't even bothered to ask me how I am feeling in two weeks."

"Do you care so little for our child that you would refuse to give him his father's name?" Rudolf asked, standing in the doorway.

"How long have you been eavesdropping?"

"Long enough to know what you are asking the duke."

Samantha rose slowly from the settee and gave her aunt a quelling look. Then she limped across the drawing room toward the door. She would find no help here.

"Your guardians are only doing what is best for you," Rudolf said as she passed him.

"You are *not* what is best for me, sir."

"I am sorry to hear that, Princess," Rudolf said in a quiet voice. "I was hoping to attend your picnic."

Samantha gazed into his dark eyes. He was patronizing her because she was pregnant. The prince felt sorry for her. Being pitied was an old friend whom she would recognize anywhere.

"The picnic has been canceled."

Rudolf cocked a dark brow at her. "Why?"

"Lack of interest."

Raising her chin a notch, Samantha left the drawing

room and climbed the stairs to her bedchamber. She locked the door and sat on the chaise.

I should never have gone into the study and forced the issue, Samantha thought. The prince did not want to marry her, nor did he love her. He had shown her that in dozens of different ways since returning to London. He tolerated her for what she carried within her body. She suffered the awful suspicion that she was about to marry the prince and live alone.

Not quite alone, Samantha reminded herself. She had Grant, Drake, and Zara to love as well as the baby she carried.

Samantha smiled without humor. Her family life would be a distortion of her dream. God had found a way to torment her with what she wanted. She should have been more careful what she wished for.

If she wasn't such a coward, Samantha thought, she would pack her bag and run away. But how could she abandon Grant and Drake? They'd already had one mother abandon them.

Bang! Bang! Bang!

Samantha knew who stood outside her door. The prince had come to reprimand her disrespect in front of others. With a defeated sigh, she rose from the chaise and limped to the door.

"Who is it?" she asked.

"May I come inside?" the prince asked.

"No."

"I want to speak to you."

"Then speak."

"I cannot speak through the door," he said. "Please."

Samantha hesitated for a brief second but then unlocked the door. She opened it and stepped aside so he could enter.

"Leave it open," she said, walking away from him.

"How do you feel?" Rudolf asked.

Samantha ignored his question. "Your Highness, what do you want?"

"I want to know how you feel."

"Why?"

Rudolf shrugged. "For the usual reasons."

"And those reasons would be?" she asked.

"Princess, you are carrying my child."

"Please, Your Highness," Samantha drawled, holding her hand up, "do not remind me of my folly."

His lips quirked as if he wanted to smile. "I want to apologize for my rudeness," Rudolf said. "I was hoping you would forgive me."

"Forgive you for your rudeness?" Samantha echoed, her voice dripping with sarcasm. "Or those balls you attended? Perhaps the opera? Surely, you want my forgiveness for that intimate supper with the actress?"

"Your sarcasm is understandable but unbecoming," Rudolf told her.

"Do yourself a favor," she said. "Find yourself a bride who can't read."

"You sound like a jealous wife," he remarked.

Samantha smiled. "I passed jealousy last week."

"What lies beyond jealousy?" he asked.

"Dislike," she answered, unable to say the word hate. "I don't like you."

The man had the audacity to look hurt before he shuttered his expression. "In two weeks, you will be married to a man you dislike," the prince told her. "Prepare yourself." At that, he quit the chamber.

During the next two weeks, Samantha turned the tables on the prince by avoiding contact with him. The prince turned the tables on her by seeming to dog her every step. He didn't speak to her unless she spoke to

him, but his constant watching was beginning to un-
nerve her. She almost wished he would resume his social life. *Almost.*

Though confused by his behavior, Samantha knew
one thing for certain. When the moment arrived, she
could not walk down the aisle to marry a man who
cared nothing for her. . . .

He could not marry her unless she knew the truth.
Rudolf knew that as surely as he knew his wedding day
had arrived.

Early on April twenty-third, so early only the servants
were up and about, Rudolf climbed the stairs to the
third floor. He carried two objects for his betrothed.
The first was a plate holding a piece of bread, and the
other was a large velvet pouch containing the jeweled
tiara his grandmother and his mother had worn on
their wedding days.

Rudolf knew he loved Samantha but could never tell
her. Once a woman knew a man's tender feelings, she
used them against him.

True, he hadn't wanted to marry. Losing Olga had
left him bitter. Had he ever been as idealistic about love
as Samantha? If he had, he'd lost his innocence a long
time ago, long before he'd even met Olga, probably
when his father had his mother confined to the asylum.

Marrying Samantha under false pretenses would be
unfair, Rudolf told himself as he walked down the third-
floor corridor in the direction of her chamber. Poor
Samantha had almost no choice about marrying him.
He would give her a choice this morning, though. There
was no other alternative for him because he couldn't
live with her unless she could live with the truth. He
had stayed away from her this past month deliberately

because he knew this moment would come. Vladimir had seen to that by showing up in the duke's garden that day.

Without bothering to knock, Rudolf opened her door and crossed the chamber to her bed to leave her bread as he'd done each morning. Only this day was different. She was awake.

"What are you doing?" Samantha asked.

Rudolf sat on the edge of the bed and offered her the bread. She sat up, leaned against the headboard, and lifted the bread off the plate.

"You left me the bread each morning?" she asked with a smile.

Rudolf inclined his head. "We must discuss a matter of some importance before we marry."

Samantha set the bread aside and waited for him to speak.

"I am going to tell you something," Rudolf said, staring into her eyes. "Afterward, I will not object if you want to cancel the wedding. My own preference is to marry and then divorce once the babe is delivered."

He was frightening her. Was he trying to get rid of her before she even married him?

A woman's wedding day was one of life's milestones and should be one of her happiest memories. Apparently, that was not to be. Already, two of her oldest acquaintances, heartache and anguish, were making their presence known. She should have known this moment would come. He hadn't wanted to marry her.

With her heart breaking, Samantha watched the prince stand and cross the chamber to gaze out the window. He couldn't even look at her as he let her down.

Rudolf turned around and told her, "I am not the man you think I am."

"You aren't Prince Rudolf Kazanov?" Samantha asked, bewildered.

"I meant, I am not my father's son," Rudolf explained. "I am a bastard."

Samantha closed her eyes against the pain etched across his face as a soft moan escaped her lips. His startling revelation explained many puzzling things. Now she knew why the prospect of fathering a bastard had upset him, why his brother wanted the Kazanov Venus, why his mother had been locked in an insane asylum.

Opening her eyes to look at him, Samantha felt her heart breaking. The prince had turned his back on her and stood facing the window. Pride made him keep his head held high and his shoulders squared, but he seemed so alone.

"Which will it be, Samantha?" Rudolf asked, without looking at her. "Shall we cancel the wedding or divorce after you deliver the babe?" When she remained silent, he continued, "If you cancel the wedding, I will support you and the child for as long as you live. Money is no problem."

Samantha knew she needed to choose her words carefully. Her prince was in pain but needed to be soothed with no trace of pity. She slid out of the bed and padded on bare feet across the chamber. Her heart ached when she remembered that she had called him a bastard.

Samantha prayed for the correct words. If he thought she pitied him, their marriage would be over before it began.

"Well, Samantha?" Rudolf said. "Has my bastardy shocked you into silence?"

"No, Your Highness," Samantha said, standing directly behind him. "What has shocked me is your *stupidity*."

Rudolf whirled around. They stood mere inches apart, and she could see how tense he was.

"I beg your pardon?" With her open hand, Samantha slapped him hard, and then said, "I hope that knocks some sense into you."

"I understand your anger," Rudolf said, narrowing his gaze on her. "You have not answered my question."

"You understand nothing," she told him.

"Enlighten me."

"Neither of your choices appeals to me," Samantha said. "Is there a third?"

She saw his jaw and facial muscles relax. When he spoke, his voice sounded less strained. "The third choice is to marry until death us do part."

"That's the one I want," she told him.

He wasn't ready to believe her. She saw that right away.

Rudolf searched her eyes for the truth. "Are you being kind to me?"

"Why should I be kind to a man who hasn't been kind to me?" she countered.

"Do you feel sorry for me?" he asked.

"Why should I feel sorry for you?" she asked in an annoyed tone. "I'm the cripple who was forced to pick pockets in order to eat. I'd trade my limp for your bastardy any day of the week."

He believed her. She could see it in his eyes.

With a groan of relief, Rudolf yanked her into his arms. He lowered his head to kiss her, but she held up her hand.

"Your lack of trust offends me," Samantha told him.

"Forgive my lapse in judgment," Rudolf said, a smile touching his lips. "How can I make it up to you?"

Love me, Samantha thought, but said, "Stop attending balls and operas without me. No more actresses."

Rudolf laughed. His mouth covered hers, pouring all of his need into that soul-stealing kiss.

"I love you," Samantha told him.

Rudolf held her tightly, his arms encircling her, as if he would never let her go. "I do not deserve your love," he said.

Samantha felt her heart breaking. She needed to hear those words from him.

Resting her head against his chest, Samantha said, "That was why your father preferred Vladimir."

"Yes."

She looked up at him and smiled. "Let's toss Venus into the Thames."

"I could never do that," Rudolf said. "Perhaps I should give it to Vladimir."

"If you give it to him," Samantha said, "I won't marry you."

Amusement lit his dark eyes. "Why?"

"Vladimir is unworthy of such a gift," Samantha answered. "Besides, if the medallion is true to legend, think of all the little Vladimirs we will be setting loose on an unsuspecting world."

Rudolf smiled but then grew serious. "There is another matter."

Samantha gazed into his dark eyes and waited. Nothing could shock her now.

"I know the identity of my natural father," he told her.

"And?"

"The Duke of Inverary sired me."

Samantha swayed dizzyingly on her feet but managed to fight off a swoon. "Does he know?"

"Yes, but I prefer to keep it a secret because"—he dropped his hand to her belly—"because of my children."

"No wonder he refused to cancel the wedding when I asked," Samantha said. "His Grace wanted wonderful me to marry his son."

"You *are* wonderful," Rudolf replied. His lips touched hers.

The door swung open, admitting Aunt Roxie, who cried, "Your Highness, what are you doing here? Seeing the bride before the ceremony is bad luck in the extreme."

"I have a feeling that my bad luck days are gone forever," Rudolf said, smiling at Samantha. He looked at her aunt, adding, "I brought my bride something I want her to wear today."

Rudolf put his arm around Samantha and drew her across the chamber. Lifting the velvet pouch off the bed, he produced a jeweled tiara, encrusted with diamonds, sapphires, and other precious gems.

"My grandmother and my mother wore this tiara when they married," Rudolf said. "Will you wear this as your headdress?"

"You know I will."

Rudolf raised her hands to his lips. "I will see you at the church."

At ten o'clock that morning, Samantha stood in the nave of Saint Paul's Cathedral. With her were her aunt and the duke. The sounds of violins playing wafted through the air to her.

Samantha wore her mother's wedding gown of white silk, embroidered with seed pearls. Its bodice had a low-cut, squared neckline and long, flowing sleeves. On her head was the jewel-encrusted tiara, and in her badly shaking hands, a bouquet of orange blossoms.

"Aunt Roxie, does my belly stick out?" Samantha asked. "I wouldn't want anyone to guess the reason for this hasty marriage."

"You look radiant, my darling," her aunt gushed. "Oh, I cannot believe my sweet Samantha will be a princess."

"Well, my dear, she won't be a princess if you don't take your seat," Duke Magnus said.

Her aunt left, and the duke escorted Samantha to the head of the aisle. Hundreds of guests filled the cathedral, lit by thousands of candles.

Samantha stared down the aisle. It seemed a great distance to traverse with all of those guests, mostly strangers, watching her.

"Are you ready, my dear?" Duke Magnus asked.

Samantha shook her head. She looked at him with anguished eyes. "I can't go down that aisle."

"Samantha, I know you love Rudolf and want to marry him," the duke said in a soothing voice.

"I do love him, Your Grace," she replied, "but limping down that aisle in front of all those people terrifies me."

"My dear, the only way to reach the prince is down that aisle."

Samantha shifted her gaze from the duke to the aisle. Then she nodded and placed her hand in his.

Holding her hand in a firm grip, Duke Magnus gently forced her forward. If she wanted to stop, she would need to struggle.

Samantha felt dizzy. Fright and the babe made her feel queasy.

Ignoring the sea of faces turned toward her, Samantha kept her gaze on Rudolf standing at the altar with the Bishop of London.

He was watching her. Though he wouldn't give voice to the words, Samantha saw the love shining at her from the prince's eyes.

Startling her and everyone else in the cathedral, Prince Rudolf took the unprecedented action of walking ten paces down the aisle to meet her. He raised her hand to his lips and smiled, saying, "Hello, Princess. Are you ready to become my wife?"

"Yes, Your Highness," Samantha answered, returning his smile, a high blush staining her cheeks.

The cathedral resounded with a collective sigh from those ladies within hearing distance. The groom and the bride ignored them, as if they were the only two people in the world.

When the bishop cleared his throat, Rudolf escorted Samantha to the altar. The Bishop of London smiled at her and opened his prayer book.

"Dearly beloved," the bishop began, "we are gathered together here in the sight of God, to join together this man and this woman . . .

" . . . therefore if any man can show just cause, why they may not lawfully be joined together, let him now speak, or else hereafter forever hold his peace."

"I can show just cause," said a voice from somewhere behind them.

Rudolf and Samantha whirled around. Samantha saw a strikingly beautiful blonde, richly dressed, advancing down the aisle. She walked with grace and confidence.

"Who are you?" the bishop asked.

"I am Prince Rudolf's wife," the blonde said with a smile. "I believe that is just cause."

Stunned, Samantha stepped back two paces as if she'd been struck. She heard her aunt's and her sisters' gasps, mutterings from the duke and the marquess, and the excited murmurings of several hundred guests.

Great Giles' ghost, the prince's wife was alive and standing here. A soft groan escaped Samantha, and she wished she could swoon to escape her humiliation and loss.

"Olga," Rudolf said.

"Really, Rudolf, you always had such discriminating taste in women," the princess said. She flicked a glance at Samantha and then asked him, "Are you so desperate you would marry a pathetic cripple?"

Samantha stared at the blonde. An entire lifetime of pain, disappointment, and humiliation was nothing compared to this.

Please, God, Samantha prayed, *send me a swoon. I cannot bear the pain.*

She tried to yank her hand out of the prince's, but he wouldn't let her go. "This isn't what you think," Rudolf said. "Olga and I—"

Instead of the prince's voice, Samantha heard the sound of ocean waves crashing in her ears. The floor rushed up to meet her as God blessed her with a swoon.

CHAPTER 16

"Is Samantha dead?"

"No, she's breathing."

"That swoon has lasted much too long."

Surfacing from the depths of unconsciousness, Samantha heard her aunt's and her sisters' voices as if from a great distance. There was something she didn't want to remember.

Moaning softly, Samantha opened her eyes and recognized her own bedchamber. What was she doing here? Why wasn't she with her husband?

Harsh reality came rushing back to her in a tidal wave of pain. She remembered turning around and the blond woman saying that she was the prince's wife.

"Welcome back, darling," Aunt Roxie said. "You gave us a fright."

Samantha looked at her aunt and sisters. Concern mingled with relief shone from their expressions. They pitied her.

A pathetic cripple. That's what Rudolf's wife had called her in front of six hundred aristocrats.

"Why couldn't you just let me die?" Samantha moaned.

"Darling, you have everything to live for," her aunt told her.

In response, Samantha rolled away and closed her eyes. She had nothing to live for. She wished she could go home to the cottage and live out her days there. Each time her dream was within her grasp, it slipped from her fingers. Perhaps it was time to let go of the dream.

"Listen to me," Aunt Roxie said. "The prince loves you and intends to make you his wife. Grant and Drake, even Zara, adore you. Within the year, you will deliver your own baby. What else could a woman want except gowns, furs, and jewels?"

A ghost of a smile touched Samantha's lips. She could always depend on her aunt to put a practical spin on an outrageous situation.

"Thank you for trying to cheer me up," Samantha said, sitting up. "Rudolf is married to another woman, and the children do not belong to me."

"Their hearts belong to you," Aunt Roxie said. "Let's get you undressed. Victoria, fetch your sister's night-shift."

Samantha stood up slowly so they could help her remove the wedding gown. Her aunt pulled the nightshift over her head and then helped her into bed again.

"Rudolf is beside himself with worry," Aunt Roxie told her.

Samantha said nothing, but fresh hot tears sprang to her eyes.

"Your prince insists he has documents to prove he is divorced," Aunt Roxie added. "Without corroborating evidence, he needs to wait for his brothers to arrive in England to bear witness to the documents' validity."

"That doesn't matter to me," Samantha said, and then sighed heavily. "I'm not going to marry him."

"Of course you'll marry," her aunt said, holding her hands. "You are expecting his child."

Samantha felt herself losing control. Her bottom lip trembled with the effort to keep from weeping.

"I don't want to marry the prince," Samantha cried, beginning to sob. "I can't trust him. He led me to believe his wife was dead."

"Listen to me," Aunt Roxie said, irritation tingeing her voice. "Whether you trust him or not, you will marry him."

"You can't force me to the altar," Samantha sobbed.

Victoria leaped to her sister's defense. "Samantha is correct, Aunt—"

"Keep those lips closed," her aunt snapped. "Go to the kitchen and tell Cook your sister needs soup, toast, and tea."

"Why do I always need to—"

"I'll go with you," Angelica offered, slipping her arm through her sister's.

"You are going to marry the prince even if His Grace and I need to drag you, kicking and screaming, down the aisle," Aunt Roxie told her. "You will not embarrass His Grace and me by bearing a child out of wedlock. If you want to live apart from the prince after you're married, that's your business."

"I don't want to live separate lives," Samantha sobbed. "I want him to love me."

"He does love you," Aunt Roxie said, patting her hands. She rose from the edge of the bed, saying, "I'll send the prince up. He wants to speak to you."

"I don't want to speak to him."

"When did you become so infuriatingly stubborn?" Aunt Roxie asked. "I would expect this recalcitrant behavior from Victoria, but never from you. Listen to what the prince has to say. You owe him that much."

"I owe him nothing," Samantha said, sobbing. "Why can't you leave me alone in my misery?"

Samantha rolled onto her side, turning her back on her aunt. Covering her face with her arm, she surrendered to tears.

Downstairs, Prince Rudolf sat in the study with the Duke of Inverary and the Marquess of Argyll. The three men drank whiskey and sat in silence while awaiting the duchess's return from Samantha's bedchamber.

"I think we should call a physician," Rudolf said. "A swoon doesn't last this long. Something could be wrong with the baby."

"Women and babies are stronger than we men believe," Duke Magnus said.

"Samantha has had a shock," Robert said. "Perhaps she's not in any hurry to wake up."

"The poor child was so frightened," the duke remarked. "I had the devil of a time getting her down the aisle."

Rudolf snapped his black gaze to the duke's. "She didn't want to marry me?"

"Oh, she wanted to marry you all right," Duke Magnus answered.

Rudolf relaxed at his words.

"Finally, I told her the only way to reach you was down that aisle," the duke went on. "She moved fast enough after that."

Rudolf smiled at that.

"Her hand shook like she had the palsy, but she summoned her courage because she desperately wanted to get to you," the duke told him.

The three men fell silent again.

Though young and vulnerable, Samantha had an

iron backbone, Rudolf thought. Because she loved him, she had faced her worst fear by limping down the aisle in front of six hundred wedding guests. This was how her bravery was rewarded. He couldn't blame her if she didn't want to do it again.

"Why would Olga do what she did?" Robert asked.

"Vladimir wants the Kazanov Venus that I took when I left Russia," Rudolf answered. Seeing their puzzled expressions, he explained, "The Kazanov Venus is a gold medallion engraved with Venus holding her son's hand. This has been in the Kazanov family for five hundred years and is always passed from father to firstborn son, which Vladimir contends should be his."

"What is so important about this medallion?" Robert asked.

"Legend says that who possesses the medallion is blessed with prosperity and fertility," Rudolf told him.

"Do you actually believe that?"

Rudolf shrugged. "What I believe is unimportant. Apparently, my brother believes the legend and is desperate to retrieve it. He visited Samantha and asked her to steal it."

"He did?" Both the duke and the marquess exclaimed simultaneously.

Rudolf nodded. "Samantha was sitting in the garden when Vladimir appeared and made her an offer. I interrupted them." Rudolf smiled at the memory. "Your sweet, biddable sister-in-law had drawn her stiletto on my brother."

Both the duke and the marquess smiled. Then the marquess said, "She becomes more like her older sister every day. I pity the man who marries Victoria."

"Why is that?" Rudolf asked.

"Tory is the least biddable of all three, and she isn't

even eighteen yet," Robert said. "Some poor soul is going to have his hands full."

Duke Magnus cleared his throat. "I do believe my wife desires a union with—er—Alexander Emerson."

Rudolf snapped his dark gaze to the duke's. "Is she disappointed to get me as a husband for Samantha?"

"Not in the least," the duke assured him. "Victoria needs a man strong enough to control her. As a matter of fact, Roxie never thought Alexander and Samantha would suit. She wanted Alexander for Victoria."

As if speaking her name had conjured her, Roxie opened the study door without knocking. Before saying a word to anyone, the duchess marched to her husband's desk and grabbed his glass. She poured a splash of whiskey into the glass and gulped it down. Then she poured herself another.

"Problems, my dear?" Duke Magnus asked, with laughter lurking in his voice.

"My nieces will be the death of me yet," Roxie told him. "All three are determined to put me in an early grave."

"How is she?" Rudolf asked.

"Samantha has regained consciousness," Roxie said. "And I wish to hell she had stayed swooned."

"I must speak with her," the prince said, rising from his chair.

"I wouldn't do that if I were you," Roxie warned him.

"Is she angry?" Rudolf asked. She had every right to be angry with him. He should have told her he was divorced instead of letting her think death had claimed his first wife.

"I don't know what the twit is," Roxie said. "First, she wants you to love her, and then she doesn't want to marry you. She would prefer to live with the boys in the old cottage. This whole day has upset her to the point where she doesn't know what she wants. Cook is preparing a tray for her, but I cannot guarantee what your reception in her chamber will be. You have your work cut out for you."

Without a word, Rudolf left the study. A few minutes later, he stood outside her chamber. He carried a tray with a bowl of broth, two slices of toast, and tea.

Without knocking, Rudolf opened the door and stepped inside. Samantha was lying in bed with her back to the door.

Rudolf paused, his heart breaking, when he realized she was sobbing dryly. Her tears had been spent, but she couldn't stop her involuntary sobs.

"Leave it on the table," Samantha whispered on a sob. "I'll eat later." Another sob.

Feeling helpless, Rudolf set the tray on the table. He stood beside the bed and stared down at her. How could he possibly comfort her when she was so consumed by pain? What words would soothe her?

"Princess, let me help you," Rudolf said, sitting on the edge of the bed. "Your unhappiness will sicken the baby."

Over her protests, he gathered her into his arms and held her tight against his chest. "Don't struggle, *ma ly-oobof*, please."

When she settled, Rudolf rocked her back and forth while she wept with her face buried against his chest. "I wish I could take away your pain," he said, in a voice raw with emotion.

Rudolf tilted her face up and winced at the sight of her swollen eyes. "Olga and I divorced when she learned that I am a bastard," he told her. "Because of my origins, she has never taken an interest in Zara."

"She's very beautiful," Samantha said in a soft voice. "You loved her."

"I loved her because I thought she was you," Rudolf said. "Olga wanted to marry the heir. She pretended to be everything you are—loving and caring and nurturing and loyal."

"Thank you," she whispered.

With one hand, Rudolf tilted her face up, and his mouth descended to hers. His kiss was long, slow, healing. Aching love for the woman in his arms swelled in his chest.

Samantha gazed at him, all the love she felt for him shining from her enormous blue eyes. "Don't blame yourself for this. You couldn't have known."

Rudolf groaned and clutched her tightly. All she had ever wanted was his love. He was the prince who would rescue her from an unkind world, from a lifetime of pain. All he had managed to do was bring her more pain. Somehow, some way, he would make this up to her.

"We will put this behind us when my brothers arrive and testify to the validity of my divorce papers," he told her. "Unless . . . Perhaps I should give Vladimir the Venus and be done with it."

Samantha shook her head. "Vladimir and Olga do not deserve to be rewarded for their bad behavior."

A smile touched his chiseled lips. She sounded as if she would be a good mother, strict but gentle.

"You must eat now," Rudolf told her.

"I'm not hungry."

Rudolf dropped his hand to her softly rounded belly. "Please eat, *ma lyoobof*. The baby needs the nourishment."

Samantha sat up and leaned against the headboard. Rudolf dipped the spoon in the soup and brought it to her lips.

"What are you doing?"

"I am feeding you."

"You don't need to do that," she told him.

"I want to do it," Rudolf replied. When tears welled up in her eyes, he said, "I will not do it if it makes you cry."

"I'm not crying," Samantha said on a choked sob.

"You cannot imagine how proud I was when you walked down that aisle to me," Rudolf spoke as he fed her. "Your beauty and bravery were one of the world's wonders."

"My aunt was correct about one thing," she said. "We did have the wedding of the decade. No one will soon forget it."

Rudolf smiled and offered her the tea. She took three sips and handed it back to him.

"I'll eat more later," she promised.

Rudolf sat beside her and leaned against the head-board. He took her into his arms and held her against his chest. When she sighed, he smiled at the top of her head.

"You are more noble than any lady sitting in that church," Rudolf told her. "You retained your dignity in the face of extreme provocation."

Finally, Samantha slept. Rudolf eased himself off the bed and gently laid her back. His heart ached as a sob escaped her in sleep.

An hour later, Samantha awakened with troubled thoughts. Though she'd encouraged the prince not to give his brother the Kazanov Venus, she feared what would happen if he didn't turn the medallion over. Vladimir might finally succeed in killing Rudolf. Olga might keep denying their divorce so the baby would be born a bastard. The woman must know how Rudolf felt about his own bastardy and siring a bastard.

What she needed was to give Vladimir the Kazanov

Venus, but that meant betraying the prince. How could she give Vladimir the Venus without really giving it to him?

Samantha rose from the bed and limped across the chamber to the door. Opening it a crack, she peered into the deserted corridor. Then she stepped outside and closed the door behind herself.

Praying that no one would appear in the corridor, Samantha scurried to the door of the prince's chamber and pressed her ear against it. No sound came from within.

Samantha stepped inside his bedchamber and closed the door. She didn't know how much time she had, only that she needed to be quick.

With grim determination, Samantha limped across the chamber to the highboy. She checked each drawer but found nothing.

Next, Samantha went into the dressing room. Staring at his clothing hanging neatly, she couldn't help but remember how her own clothing had hung beside his when they shared a chamber in Scotland.

The memory brought a smile to her lips. Without thinking, she began to touch his clothing as if that could bring them closer.

Samantha told herself that she was wasting time. Each moment's delay could bring the prince back to his chamber. Then how would she explain herself?

Spying a leather case on the floor, Samantha dropped to her knees. She lifted his boots off it and opened the lid. Several documents lay on top of the contents; she lifted them out and realized they were written in Russian.

There was another case beneath the documents. Lifting its lid, Samantha spied several pieces of jewelry and a black velvet pouch. She opened the pouch and peered inside.

Smiling at her discovery, Samantha lifted the gold medallion out of the pouch. She stared at it for a long moment, unable to believe such a small ornament could create trouble.

The medallion didn't cause the trouble, Samantha told herself. The desire to own the medallion was the root of this trouble.

Dropping the medallion into the pouch, Samantha placed the documents into the leather case. Then she and the velvet pouch returned to her chamber.

She was going to need her sister's help.

Samantha slept surprisingly well that night after Victoria promised to help her the next afternoon. She rolled over in bed the following morning and smiled at the slice of bread.

Rudolf had come into her chamber while she slept and left her the bread. He cared for her and would care for her even more when she solved his problem for him. She couldn't let him know what she planned, though. He would never allow her to go into Montague House to face Vladimir and Olga.

After eating the bread, Samantha rose from the bed and dressed in her blue gown, the one the prince had bought for her. She thought of going downstairs to breakfast but decided against it. Seeing pity in the servants' gazes was something she couldn't face yet.

Samantha sat on the chaise near the hearth and waited for the hour when Victoria and she would leave. She was hungry. Perhaps her aunt or the prince would come to visit and order food sent to her.

"Tinker told me you haven't eaten breakfast."

Samantha turned at the sound of the prince's voice. "Would you have Cook send something up to me?"

"Breakfast is served in the dining room," Rudolf told her, crossing the chamber to stand in front of her.

"I don't want to go down there," she told him.

"You will if you want to eat," he said.

"I'm never leaving this room again."

Rudolf laughed out loud.

"Well, I'll probably leave sometime but not this morning," she amended herself.

"Why don't you want to go downstairs?" he asked.

"Everyone knows I'm a pathetic cripple," Samantha answered, her gaze fixed on the carpet.

Rudolf knelt in front of her. "Princess, no one believes you are pathetic except yourself. The longer you put off facing people, the more difficult it will be."

"I'll come down for dinner," she said.

"You will come down now," he insisted.

Samantha knew from that implacable set to his jaw that he would not let her escape going down to the dining room. She wet her lips nervously. "I'm not hungry," she lied. "I don't think I could eat a thing."

"The baby needs nourishment," Rudolf said.

The prince held his hand out to her as he had done on the night of the Emersons' ball. She looked into his eyes and saw the tenderness there. "Trust me, Princess."

And she did.

Samantha looked from his dark eyes to his offered hand. Like the night of Emerson's ball, she placed her hand in his and her trust in him.

"Good morning, Lady Samantha," Tinker called when they walked into the dining room.

"Good morning," Samantha answered, her gaze glued to the carpet lest she see the pity she knew the major-domo felt for her.

Rudolf put his arm around her and leaned close to

whisper, "Are you greeting Tinker or the carpet?" He escorted her to a chair and said, "I will serve you."

Samantha watched the prince walk to the sideboard and grab a plate. With a sigh, Samantha realized how deeply intense her love for him was. Too bad the prince didn't love her. Who could love defective merchandise? He had a fondness for her, but he probably had a fondness for his dogs and his horses.

Rudolf looked over his shoulder and called, "Kippers, my lady?"

Samantha smiled through her misery and shook her head. Rudolf placed the plate on the table in front of her and then sat beside her.

She looked at the contents of the plate: a large scoop of scrambled eggs, three slices of ham, a roll accompanied by butter and strawberry jam. "I don't think the baby's appetite is large enough for this."

"Stop eating when he has had enough," Rudolf said, his eyes gleaming with humor.

"Or she," Samantha corrected him. "Where is the *Times?*"

"We don't have the paper today," he told her.

"We have it every day."

"Not today."

"I want to see that paper," Samantha insisted. "Mr. Tinker, please bring me the *Times.*"

Samantha watched the majordomo shift his gaze to the prince and suddenly knew how horribly insulting the gossip would be. She needed to know, though.

Rudolf stared at her for a long moment and nodded at the servant. Tinker handed the prince the paper and then left the dining room, closing the door behind himself.

Watching the majordomo leave, Samantha was filled with embarrassed dread. Somehow, Rudolf had signaled the servant to leave, which meant he expected her to become hysterically upset.

"That bad, huh?"

"Bad is a relative thing, Princess."

Samantha promised herself that she would remain calm and casually aloof. She promised herself to adopt a humorous attitude toward her wedding day fiasco. She promised herself not to weep.

Rudolf handed her the folded newspaper. Samantha opened the newspaper slowly, glanced at the headline, and felt her stomach lurch.

It was worse than she could ever have imagined. In bold black, the *Times* headline read, *Marriage, Russian Style*.

Samantha paled and trembled as she began to read the front page article. The reporter was surprisingly factual, ending with Princess Olga's words that the bride was a pathetic cripple.

Humiliated almost as much as the previous day, Samantha closed her eyes. She knew one thing for certain; she could not keep the promises she made to herself three minutes ago.

Samantha pushed the plate of food away. Resting her arms across the table, she lowered her head to hide her face and wept.

"I promise we will soon marry," Rudolf said, stroking her back soothingly. "This will be forgotten."

Samantha turned her head to look at him. "I-I w-want to g-go home," she sobbed.

"Princess, you are home."

"N-No, I want to g-go home where I b-belong."

"You belong with me."

Samantha shook her head. "I belong at the cottage. You didn't want to marry me. You wanted to give your baby your name."

"Come here," Rudolf said, taking her hand and gently but firmly forcing her out of her chair and onto his lap. He folded her within the circle of his embrace and said, "The truth is I did want to marry you. I fought my feelings because I did not want to want you so desperately." He tilted her chin up and waited until she raised her gaze to his. "Your love for me has brought you only pain. I plan to pass the next fifty years making that up to you."

Wrapping her arms around his neck, Samantha leaned her head against his shoulder. She pressed her lips to his throat.

"I will return you to your chamber," Rudolf said. "Later this afternoon, you may sit in the garden with the children, who are worried about you."

Later, alone in her chamber, Samantha sat on the chaise and stared at the gold medallion depicting Venus and her son. The door opened, admitting her sister.

Victoria stepped inside the chamber and whispered, "Do you still want to—?"

Samantha's expression was grim. "Yes, we are going to Montague House."

CHAPTER 17

"I am going to shoot them."

Wearing a grim expression, Rudolf marched across the duke's study to the pistol case. He opened it, grabbed a pistol, and reached for the ammunition.

The Duke of Inverary and the Marquess of Argyll turned from their business discussion when the prince barged into the study. They watched as the prince, muttering in Russian, began loading the pistol.

"Who are you going to shoot?" Robert asked.

Prince Rudolf looked at the two men as if just noticing them. "First, I am going to shoot Vladimir and Olga," he answered. "Then I will look for that *Times* reporter."

Robert bolted out of the chair and placed himself between the prince and the door. He held out his hand, saying, "Give me the pistol."

"Samantha is hurting," Rudolf said.

"If you commit murder, Samantha will be left an unwed mother," Robert reminded him.

Rudolf passed him the pistol, asking, "Do you know of a good assassin?"

"You would still be the chief suspect," Robert said, grinning.

Rudolf inclined his head. He crossed the study and sat in one of the chairs in front of the desk. "What action do you suggest I take?"

"*If* you are sufficiently calmed by this afternoon," Robert told him, "we'll visit Montague House and apply some pressure."

"*We* will go?"

"I insist on accompanying you," Robert said.

"This is not your fight," Rudolf told him.

"You are my brother," Robert said. "Your fight is my fight."

Rudolf couldn't believe how easily these men had accepted him. He had lived his entire life without anyone's approval or support, except for his three youngest brothers.

"I accept your offer," Rudolf said, and inclined his head at the marquess.

Upstairs, Samantha had wiped her tears away. With her cloak draped over one arm and the black velvet pouch safely hidden inside her reticule, she sat on the chaise in her chamber and waited for her sister.

She supposed there was nothing she could do about being the laughingstock of London. Only . . . for her entire life people had considered her a pathetic cripple and pitied her. It hurt horribly to know that all of London, from the lowest street urchin to the Regent himself, would read in the *Times* that she was a pathetic cripple.

The door opened, admitting Victoria, who whispered, "Are you ready?"

Samantha cast her sister an amused look. "Tory, we aren't thieves sneaking around in the night," she told her.

Victoria arched a copper brow at her and asked, "Didn't His Highness give you orders not to leave this house without his permission or escort?"

"Yes, he did."

"Do you have his permission?"

"No."

Victoria gave her a jaunty smile. "Do you actually believe that His Highness would consider me a proper escort?"

"I see your point," Samantha said, crossing the chamber to the door. "We'll need to use the servants' stairs and keep our voices down. You lead the way. You're much better at sneaking around than I."

Victoria opened the door a crack and peered into the corridor. "Let's go," she whispered.

Hand in hand, the two sisters hurried toward the far end of the corridor and the servants' stairs. It was just on this type of occasion that Samantha especially wished she didn't limp.

Reaching the ground level, Victoria led the way through the kitchen. "Just passing through," she called to the startled servants.

"Excuse us, please," Samantha added with an apologetic smile.

Once outside in the garden, Samantha and Victoria hugged the house with their backs lest someone spy them from a window. They reached the safety of the alley and walked the short distance to Park Lane.

Victoria waved at a passing hackney coach, which stopped for them. Samantha climbed inside first, followed by her sister, who ordered the driver, "Bond Street, please."

"I don't believe I have the constitution for this type of activity," Samantha whispered.

"Sister, leave everything to me," Victoria said, patting her hand. "I thrive on excitement."

A short time later, the coach started down Bond Street. Victoria leaned forward and told the driver, "Stop at the first jeweler's."

When the coach stopped, Samantha started to open her reticule to pay the man, but Victoria stilled her hand. "We are only making this one stop and then going on to Montague House," Victoria told the driver. "Would you consider waiting for us? Our errand may take some time."

"I've all the time in the world if you've the money to pay me," the man said.

Victoria smiled. "Indeed, we do."

Opening the door, Victoria stepped down from the coach and then turned to help Samantha. "His Highness won't be happy if I let you fall," she said.

Samantha laughed nervously. "His Highness won't be happy if he discovers I've left the house."

"Don't worry," Victoria said, slipping her arm through Samantha's. "He'll never find out."

"Why did you ask the driver to wait?" Samantha asked.

Victoria gave her a pointed look. "You don't want to be seen hailing a hackney on Bond Street, do you? Someone would tell Rudolf."

Samantha paled at the thought of what Rudolf would do. Kind and gentle unless thwarted, the prince possessed a formidable temper. She knew from experience how sharp his tongue could be. Why, he would probably lock her up and throw the key away if he knew what she planned.

"What would I do without you?" Samantha asked.

Victoria smiled. "Not very well, I'm afraid."

Thankfully, the exclusive jewelry shop was empty at that hour of the day. Wearing an ingratiating smile, the proprietor greeted them, asking, "May I be of service, ladies?"

"We certainly hope so," Victoria said, taking charge. "Tell him what you need, sister."

Samantha smiled at the man and reached into her reticule for the black velvet pouch with the Kazanov Venus. She handed it to him, saying, "I need a replica made of this piece. You see, the woman is the goddess Venus holding her son's hand."

The jeweler examined the piece thoroughly and carefully. He rubbed his finger across the raised goddess and her son. Finally, he looked at them and said, "I could do the job for you."

"How long will it take?" Samantha asked.

The jeweler shrugged. "A week or two."

"We have only one hour," Victoria said.

"This is a life or death emergency," Samantha added.

The jeweler shook his head. "No one could complete this job in an hour."

Victoria narrowed her blue gaze on him. "Do you have a gold medallion approximately the same size?" she asked.

The jeweler nodded. "I believe so."

"Do you have any gold replicas of Venus and Cupid that would fit on the gold medallion?" Victoria asked him.

"Possibly. I could look."

"I don't understand," Samantha said. "What are you thinking?"

"He could lift Venus from one piece, Cupid from another piece, and then glue them to a gold medallion similar in size to this," Victoria answered.

"Sister, you are so wonderfully clever," Samantha said with a smile.

"I know."

"You realize, of course, that you would be required to purchase the other pieces," the jeweler told them.

"Sir, my sister is betrothed to Prince Rudolf Kazanov," Victoria announced. "Money is no object."

Lightened by one thousand pounds, Samantha and Victoria left the jeweler's an hour later and climbed into the coach. The Venus replica was wrapped inside a white velvet pouch inside Samantha's reticule.

"Montague House," Victoria called to the driver.

A short time later, the coach halted in front of Montague House. Samantha glanced at the mansion and remembered the night Rudolf and she had come here before fleeing to Scotland and succumbing to the prince's charms.

"Are you all right?" Victoria asked.

Samantha nodded.

"Wait for us," Victoria instructed the driver. "We'll be returning to Park Lane shortly."

Victoria opened the door and climbed down. Then she turned to assist her sister.

Trembling almost uncontrollably, Samantha walked up the stairs beside Victoria. If her sister hadn't been with her, she never would have had the courage to do this.

"Let me handle this," Victoria said.

Samantha shook her head. "This is my problem." She hesitated and then asked, "Did you bring your dagger?"

"It's strapped to my leg," Victoria said with a smile.

With a badly shaking hand, Samantha lifted the knocker and banged it. A moment later, a familiar figure opened the door.

"Igor," Samantha said in surprise.

"Prince Rudolf's lady," Igor said. "What do you want?"

Samantha squared her shoulders. "I want to see Prince Vladimir."

"I cannot guarantee your safety," he warned.

"As I recall, *you* threatened my safety the last time I saw you," Samantha said. "I am ready for the unexpected this time. I've brought my sister with me."

The Russian giant shifted his gaze to the petite red-head who stood beside her. His lips quirked with amusement.

"Victoria is tougher than she appears," Samantha said. Then she ordered, "Open the door and let us pass."

Igor stepped back and allowed them entrance to the foyer. "Follow me."

The Russian led them down the corridor to the dining room where she had sat with Rudolf on New Year's Eve. When they walked into the room, Prince Vladimir and Princess Olga looked up in surprise.

In that moment, Samantha compared herself to the prince's former wife and came out lacking. Olga was everything that Samantha could never be—strikingly beautiful, gracefully poised, blond.

"If it isn't the pathetic little cripple," Olga said.

In a flash of movement, Victoria bent and lifted the bottom edge of her skirt to draw the dagger. "Kindly refrain from insulting my sister, or I shall be forced to cut your tongue out," she threatened the other woman. Victoria turned to the right suddenly and pointed the dagger in the general vicinity of Igor's groin. "You stay where you are, or you'll be a candidate for the opera's soprano."

"I have my pistol in my reticule," Samantha lied in a quavering voice.

Prince Vladimir inspected Samantha from head to

toe and waved the giant out of the room. "How can I be of service?" he asked.

Before Samantha could reply, Princess Olga spoke up, "I understand congratulations are in order."

"What do you mean?"

Olga smiled coldly. "In a few months, we will have something in common—bearing the bastard's child."

Samantha flinched at the word *bastard* and wondered how she knew about the pregnancy. Nobody with an ounce of kindness who had seen the prince's anguish could ever use that horrible word. The beautiful, graceful blonde had no heart.

Instead of replying to the princess, Samantha said, "Victoria, if this witch uses the word *bastard* again, cut her tongue out."

Victoria smiled. "With pleasure, sister."

Prince Vladimir chuckled, earning himself a glare from the blonde. "Does my brother know you are here?" he asked. "Ah, I see from your expression that he does not."

"Will you leave England and Rudolf in peace if I get you the Kazanov Venus?" Samantha asked.

The princess spoke instead of the prince. "You don't want to bear him a—" With dagger in hand, Victoria took a step toward the blonde. "You don't want to bear a child without benefit of marriage?"

"Olga, be quiet," Prince Vladimir said. He looked at Samantha, saying, "I already told you I would leave my brother in peace if I get the Venus. I wish Rudolf no harm. We share a mother, after all."

Samantha opened her reticule and withdrew the white velvet pouch. She placed it on the end of the table. "There is your Venus. Now kindly remove yourself from England. Let's go, sister."

With their heads held high, Samantha and Victoria

left the dining room. Once out of the prince's sight, they raced down the corridor and into the bright sunlight outside. Neither sister stopped moving until they'd closed the coach's door.

"Park Lane," Victoria called to the driver.

While Samantha was sneaking into the prince's chamber to return the Kazanov Venus, Rudolf and Robert were on their way to Montague House. With his half brother's support, Rudolf intended to persuade Vladimir and Olga to admit to the divorce and return to Russia. He would let them name their price but would not relinquish the Venus to them. That was reparation for his mother because Rudolf knew the missing piece was important to Fedor Kazanov.

"This seems to be a day for visits," Igor said, opening the front door.

"I want to speak to Vladimir," Rudolf said.

Igor stepped aside to allow them entrance. The hint of a smile touched his lips when he asked, "Your Highness, I am curious about how—"

"Lady Samantha lifted the key out of your pocket," Rudolf interrupted. "She is an expert pickpocket."

Igor's chest rumbled with thunderous laughter. "Your lady seemed so meek."

Rudolf smiled. "My offer of a job is still open."

"I will consider it," Igor said, leading them upstairs to the drawing room. "Follow me."

"I hope you are enjoying my hospitality," Rudolf said, walking into the drawing room.

"You are looking well, brother," Vladimir said.

"I have never felt better," Rudolf replied.

"A bastard for a bastard," Olga spoke up. "How quaint."

Surprised by her knowledge, Rudolf looked at his former wife for the first time. His gaze on her was pure hatred.

How he wished he had never been fooled by her beautiful face, Rudolf thought. She was more ruthless than any ten men he had ever known. There was no softness, no heart in her. The bitch had never even taken an interest in her own daughter. Samantha was a queen compared with this monster posing as a woman.

"Don't look so surprised," Olga told him. "Servants talk to other servants who, in turn, talk to other servants. You should know that."

"You just missed your lovely betrothed," Vladimir said with a smile. "Lady Samantha and her sister stopped by for a visit."

Rudolf stiffened at the mention of Samantha, every muscle in his body tightening, ready to leap at his brother. He felt Robert touch his arm, warning him to remain calm.

"I do not believe you," Rudolf said, his jaw clenched.

Olga drew his attention. "Lady Samantha wants to be certain she doesn't whelp a bastard. She brought her sister along for protection. Her *red-haired* sister."

"Darling, what color gown was she wearing?" Vladimir asked, touching the princess's hand. "Blue, wasn't it?"

"Yes, the gown was definitely blue."

Though he kept his face expressionless, Rudolf felt the surge of anger coursing through his body. Samantha *had* been wearing a blue gown, and he had forbidden her to leave the house without his permission and escort. What, in the name of God, had incited her to disobey him and come here today? He was going to give her a stinging lecture when he returned home, and then he would punish her. Solitary confinement in her chamber for a few days seemed appropriate.

"I will not surrender Venus to you," Rudolf told them.

"Actually, we have begun packing and will leave England in a few days," Vladimir told him. "Lady Samantha was kind enough to bring us the Venus."

Rudolf struggled for control. "You lie," he said through clenched teeth, his hands in fists at his sides. "Samantha would never—"

Vladimir produced a pouch. Opening it, he removed the gold Venus medallion and held it in the palm of his hand for Rudolf's inspection.

Rudolf couldn't believe what he was seeing. Samantha had betrayed him. Her kind and nurturing acceptance of him had hid an unscrupulous heart. He had trusted her, and she had betrayed him. The proof lay in the palm of his brother's hand.

That was her folly. Starting today, she would live to regret her betrayal. He would marry her because of the baby and then lock her away at his estate on Sark Island. She would never get another chance to betray him.

"Since you have the Venus," Robert spoke up, "you won't mind signing a document stating that Rudolf and Olga are divorced. My sister-in-law has nothing to do with your quarrel and should not be punished by bearing a child out of wedlock."

Vladimir inclined his head. He rose from his chair and crossed the drawing room to a table, returning with parchment, ink, and quill.

"You are not going to do that?" Olga asked. "Let the bastard sire a bastard."

"Lady Samantha seems to be a sweet child with her heart in the right place," Vladimir said. "You, my dear, have no heart."

"I will not sign it," Olga insisted.

"You will sign it or you will regret it," Vladimir threatened.

"I want to visit Zara before I leave England," Olga said, turning suddenly to Rudolf.

"You may see her in my presence only," Rudolf told her. "Come to Campbell Mansion tomorrow."

Vladimir passed the parchment and quill to Olga. "Sign it," he ordered. Then he handed it to Rudolf, saying, "This is for Lady Samantha, not you."

"I would not have expected otherwise," Rudolf said, staring coldly at his brother.

"Do not be too hard on her," Vladimir told him. "She had good reasons for giving me the Venus."

Rudolf turned away and left the drawing room. Climbing into the coach, Rudolf stared straight ahead. He was furious and humiliated. He needed to think of a suitable way to punish Samantha. God, how he despised her. He'd been fooled by her simperingly sweet, accepting manner. Why, she had even had him loving her, and all the while she'd plotted to betray him.

"From your expression, I would say that Samantha is in trouble," Robert said. "I urge you to remember that she is carrying your child."

"I have forgotten nothing," Rudolf said. "Tell your man to take us to the bishop. Samantha and I will marry at Campbell Mansion this afternoon. Will you be my best man?"

"I would be honored as long as you promise not to beat her," Robert said. "I do not consider spanking as a beating."

"The thought of spanking her and her sister is very tempting," Rudolf replied. In an awful voice, he said, "When I am finished with her, Samantha will wish for a simple spanking."

* * *

Later that afternoon, Samantha sat in the small drawing room and knitted a blanket for her baby. The prince could afford to purchase a thousand such blankets if she asked, but this one was made with love.

With her in the drawing room were Mrs. Sweeting, the children, and Giles. Victoria entertained them with a concert on her flute.

"Sweeting, take the children upstairs," Aunt Roxie ordered, hurrying into the drawing room. "Samantha and Victoria, your presence is required in His Grace's study."

Samantha felt an inkling of fear, especially when she noted the worry in her aunt's eyes. She glanced at her sister, who shrugged and shook her head.

When she limped into the study, Samantha stopped short. Not only were Duke Magnus, Robert, and Rudolf there but also the Bishop of London.

One look at the prince's face told Samantha something was terribly wrong. His facial muscles were tensed, his expression forbidding, and his right cheek muscles began twitching when he looked at her.

"Stand here," Rudolf ordered, his voice mirroring his anger. "The bishop is going to marry us."

Suddenly frightened, Samantha filled with foreboding, and her heart beat faster. "Marry now?" she said. "I don't understand."

"There is nothing to understand," Rudolf snapped. "The bishop has come to marry us."

Samantha shook her head, saying, "I want to wait."

"Until you whelp the brat?" Rudolf asked.

Samantha stared in surprise at him. Except for the day they had returned to London, Rudolf had never said anything so crude to her or anyone else.

Why was the prince behaving like this? He was frightening her. She could see him struggling against a rage but didn't know how to pacify him.

"We are waiting," he said.

Shaking her head, Samantha backed away. Rudolf grabbed her upper arm in a tight grip and yanked her beside him.

"You will marry me now, or I will beat you," Rudolf told her. "No one in this room will intercede for you."

Samantha looked to her aunt for help, but she looked away. Silently, she appealed to the duke, but he also looked away. Knowing the marquess would refuse her, she said to the prince, "You can release my arm. I am willing to marry you."

Rudolf glanced at her but refused to release her arm.

"Please, you are hurting me," she said.

Rudolf loosened his grip but held on. He nodded at the bishop.

Within surprisingly few minutes, the Bishop of London pronounced them man and wife. Duke Magnus instantly grabbed the cleric's arm to escort him from the study, saying, "Let's all go to the drawing room and toast the happy couple."

The happy couple? Samantha thought, her panic rising as a horrified giggle threatened to bubble up in her throat. The prince appeared ready to murder her.

Everyone was behaving so strangely. She saw her aunt grab her sister's wrist and force her from the study. Robert followed them out, closing the door behind him, leaving her alone with her husband.

Since fleeing seemed wiser than fighting, Samantha turned to leave. Her husband's voice stopped her.

"You will remain here," Rudolf ordered. "We have an important matter to discuss."

Samantha looked him straight in the eye and then

wished she hadn't. The prince was furious with her. She wanted—*no, needed*—to get away from him.

"I'm not feeling well," she told him. "Could we postpone this discussion until later?"

"No." The word fell between them like an axe.

Samantha forced herself to incline her head, instead of scream for help. "What did you wish to discuss?"

"You disobeyed me," Rudolf said, grabbing her chin in an iron grip and staring coldly into her eyes. "Do not bother to lie. I know you left the house without permission or escort."

"I had an escort," Samantha defended herself.

"I do not consider your sister a proper escort," Rudolf said.

"I'm sorry," she said. "I didn't mean to disobey—"

"Where did you go?" Rudolf asked.

Samantha felt confused. Great Giles' ghost, what was he accusing her of? "Do you think I was meeting a lover or—"

"Do *not* be ridiculous," Rudolf snapped. "I am the only fool in London to be gulled by a pa—" He broke off, unwilling to say the two words that would wound her.

Knowing what he'd almost said, Samantha felt as though he'd kicked her in the stomach. She flinched and began to tremble, and her bottom lip quivered in her struggle to fight back tears.

"You think I am a pathetic cripple," Samantha cried, her voice filled with pain. "Why are you doing this to me?"

Still, Rudolf refused to say the words. With both hands, he yanked her against his hard, unyielding body. "I know you stole the Venus and delivered it into my brother's hands."

"No, you don't understand," Samantha said, her expression clearing. "I can explain—"

Losing control, Rudolf shook her until her teeth rattled. He released her so suddenly, she lost her balance and nearly fell. In an instant, his hand was there to steady her.

"Go to your chamber while I join the others to toast the happy couple," Rudolf ordered. "I will deal with you later."

Too frightened to argue, Samantha limped toward the door. She paused there and tried again, saying, "Please, let me explain. I'm begging you to listen."

"Get out of my sight before I do something I will regret," Rudolf ordered, hatred leaping at her from his black eyes.

Defeated, Samantha opened the door and left the study. Tears welled up in her eyes and rolled down her cheeks as she limped down the corridor to the stairs.

When she reached her chamber, self-preservation demanded she lock the door. Then she lay down on the bed to wait for whatever punishment her husband had planned.

Samantha knew one thing for certain. She would always look back in bitterness on her wedding day, a day that should have been one of the happiest of her life.

Rudolf thought she was a pathetic cripple. She had trusted and loved him, and he had nearly thrown the two words she most despised into her face.

For the first time in her life, Samantha didn't bother to thank God for a blessing. She had none.

CHAPTER 18

Why wouldn't Rudolf listen to her?

Samantha asked herself that question for the hundredth time since being sent to her chamber.

Sitting on the chaise in front of the hearth, Samantha looked down at her nearly transparent, light-as-gossamer nightgown. The gown had been made for her wedding night and meant to entice.

Her aching heart sank in despair. Once she'd recovered from her crying jag, Samantha had freshened up and donned the nightgown. This was her wedding night, and the prince would surely come to her. Then she would explain what really happened.

Hours had passed since then. The sounds of supper had quieted many hours earlier, and now the household slept.

Not Samantha. Though bone weary, she couldn't find release from her pain in sleep.

Why shouldn't she go to him? Rudolf was her husband. There was nothing improper about seeking him. He would be drowsy with sleep and more amenable to listening.

Determined to set things right between them, Samantha rose from the chaise and lifted the candle off the table. Then she limped to the door.

Samantha hesitated a fraction of a moment before she opened the door to his bedchamber. There was nothing to fear, she told herself. She loved him and he cared for her. He was angry but would listen to the woman who carried his seed in her body.

Stepping inside the dark chamber, Samantha walked to a table to set the candle down. Then she turned toward the bed.

The bedchamber was empty. The bed was unused.

Samantha stared in confusion at the bed. Where was he? Had he moved his chamber to get away from her?

Turning to leave, Samantha froze, and her breath caught in her throat. Looking heartbreakingly handsome in his formal evening attire, Rudolf stood just inside the doorway and stared at her.

"Are you looking for something to steal?" Rudolf asked.

"Why are you dressed like that at this hour?" Samantha asked.

Rudolf sauntered across the chamber. His hot, intense gaze raked her body enticingly enfolded in the flimsy nightgown. There was no love in his expression, not even lust, only barely suppressed rage.

"I will ask the questions," Rudolf said coldly. "Are you here to steal something else?"

"I thought you would come to my chamber," Samantha said, lifting her chin a notch.

His smile chilled Samantha. "Our marriage was consummated before the ceremony," he said. "The proof grows inside you."

Samantha remained silent, unable to think of a suitable reply. She searched her mind for the magic words that would bring down the wall he had built to shut her out.

"I want to explain about today," Samantha said, holding out a badly shaking hand to him.

Rudolf dropped his gaze to her shaking hand, held out to him in supplication. He turned his back on her and removed his jacket and cravat, tossing them aside even as he was tossing her aside.

"I have no desire to hear lies at three in the morning," he said. "Return to your own chamber."

"I need to explain."

Rudolf looked at her, pinning her to the spot where she stood. "You are trying my patience, Princess." He reached out to lift her chin and stare into her eyes. "Today, you swore before God to obey me. Are you breaking your vows already?"

Samantha stared in silence at him. She saw no love, no warmth in his black gaze, only a desire to hurt her.

Long, silent moments passed. The prince folded his arms across his chest.

Samantha hesitated for another fraction of a second and then limped toward the door. "Why won't you listen to me?" she pleaded, before leaving.

Rudolf ignored her question. "If I find you in my chamber again," he warned, "I won't be so kind."

Samantha dropped her gaze to the carpet. She knew he was punishing her. Maybe she needed punishing. She *was* a pathetic cripple.

"I have no use for you tonight," Rudolf said. "You are dismissed."

"You will regret this," Samantha told him, her voice mirroring her pain. "I will never forgive you." And then she left the chamber.

I am a *bastard*, Rudolf thought, anguished by his own cruelty to the woman he loved. But Samantha had betrayed him, had stolen the Venus medallion and given it to his brother and former wife. She had known how important keeping it was to him.

Rudolf could not forgive her for that. He needed to hurt her as she had hurt him.

When she awakened the next morning, the first thing Samantha did was reach for the bread on the table. There was none.

Samantha felt heavyhearted. Her husband of one day hated her. The dream she'd cherished for all of those years crumbled beneath the pain of her husband's hatred.

Why had God chosen to torment her by giving her a husband who hated her? Yes, she had picked more than a few pockets, but she wasn't a bad person.

You are a pathetic cripple, she told herself. Even her husband thought so.

Samantha forced herself to get out of bed and dressed. Perhaps she would have an opportunity to explain herself over breakfast.

And then her Douglas pride swelled within her. After what he'd said to her the previous day, Rudolf deserved no explanation. Let him think whatever he wanted. In fact, she hoped he had already eaten and left the dining room. She needed peace of mind more than she needed him.

Trying to lift her spirits, Samantha dressed in a petal pink gown and went downstairs. She tried to keep her face expressionless when she walked into the dining room and saw her husband sitting at the table.

Ignoring him, Samantha limped to the sideboard. "Good morning, Tinker," she greeted the majordomo with a warm smile.

"Good morning, Lady Samantha."

"She isn't Lady Samantha," Rudolf snapped.

Both Samantha and Tinker looked in confusion at the prince. "Who is she?" the majordomo asked.

Rudolf looked at her almost reluctantly, his expression telling her how disgusted he was by her presence. "She is Her Highness, Princess Samantha."

"I apologize profusely, Your Highness," Tinker said.

"You don't need to address me like that," Samantha told him.

Rudolf banged his fist on the table, making them jump. "He does if I say he does."

Samantha said nothing. Though her husband had stolen her appetite in less than two minutes, she spooned scrambled eggs onto her plate and then a roll with butter.

Turning to the table, Samantha chose not to sit beside him. Instead, she sat at the far end of the table.

Samantha forced herself to eat but kept a wary eye on her husband. She had no idea what he would do next.

Tinker appeared at her side and placed the morning paper beside her plate. "His Highness sent you this."

"Thank you, Mr. Tinker."

Samantha looked at the headlines and then turned nonchalantly to the society column on page three. She hoped the reporter had found someone else to malign.

The remarks about Lady Randolph's ball caught her attention:

Abandoning both wife and betrothed, Prince Rudolf Kazanov attended Lady Randolph's ball and danced

*until dawn with London's most sought after beauties.
Judging from his many female admirers, this reporter believes the prince has joined the ranks of London's most
sought after. Is he available or not?*

Samantha felt the first flush of fury. Her groom had
passed their wedding night dancing with London's most
sought after beauties.

"Your Highness, are you trying to give me ideas?"
Samantha asked, gesturing to the newspaper.

"What do you mean?" Rudolf asked coldly.

"I may decide to follow your example," she told him.

"Do not even consider playing games with me," he
replied. "You cannot win."

Samantha arched an ebony brow at him. "I'm perfectly serious."

"Try it, and I'll send you—"

Samantha bolted out of the chair so fast it toppled
over, surprising him. "Will you send me to an insane asylum?" she cried. "You are the insane one here. You passed
our wedding night dancing with London's most sought
afters. God, how I wish I had never met you."

"Are you finished with your theatrics?" Rudolf asked,
the ghost of a smile flirting with his lips.

Samantha didn't answer. Tears welled up in her eyes,
and her hand flew to her throat as she fought the nausea. Then she limped toward the door.

"Stop," Rudolf ordered.

Samantha stopped short and turned around. She
couldn't control the hope and the love shining in her
eyes.

Rudolf leaned back in his chair. "Christ, you are becoming tedious," he told her in a voice filled with contempt. "Are you capable of anything besides weeping
and vomiting?"

Desolation replaced hope and love. Her shoulders sagged beneath the weight of his cruelty, but she couldn't bring herself to call him a bastard. She couldn't hurt him.

"Well?"

"Apparently not." Samantha turned and limped out of the dining room.

"Bravo, Your Highness," Tinker said from where he stood at the sideboard. "Will there be an encore?"

"I beg your pardon," Rudolf said, turning to stare at the man.

The majordomo said nothing.

"Bring me another cup of coffee," he ordered.

Tinker looked down his nose at the prince and told him, "Get it yourself." Then he stalked out of the dining room, too.

Later that afternoon, Samantha sat on a stone bench in the garden. Beside her sat Mrs. Sweeting and Giles. Grant, Drake, and Zara gamboled around and around the garden, reminding Samantha of puppies and kittens at play.

"Drake, don't push Zara," Samantha called. "You need to be gentle with little girls."

"Lady Samantha, may I join you?" a familiar voice asked.

Samantha turned and saw Alexander Emerson walking in her direction. She gave him a sunny smile. Here was a friend who had always been kind to her.

"I'd like to speak privately if possible," Alexander said, taking her hand in his.

Samantha nodded and said, "Sweeting, would you take the children inside and give them cider?"

"Come, children," the nanny called. "We're going to have cider now."

Samantha watched them walk into the mansion and then patted the bench beside her. "Sit down, my lord. It's good to see you again."

"I have business with His Grace and thought I'd come a few minutes early to see you," Alexander said. "How are you feeling?"

Samantha tried to smile, but her bottom lip quivered. Tears brimmed over her eyes.

"That good, huh?"

Samantha gave him a wobbly smile. "You must have seen the article in the *Times* about my wedding day fiasco."

"Samantha, I think your aunt wants to propose a match between me and Tory, but if you need a father for your child, I would be proud to marry you and care for you and the baby," Alexander said, his hazel eyes filled with compassion.

His kindness was her undoing. He had always been kind, and she had repaid him by climbing into the prince's bed.

Samantha burst into tears. Alexander put his arm around her.

"Tell me what's wrong," he said. "If I can help in any way—"

Samantha shook her head. "Rudolf and I wed yesterday here at the mansion. I wish I had never met him."

"Tell me what I can do for you," Alexander said.

"The first thing you can do is take your hands off my wife," Rudolf said, walking toward them.

Frightened, Samantha leaped away from Alexander. There was no telling what the prince would do now.

Alexander stood to face the prince. "Why is your bride of one day reduced to crying in someone else's arms?" he challenged the prince. "What have you done to her?"

"My marriage is none of your business," Rudolf replied.

"I am making it my business," Alexander told him.

"I'll countenance no violence on my property," Duke Magnus said, materializing from inside the mansion.

"Your Grace, I simply asked Lady Samantha how she was feeling, and she burst into tears," Alexander told the duke. "Something is definitely wrong."

"Whatever is wrong is Samantha's fault," the duke told him. He turned to the prince and said, "I have business with Alex and invited him here. There's no need for any challenge. Why don't you see to your wife." The duke leveled an irritated look on Samantha that told her the enmity between the two men was her fault.

"Will you be all right if I leave you with him?" Alexander asked.

Samantha nodded but didn't trust herself to speak. She dropped her gaze to the ground, afraid to look into her husband's eyes.

When Rudolf spoke, his voice was not unkind, "I have decided your punishment."

"You wouldn't do anything to hurt my baby," Samantha asked, raising her gaze to his.

Something flickered in his dark eyes. "I would never strike you, Princess." He held out his hand as he'd done the first night they met at the ball. Samantha placed her hand in his and rose from the bench.

"Come with me," Rudolf said, leading her by the hand. "You will be confined to your chamber until Vladimir leaves London. Once he's gone, I will be moving into Montague House, and you will be sent to live in seclusion at my estate on Sark Island. I will, of course, return for the birth of our child."

Reaching the third floor, Rudolf opened her chamber door for her. She turned to him before going inside and asked, "What will you tell the children?"

"I will think of something plausible," he assured her.

Samantha nodded and walked into her chamber. She whirled around when he locked the door. She really was his prisoner, and he was determined to banish her from his life. It would be worse on Sark Island. Everyone there would be on the prince's payroll. There would be no friendly face.

Samantha sat on the chaise and took up her knitting. Sometime later, she heard a knock on her door and limped across the chamber.

"Who is it?" she asked,

"Tory."

"The prince has locked me in here," Samantha told her sister. "In a few days, he's sending me to his estate on Sark Island."

"Where will he be?" Victoria asked.

"He's remaining in London."

"I'll make him listen to the truth."

"Don't bother," Samantha told her sister. "After last night, I don't want him anymore."

"What happened last night?"

"I went to his chamber just as he was returning home from his social schedule," Samantha answered. "He refused to listen to any explanation and ordered me out of his chamber. Her voice broke when she added, "He hurt me, and I want to go home."

"You *are* home."

"No, I want to go home to the cottage."

"Will you live there alone?" her sister asked.

"I promise I'll come back eventually," Samantha said. "Perhaps, if I'm gone, Rudolf will see things differently and forgive me."

"He should be begging for your forgiveness," Victoria said in an angry voice. "I'll sneak some supplies out there today. Tomorrow, I'll help you escape."

"How will I get through the locked door?" Samantha asked.

"You'll climb out the window and down the tree," her sister answered.

"It's three stories down," Samantha cried softly. "What if I fall?"

"Then you won't need to worry about the prince anymore."

"What?" Samantha was already beginning to panic.

"Don't be a twit," Victoria said. "I'll simply climb up and get you. Put a few belongings in a bag tonight."

"Tory?"

"What?"

"I love you, sister."

"I love you, too."

Samantha immediately grabbed a few necessities, packed them into a satchel, and hid the satchel under the bed. Then she changed into a nightgown and lay down on the bed to worry about the next day.

Would she reach the ground safely without injuring her baby? Would Grant and Drake believe she had abandoned them? What would Rudolf do when he discovered her missing?

Later that evening, Samantha heard the sound of the door being unlocked. Sitting on the chair near the window, she knitted a blanket for her baby. Though she didn't look up, Samantha felt her husband's presence with her whole body.

Rudolf set the tray with her supper on the table. She looked up at him then. He stood there with his hands in his trouser pockets and watched her.

312   *Patricia Grasso*

"How can you see without daylight?" he asked.

"I don't need to see what I'm doing," she told him.

"What are you knitting?"

"A blanket for my baby."

"Blue for a baby?" he asked, the hint of a smile touching his lips.

"You already have a daughter," Samantha said. "I assumed you would want a boy. If you would prefer a pink blanket . . ."

"I have no preference."

His wife seemed eager to please him. Too eager. She feared him. He thought he would feel better if she feared him, but he was wrong. He felt worse.

"Good night," he said, and walked toward the door.

"Good night, Your Highness."

It was late when Rudolf climbed the stairs to the third floor again. He'd purposefully gone to several balls and danced every dance so that his wife would read about his social life in the *Times*.

Pausing at her bedchamber door, Rudolf reached into his pocket and pulled out the key. He let himself into her chamber and stood by the bed to stare down at her.

Samantha appeared angelic in her sleep. He was hard-pressed to believe she could be so treacherous.

Drawing the coverlet away from her body, Rudolf touched her belly where his child grew. He wished things could have been different. What was it about him that made women want to betray him?

He had made such a mess of things. He should never have trusted her. For all of those years since Olga's betrayal, he had guarded his heart, and then Samantha had limped into his life.

"My prince," Samantha said on a sigh, her eyes opening. "Stay with me."

Rudolf gazed down at her. If he didn't know better, he could almost believe she loved him.

Feeling as if she'd won this battle, Rudolf left the chamber.

The heart-wrenching sound of her sobs dogged his every step.

CHAPTER 19

No bread, Samantha thought, awakening the next morning. She'd been so certain that the prince would leave her bread.

Samantha rose from the bed and, after washing, dressed in an old gown, the one she would wear when she returned to the cottage. Wearing one of the gowns the duke or the prince had purchased was out of the question. She didn't want to call attention to herself while staying at the cottage.

Limping across the chamber, Samantha opened the window and breathed deeply. Spring was in the air. Down below in the garden a forsythia bush bloomed with yellow flowers.

Samantha heard the door being unlocked but remained at the window. Great Giles' ghost, she couldn't wait to feel the sun on her face. This afternoon, she thought, at the old cottage.

"Breakfast, Princess," Rudolf said.

Samantha turned away from the window and asked, "Are you actually going to keep me prisoner?"

Rudolf ignored the question. "Eat your breakfast."

Samantha sat down and looked at the tray. The prince had filled the plate with a mountain of scrambled eggs, several slices of ham, and two rolls with butter. Beside the plate lay a copy of the *Times*.

"Were you feeling generous this morning?" Samantha asked, looking at the heap of food. "Or did you think my appetite had increased overnight?"

When Rudolf said nothing, Samantha broke off a piece of roll and ate it. The prince seemed reluctant to leave. With his arms folded across his chest, he stood near the window and watched her.

"Have you given up reading the morning paper?" Rudolf asked.

Samantha glanced at him and then down at the *Times*. Apparently, he wanted her to read the paper, which meant there was something in it about him. He'd been wearing formal evening attire when he'd come to her in the night.

Giving him one of her sweetest smiles, Samantha said, "I am no longer interested in your social life."

"This is a complete reversal," Rudolf said, cocking a dark brow at her.

He was taunting her.

"I am no longer interested in your social life because I am no longer interested in you," Samantha told him.

"I am so disappointed," he drawled.

Because she couldn't find a crack in his armor, Samantha lashed out in frustrated anger. She swiped the tray, sending it and its contents onto the floor.

Rudolf didn't move a muscle. In fact, he appeared amused. "You really ought to control these fits of temper," he said.

"I didn't have fits of temper until I met you," she snapped.

"Have yourself a nice day, Princess," Rudolf said, walking toward the door.

Samantha heard him locking the door. She grabbed the *Times* and opened it to the society column. And then she wept.

Later, Samantha heard a light tapping on her door. She crossed the chamber and asked, "Who is it?"

"I have the gig in the alley," her sister whispered. "Are you ready?"

"Yes, I'm ready."

"Toss your satchel out the window," Victoria instructed her. "I'll come around and help you down."

"I don't want to be caught," Samantha said. "Do you know where my husband is?"

"He's downstairs with Zara," Victoria answered. "Princess Olga is expected to visit her daughter. I'm leaving now."

Samantha grabbed her satchel and tossed it out the window. Next went her cloak.

Victoria appeared a few minutes later. Samantha watched as her sister climbed the oak tree.

"Good morning, sister," Victoria said with a smile, sitting on a branch outside her window.

Samantha looked down. "Tory, I don't think I can do this."

"Do you want to be banished to Sark Island while Rudolf remains in London and makes love to the acclaimed beauties?" her sister asked.

"If I fall, my baby will be hurt," Samantha argued.

"You won't fall as long as you don't look down," Victoria told her. "We're going to take this tree one branch at a time."

Samantha nodded. "I understand."

"Climb arse-first out the window," Victoria instructed her. "Only one leg first, though. Then sit on the branch like you would sit astride a horse. Hold on with both hands."

Samantha watched Victoria descend to a lower branch. Then she climbed out the window as instructed.

"Sister, I think I may be stuck here," Samantha called softly, and giggled nervously. "You'll need to fetch my husband to get me down."

"You are doing fine," Victoria said. Then instructed her, "Move your arse back toward the tree trunk when I drop to a lower branch. Then lean to the left and lower your left leg to the branch I'm standing on now. You will dismount the branch as if you were dismounting a horse."

"I understand." Samantha watched her sister descend to a lower branch, and then she moved.

By slow degrees, Victoria guided Samantha down to the last branch. "Drop to the ground," she said. "I'll break your fall."

Samantha let go and dropped into her sister's arms. They looked at each other and smiled.

Victoria grabbed the satchel and took Samantha by the hand. Hugging the house with their backs lest they be seen from a window, the sisters moved around the house. They cut through the garden to the alley where the gig was parked.

Victoria climbed into the driver's seat, and Samantha climbed up beside her. Samantha took a deep breath. She was finally free.

Her heart ached for her husband, but leaving him was best for both of them. She couldn't endure his cruelty another day. He needed time to realize that he should have listened to her explanation before judging her guilty of betraying him.

When they reached Park Lane, Victoria steered the gig west in the direction of Primrose Hill. Neither

318 *Patricia Grasso*

noticed the strikingly beautiful blonde in the coach that had just pulled to a halt in front of Campbell Mansion. Nor did they see the woman's coach move to follow them at a discreet distance.

Twenty minutes later, Victoria halted the gig in front of the old cottage. Samantha looked at the cottage and saw Rudolf as he'd been on New Year's Eve, not so long ago, when they'd passed the night here before traveling to Scotland.

"Are you coming?" Victoria asked, drawing her attention.

With a heavy heart, Samantha climbed down from the gig. She missed him already. Even when he was at his most disagreeable, she loved her prince with her whole heart and soul.

"I brought food here yesterday," Victoria told her, handing her the satchel. "I'll bring more in a week or so. Do you want me to stay with you?"

Samantha shook her head. "I need to be alone."

"How long will you stay?" her sister asked.

"I need some peace of mind," Samantha said with a shrug. "Will you do me another favor?"

Victoria smiled. "Anything."

"I need you to reassure Grant and Drake that I haven't abandoned them," Samantha said. "Tell them I'll be home in a few days. Don't let the prince know where I've gone."

"I will die before I breathe a word of your whereabouts," Victoria promised.

"Keeping silent won't be easy," Samantha warned. "Rudolf will know that you know where I am."

"Torture won't make me tell," Victoria said.

Samantha hugged her, saying, "Thank you, sister."

Victoria climbed into the gig, waved good-bye, and turned the horse in the direction of London. Samantha watched her sister drive away. Then she lifted her satchel off the ground and limped into the cottage. She hoped she was doing the right thing.

At Campbell Mansion, Rudolf paced back and forth in front of the hearth in the small drawing room. He halted abruptly and checked the time on his pocket watch.

Damn Olga to hell, Rudolf thought, resuming his pacing. She was forty-five minutes late. Now he would have to speak with Samantha after his scheduled meeting with the duke and the marquess. He couldn't live like this for the rest of his life, and he was damned tired of going to all those balls and society functions. If another simpering blonde clung to his arm, he might do her bodily harm.

Rudolf recalled the way Samantha had asked him to stay when he'd gone to her during the night. In spite of his cruelty during the past several days, she had refused to hurt him with the word he despised most, bastard.

There was not a shadow of a doubt in his mind that his wife loved him. He owed her the respect of listening to her explanation of why she'd given the Venus to Vladimir. Perhaps she hadn't truly understood the significance of her actions.

"Your Highness, Princess Olga has arrived," Tinker announced.

"Bring her here, and then fetch Zara and Sweeting."

A few minutes later, Olga strolled into the drawing room. Rudolf couldn't understand how he could ever have loved her. Yes, Olga was strikingly beautiful but so, too, were many poisonous snakes. Only this one walked on two legs instead of crawling on her belly.

"Rudolf, how good to see you again," Olga greeted him, offering her hand.

Rudolf ignored the hand and the greeting. "Zara is on her way down."

"Have you married the little cripple yet?" Olga asked.

Rudolf felt his muscles tense at the word *cripple*. His former wife was looking for an argument. He decided to disappoint her and inclined his head in the affirmative.

"Where is the new princess?" Olga asked. "I assumed she would be here, too."

"Samantha has other duties and would never intrude on your visit with Zara," Rudolf said stiffly.

"I do hope you manage not to lose this wife through inattention," Olga said with false sincerity.

"What does that mean?" he asked.

"I've been keeping up with your busy social schedule by reading the *Times*," she answered.

Rudolf said nothing.

"The red-haired sister should be spanked for her insolence," Olga told him.

Rudolf raised his brows. "You mean, Lady Victoria?"

"Victoria is no lady," Olga said. "Why, she had the audacity to threaten me with a dagger."

Rudolf smiled at that. He must remember to thank his young sister-in-law for her loyalty to his wife.

"Did you beat your wife for her betrayal?" Olga asked.

"Have you come here to badger me about Samantha?" Rudolf asked. "Or did you want to visit Zara?"

Princess Olga smiled. "Dearest Rudolf, I came here today to do both."

"Why do you want to visit Zara?" he asked. "She barely knows you. After all, you wanted nothing to do with her after you learned that I was—"

"A bastard," she finished for him.

Rudolf looked past her. "Here they are now. Sweeting, come in and close the door behind you."

"Zara, my sweet, come and give your mother a hug," the princess said.

Frightened, the little girl clung to her father's hand. "Where is the other mother?" she asked him.

"*I* am your mother," Olga told her.

Zara shook her head. "The other mother plays with me. We watch cloud pictures together."

"Zara is referring to Samantha," Rudolf said.

"She plays with children?" Olga said. "How bourgeois." She looked at the little girl, saying, "Lady Samantha is not your mother. I am your mother."

Zara shrank back from her. "Is Samantha my mother?" she asked, looking up at her father.

"Yes, sweetheart, Samantha is a real mother who takes delight in her children."

"You have been too indulgent with her," Olga said, clearly irritated. "She needs to learn proper manners."

"Sweeting, do not let Zara out of your sight for any reason," Rudolf ordered, turning to the nanny suddenly. He grabbed his former wife's arm, saying, "Your time is up, Olga. Zara wants nothing to do with you. Go home to Vladimir."

At that, Rudolf forcibly escorted his former wife down the stairs to the foyer. Instead of waiting for the majordomo, he opened the front door himself and shoved his former wife outside.

"Good to see you again, Olga," Rudolf said, echoing her words to him.

Closing the door behind her, Rudolf turned to Tinker and instructed, "If that woman ever shows her face here again, do not allow her entrance to this house."

"I understand, Your Highness."

Rudolf took the stairs two at a time. The sooner he met with the duke, the sooner he could speak with his wife.

Knocking on the study door, Rudolf entered when he heard the duke call out to him. The marquess was already there.

"Would you like a shot of whiskey?" Robert asked.

Rudolf nodded. "I have just endured an interview with my former wife." He reached for the glass of whiskey and gulped it down. "I gave Tinker instructions not to allow her entrance again."

"Your Highness, are you and my niece still not in accord," Duke Magnus asked.

"I see you have a copy of the *Times* there," Rudolf hedged.

"I am beginning to doubt the wisdom of giving her to you in marriage, pregnancy or not," the duke said.

"I am on my way to have a long talk with my wife," Rudolf told him. "I think that she did not understand the implications of her actions."

"I am glad to hear that," Duke Magnus said, smiling with relief. "The birth of your baby will settle any lingering differences you have."

"There is nothing like motherhood to calm a woman down," Robert agreed.

Rudolf smirked. "Oh, really?"

"The extra energy a spirited female has to argue with her husband is spent on nurturing the babe," Robert told him.

"I never found that to be true," Rudolf replied, the hint of a smile touching his lips. "As I recall, after she recovered from the birth of Zara, Olga began an affair with my brother.

Robert flushed. "Oh, perhaps some women are different."

"Do not concern yourself with Olga," Rudolf told him. "If she hadn't fallen into Vladimir's bed, I would never have met and married Samantha."

"Before we turn to business," Duke Magnus said, "I have another matter to discuss."

Rudolf raised his dark brows at the duke. "Speak freely, Your Grace."

Duke Magnus cleared his throat. "I would like to know if you can set aside your animosity for Alexander Emerson and welcome him into the family at some future time."

"Are you considering adoption, or is he another of your by-blows?" Rudolf asked.

"Roxanne wants a marriage between Alexander and Victoria," the duke said. "My wife's youngest niece is impulsive and has a wild streak. She was allowed an unusual amount of freedom at an early age. She is exceptionally undisciplined and unruly. Roxanne feels that Alexander is strong enough to control Victoria."

"I can stomach the man as long as he stays away from my wife," Rudolf answered.

"I am relieved to hear you say that," Duke Magnus said. "Alexander and I settled on a betrothal agreement yesterday. Of course, we'll give her another year to mature."

"Does Victoria know she's betrothed?" Robert asked.

"Good God, no," the duke exclaimed. "Alexander insists on courting her first so she won't fight him."

"And if Victoria does not develop a fondness for Emerson?" Rudolf asked with a smile.

"She'll go down the aisle anyway, but she'll fight us all the way," Duke Magnus said, his expression grim. "I can't begin to tell you how infuriating Victoria can be."

Robert laughed out loud. "Poor Alexander thought he was getting sweet, biddable Samantha but ended up with the family's hellion. I can almost hear the sound of crashing crockery."

"Samantha is nothing like her younger sister," Rudolf said. "Except for that lapse in judgment, she would never do anything contrary to my wishes. I know where she is and what she is doing at all times."

Robert hooted with laughter. "That's because you've locked her in her chamber."

There was a knock on the door, and Tinker entered, saying, "Your Highness, three gentlemen are asking for you. They claim to be your brothers."

"Send them in," the duke told the majordomo.

Rudolf grinned. It was about time. Too bad they hadn't arrived a few days earlier. He would still have the Kazanov Venus.

And then they were there. Rudolf rose from the chair and hugged each brother in turn. "Your Grace," he introduced them, "these are Viktor, Mikhail, and Stepan. Brothers, this is my wife's uncle, the Duke of Inverary, and his son, also my brother-in-law, the Marquess of Argyll."

The three princes shook hands with the duke and the marquess. Robert remarked, "Viktor looks exactly like Vladimir."

"They are twins," Rudolf explained. "Unfortunately, Vladimir is older by two minutes."

"They have the look of you except for the blue eyes," Duke Magnus said. "Sit down, please. Robert, pour them whiskeys."

"Vladimir tried to kill me to get the Venus," Rudolf said in English for the benefit of the duke and the marquess. "Olga is in London with him."

"They married after you left Russia," Viktor told him.

"How long have you been married?" Mikhail asked.

"Two days."

"Why are you speaking with us instead of getting a son on your wife?" Stepan asked.

Rudolf's eyes lit with amusement. "I took care of that *before* the wedding."

"What is her name?" Mikhail asked.

"What is she like?" Stepan asked. "We want to know everything."

"Samantha is an angel, everything Olga was not," Rudolf told them.

"We went to Montague House first," Viktor said. "Igor directed us here. He asked me to tell you he is accepting your offer as soon as Vladimir leaves England."

"Who is Igor?" Duke Magnus asked.

"Igor is the man who abducted Samantha and me from your estate," Rudolf said. "I offered him a job while he had us locked in that cellar."

"You trust him to work for you?" the duke asked.

Rudolf nodded. "I always liked Igor. Besides, he had the opportunity to kill us but didn't."

"Let's join the ladies for tea," Duke Magnus said. "Your Highnesses?"

The Kazanov brothers looked at each other and laughed. "Call me Viktor," the twenty-seven-year-old said.

"I am Mikhail," said the twenty-five-year-old.

"Stepan, if you please," the twenty-three-year-old said.

The prince turned to the duke and said, "Call me Rudolf."

Duke Magnus was obviously touched. The two men shook hands.

"Can I call you Rudolf, too?" Robert asked.

Rudolf grinned and teased the other man, saying, "No, you may call me Your Highness."

Laughing and talking all at the same time, the six

men walked down the corridor to the drawing room. The duchess sat in a high-backed chair, and Victoria sat on the settee.

"Your Grace, I would present my brothers, Viktor and Mikhail and Stepan," Rudolf made the introduction.

"I am so pleased to meet you finally," Lady Roxanne told them.

"And this young lady is my wife's younger sister, Victoria," Rudolf added.

Victoria gave them an easy smile and said, "Welcome to England."

"What an interesting color hair," Mikhail said, admiring her fiery mane. He sat beside her on the settee.

"I saw her first," Stepan told his older brother, sitting on Victoria's other side.

Victoria laughed, pleased by their attention.

"Be careful, Victoria," Rudolf said, laughing. "My brothers could charm the virginity out of a celibate."

"I wish the settee had space for four," Viktor complained.

"I'll get Samantha," Rudolf said. "She's upstairs." He turned to leave the room, but his sister-in-law's voice stopped him dead in his tracks.

"You won't find her there, Your Highness," Victoria announced. "She's gone."

Everyone except for his brothers looked stunned. And then his sister-in-law had the temerity to inform his brothers, "His High-and-Mighty Highness locked my sister in her bedchamber."

"Where did she go this time?" Rudolf asked, his irritation apparent in his voice.

Victoria looked him straight in the eye, and there was no mistaking her hostility when she answered, "I have no idea."

Rudolf felt his temper rising. The sister knew where Samantha was hiding.

He impaled her with his black gaze and knew he'd frightened her when she shrank back into Stepan. "I will protect you," his brother whispered.

"Stepan, mind your own business," Rudolf ordered. He looked at Victoria and asked, "How did she escape from a locked room? You stole the key and opened the door, didn't you?"

"I did not," Victoria said, lifting her nose into the air. She gave him a smug smile, adding, "Samantha climbed out the window and down the tree."

"Samantha did that?" the duchess asked, her surprise obvious.

"With my assistance," Victoria amended. She gave Prince Stepan a sidelong glance and said in a loud whisper, "I needed to climb up the tree to get her down. She was desperate to get away and—"

Rudolf was heartened to see her pale when she looked at him. He was enraged by her bragging about disobeying his orders. He could feel his cheek muscles twitching. His hands itched to spank both sisters, especially this one who had obviously encouraged Samantha to endanger herself by going out the window.

He watched the girl turn to her aunt and say, "Perhaps climbing down the tree was not a sterling idea." She turned suddenly and looked him straight in the eye, saying, "I don't blame her, though. You *are* a tyrant."

"I commend your loyalty to your sister," Rudolf said, his lips quirking with amusement. "However, you have no idea of the seriousness of her actions."

"You don't know what her actions were," his sister-in-law told him. "You judged her guilty without giving her a chance to explain herself."

"What did the lady do?" Viktor asked.

"My wife handed the Venus over to Vladimir," Rudolf answered his brother.

"The Venus is merely a piece of metal," Mikhail reminded him.

"The medallion is important to Fedor," Rudolf said.

"When will you stop fighting that war?" Stepan asked.

"Have you forgotten what Fedor did to our mother?" Rudolf replied.

"We have forgotten nothing," Viktor answered quietly.

Rudolf turned to Victoria, intending to frighten her into telling him where Samantha was, but he was unprepared for her verbal attack. "You ruined her wedding day, and you ruined her wedding night," Victoria accused him, her voice rising with anger on her sister's behalf. "When she tried to explain herself, you hurt her."

"You hurt Samantha?" the duchess asked.

"I hurt her pride," he answered.

"Pride was all she had," Victoria shouted.

Rudolf snapped his black gaze to his young sister-in-law. Her words rang with truth, but his anger had blinded him to the fact that Samantha was not Olga.

"Suppose you tell me what exactly her actions were," he said.

The twit had the audacity to lift her nose into the air and tell him, "Your willingness to listen comes two days too late. My sister doesn't want to explain now. She only wants to be left in peace."

"You are going to be left in *pieces* if you don't start talking," Rudolf growled. *"Now."*

He could see the seventeen-year-old trembling with fear, but she put a brave face on. "Your oh-so-treacherous wife took her entire life's savings of one thousand pounds—"

"How did Samantha manage to save one thousand pounds?" Aunt Roxie asked.

"I will begin at the beginning," Victoria told Rudolf, "but you will not like yourself very much by the time I finish."

Rudolf inclined his head. "I will chance that."

"Since we became wards of His Grace, he has been kind enough to give us a monthly allowance," Victoria said. "Samantha saved hers, never even spent a penny."

That surprised Rudolf. Women were notorious for squandering money, and his wife hadn't spent a penny.

"What was she saving for?" he asked.

Rudolf watched his sister-in-law's expression change from jaunty impertinence to remembered pain. Suddenly, he felt a tremendous weight settling around his heart. He knew he didn't want to know the rest of her story, but he needed to hear it.

"I asked her that once," Victoria said. "Samantha told me she was saving for her old age."

Everyone laughed, including the prince. "Old age?" he echoed.

"Samantha said she was already a pathetic cripple. She didn't want to add the word *burden* to describe herself," Victoria said. "I tried to persuade her to buy a few hair ribbons that she had been admiring." The seventeen-year-old's voice cracked with emotion, adding, "Samantha insisted that, in her case, buying ribbons was a waste of money. No matter how many pretty ribbons she wore, she would always be a pathetic cripple, and no man would want to marry her. She said she needed to save her money to support herself when she was an old spinster."

"Oh, dear God," Aunt Roxie exclaimed.

"The poor child," Duke Magnus said.

Rudolf felt sickened by the story. His heart was breaking for his wounded princess. His sister-in-law was correct; he didn't like himself very much.

Rudolf cleared his throat. "What does this have to do with the other day?"

"On the day in question, Samantha took her entire life's savings of one thousand pounds for her old age and asked me to accompany her to Bond Street," Victoria continued. "She paid a goldsmith the whole thousand pounds to make a replica of your stupid Venus medallion. Then we went to Montague House and gave the replica to your brother. If you don't believe me, go upstairs and look. Samantha put the real medallion back as soon as we returned home."

Everyone in the drawing room was silent. Rudolf filled with self-loathing. His wounded princess had put aside her own safety for him, and he had repaid her with cruelty.

"Why did she not tell me this?" he asked, his voice hoarse with raw emotion.

"You wouldn't listen," Victoria cried. Then she pointed her finger at him, saying, "And you owe me money for the hackney coach I hired."

"Tell me where Samantha is," Rudolf ordered.

"No."

"She is carrying my child," he tried to reason with her.

Victoria rose from the settee and walked toward the door, calling over her shoulder, "Samantha said she would return before she delivers the babe."

Rudolf felt like shaking the twit. He appealed to the duchess, saying, "Make her tell me where Samantha is."

"Victoria, tell His Highness where you have put his wife," Aunt Roxie ordered.

Victoria turned to the prince and smiled. "I have put her in a safe place where you can't hurt her," she told him. "I will not betray my own sister."

Rudolf couldn't believe it when his brothers seemed to side with the twit. Viktor walked over to her and kissed her hand. "You are too amazing for words," he complimented her. "Will you do me the honor of becoming my wife?"

Victoria looked confused.

"Viktor is too old for you," Mikhail told her. "Marry me."

"I am younger than they are," Stepan said. "I have more endurance. Marry me."

His sister-in-law apparently didn't know what his brother meant by endurance. She smiled at each in turn and said, "I am flattered." Then she glared at him, adding, "However, I would never wish to marry a man even remotely related to that monster."

Rudolf inclined his head. He had it coming. He had treated his wife abominably.

"If you have misplaced your wife, Your Highness," Victoria said, "I suggest you look for her *without my help.*"

CHAPTER 20

Please, God, keep her safe, Rudolf thought, staring at the Venus medallion in his hand. He'd passed a troubled night in his wife's chamber, sleeping fitfully on the chaise because he felt closer to her there. Now, as the sun streamed into the window, he wondered where he could start looking for her.

His beautiful, wounded princess. . . .

Rudolf remembered how shy she was the night at Emerson's ball. He'd thought she was a proper English lady until she picked Igor's pocket and began to reveal another side to herself.

He smiled at the memory of their coach ride to Scotland. How appalled she was at the prospect of sharing his bed. He'd had a wonderful time seducing her. He loved her sweetness and savored her surrender. She had welcomed him into her heart, her soul, her body. And still she had enough love to share with Grant, Drake, and Zara.

Samantha was shy and obedient but fierce when those she loved were endangered. She had accepted him completely in spite of his bastardy. When he was acting like a bastard, she had refrained from using that word on him. He had almost called her a pathetic cripple. He would never forgive himself for that.

His wife had bravely subdued her fear and limped down the church aisle in front of all those aristocrats. Her reward had been humiliation, which he had compounded by resuming his social life so that she could read about it in the *Times*.

Rudolf smiled, remembering how she had rebelled by eating those kippers. God, he had let her learn a hard lesson that day.

He loved her but had never spoken the words she needed to hear. When he found her, he would tell her he loved her every day for the rest of his life.

After Olga had ruined their wedding, Samantha had wept when she read the *Times*. His wounded princess had told him she wanted to go home and—

Rudolf sat up straight. Samantha had wanted to go home to the cottage.

His princess was in pain and had gone home.

Rudolf looked at the Venus medallion and put it in his pocket. He was going to the cottage to collect her, and then he was going to give her the medallion to toss in the Thames.

His expression darkened. If Vladimir ever realized what Samantha had done—

While Rudolf was ordering his horse saddled, Samantha was just awakening. She sighed and touched her belly, saying, "You'll get your bread as soon as I get up."

She lay there for long moments that stretched into an hour. She tried to summon her energy, but depression weighed her down. Finally, she rose from the bed and limped into the kitchen.

"You'll have oatmeal in a little while," Samantha told her belly, sitting at the table to eat her bread. Tonight, she would remember to bring a piece of bread to bed with her, and then she could eat it before she arose.

After washing and dressing, Samantha made herself a breakfast of oatmeal and tea. It wasn't the duke's dining room, but she would survive.

Samantha wondered what Rudolf was doing. Did he know that she had gone? If he did, how was Victoria bearing up under the pressure he was assuredly putting on her?

The kettle boiled, and Samantha poured hot water into her teacup. She put the kettle back and sat down, but her spoon slipped out of her hand and fell beneath the table.

Samantha crawled beneath the table to recover the spoon and never saw the cottage door open. Then she noticed the boots planted on the floor beside the table.

Surprised, Samantha started to rise but hit her head on the table. "Ouch," she cried, and backed out from under the table.

Kneeling on the floor, Samantha looked up into black eyes. Rudolf knelt and touched her head, asking, "Did you hurt yourself?"

Samantha shook her head. She didn't know what to do and had not expected her husband to find her this quickly or to be so amenable when he found her.

"Victoria did not tell me where to find you," Rudolf said with a wry smile. "I did my best to frighten her, but she is not as easily frightened as you or the children."

Samantha smiled at that. "How did you find me?" she asked in a whisper.

"I remembered that you considered the cottage your home," he told her.

Samantha worried her bottom lip with her teeth. "How will you punish me this time?"

"How does a mortal punish an angel?" Rudolf asked.

Samantha blinked and shook her head as if trying to clear it. Apparently, she was having a delusion or dream. That must be it. She was still in bed and enjoying a wonderful dream.

Rudolf looked puzzled. "What is wrong? Is it the baby?"

Samantha placed her hand on his chest and said, "You feel solid and real."

"Of course, I am real."

"What's wrong with you?" she asked. "You aren't the same."

"I have been an ass," he admitted.

"Yes, you have." Samantha nodded her head in agreement.

Rudolf burst out laughing. He yanked her into his arms and held her tightly. His lips descended to hers in a devouring kiss.

"I brought you a gift," he said.

Samantha smiled in confusion. "A gift?"

Rudolf stood and offered her his hand as he'd done on the night of Emerson's ball. Samantha dropped her gaze from his black eyes to his offered hand. Almost shyly, she placed her hand in his and rose from the floor.

Wrapping his arms around her, Rudolf kissed the crown of her head. Desperation tinged his voice when he said, "Please, Princess, do not ever leave me again. I love you too much to live without you."

Samantha hid her face against his chest and wept. He had said the words she longed to hear. He loved her. She had never felt this happy in her life.

"I am glad that Grant is not here," Rudolf said, stroking her back soothingly. "He would be complaining about how stupid girls are."

Samantha laughed and pushed away from his chest. She looked up at him through enormous blue eyes glistening with tears. "I was about to eat breakfast. Would you like a bowl of oatmeal?"

"Did you make it?"

Samantha nodded.

"I would love to eat your oatmeal after you open your gift," Rudolf said. "Sit down, and I'll get it."

With a smile playing on her lips, Samantha watched him step outside and lift something into his arms. He was back in an instant and, after she pushed the bowl of oatmeal aside, set the large box on the table.

"Open it."

"It's quite large," Samantha said. "Did you buy something for the baby?"

"No, *ma lyoobof*, I bought this for you."

"If you buy something for the baby," Samantha corrected him, "then you are buying it for me." She opened the lid. The box contained hundreds—no, thousands—of hair ribbons in every color imaginable.

She looked up at him, a confused smile on her lips. "You bought me hair ribbons?"

Her heart ached when she saw him swallow a lump of emotion, and his black eyes shone with unshed tears. "I have never seen you with a hair ribbon and thought you might want a few."

Samantha laughed. "A few?"

"Do you like them?"

"I love them," she answered. "I would love anything you gave me." She reached inside and pulled out a handful of ribbons. "These are very fine hair ribbons."

"I did not know which colors you preferred, so I bought all of them," Rudolf told her.

"All of the ribbons in the shop?"

Rudolf nodded. "I cleaned them out and then went to the next shop. And the next and the next and the next. You own a monopoly on hair ribbons at the moment."

Samantha burst out laughing. She rose from the chair and entwined her arms around his neck. Pulling his head down, she poured all of her love into that single kiss.

"Princess, I want you to know——"

Samantha placed a finger across his lips. "We don't need to speak about it."

"Yes, we do." Rudolf lifted her hand to his lips. "I want you to know that, after I calmed down yesterday, I planned to listen to your account of that day. You had already gone."

"Thank you."

"I will become angry sometimes over the next forty or fifty years," Rudolf told her. "When I do, I want you to remind me what an arrogant, insufferable, pigheaded lout I can be."

"I don't think I would want to say that to you when you're angry," Samantha said, a smile on her lips. "Your expression is always so forbidding."

"I tried not to love you," Rudolf said, holding her close. "I did not want to marry you because I wanted to marry you too much. After Zara was born, Olga learned of my less-than-noble origins. She began an affair with Vladimir. I found them in my bed together. That is why I guarded my heart for so long and struggled to keep from giving my love to you."

Samantha reached up and touched his cheek. "I loved you from the moment you forced me to dance at Emerson's ball."

"You will never know how grateful I am to Igor for abducting us," Rudolf told her, making her smile. He dropped his hand to her belly, asking, "How is my baby?"

"Hungry."

Rudolf sat at the table, and Samantha served him a bowl filled with oatmeal. After tasting it, he exclaimed, "This is the best oatmeal I have ever eaten."

"How much oatmeal have you eaten?" she asked him.

"None." Rudolf glanced around the cottage and said, "I am going to purchase this cottage. Every year the two of us will return for a week or two and pretend we are ordinary people."

"That is the best offer I have ever had," Samantha said, her blue eyes shining with love. "By the way, you owe me one thousand pounds and whatever Tory paid for the hackney."

"Your sister is lucky that I am letting her live after she confessed to supervising you climbing out the window and down the tree," Rudolf said.

Finished with his oatmeal, Rudolf stood and offered her his hand as he had done the night they met. Samantha knew what he was asking. She smiled shyly and placed her hand in his.

Together, they went into the tiny bedroom. Rudolf pulled her against his hard, muscular body. "Today is yours, my love," he whispered.

Rudolf kissed her thoroughly while his hands unfastened her buttons. Then he slipped the gown off her shoulders and let it pool at her feet. Rudolf looked down at her leg and laughed, saying, "I have never made love to a woman who was wearing a dagger." He bent down and unstrapped the leather garter that held the dagger.

"My turn, Your Highness," Samantha whispered.

He stood to let her unbutton his shirt. Sliding it off his shoulders, Samantha placed little nipping kisses across his chest.

Rudolf sucked in his breath at the sensation and pushed her chemise down until she stood naked in front of him. "You are not wearing anything else," he said.

"Stockings and garters and other fancy unmentionables are for the wealthy," Samantha said. "While here, I am a simple girl."

"There is nothing simple about you," he said.

Rudolf placed her gently on the cot. His hands moved to her swollen breasts with their darkened nipples. "I can hardly wait to see my baby suckling on your nipples."

Samantha sighed. Her husband was everything she had ever wanted. Her long-cherished dream was coming true.

Rudolf quickly discarded his boots and trousers and then lay down beside her. The cot was so small, he was forced to lie on his side.

Sliding his hands down her body, Rudolf caressed her breasts, the curve of her hip, the wet folds between her thighs. "Princess, lie on top of me," he said in a husky voice.

When she moved over him, Rudolf cupped each breast and brought them down to hover near his lips. He suckled each lingeringly, enjoying his wife's throaty moans. She had wonderfully sensitive nipples.

"Ride me, wife," he whispered.

"Oh, yes."

Samantha lifted herself into position and slowly impaled herself, inch by exquisite inch. Then she rocked back and forth while he grinded himself deep inside her.

"You are beautiful, *ma lyoobof,*" Rudolf told her.

Samantha cried out as spasms shook her body. Only then did Rudolf lose himself in her, holding her hips while thrusting upward again and again and again.

Later, after they'd napped, Samantha caressed his face. Rudolf turned his head and kissed her hand. "Husband, there is something I've been wanting to ask you," she said.

Amusement lit the prince's dark eyes. "My answer is no."

Samantha felt confused. "No, what?"

Rudolf smiled. "No, I did not make love to that actress."

"Your Highness, you are exceedingly conceited," she told him.

"I know, but you love me."

Samantha laughed but would not be deterred from her question. "Seriously, I want to know something."

"What is it, Princess?"

"Do you remember on our way to Scotland when we went shopping?" she asked.

"Yes."

"Why *did* you purchase that ostrich feather?"

Rudolf shouted with laughter and hugged her close. "Princess, I forgot I bought that. I will show you what the feather is used for when we move into Montague House."

"I don't understand," she said, looking into his dark eyes.

"Darling, the feather is used as a toy for adults," Rudolf told her.

"An adult toy? What is it used—*Oh.*" Samantha felt her cheeks grow warm. After a time, she said, "We should get up and return to His Grace's."

"We can stay here for the night if you wish," he said.

"I would like that very much," she answered, "but everyone will be worried."

Samantha rose from the cot and drew her chemise over her head. Then she strapped the leather garter with its deadly dagger to her leg.

"Is that necessary?" Rudolf asked, watching her.

"One should always be prepared," Samantha replied, reaching for her boots. It was then she noticed the star ruby had darkened to the color of blood, and a chill ran down her spine. She pulled her dress over her head and sat on the edge of the cot.

"My aunt's star ruby has darkened," she told him. "We may be in for some trouble."

Rudolf burst out laughing but then said, "I can handle anything that threatens us."

Rising from the cot, Rudolf dressed and walked into the main room. After smothering the dying embers in the hearth, he lifted the box of ribbons off the table and followed her to the door.

When Samantha opened the door, Olga stood there. Behind her stood Vladimir with a pistol in his hand.

Olga slapped her hard. Samantha fell back against her husband, who kept her from falling.

"Princess Samantha, I thought you were such a sweet, innocent child," Vladimir said, gesturing them inside with his pistol. "That angel's face hid a devious mind. I never would have guessed you would be so wily as to fool us with an imitation."

Rudolf set the box of ribbons down on the table. Then he gently pushed Samantha behind him.

"Isn't that sweet," Olga said snidely. "The bastard is protecting her. Too bad, but both of you will be dead in a few minutes."

"Brother, please excuse my wife," Vladimir said. "She

gets carried away sometimes. If you will hand me the real Venus, we will leave you in peace."

Rudolf inclined his head, reached into his pocket, and produced the black velvet pouch. He handed it to his brother, who placed it into his jacket pocket.

"Kill them," Olga said.

"I will not kill my own brother," Vladimir told her.

"Give me the pistol, and I'll kill them," Olga ordered.

"Owww," Samantha cried, falling to the floor in a faint, drawing their attention.

At the same moment, Rudolf knocked the pistol out of his brother's hand. It slid into the princess's shoe.

Olga bent to pick it up, but Samantha was faster. Drawing her dagger, she pointed its sharp tip against the blonde's cheek.

"I don't think so," Samantha told the blonde.

Rudolf retrieved the gun and leveled it on his brother. He glanced at his wife, asking, "Are you injured?"

"No." Samantha put the dagger back in its sheath.

"You clumsy idiot," Olga snapped at her husband.

Vladimir slapped her hard, effectively silencing her. "I suppose you want this," Vladimir said, offering the black velvet pouch to his brother.

"You keep it," Rudolf said. "I have everything a man could want."

The door opened unexpectedly, admitting Igor. The big Russian looked at the pistol in the prince's hand and said, "I see that my services are not required."

"My wife and I could have been killed if we waited for you to rescue us," Rudolf told him. "Make certain my brother and his charming wife board a ship leaving England today."

"I understand, Your Highness," Igor said.

Vladimir and Olga turned to leave.

"Ooops," Samantha cried, tripping into Vladimir as he passed her. He instinctively reached out to break her fall.

"I apologize, Your Highness," Samantha said, blushing furiously. "The babe makes me dizzy."

Vladimir inclined his head. "I wish you well with your new baby."

"Thank you, Your Highness," Samantha murmured, dropping her gaze to the floor.

Vladimir and Olga walked outside the cottage, but the big Russian paused to look at her. Suddenly, Igor let out a thunderous bellow of laughter and walked out of the cottage.

"I'm not certain I want to remain married to you," Samantha said.

"Why?" he asked, a smile flirting with the corners of his lips.

"I always hoped for a boring husband," she told him.

"Princess, I promise to bore you to tears," Rudolf said, pulling her into his arms. "I will be the most boring husband who ever lived." He planted a kiss on her lips and asked, "May I have the Venus now?"

"Of course, darling." Samantha handed him the black velvet pouch. "Aren't you glad you married me?"

Rudolf lost his smile, his dark gaze becoming intense. "I meant what I said to my brother about having everything a man could want. I have waited for you forever."

"I love you, too," Samantha said. "Forever."

Sark Island, November

Samantha set her teacup on the table and stared at her pregnancy-swollen belly. She glanced at her husband, who sat on the edge of her chair.

"You have never looked more beautiful," Rudolf whispered.

Samantha glanced around the drawing room. Her whole family had come from London for the birth of her child. Only, her child wasn't cooperating.

A whoop and a shriek of excitement caught her attention. Victoria and Rudolf's brothers were engaged in a game of tag with the children. A rather wild game of tag.

Samantha crooked her finger at her husband, and he leaned close. "I think your brothers are taking advantage of my sister," she whispered in his ear. "I just saw Stepan tag her breast, and a few minutes ago, Mikhail tagged her posterior."

"I will speak to them about their behavior," Rudolf said, nuzzling her neck.

"I don't think that will do much good."

"I pity Emerson," Rudolf said. "Your sister is going to have him tied in knots."

Samantha smiled. She looked at her aunt, who sat holding Rudolf's mother's hand but was watching her sister's outrageous game of tag with the princes and the children. Her aunt wore a worried expression.

Samantha crooked her finger at her husband again. When he leaned close, she whispered, "I don't think my aunt has the constitution for another courtship." That made him smile. "I also think my time has come."

"What about time, sweet?" Rudolf asked.

Samantha closed her eyes as the beginnings of a contraction swept through her. The panic hit her as soon as the pain passed. Great Giles' ghost, she had experience with pain and knew what was coming. She wasn't sure she could bear it.

"Samantha?"

She grabbed his hand, pleading, "Don't leave me, please."

The realization of what was happening slammed into the prince. He lifted her into his arms, calling over his shoulder, "Roxie, the baby is coming. Stepan, get the physician."

Upstairs, Rudolf gingerly laid Samantha on the bed just as another contraction hit. She clung to his hand and panted.

"That's a good girl," Rudolf soothed her. "I won't leave you. There's nothing to fear."

Aunt Roxie raced into the bedchamber, a nightgown in her hand. Angelica appeared with bed padding.

"Rudolf, lift her so we can put this on the bed," Angelica said.

"We'll need to change her into this," Roxie said.

Rudolf undressed his wife gently and pulled the nightgown over her head. "I think we should walk around the room, *ma lyoobof.*"

Samantha looked at him in confusion. "Walk?" she echoed.

"Yes, Princess, we will walk around the chamber," Rudolf said, putting his arm around her and beginning to circle the room. "You will go to bed when the pain becomes intense."

"Intense?" His wife had the look of a trapped animal.

"Really, Rudolf, I think she should lie down," Roxie said.

"The prince knows how to care for his wife," Angelica said. "He knows what's best. Let's wait outside until we're needed."

Rudolf sent his sister-in-law a look of gratitude. The duchess was so excitable, she would only make the situation worse. When his wife needed to go to bed, he would call for them.

With his arm around her, Rudolf passed the next two hours walking his wife around the chamber. When the pains came, he held her steady as she leaned into him.

"Rudolf?"

"Yes, love?"

"I need ribbons."

Rudolf looked at her in confusion. "Ribbons?"

"I need two of the ribbons you bought me," she said softly.

Rudolf helped her to sit on the bed, asking, "What colors do you want?"

"Pink and blue."

Rudolf ran for the dressing room. He found the box on the floor and rummaged through it until he caught one pink and one blue ribbon.

When he returned to the bed, Rudolf found her in the midst of another contraction, worse than the others. "You need to lie down now," he said when the contraction passed.

"First, pull my hair back and tie the ribbons in my hair," she said.

"Samantha."

"Please."

Rudolf tied her hair with the ribbons and gently pushed her back on the bed. Then he hurried across the chamber, opened the door, and nodded at her aunt, her sister, and the physician.

"You need to leave now," Aunt Roxie told him.

"I am not leaving her."

Rudolf sat on the edge of the bed and held his wife's hand while she writhed in pain. "I am sorry, *ma lyoobof,*" he said. "I am sorry to put you through this."

"Oh, God," Samantha cried as the worst contraction yet caught her. The contractions were rolling into her like great tidal waves of pain.

And then Samantha shocked not only her husband

but her aunt and her sister as well. She looked at her worried husband and screamed, "You son of a no-good bitch. Look what you've done to me. You don't love me. You just wanted to stick yourself in me . . . Aunt Roxie, he tricked me, the lying arse."

Hiding a smile, Angelica put her arm around the stunned prince and guided him toward the door, assuring him, "Samantha will feel differently in the morning." She slammed the door in his face.

Rudolf stared at the door. He hadn't realized his wife knew those curse words. God, he needed vodka.

Slowly, Rudolf walked downstairs and into the drawing room. Duke Magnus put a glass of vodka in his hand.

"Has Samantha started cursing you yet?" Robert asked with a smile.

Rudolf snapped his gaze to his brother-in-law. "Do all women do that?"

Robert nodded.

"Every time?"

Robert nodded again.

"The only cure for it is in your hands," Duke Magnus told him. "Drink up, son."

Long hours passed. Rudolf frequently walked to the bottom of the stairs and looked up as if he could see what was happening in his bedchamber.

The physician appeared in the drawing room where the men were drinking. Drying his hands on a towel, he announced, "Your Highness, you have a son . . ."

The men cheered and raised their glasses, but the physician wasn't finished yet.

" . . . and a daughter."

The glass of vodka slipped from the prince's hand. Rudolf Kazanov, Prince of Russia, fainted.

The next afternoon after the family had inspected

the babies and gone downstairs for tea, the proud parents sat in their bedchamber and watched their babies sleeping. Sitting on the edge of the bed, Rudolf held his daughter in his arms while Samantha cuddled their son. A knock on the door drew their attention.

"Come in," Rudolf called.

Another knock sounded on the door. Again, Rudolf called a little louder, "Enter."

When the door remained closed, Rudolf looked at his wife. Samantha shrugged and returned her attention to her baby.

Boom! Boom! Boom! Louder and more insistent, more knocking sounded on their door. Cursing in Russian, Rudolf cradled his daughter in his arms and walked across the chamber to yank open the door.

No one was there.

And then he heard his wife's laughter.

"If you look on the other side of the door," Samantha called, "I think you will find a potato."

It was then Rudolf heard the sound of children's giggling. Smiling, he called to his wife, "Samantha, if I find the culprit, I will give him or her a spanking to remember."

Rudolf heard the muffled scuffling of feet as the culprits sought the safety downstairs. He closed the door and returned inside to place his daughter in her cradle. Then he lifted his son out of his wife's arms and placed him in his cradle.

Sitting on the bed, Rudolf leaned back against the headboard and put his arms around his wife. She looked up at him and said, "You were correct. When they put the babies in my arms, I forgot the pain."

Rudolf lifted her chin and gazed with love into her eyes. "When you are recovered, I am going to wash your mouth out with soap."

Samantha laughed. "For what?"

"You called me a lying arse and a son of a no-good bitch," he told her.

"I never did that," she insisted.

"Shall I say the words now?"

"Please do."

"I love you, Princess."

"And I love you, my prince."

ABOUT THE AUTHOR

PATRICIA GRASSO lives in Massachusetts. She is the author of ten historical romances and is currently working on her eleventh, TO CATCH A COUNTESS (Victoria's story), which will be published by Zebra Books in June 2004. Pat loves hearing from readers, and you may write to her c/o Zebra Books. Please include a self-addressed stamped envelope if you wish a response.

Embrace the Romances of

Shannon Drake

__**Come the Morning** $6.99US/$8.99CAN
  0-8217-6471-3

__**Blue Heaven, Black Night** $6.50US/$8.00CAN
  0-8217-5982-5

__**Conquer the Night** $6.99US/$8.99CAN
  0-8217-6639-2

__**The King's Pleasure** $6.50US/$8.00CAN
  0-8217-5857-8

__**Lie Down in Roses** $5.99US/$6.99CAN
  0-8217-4749-0

__**Tomorrow the Glory** $5.99US/$6.99CAN
  0-7860-0021-4

Call toll free **1-888-345-BOOK** to order by phone or use this coupon to order by mail.

Name_____

Address_____

City_____ State _____ Zip _____

Please send me the books that I have checked above.

I am enclosing $_____

Plus postage and handling* $_____

Sales tax (in New York and Tennessee) $_____

Total amount enclosed $_____

*Add $2.50 for the first book and $.50 for each additional book. Send check or money order (no cash or CODs) to:

Kensington Publishing Corp., 850 Third Avenue, New York, NY 10022

Prices and numbers subject to change without notice.

All orders subject to availability.

Check out our website at **www.kensingtonbooks.com.**